TRAPPED

Piper looked up. She could see a faint shaft of light far above her in the open trap door. She grabbed the side of the ladder and tested the bottom rung with her left foot. It felt shaky. Two rungs later the ladder collapsed under her. She blinked her eyes, terrified.

It wouldn't help to yell; no one would come. Piper's mouth was dry, her legs weak, but she tried—in vain—to jump up and grab the trap door. It was impossible.

She leaned her body against the damp earthen walls and then, to her absolute horror, she felt something move across her foot. Claws dug into her skin; the rodent scurried up her leg. Then her thigh.

Piper doubled her fists and whacked the rat, knocking it to the floor. She stood rigid, tried not to breathe hard, and shielded her throat with her hands. Her ears hummed.

Above her, the shaft of light faded. Then she heard a thump and a click as the trap door slid into place . . . and the bolt slid home.

CLOAK
OF
DARKNESS
ANN BRAHMS

ZEBRA BOOKS
KENSINGTON PUBLISHING CORP.

ZEBRA BOOKS

are published by

Kensington Publishing Corp.
475 Park Avenue South
New York, NY 10016

First printing: March 1992

Printed in the United States of America

I dedicate this book with love to my parents Don and Audrey Allen and to my husband Paul—who really was the best boy. To my niece Pam Kane and to Crutches, a loving, happy-go-lucky Newfoundland.

Special thanks to Jeff Harmon of the Maine State Police and to his wife Lisa. Thanks also to my brother Don Allen and his wife Linda and to Roger and Marion Wilmot and their kids. What fun we had with the chili. I must not forget my friend Susan Winslow who dislikes exclamation points and who created my favorite—Grandpa Scarecrow.

CONTENTS

and the candle caught. Another strong smell of sulphur, mixed now with burning wax, filled the air. She blinked her eyes and then she saw it. "Is it real?" she asked.

"Yes. And it's for you."

"Quit that. That's not funny. You're scaring me. I'm getting out of here."

"No. Wait. Let me open it for you so you can see what's inside."

"No thanks. It can wait until later. I'm leaving." She turned around and tried hard not to bolt for the door. It seemed to take forever to reach the door. She was almost there when she heard a *whoosh*. Something dropped down over her head and tightened around her throat. She was yanked backwards; her feet lifted off the ground, and her lollipop and teddy bear flew across the room. She tried to pull the thing away from her throat and failed. She tried to scream but only horrible gagging sounds escaped. Precious air was shut off. The last thing she saw were black specks floating in front of her eyes and then everything went dark.

"That's a good girl. You made it so easy for me. Now what is that old saying? I think it goes something like this: *Whenever you see a hearse go by—you know some day you're gonna die. The undertaker, tall and thin, looks down at you with a slimy grin. He'll wrap you up in a dirty white sheet and throw you under six feet deep. The worms crawl in—the worms crawl out . . ."*

She was dead in just a few minutes.

Her slim, limp body was easily dragged across the floor. The hardest part was lifting her. Her arms flopped like those of a rag doll. Her lollipop was found and placed in her left hand; her teddy bear was returned to her pocket. There was no time to fix her curls.

It had been too long since the last murder. It felt good to kill again.

Chapter One

Rag Dolls

Maine in October: warm days—crisp nights. Folks could see their breath in the morning. The wash felt a bit stiff on the line. A hint of winter in the air brought mothball-scented, fleece-lined jackets, wool caps, and sweaters out of storage in dusty attics. Blue ribbons had been handed out at the county fairs for the best homemade quilts, pickles, and the biggest vegetables. Some vendors made money selling pink cotton candy. Others sold fried dough brushed with melted butter, lots of sugar and cinnamon, and just a smidgen of nutmeg. Garden plots had been plowed under. Geraniums in window boxes and fields of wildflowers had been nipped by frost and drooped lifelessly. Shaws and Shop N Save grocery stores had stocked in plenty of fresh butternut and acorn squash. There had been lots of folks apple-picking in neighboring orchards. Some left carrying jugs of sweet cider—cider that promised to go hard and make one tipsy if not soon enjoyed with a box of plain donuts. The tantalizing aroma of homemade apple pie made one's mouth water.

Rugged men clad in colorful, warm chamois shirts and stone-washed jeans stacked cords of wood for the upcoming winter. At dusk, pine-scented smoke rose from red brick chimneys and drifts through near naked tree limbs. A harvest moon hovered over Maine. Blankets of fallen leaves crunched underfoot and covered the earth in red and gold.

Piper Jordan and Kelly Stewart were enjoying the fall. Sweater weather, they called it. They had recently turned twenty-five; Kelly was the oldest by a month. Her birthday was in August and Piper's was in September. They'd grown up on Spruce Street on the west end of Portland, their houses only four doors apart. Piper's mother used to say that the two were so close they might as well have been twins, though Piper was blond and Kelly dark-haired. Their eyes were the same shade of blue, their lashes long, thick, and black. They were exactly the same height and weight, sounded almost alike, and could wear one another's clothes, though not their shoes—Piper's feet were a size larger. Kelly liked cats. Piper liked cats and dogs. They both loved expensive clothes, pizza, strawberry frozen yogurt, reading, and a walk on the beach just after a storm. Kelly collected driftwood carried to shore on incoming waves. Piper always gathered sea glass (purple was her favorite color).

Kelly was the one with the fiery temper. It didn't take much to set her off, but Piper knew how to keep her in line. Though both looked innocent, they had an impish side. Years ago, their parents were motified when they were kicked out of the church choir the rainy Sunday when Piper disrupted the congregation when her pet, a foot long green garter snake, slithered out of her choir robe pocket. To this day, she and Kelly would get the giggles when they remembered how the old lady seated beside Piper screamed when the snake crawled across her lap. The other two women in the pew had screamed when they spied the snake, and the congregation had scattered because they'd no idea what was the matter. The Reverend Bartlett displayed no sense of humor about the incident, and the girls were told they could never sing in the choir again.

Piper and Kelly knew each other's deepest, darkest secrets. If one suffered, the other felt the pain. Kelly had grieved as much as Piper when Piper's parents died. She had moved out of her own parents' house and into Piper's so her friend wouldn't be alone, and she didn't move back home until Piper sold the house and moved into a spacious, second floor apartment on Pine Street, near the elite Western Promenade.

That's when Piper met Jeremy and he moved in with her. Later, when she realized she didn't love him, she was so depressed that there were moments she almost gave up on terminating the relationship, but Kelly helped her straighten out her head. Still, Piper was lonely after Jeremy moved out. "Absence makes the heart grow fonder," Kelly told her over and over and tried to keep Piper busy so she wouldn't slip back into such an unhealthy relationship. She constantly reminded Piper of how miserable she'd been when she lived with him.

And eventually, Piper gave the same support to Kelly when she broke her engagement with Tim.

Recently Kelly had expressed an interest in moving in with Piper again. She was too old to be living with her parents she said, and she meant it but another reason for wanting to move was that she knew Piper was having difficulty making ends meet. Her rent was expensive and she had to pay for the utilities. Both women agreed that it would be a shame to have to give up such a splendid apartment.

Piper and Kelly had taken jobs in a new dress shop called Tatjana's on Exchange Street in the old waterfront section of Portland. Tatjana, their boss, owned several stores in New England and in New York, where she had a swank apartment on Fifth Avenue. She stayed in Portland just long enough to train Piper, Kelly and Mona Hadley, the manager. Once Mona knew how to operate the business, Tatjana left for New York.

Mona was a perfectly manicured, expensively dressed woman, who loved to complain and to brag. She was also very secretive about her past, though Piper and Kelly had managed to find out that she'd moved to Portland from the midwest in '89, and that shortly afterwards she'd married Steven, a well-to-do contractor. Like Mona, he, too, had come from out of state and like his wife, he never talked about his background. He and Mona owned a magnificent house not far from the ocean in fashionable Cape Bethany, a bedroom community of Portland. Mona often said she worked because she was bored and because she loved clothes. This appeared to be true, because sometimes she flew to New York to shop at Tatjana's or at Bergdorf Goodman's; Everyone knew that that store was where the chosen few did their really important shopping.

Piper and Kelly soon found out that Mona was given to frequent mood swings. One minute she was happy and smiling, and then for no apparent reason she would be sullen and make nasty remarks—especially to Piper.

Piper tolerated such bad treatment because she understood why Mona acted the way she did. It was obvious she was jealous because of Steven's behavior. There wasn't a time that they were together socially, that he didn't try to make a pass at Piper. She'd been afraid of Steven ever since the night he'd tried to corner her in his bedroom during a dinner party at his house. That's when Mona slapped her face. Kelly told Piper that she should've told both of them to go to hell. Piper didn't because she was afraid she'd lose her job. Besides, Mona apologized and she didn't see Steven that often. And, no sooner would Mona be mean to her than she would have a change of heart and be sweet. And besides, the Hadleys' hosted the best parties Piper and Kelly had ever attended.

Mona and Steven's last Christmas get-together had been a real spectacle. Their house had been decorated so beautifully that it could've been featured in *House Beautiful*. Mona wasn't satisfied with having just one perfectly shaped tree—she had three—and the ornaments that dangled from the branches were exquisite. Piper especially liked the little red sleds and the Austrian clear glass balls with silver tinsel inside.

The food was out of this world. The caterer, Cathy, was the best around, and she had outdone herself preparing platter after platter of hors d'ouerves. The main course had been fresh Maine lobster, and there had been tray after tray of shrimp and crabmeat served with huge bowls of tossed salad and with bottles of expensive wine to wash it down. There had been enough seafood to sink a battleship, and Cathy's homemade rolls, cakes, and decorated Christmas cookies from several nations disappeared so fast that Piper hadn't had a chance to try any.

Kelly couldn't wait until they went to Mona and Steven's Halloween party. Mona said it was to be a costume party, and she warned that guests who didn't wear costumes would be turned away. She dropped hints at work that things were going to be really spooky. Piper really didn't want to go because she knew that Steven would make a pass at her, but Kelly pestered her until she gave in. "Okay, Kelly," she'd said. "But if Steven pulls anything that's it for me. I swear I'll leave Tatjana's."

"Me, too," Kelly vowed, and then she thought over what she'd just said and had second thoughts. "Keep your fingers crossed the jerk behaves."

Piper on the other hand was serious. If anything happened at the Halloween party she knew that she'd have to quit her job because Mona would make her life miserable. The more she thought about that happening, the more she wanted to tell Kelly that she wasn't going to the Halloween party. But Kelly was counting on going and she didn't have the heart to disappoint her.

Piper didn't have much enthusiasm about putting together a costume. Kelly was the one who came up with an idea. The brainstorm hit her at Tatjana's one Monday morning. She made certain that Mona wasn't around to hear, and then she called Piper over to her and whispered, "I figured out what we can wear to the party."

"What?" Piper whispered back.

"You're going to love it. Look. We have the same color eyes; we're the same height, and we'd be the same weight if you hadn't eaten two hot fudge sundaes this week," she teased. "Anyway, we can go dressed as twin rag dolls. What do you say?"

"It's a great idea, Kelly. But what about our faces and hair? I don't know any identical twins where one is blond and the other dark."

"That's no problem. We can wear wigs. I saw just what we need out at the mall in South Portland. Let's go there after work tonight. How about it?"

Piper agreed, although she still wasn't keen on wearing any costume because of what had happened to her last Halloween at Mona and Steven's. She'd dressed as a black cat. She'd made the costume herself, out of silk, and had gone to great lengths to make an extra long tail—she even took the trouble to put wire inside to make it rigid, and yet flexible. Piper had been proud of her outfit until the tail caught one of Mona's expensive hand-painted Oriental lamps and sent it crashing to the floor. Her precious tail ended up costing her $150.00. She could only hope that dressing like a twin rag doll wouldn't wind up costing her her whole paycheck.

Finally, the day of the party arrived. Kelly was due at Piper's to get dressed. Piper told her to come at six. Kelly was so excited she arrived at five, which was just as well because it took them a long time to get ready. When finished, they stood pigeon-toed before Piper's full-length bedroom mirror, wearing the same little girl masks, mustard yellow wigs with thick curls and oversized, hot pink bows plunked on top. Teeny-weeny teddy bears peeked out of the pockets of their stiffly starched white bib aprons. Kelly had made them matching calico dresses. Piper bought their white tights and black patent leather flat shoes with straps. Both had to admit that they looked exactly alike, so much alike that they couldn't tell each other apart. They toasted their cleverness over glasses of Glen Ellyn Proprietor's Reserve white wine.

"Piper," Kelly said excitedly. "You know how jealous Mona is. Well, she's sure going to turn green when she sees us. I bet we win first prize for the best costume."

"Heaven forbid," Piper said and rolled her eyes. "Mona will have a fit. Oops. I forgot something. I'll be right back." She left the room and returned immediately carrying a small plastic bag.

"What's that?"

"You'll see," Piper replied and pulled out two oversized

18

red lollipops. "I bought these at Margo's down on the waterfront." She handed Kelly hers, and together they ceremoniously peeled off the cellophane wrappers, took sticky licks, and rolled their eyes.

Kelly licked her lips and said, "Yummy. Isn't it fun to be a kid again?" They both laughed so hard it hurt. Piper glanced at the clock on her nightstand; it was time to go, and arm in arm the twin rag dolls went out the door. Little did they realize that they were about to walk into hell.

Chapter Two

The Party

A thick fog had crept off the open sea during the night, covering quaint Cape Bethany like a shroud. The dampness seeped into the bones and made you feel as if you'd never get warm. The WMGX weatherman promised it would lift before evening and then a harvest moon was expected. There was no wind blowing off the white-capped Atlantic. All was quiet—too quiet. It was as if the eerie weather had been especially ordered for Mona and Steven's costume party. How perfect.

Mona and Steven had risen at five because she was too excited about the party and couldn't sleep. Now they were seated at their white-tiled kitchen table having their morning coffee. He was already dressed in jeans and a red plaid flannel shirt. Mona, clad in a peach silk nightie and matching robe, was engrossed in last evening's paper. She was totally unaware that Steven was watching her. They'd been married for almost two years now, he thought. Two fucking years of hell. What a fool he'd been to tie up with the likes of her. What a nightmare! He knew exactly what kind of advice he'd offer single men about marriage, if asked. He'd say think with your head—not your pants. He'd married Mona out of lust. Once their passion ebbed, he'd soon discovered what a twisted, jealous bitch she was. And if the opportunity ever arose he'd offer another piece of information: never marry a woman who won't tell you about her background. He'd have sworn that Mona escaped from a looney bin.

He really knew very little about her. She always changed the subject when he brought up her past. When they were first married, he'd managed to find out that she used to live in St. Louis. He'd discovered this one night after she'd had too much wine. She'd told him that she'd come to Maine after a broken relationship. She'd mumbled something about a redhead and how she'd fixed her wagon. He'd tried to probe for details, but Mona wouldn't say another word. Her silence hadn't intrigued him then. It was her body that held his interest, and he had to admit that she was good in bed.

Lately, he'd toyed with hiring a private detective to find out about her past for him, because she was acting more and more peculiar. He'd catch her muttering to herself about Piper Jordan. She seemed to be obsessed with jealousy over Piper ever since that night she'd caught him trying to kiss her, up in the bedroom. Worse, Mona was becoming more and more short-tempered and violent. One wrong word and she was off. Yesterday she'd flown into a rage because he said he didn't like the color of her new dress. Now he looked at both arms and followed the tracks where her long fingernails had left a ragged path. He touched his head and winced as his scalp was still sensitive where'd she'd yanked his hair almost out of his head.

To be truthful with himself, Steven knew that he didn't need to hire a detective—he needed to run away. Five years in Maine had been long enough. The thought of spending the rest of his life here made him break out in a cold sweat. It was time to dump that crazy bitch before he did something he'd be sorry for. He would leave town just as soon as he could.

A smile came. The thought of having his freedom was exhilarating. Happy days were just ahead. And if he had his way, Piper Jordan would be part of his plan.

Steven sighed and continued to stare at Mona across the

table. He hoped that the Halloween party they were hosting that night would continue to keep her in a good mood. Once again he thought about leaving her. He made a vow that there would be no more stalling.

After all, he'd done it before—with the last wife in Colorado. Hell, he'd never even bothered with a divorce. The image of her stretched out on the bed with ugly purple bruises all over her throat flashed in his mind. What had he called himself then—Mark Smith—or was he Mark in Arizona? He had planned to move to California or Hawaii but chose Maine at the last moment because the rugged outdoors appealed to him. And it was like being in the last outpost. He'd assumed that the cops would be stupid hicks.

It had been easy for him to take on a new identity and start a thriving construction business. Thank God he'd had that background, but of course he'd brought so much money with him to Maine that when he opened an account, the banker's eyes had bulged out of his head. He'd told the jerk that he'd sold a couple of houses in New York and the banker didn't ask any questions. Money talks. He'd worried about the IRS but so far so good; he'd made a fortune and his credit was better than a lot of lifelong natives. And Mona had never, not once, asked him about *his* background. She just wasn't interested. If only she knew . . .

He glared at Mona. She could have the house, he said to himself. Ouch. That hurts—but he knew he didn't have any choice, because she'd never leave. In the meantime, he'd empty the bank accounts and try to keep her in a good mood. That was his biggest problem; if he pushed the wrong button he might end up bald as an eagle. He touched his tender scalp again and winced.

He recalled the night of that damned dinner party Mona gave last month, when her jealousy over Piper erupted. He'd tried to convince her that he'd hustled Piper because he was drunk. That wasn't a lie; he'd been tanked. He'd sobered fast when Mona came into the bedroom, charged across the floor, yanked Piper by the hair, spun her around, and slapped her face so hard she left the imprint of her fingers on her cheek. He'd known better than to say a word.

Poor Piper. She was so innocent. "Mona," she'd said. "What are you doing? Stop. It's Steven's fault."

"You slut," Mona snarled. "I've been watching you flirt with Steven all evening."

"No I haven't. It's his fault. I came up here to use the bathroom. He must've followed me."

"Liar," Mona said.

Piper was angry now. "Don't call me a liar," she shot back. "I'm not interested in him." Steven had pouted when he heard that.

"Get out of my house," Mona ordered. "I hate you." Steven had never seen Mona in such a frenzy. He'd been afraid she was going to scratch Piper's eyes out or do some other godawful thing to her. But Piper wasn't about to hang around to find out. She grabbed her coat, and Kelly's, off the bed and made a fast exit, leaving Steven alone to face the music.

Before he could continue with his thoughts, Mona rustled the paper, turning a page which ushered him back to the moment. He picked up his coffee cup and took a sip. His eyes rested on the black and orange candles and a perfectly shaped pumpkin on the table. He knew that Mona would soon ask him to carve a face on it and probably twenty more for the party. His hands would be blistered by night, but it would be worth it if it would keep the bitch happy. He'd do anything to keep her off his neck, and preparing for the Halloween party had been his salvation. He hadn't even complained when she sprung on him that she'd had the cleaning lady come an extra day. He'd wanted to yell, "Jesus, Mona. Don't be so stupid. That broad costs ten dollars an hour and she stays all day." But once again he'd suppressed his anger to keep peace in the house, skin on his arms, and hair on his head. And he didn't complain when she told him that she'd spent a small fortune on party favors and hired one of Portland's finest caterers, Cathy something or other. At least she had good taste when it came to food. But he could bet that she'd insist on making her goddamned chili. She always made that for parties. Worst-tasting stuff he'd ever had, but he wasn't about to tell her so.

Mona looked up from the paper and said matter-of-factly, "I bought more decorations for the party. Do you want to see them?"

"I can hardly wait," he said with feigned interest.

"Before I show them to you—you promise you won't get angry?"

"Why should I get angry?"

"Because they cost plenty."

"I won't say a word." He forced a smile though he really wanted to leap across the table and choke the life out of her.

"Follow me." She got up from the table and walked out of the kitchen into the dining room.

Steven followed. They came to an abrupt halt the minute they stepped into the dining room. Steven gasped when he saw what was facing him. "Where did you get it? Jesus, Mona. That looks real," he said with disgust.

"I ordered him through a catalog. He's real. I named him Stanley. He cost an arm and a leg," she giggled. "He was about your age when he died, Steven. Let me introduce you. Stanley, this is my husband, Steven." She grabbed the six-foot-tall skeleton by his left hand and waved it.

"Quit that," Steven said and made a sour face. "You mean to tell me that—that thing used to be a real person?"

"Of course," she said, glancing lovingly at the skeleton, and then she pouted. "Now you've offended him, Steven. He doesn't like to be called a thing. Stanley," she said sweetly, "If you'll excuse us, I want to take Steven to meet your two friends." Mona turned and left Steven in the room with Stanley. Steven didn't linger.

He found Mona waiting impatiently for him in front of a closet in the hallway. She faced him and said, "Close your eyes. Don't open them until I tell you to. You're going to love what I have in here." He could hardly wait.

Mona twisted the brass knob and opened the door wide. "You can look now."

Steven opened his eyes. "Jesus!" he said and shook his head. "Where in hell did you get them?"

"Aren't they great? I borrowed them from Tatjana's."

Steven stared at two, full busted naked female mannequins. One was blond and the other dark-haired. "What are you going to do with them?"

"Well," she said. "The dark one is going to be a witch. She'll stand next to the punch bowl in the dining room. I thought you might like to think of something special for the blond. Any ideas?"

"Maybe."

"Maybe?" Mona snapped losing her good mood over his less than enthusiastic response. "For Christ's sake, Steven. At least think about it. She's yours."

"Thanks."

"You're welcome."

"She looks like Piper," he said without thinking. The minute the words popped out of his mouth he thought all hell was going to break loose. Mona frowned, and her face flushed beet-red, but she didn't go into one of her usual tirades.

"The dummy is prettier," is all she said, coldly.

Steven exhaled slowly. That was a close call.

Mona concealed her anger because she didn't want anything to spoil the party. Everybody that had been invited said they were coming; it was going to be the best costume party in the world. Her enthusiasm overflowed and she gushed, "Let's finish decorating now."

"I can't," Steven said. "I have to go out."

"Out?" Mona whined. "You can't be serious. We have too much to do."

"Sorry. But I have a couple of important errands to run."

"What kind of errands?"

"Can't tell you. It's a surprise."

"I want to go."

"Nope. I already told you. It's a surprise. I'll be back in a couple of hours." He reached into the closet to get his brown leather jacket and quickly exited before she had a chance to nag him further.

Mona didn't have any idea what kind of a surprise Steven had planned, and at that moment she didn't care. She wandered into the living room to look out the bay window so she could watch him drive away. That's odd, she thought. Why is he taking the pickup instead of the Jag? She knew then that he must have a big surprise lined up. He only drove the truck when he had to haul supplies or when he carted the trash to the Cape Bethany dump every Sunday morning. Lots of businessmen gathered at the dump to talk. "Going to your country club again?" she'd say snidely.

She was glad Steven wouldn't let her go with him. Having him out of the way put her in an even better mood than before and she could decorate in peace. She'd made the invitations; she'd been so proud of those little haunted houses with the bright orange envelopes and black writing. And every one of her ten rooms, including the three bathrooms, were going to be decorated with ugly, black rubber spiders on fine-spun, silver webs. She would have them clinging to mirrors and paintings. Some would be fixed so that they dangled from the ceilings. When Steven came home she would have him carve all the pumpkins she'd bought at Skillin's Greenhouse on the Foreside Road out in Falmouth. She must be certain to tell Steven that the pumpkins must have crooked teeth. When Cathy, the caterer, arrived with her crew, she'd have them set the table with her rented black-and-orange china plates, napkins, cups, and flatware with black enameled handles. And she must not forget to have all the balloons blown up.

Mona continued to daydream while staring out the window. Finally she noticed that the fog was lifting. Now she could see the tiny, mock graveyard she and Steven had made on their dew-covered front lawn. Several evenings after work, she and Steven had sat at their kitchen table to make seventy tiny tombstones out of gray plastic. She'd

26

painted RIP and drew skulls with crossbones in phosphorescent green. Then she'd written the name of each guest, their birthday (information she gathered over a period of weeks) and date of death, which of course, was today—the day of the party. She frowned when she recalled that she'd had to pester Steven to make a small fence for the cemetery. He finally made one out of the white plastic fencing that she ordinarily used around her flower beds. After that was done, she'd pushed him until he constructed an arched entrance out of latticework. Over this she'd tacked a huge sign also written in phosphorescent green that said, "Memory Gardens."

Mona had placed Piper's tombstone in the very front row next to Kelly Stewart's because those two bitches were always together. On all the graves she put small black baskets filled with dead flowers. Then came her pride and joy: Mona had spent a lot of time creating a huge, papier-mâché angel that she named Mazie. Mazie had full, wide wings, a long haired, straight gray wig on her head, and a face painted pasty white. Her eyes were black buttons, and her thick lips were painted bright red, offsetting the paleness of her face. Mona had dressed the angel in one of her cast-off full-length, white silk nightgowns that accentuated her full breasts. Steven had nailed Mazie's feet to a wooden box and positioned her in the middle of the cemetery so she would appear to watch over the tombstones. Now, she looked wilted from the dampness. Her papier-mâché face was caving in. This made her look more frightening, but Mona was concerned that she might not last until the party.

Steven had placed two floodlights at each end of the fence. Next, he rigged two speakers in the bushes in order to broadcast somber funeral music for the benefit of the arriving guests as they passed by the cemetery on their way to the house.

The phone shattered the silence, and Mona ran to answer it. Cathy, the caterer, was calling to clarify some last minute details. When Mona hung up she glanced at her watch. She went upstairs to shower and dress, making a mental note not forget to put her chili on the stove to simmer. It was the best she'd ever made. Cathy offered to make it but she wouldn't hear of it. Mona didn't know why she always served chili at a party—she didn't even like the stuff. She thought perhaps there was something about the color that appealed to her.

After showering, Mona raced downstairs to get the pot of chili out of the refrigerator and onto the stove. When it had finally heated enough she took a wooden spoonful and tasted some of her concoction. The instant the spicy flavor hit her taste buds she was carried back to the time she'd slapped Piper's face, the night she'd caught her and Steven upstairs in the bedroom. The memory depressed her, and a minute later, while fixing herself a cup of coffee, she sat down at the table and relived that awful moment. The next day her friend Lucy had phoned and eagerly let her know that she'd seen Piper come into the living room to get Kelly Stewart, who was in a corner chatting to a handsome bachelor she'd been flirting with all evening. Piper had asked to speak to Kelly in private, and the bachelor had excused himself and said he'd go get a fresh drink. Lucy said she'd overheard Piper tell Kelly that she wanted to leave right away. Lucy couldn't understand the rest of what Piper told Kelly, but she had heard Kelly say that she wanted to stay because she had some electricity going with the man she'd been talking to. Piper had gotten angry and told her that she'd have to catch a ride home with someone else and she started to leave. Kelly had followed. Mona's face flushed thinking about that embarrassing evening.

Steven had made himself sick from drinking too much; he'd barely made it to the bathroom. She'd followed him. He'd laid his head on the floor in front of the toilet after he vomited. By then her anger had subsided. She thought about wetting a face cloth to wash his face but decided against it. He could die for all she cared. Next, she went into the bedroom and filled her arms with coats.

Steven didn't find out until the next day that she had

taken the coats downstairs and informed everyone that he was ill and that it was time to call it a night. She couldn't find Piper or Kelly. When she asked someone where they were she was told that they had left. "Oh," she'd said with a fake smile, smoothing her hair. "You probably heard me yelling at Piper. We had a little tiff. It's nothing serious. I'll phone her. Night everyone."

Mona never did tell Steven that after the last guest went out the door she'd gone to the kitchen, poured herself a glass of white wine, and sat down at the table to think. When she felt in control of her temper she'd decided to phone Piper and apologize. If she didn't, they'd both be miserable at work on Monday. She got up from the table and lifted the receiver off the wall phone. Seconds later she heard a sleepy, familiar voice say, "Hel—hello."

"Piper," Mona said sweetly, as if nothing had ever happened. "I'm sorry to wake you but I had to call and apologize for slapping you." All Mona heard was a deep sigh on the other end of the line and silence for several seconds.

Finally, Piper said, "It's okay, Mona."

"Oh, thanks," Mona said. "I know it was Steven's fault. Did I hurt you?"

"No," Piper yawned. "I'm fine."

"Good," Mona said and then she paused. "Piper," she continued, "Steven didn't know what he was doing. You know how he gets when he drinks too much." There was no response. "Piper. Are you there?"

"Forget it, Mona." Piper said coolly. "But tell Steven he should watch it."

"Watch what?" Mona bristled, not knowing what was to come.

"What?" Piper said coolly. "Steven is a diabetic, isn't he? Diabetes and booze don't mix. He's going to kill himself if he's not careful."

"I know," Mona said, faking concern. "I tell him that all the time. Look, Piper. It's late and we need to get some sleep. Like I said. I just wanted to call and apologize."

"It's okay, Mona."

"Good. I'll see you at work on Monday." Mona cradled the receiver, turned off the kitchen light, and went upstairs.

Steven had managed to find his way to bed. She'd gone into the bathroom to shower. When she climbed into bed Steven never stirred. She had an urge to yank his hair out of his head but she was too tired to make the effort. She rested her head on her pillow and tried to think about more pleasant things. She concentrated on her wardrobe. It would soon be fall. Time to go shopping in New York. Heaven forbid that she be seen in last year's clothes. Fall meant Halloween. Maybe she should have a costume party. She'd fallen fast asleep trying to dream up a fantastic costume.

The next morning Steven had woken up with a terrible hangover. The first thing he did when he came downstairs to the kitchen was to get a bottle of aspirin out of the cabinet. He poured himself a glass of water and swallowed two pills. Mona was seated at the table dressed in a red and gold floral robe. She stared coldly at him. "I hope you're hung over big time, Steven."

"Thanks, Mona. I appreciate your sympathy."

"Asshole."

"Such flattery will get you nowhere, my dear."

"Don't try to be funny. About last night," she said with ice dripping from her words.

"What about it?" He acted a bit sheepish now.

"You're so fucking stupid."

"Why do you say that?" he asked in a bored tone.

"Because of your diabetes. You're gong to kill yourself one of these days." He flinched. She knew that he hated the very mention of the word. "Oh, by the way, Steven. I have a good idea."

He doubted that but he asked her what it was anyway.

"Next month is October."

"So what?"

"That means Halloween. I've decided that we should have a party."

"C'mon, Mona. Not another party. Jesus."

30

"I don't care what you think. I'm going to have a costume party whether you like it or not."

"I don't give a damn what you do." He wanted to tell her that living with her was like Halloween every day.

"I'll start making plans today."

Steven didn't want to listen to her flapping mouth. He got up from the table to prepare his insulin shot. It was only a few months since he'd been diagnosed as having adult-onset diabetes, and the very idea of pricking himself with a needle still made him break out in a cold sweat. Not that it was any surprise; his father had been cursed with the same problem, and he'd been suspicious of his own symptoms for a long time. Night sweats had plagued him, and so had constant thirst and listlessness. He'd finally gone to a specialist who tested him and confirmed his worst fears.

Steven had tried to educate Mona about diabetes. He showed her how he tested his blood sugar with a device called a glaucometer, and he showed her how much insulin he needed and how to inject it into his body in case he ran into a problem and couldn't do it himself. He knew that drinking and diabetes didn't mix—that his blood sugar could soar to a dangerous level. He knew he could slip into a coma and die. But whenever he'd get his drinking under control, Mona would start in, and he'd hit the bottle again.

Mona watched Steven inject himself. She smiled, remembering how rough she'd been when he'd had her give him a shot. "Fuck," he'd yelled. "Mona. Jesus Christ. Can't you be more gentle?"

She had pulled the needle out of his arm and thrown it across the kitchen. "Do it yourself," she screamed. "Your diabetes is your problem—not mine."

She was right about that, she thought. His diabetes was his problem. And his answer to that was that he often ignored the fact that he had it. She knew that was another reason why he made certain he got into the sauce. She never missed an opportunity to nag him that he drank so much that it was impossible to tell if he was having a

31

diabetic reaction or was he just plain drunk. She loved to remind him that he was "in denial," as shrinks called it. He'd told her that he'd had nightmares about his illness. In those dreams, he would suddenly go blind—which happens to many diabetics. Others involved having his legs amputated due to poor circulation. He would wake up in a cold sweat feeling for his legs. Once he was awake, he'd say that he was going to be careful about his health, as if she cared. Weakling that he was, he always went right back to the bottle.

He hadn't screwed her in ages—another side effect of diabetes. She was beginning to feel like a nun. No matter; she had a new lover picked out. The first time she saw their new gardener she got the hots for his body. The next time he came to do the weeding she'd be certain to offer to pluck a few for him.

Sometimes Steven told her that he was going to join a self-help group, but each time he picked up the phone to call he lost his courage. She hadn't helped. She'd rave that people spilling their guts to one another was sissy stuff. Only marshmallows had to ask for help. She knew that his doctor had recently laid the gruesome facts on the line to him. He'd warned that Steven had better quit his drinking, stop eating sugar, watch his diet, and to be certain to take his insulin regularly twice a day—or he *would* go into a diabetic coma—and probably die.

Steven did the opposite of what was right for him. He was late taking his shots, he ate too much sugar, and he drank heavily. Too often his memory failed him.

The neighbors' German shepherd barked and brought Mona crashing back to the moment. It was time to stop daydreaming about nonsense and finish decorating. Then the phone rang again. It was Cathy. She said she had forgotten to tell her that she might be a little bit late.

Meanwhile, Steven drove his truck toward Portland and complimented himself because he'd been pretty careful not to mention Piper until this morning. He had to admit that the blond mannequin did look like her—especially the curves and tits. The dark one didn't look a thing like Kelly Stewart. Steven scowled. Kelly was another story. He knew that she'd told Piper he'd tried to screw her last spring. Kelly, he thought. God, he hated her. She was the one who had ratted to Mona about Gina. Great legs on that broad. He shook his head; Kelly had made his life miserable for months by opening her big mouth to Mona.

Steven finally reached his destination. He pulled into the large blacktop parking lot and shut the engine off. Before he climbed out of the cab of his truck, he had to muster the courage to accomplish what he was about to do. These places always gave him the creeps, and he wondered, for a moment, why he was carrying out this plan. He was getting as bad as Mona. They were both nuttier than two March hares. Still, the more he thought about it he knew he couldn't pass this one up. Mona was going to die when she saw his surprise.

He returned to Cape Bethany an hour later than expected, and Mona was livid that he was late. He saw her standing in the bay window.

She stomped out of the living room to meet him, and Steven had no sooner climbed out of the truck than he heard Mona yell out the front door, "What the hell took you so long? Jesus, Steven." Then she spied what he had in the back of the truck, and her eyes lit up. "Where did you get it?" she cried, and felt her anger fade. "It's fantastic! Where did you get those chairs?"

"I have connections," he said. "Come on, Lady Dracula. Don't just stand there. Help me carry the thing into the living room."

"Is it heavy?"

"No. You'd be surprised at how light it is. Why don't you help me unload the truck."

After everything was in their living room Mona said, "God, Steven. What are we going to do with all this stuff?"

"You'll see," he promised with a sly grin.

Ten minutes later, Steven had finished making even rows out of the folding chairs that now faced his big surprise. Mona couldn't get over it. Right before her very eyes, in the bay window area of her living room, rested a six-foot-long pine casket. Steven pulled the window shades to darken the scene. He lifted the coffin lid, and when he did, the hinges squeaked.

Mona cringed from the irritating noise. "What are we going to do with all this stuff?"

"I thought you might've guessed by now," he said. "The answer is we're going to hold a funeral tonight."

Mona smiled and did a little dance. Steven hadn't seen her so overjoyed since he'd married her. "Steven. Sometimes you're so clever."

He puffed with pride. "Genius is more like it. I'll be right back," he said and promptly left the room. He returned right away carrying the blond Piper-like mannequin. "Found a use for her," he said and lowered her into the coffin. He still couldn't get over how much the doll resembled Piper. *Christ,* he said to himself. *She'll get the creeps when she gets a sneak preview of what she's going to look like when she croaks.* "Mona," he said and turned and faced her. "I think we ought to save the funeral for last. We should keep the room dark and lock the door. Don't you tell a soul."

She crossed her heart. "I won't."

"You didn't get it," he pouted.

"Get what?"

"My joke."

"What joke?"

"Don't tell a soul."

"Not funny," she snapped and then she said, "This casket is going to be the hit of the party."

He waved his index finger at her. "Don't call it a casket."

"Why?"

"I just learned the difference. It's called a coffin and a coffin is a trapezoid."

"What's a trapezoid?" she asked, impatiently. "I used to know but I can't remember."

"A trapezoid is a plane figure with four sides, two of

34

which are parallel."

"So what's a casket?" Mona asked.

"A casket," he said in a deep, eerie sounding voice, "is a box used for precious things."

"Who cares?"

"I do. Don't be such a bitch."

She let that pass. She was in such a good mood over Steven's surprise that she decided to be nice to him for a change. She told him that she'd fix him lunch. While she went to the kitchen, he fussed with the coffin. He could hear her humming some goofy off-key tune. "Damn, I hate her," he muttered to himself. She was being sweet, but he knew it wouldn't last. He could hardly wait to pack his bags and leave. Once again, he dreamed about being free. San Francisco was his first choice. San Diego would be second. Piper had to go with him. He knew that he could convince her to go as long as Kelly kept her mouth shut and didn't interfere. That was going to be a problem. To be with Piper all the time would be fantastic. He tried to imagine what it would be like to have her in his bed.

After lunch, Mona got four of her very best brass candlesticks out of her china closet in the dining room and put them on matching end tables at each end of the coffin. But it still looked too plain. She phoned a local florist and ordered four large baskets of flowers. After she hung up, she made a mental note to be certain to take an allergy pill or she would have swollen, itchy eyes and go into a fit of sneezing.

Afternoon turned into evening. It was time for Mona and Steven to go upstairs and get dressed in their costumes. At the top of the stairs, they separated. She went into her dressing room and he into his.

A half hour later, Mona stared at her image in her full-length mirror. It was obvious that she'd gone to great lengths to perfect her costume. Had she been invited to a party she knew she would win first prize. What a sight! She waved at her image. "How ya doin, Joe?" Her voice sounded so sexy.

"Just fine, Stella," Mona deepened her voice to sound

like a man.

In the meantime, Steven was in a terrible frame of mind over getting ready. He hadn't wanted to dress up like an absentminded psychiatrist. That had been Mona's idea. He wanted to be an Egyptian mummy, but Mona wouldn't hear of it, and she'd badgered him until he'd relented. He'd borrowed a white coat from a doctor friend, a black stethoscope, and a thermometer to put in his lapel pocket. Now, he was ready. He took one final glimpse of himself in his mirror before he went to find Mona. "Stupid looking outfit," he mumbled, "The mummy would've been great."

He tapped lightly on Mona's door. "Come in," she said sweetly.

He was fiddling with the top button on his white shirt. "Collar is too tight," he grimaced. The minute he looked at Mona he had to laugh. "Mona. Sometimes you're so clever."

"Steven. I want you to meet Joe and Stella."

Steven waved. He took Mona's costume in from top to toe. Joe had short hair (Mona had pulled her long hair back on that side of her head and pinned it) and sported half a mustache on his face. She'd used a heavy black eyebrow pencil to draw a straight line down the middle of her forehead, chiseled nose and dimpled chin to separate the two halves. Stella had long hair and wore flaming red lipstick. A round dab of hot pink rouge dotted one cheek. Heavy green eyeshadow and black liner was on her eye, offset by a pair of exceptionally long false eyelashes. A huge silver hoop earring dangled from her ear.

Steven said, "I just thought of a name to call myself. Do you want to hear it?"

"Of course," she said.

"Well, since you're dressed as a split personality, I'll be Dr. Duet."

"That's great Steven," Mona smiled and then she pouted. "You don't know how lucky you are that your costume was so easy to put together. Mine was a pain in the ass. Do you know how difficult it is to attach half a man's white shirt, black tie, and one gray pantleg to half of a blue silk evening gown?" She talked so fast she was out of breath.

"No, I can't imagine," he said to pacify her. He recognized Stella's gown. Mona had bought it last year at Bergdorf Goodman's while on a shopping trip to New York. As well as he could recollect, she'd only worn the thing once. She'd never dream of wearing the same outfit twice. He also noticed that she'd stuffed something, probably cotton, into one bosom to give Stella a big bust. He'd like to bust her, he thought. Right in the fucking mouth.

"And then," Mona was still talking, "came the finishing touches. One black cuff link for Joe's shirt, a cigar for his side of the mouth, one white sock and a black shoe. Do you think his hair looks okay?" She didn't give Steven a chance to answer. "I chose a rhinestone bow for Stella's wig. Don't you think her hair looks great?"

Steven nodded. "Isn't that a Jackie Kennedy hairdo?"

"Yes. Right out of the sixties," Mona touched Stella's hair. Steven noticed that the rhinestone bracelet she was wearing matched her bow.

"And," Mona continued, "I had to stitch this silk scarf to the necktie—let alone the problems I had with this," she tapped her leg, "damned knee-high stocking. What a devil that was to sew."

Steven looked down at Mona's feet. He saw that Stella wore a silver flat shoe. This made sense. He knew Mona wouldn't wear a high heel because that would've made her much taller than Joe.

". . . but it was worth it," Mona said. "I'm positive that I'll have the best costume tonight." She sighed pleased with herself and then she picked up a small silver evening bag off her nightstand and clutched it in Stella's hand. "Joe was the hardest . . ."

Steven interrupted. "Mona. It's almost time for our guests to arrive. Don't you think that we'd better go downstairs to greet them?"

"You're quite right, Dr. Duet," she said in a deep voice.

"That was Joe speaking in case you're wondering." She couldn't stop laughing until she reached the kitchen.

Cathy and her staff of four arrived less than ten minutes later and told Mona that her costume was absolutely wonderful. Cathy had brought along a camera and took two pictures of her. Cathy had costumed herself as a French chef, two of her men had dressed like Frankenstein, and the two women were vampires. Mona thought that the men looked the best. She admired their stringy black wigs, fanged fake teeth, deep red lips, droplets of fake blood on their chins and on the front of their white silk blouses. Steven cast his vote for the two French maids.

He made certain the caterers understood that they were not to step one foot into the living room because he wanted them to be surprised about the funeral along with everyone else. All four said they wouldn't go near that room. When they got busy, he dashed into the living room to make certain everything was in order. The minute he flipped on the light switch he could tell that things weren't right. He'd specifically told Mona that the lid of the coffin should be closed and she'd left it open. He blew the Piper-like mannequin a kiss, bent over, kissed her forehead, gave her rock-hard breasts a good feel, and then he slammed the lid. Mona had put the flower displays in the right spots. The window shades were still down. What was missing? "Aha," he said and turned on the stereo. He could hear somber funeral music coming from the outside.

Satisfied with the arrangements, Steven turned off the light and stepped into the front hall. Next he made a PLEASE KEEP OUT sign to tack on the living room door. When that was finished, he flipped the outside light switch, opened the front door, stood on the landing, and surveyed the front yard. His two flood lamps illuminated the minigraveyard. The angel, Mazie, hovered in a foggy mist over the tombstones. It was easy to read the phosphorescent names. He saw Piper's and Kelly's and . . . *Wait until they see what's coming later.* He chuckled and shut the door. It was time to have a drink before the guests arrived; maybe he'd have two. That was the only way he could muster the courage to get Piper alone and ask her if she'd consider running away to California with him. He had no idea what he was going to do if she turned him down.

Out in the kitchen, Mona had put on a white apron and was stirring her pot of chili. Cathy and one of the French maids chatted away while seated at the table arranging hors d'oeuvres on huge dolly-covered glass platters. Mona happened to see the maid sneak a cracker. She hadn't finished taking the first bite when Mona yelled, "Keep your hands off the food. I didn't hire you to pig out." The maid jumped and quickly swallowed. She lowered her eyes to avoid Mona's glare, and Cathy kicked her under the table.

Mona looked at the clock on the stove. She knew that her guests would start arriving any minute. She had already sent one Frankenstein and one vampire to stand at the front door to take coats. She wondered what Kelly and Piper were wearing for costumes. With a twinge of jealousy she hoped it wasn't anything too sexy which would take away from her creation. *And,* she thought, *Steven had better keep his mitts off Piper tonight or I'll* . . . Suddenly she heard a car pull into the driveway, and then a door slammed. She heard another car arrive, and excitement shot through her. She took off her apron, draped it on the back of a chair, smoothed Stella's hair, then Joe's, and grabbed her silver evening bag off the countertop. Head held high, she swept past Cathy and left the kitchen to greet her guests. There was no question in her mind that her Halloween party was going to become legend in Cape Bethany.

The Halloween party was in full swing, and everyone was having a great time except Piper. Steven had been trying to seduce her all evening. He kept saying that he had an important question to ask her and would she step into the living room with him for a few minutes. Piper wasn't about to fall for that one. He was so perverted. The last time he'd asked her to go with him she hadn't said a word. She'd simply walked away and left him standing with his mouth wide open. He'd caught up with her and whispered so nobody could hear him, "Sonofabitch. Say something, will you. I don't know if it's you or Kelly I'm talking to. Take off that mask so I can see your face?" Piper walked away.

Piper assumed that Steven must've finally given up on her because she hadn't seen him for about a half hour. Kelly wasn't around either. The last time she'd seen her she'd been standing next to the punch bowl. Piper assumed that she was in one of the bathrooms. She was frustrated because she wanted to tell her about Steven. She decided to go upstairs to see if Kelly was up there, but before she could, Mona came out of the kitchen into the dining room, followed by Steven. "Okay everyone," she said. "It's time to unmask so we can see who you are." Piper didn't hesitate. Her mask made her face hot.

Steven stared at Piper when he was certain Mona wasn't looking. Piper ignored him. Mona said, "Everyone line up. It's time for the big surprise of the night. Follow Steven and me. Boy. Are you going to flip out!"

Mona took hold of Steven's arm and they led the costumed parade into the front hall. They came to a halt in front of the living room door. Rumor had it that that's where the surprise awaited, and whispered excitement filled the air.

Piper was right behind Steven and Mona. There were too many guests to fit all together in the hallway, so some had overflowed into the dining room. Piper searched in vain for Kelly. She asked a clown standing beside her if he had seen a girl dressed like her. The clown said no.

Piper again scanned the crowd but there wasn't a sign of Kelly. Where was she? She was taking too long. Suddenly, an uncomfortable sensation washed over Piper. She moved out of the line. Maybe Kelly was sick. She would go upstairs and see if she was in one of the bathrooms. Before she had a chance to move, Steven began to speak.

He said, "I know that you've all been curious as to why

you couldn't go into the living room all evening, because I snooped and overheard some of you talking. Nosy. Nosy. Well, you're about to find out what's in there." He rubbed his hands together, smiled and said, "But remember folks. Curiosity killed the cat."

Mona cackled witchlike. Steven opened the door. The two of them stepped into the living room and Piper and the rest of the guests followed. The room was pitch black until Steven lit a candle. When his guests spied the pine coffin and the rows of wooden chairs all that could be heard was a lot of oohs, aahs, feminine squeals—and Mona's sneezing, because the heavily scented flowers triggered her allergies. The living room looked too much like a funeral parlor to suit Piper, and goose flesh covered her arms. There was something sinister in the air. She wanted to flee but her legs wouldn't move.

She watched in horror as one of the Frankenstein caterers walked up to the coffin, pulled a book of matches out of his coat pocket, and proceeded to light four brass candlesticks—two on each end of the coffin. Flickering candlelight created spooky, wiggling shadows on the walls. Piper glanced at Mona and Steven and scowled. They were so weird. The last of the guests came through the door and then Steven closed it.

Kelly still wasn't in sight, and Piper was angry. If she'd left with some guy without telling her she was going to wring her neck. But underneath she knew that Kelly wouldn't leave without her. Something had to be wrong.

Piper hadn't realized that she was muttering under her breath until a tall man with steel gray hair asked, "Did you say something?"

"No, no," Piper answered. "I was just clearing my throat," She was letting her imagination run wild. It was time to get hold of herself. Kelly would show up any time now.

"Step right this way," Steven said in a creepy voice, and then he laughed in a sinister way. Next, he bowed and with a wide sweep of his hand ushered his guests to their rock hard, wooden seats. Everyone sat. Piper found herself in the front row. She fidgeted. There was still no sign of Kelly.

One of the hired French maids turned on the stereo, and somber funeral music filled the air. Piper and the rest of the guests squirmed. One whispered to another, "This is too real. Jesus. Mona and Steven have gone too far."

"Let's go into the dining room and get some punch," whimpered a pretty woman costumed in a nurse's uniform, who carried a hot water bottle sporting a bandaid patch. She and the tall yellow chicken she'd been talking with hopped off their chairs and made a quick exit.

Piper felt a strong wave of panic; funerals of any kind did that to her. She found it hard to breathe. She had to get out of that room that very minute. She stood up and walked over to Steven. "I have to get out of here." Steven laughed. Everyone was watching. Mona came over to her, took her by the hand and led her back to her chair.

Mona went to stand in front of the coffin. She said, "Dear friends. One by one you must come forward and pay your last respects to the dearly departed. Let's see who will be first. She looked right at Piper. "C'mon. You lead the way."

Piper froze. She couldn't imagine what Mona and Steven had put in that pine box, and she didn't want to know. All she wanted was to find Kelly and leave. But she knew that Mona would force the issue if she didn't get up and look at her surprise. She decided to brave a quick peek and then go. Once again she stood up, and she moved hesitantly until she was about two feet away from the coffin.

Mona, always the actress, came forward and put a comforting arm around Piper's shoulders. She walked her up to the coffin. They were so close that it was impossible to take another step without bumping into it. Steven came and stood on the other side of Piper. He reached out and lifted the coffin lid. The hinges shrieked. But Piper didn't hear the noise over everyone's screams, including her own. Kelly was in that coffin! Her mustard yellow wig was cockeyed. Her mask was off, her lollipop was still in her hands, and the tiny teddy bear's head was still peeking out of her pocket. Blood oozed out of her mouth and nose. Her lifeless blue eyes were half open. Her watermelon-colored tongue protruded. Her throat looked horribly bruised and bloody. Piper reached out, touched her, and found Kelly's skin clammy and sticky as that of a dead chicken. "Get up, Kel," she cried. "Oh, Kelly. No. Please God," she said, and fainted. The party was over.

Chapter Three

Detective Matthew Carter

While Mona and Steven's Halloween party was in full swing, Detective Matt Carter of the State Police had come home from work to greet trick-or-treaters at his door. He had recently rented a four room log cabin on Soudahook Lake in Gray, so he wasn't too familiar with the area. But he knew there were lots of kids living nearby, because he saw them waiting for the school bus Monday through Friday. He'd expected to be mobbed by ghosts, witches, scarecrows, and parents. Not one kid showed up.

Tall, dark-haired Matt Carter knew that if he was ever lucky enough to have a family, he wanted to share in everything they did. He loved kids and holidays, especially Christmas and Halloween. Even though he'd put in a hard day at headquarters he'd looked forward to handing out candy. He'd had no idea how much to buy. Twenty dollars later he'd arrived home with a lot of sugar-free gum, three bags of chocolate kisses and four packages of caramels—his favorite. The sight of the huge bowl of trick-or-treat candy depressed him. "And how about all the money I spent on decorations?" he grumbled. There were cardboard witches and skinny skeletons taped to his front windows, and he'd even used a perfectly good white sheet, stuffed it full of crunchy fallen leaves he'd gathered on his property, and had it swinging from the flagpole on his front porch. "And how about that jack-o-lantern I carved? Christ. The teeth are perfect." He took off his suitcoat, grabbed a beer out of the fridge, and sat down at the kitchen table to rest a few minutes before he fixed his supper.

Matt thought about the kids he came across on his job as a detective. Most were robbed of their youth and too many lost their lives. That was the part of being a detective that bothered him the most, and he wasn't alone; his colleagues felt the same way. Some had burned out and quit before the brass decided to bring the staff some relief from the stresses by scheduling everyone three months on homicide and three on child abuse cases.

Matt recalled that he was eleven when he had his first encounter with death. That's when his friend Marty drowned in the Saco river. He'd never forget how bloated Marty looked when he was fished out of the water. He'd had nightmares for months. Yet Marty was luckier than most of the kids he came across on the job.

The first time Matt was called to a murder scene a sixteen year old girl had had her throat slashed from ear to ear. Her boyfriend had killed her because she wanted to break up with him. When Matt saw the girl's body, he'd felt dizzy and he had to run from the room before he threw up. His stomach wouldn't settle down for a couple of days after that.

And then there was that little boy who had been beaten by the mother's boyfriend . . . seeing his battered body had made him think seriously about quitting. Then he was able to solve that case, and he forgot that he'd contemplated throwing in the towel—until the next time. There hadn't been a trial for that little boy's killer. The man, a strapping 250 pound illiterate, made the mistake of pulling a gun. The detective who'd had him cornered was faster and shot the guy in the chest. *Good riddance*, Matt thought; the sonofabitch had had a history of molesting little boys.

And the mother. What an ice queen. She'd known about her boyfriend's police record and she also knew that he had been molesting the kid. She should've gone to prison for the rest of her life. Matt had heard through the grapevine that she had herself a new boyfriend and that she was pregnant. He knew a couple who'd been trying unsuccessfully for years to have a baby. Nice people. He sighed deeply.

Life made no sense to Matt. Sometimes he felt like quitting his job and going up north to live deep in the woods like a hermit. During such moments, he'd tell himself that if he was going to do it he'd better hurry. Maine was changing fast, too fast to suit him, and one of these days there weren't going to be any woods left to live in.

Matt had just started his homicide stint that morning. He'd put in a long but fruitful day. After enduring months of agonizing delays, he and his colleagues had solved a murder of a seven-year-old girl. Some twisted, fifty-year-old bastard, with a past history of molesting little girls, had kidnapped and raped her in the back seat of a totaled Chevy in an auto graveyard. Then he'd strangled her with her own belt. An employee had found her body when he went to salvage a side mirror from that car for a customer.

The medical examiner called to the scene had said that the girl's body hadn't been there too long because rigor mortis hadn't set in yet. The vision Matt now conjured up of that lifeless child stretched out on that soiled, torn seat made his eyes water. What a cute kid, he thought. Dark curly hair and dimples. She looked like she was sleeping. The sight of her had damned near shattered his composure at the scene.

Then the little girl's mother arrived. That poor thing. Who the hell was it that brought her to the scene? He heard the woman cry out in his mind, *My baby, my baby*. He had to drag her away from the car so she wouldn't contaminate the evidence, and it was one of the toughest things he'd ever had to do. She tried to bite, kick and punch him. All she wanted was to hold her little girl. Matt had to pin her arms to restrain her until she calmed down. He'd kept his cool on the surface but inside he was a mess. Finally, she tired and Matt felt her taut body slacken. Whimpering like a wounded animal, she rested her head against his chest and sobbed and sobbed. It had taken everything in him not to give in and let her go to her child. "Please, please let me go," she begged. "I want to hold my baby." Matt had to ask one of the other detectives to take over before he broke down. From that moment on, he knew that he could never look at a dead person as other than evidence. If he did otherwise, he would become too emotionally involved, and he might as well hang up his career.

Matt took another swig of beer and thought about how well he'd managed to control his emotions in front of the public. He wished he could be that successful with his memories. There wasn't a victim, child or adult, or their families, that he'd ever forgotten. The list was growing. He didn't know if his brain could store much more. Sometimes he had recurrent nightmares. There was that little girl in Kennebunk and that boy in . . . Christ, he thought. I've seen it all. Cut throats, strangulations, shootings, burns. He wondered if all the weirdos in the world had moved to Maine. He knew he was working himself into a dark depression. It was time to think about other things.

In spite of all the gore and heartache he'd seen, Matt couldn't imagine doing anything else for a living. He was cut out for police work. His father and grandfather had been detectives. Much to his father's pride, Matt had been one of the youngest troopers to make detective, right after his required three years of highway patrol. And after that he attended the NESPAC—New England State Police Administrator's Conferences in Connecticut. Next, he'd been sent down to Baltimore to take a course in medical-legal issues, and he'd taken several generic courses at the academy in Waterville, Maine. In between, there would be a murder or some other god-awful thing and he would be swamped with investigative work. "Nothing quite like on-the-job experience," Matt said out loud and realized that he was talking to himself. "That's a bad sign buddy boy."

He took the last swig of beer, got up from the table, and went into the living room. He grabbed a piece of candy out out of the huge mixing bowl he'd placed on a table next to the front door, tore off the wrapper, and popped it into his mouth. No sooner had he swallowed the last of it than he had an urge to eat another one. He counted to twenty in order to restrain himself. No will power. He ate two more. He sat down on his black leather sofa and swung his feet onto a pile of magazines stacked on top of his lobster trap coffee table with the dust-laden glass top.

He laid his head against the back of the sofa and closed his eyes. He'd been a detective for three years. It seemed like yesterday he'd graduated from the academy. What a big deal he'd thought he was that day strutting around in his uniform. He laughed over the image, and once again he thought about how life in Maine had changed. Parents didn't allow their children to do some of the things that they used to do when they were young. His active mind twirled with thoughts about Halloween night when he was a kid. He'd arrive home after trick or treating with a shopping bag full of candy and charge upstairs to his room to dump his haul onto his bed. All the good stuff—like caramels and chocolate kisses—he'd put in his top dresser drawer for safekeeping. The kind of things he didn't like he'd given to his mother. Matt smiled as he recalled that she liked sour balls. He screwed up his face as if he had just tasted one.

He quickly unwrapped another piece of candy, which reminded him again that he wasn't hearing knocks on his door. "Shit," he said. He toyed with the idea of going out for the evening. He knew he was too tired to make the effort, but he longed for some female company.

He found himself missing Laura; then remembered their last argument and decided he didn't miss her at all. He couldn't believe that a year had passed since they'd split up. Where the hell did the time go?

Matt finally admitted to himself, sitting there on the sofa, that he was lonely. It wasn't that he lacked the opportunity to date, because he knew plenty of women that he could take out. The problem was that they came wanting careers—not a husband and children. He wanted someone that didn't mind staying home and taking care of a family. Others made no bones about saying all they wanted was to get laid. Laura had practically dragged him into bed the first night they met. She was good at that. For a brief time he thought he loved her. He remembered the look on her face when he asked her to marry him; she'd laughed in his face, and that was the night they split up. A friend had told him that he'd heard Laura was living with a doctor. Not long after that, Matt started going out to bars, but he soon tired of the single-scene watering holes. He decided that he'd much rather sit at home before a roaring fire watching television or reading a good book.

But Matt knew that he'd have to start going out again or he'd never meet anyone. And he was getting old. The week before he'd found his first gray hair—what a shock that had been. Worse, his thirty-first birthday was just around the corner. Once again he wondered if he should go out for the evening. Who knows, he told himself. Maybe I'll find my dream woman. Before you can have kids you have to meet their mother, dummy.

The men at work flashed in his mind. According to them, he was married to his job. Little did they know the truth.

Matt visualized coming home from work to a wife. She would be trim and blonde with blue eyes, great legs and . . . she'd have to like kids, because he intended to spend a lot of time making babies. It would be perfect if they enjoyed the same kind of books, and music. She had to like golden retrievers. Matt could see the dog stretched out in front of the hearth. His name would be Sam. He knew for sure that his future wife, if he ever found one, was going to have to be a special kind of woman to tolerate his kind of job—like his buddies wives, if there were any left from that mold. They had to put up with interrupted plans at a moment's notice, long hours alone, and constant worry. He wondered if he should've been a ditch digger, a bank teller—or a movie star. His name could be

Matt Redford or Matt Newman. He laughed over that one and reached for another caramel, vowing that it would be his last; he'd eaten enough sugar to make his dentist cringe. It was time to fix a decent meal, watch some television, and then call it a night.

He looked forward to being able to sleep late the next morning. He could see the black wall phone just inside the kitchen door. "Don't ring," he commanded, stood up, and walked on tired feet out to the kitchen to prepare his supper. He'd bake himself some fresh haddock he'd bought at Shaw's on the way home. His mouth watered at the thought. He'd pop a couple of potatoes in the oven, make a large salad, and boil a whole bag of frozen peas.

While the potatoes baked, Matt went into the bedroom and removed his shoes and socks. When he first got home, he'd taken off his belt and black leather holster that held his loaded thirteen-shot, semiautomatic Baretta 9mm pistol. He had put it down carefully, where he always did, on top of his bureau. He changed into some baggy, gray sweats, and a blue T-shirt, and then returned to the kitchen to fix his supper.

After eating too much, Matt sat before the television and watched Peter Jennings present America with the latest news. Most all of it was about death and destruction. Then Wheel of Fortune came on and by the time that was over Matt couldn't hold his eyes open. It took all of his remaining energy to drag himself into the bedroom. He didn't bother to undress. The minute his head touched his pillow he was gone. He had nightmares about victims again, and he tossed and turned, moaned and groaned. Twice he awoke and then he immediately returned to his torture. He was too damned tired to stay awake. Any sleep was the lesser of two evils.

The hands of the alarm clock on the nightstand beside Matt's bed were almost on midnight when the phone rang. He didn't wake up right away. When he did, he had to fumble in the dark to find the receiver. "No," he mumbled. "Don't tell me." He finally found the phone, but in doing so he knocked his watch, the clock, and his wallet onto the

50

floor. "Shit. Sonofabitch," he grumbled and then he said a curt, "Hello."

"Hi, Matt, this is Jake. What did I just hear you say, old buddy? Don't you know that sweet talk will get you nowhere." He laughed but Matt didn't.

"What's up?" Matt yawned and stretched, his anger forgotten.

"Cape Bethany Police just called. Young girl bought the farm on Lighthouse Road. Ritzy area. Seems there was a Halloween party going on. She was strangled. Shoved in a pine coffin. Is that weird or what?"

"Jesus, Jake. Are you serious?"

"I'm not kidding. That's what the Cape Bethany police told me. Anyway, like I said, the place is on Lighthouse Road. Do you need directions?"

"No. I know where that is," Matt said. "I used to live in Cape Bethany. Did you call the others?"

"Yeah. They're already on the way. So you used to live out there. Rich kid, huh?"

"Nope. Poor. Sorry to disappoint you, Jake, old boy. My mother couldn't stand the snobbery out there so we moved. Look, if you get there before I do, make certain that the scene isn't contaminated. Don't let anyone mess up. I'll be there just as soon as I can." Matt didn't bother to say goodbye. He cradled the receiver and then he reached for the switch on the lamp on his nightstand. He blinked from the glare of the 100 watt bulb but he was wide awake now. "Murder in Cape Bethany. Wouldn't my mother flip. I'll be damned."

He climbed out of bed, staggered into the bathroom, wet a wash cloth with warm water, and held it against his face until it cooled and he felt refreshed. He shaved so quickly that he cut his chin. Blood trickled. He tore off a piece of tissue and held it against the scrape until it stopped. He brushed his teeth, gargled with mint mouthwash, patted deodorant under his arms and aftershave on his face. Then he charged out of the bathroom. He didn't waste any time changing his clothes. Past experience taught him that to reach the crime scene as soon as possible was essential before the vital evidence could be destroyed. He often wondered how many murderers were free because of careless cops or volunteer rescue people screwing up evidence.

He grabbed his belt and holster off the bureau and put it on. Over this he wore a tweed sports jacket. He glanced at himself in his bedroom mirror. As usual, he had to duck in order to see his head because he was a dite shy of six three. He tried unsuccessfully to flatten the two cowlicks—one in front and one on the back of his head. They always misbehaved, especially after shampooing. He never could make them go in the right direction. Women loved his cowlicks—at least that's what Laura used to tell him. She also said that women thought he was handsome, in a rugged sort of way. His colleagues teased him about his looks. "Pretty boy," Jake called him. Matt gave it right back. He was forever reminding Jake that that was the only time the truth didn't hurt.

It was time to get going. His watch read twelve-thirty. Not too bad, considering. As he went out the door he felt a familiar thud hit his stomach. He knew that the uncomfortable sensation was not caused by having eaten too much candy and supper; he suffered the same discomfort every time he witnessed an autopsy.

He remembered his first. He'd damned near passed out when the medical examiner cut into the bloodless flesh of that young guy who had been murdered by his girlfriend after an argument. Matt learned one thing for sure, and that was that a dead person didn't feel a thing. No pain killers required. No complaints from the patient. An autopsy, to Matt, was like being in a butcher shop for cannibals. Every stainless steel sink he came across, including his own, instantly caused him to recall that clinical warehouse of the dead, and metal tables made his stomach churn.

Outside, Matt climbed into his unmarked, green Chevy Celebrity and sped away. It was quite chilly but after a few minutes he was oblivious to the weather, his mind focused on what awaited him on Lighthouse Road in Cape

Bethany. When he reached the town of Gray he decided against taking Rt. 126 to Portland. It was faster to take the Maine Turnpike down to South Portland. From there he would take back roads, making use of shortcuts he'd discovered years ago before his parents sold their house in Cape Bethany. He had been in junior high at the time. That was a long time ago.

Cape Bethany, he thought and whistled long and low. Living out there meant you were as wealthy as you could possibly be—unless you had a house in Cape Bethany park, where his family had lived. Outside the park, the homes were magnificent. Sprawling lawns were rich velvet-green and weedless and gave way to breathtaking views of the open sea and stretches of rugged coast. The park, on the other hand, was inland. It was a closely knit development orginally constructed for returning veterans of World War II. The Cape Cod style homes cost under $4000 back then. People who lived there assumed they'd never go up in value. Matt smiled. He'd recently seen an ad in the Sunday paper offering a park house for $110,000. His mother would've been pleased.

Matt smiled again when he recalled how furious his mother became when she thought about her sister-in-law, on his father's side, who was fortunate enough to live in a gorgeous house right on the water. His mother never forgot what the woman had said to her when she found out their family was moving to Cape Bethany. "Why, Sarah. I can't believe you and Joe are moving to the Cape. Goodness. I don't know if you'll ever be able to get used to all the money out here. But you're moving to the park so there's nothing for you to worry about." Matt's aunt still lived in Cape Bethany. He hadn't seen her since his mother's funeral. There was no love lost as far as he was concerned. There wasn't a doubt in his mind that the old biddy jumped for joy the day his family moved. It must've been sweet relief for her when her relatives left their park house. She no longer had to apologize to her friends about where her brother and his family lived.

Matt glanced out the car window. He could tell by the

hilly landscape and some of the elegant houses that he was in Cape Bethany. It wouldn't be long and he would be on Lighthouse Road. He was pretty certain he knew the address and that the house sat on three, maybe four acres of lawn. There wouldn't be any crab grass or, heaven forbid, a dandelion showing its common face around there. Matt assumed the owners had a housekeeper. And he bet that the man of the house was a golfer and that his wife belonged to the garden club. Both probably held memberships in the local country club. They probably knew his aunt. His mother used to say that his aunt lived for the Cape Bethany clubs.

Matt's mother and his older sister often said that they'd never spent a happy day in all the years that they had to endure living in Cape Bethany. His mother yearned to be able to belong to the garden club but she was never asked to join. She used to sputter, "Matthew, that aunt of yours is no different than all the rest of the snooty women who live out here." Matt had tried to convince his mother that the mothers of his friends who lived outside the park weren't at all like the picture she painted.

His mother got furious with him every time he defended the women of Cape Bethany. And if he went too far in their defense, she'd remind him about what happened to his sister. He could hear her plain as day saying, "All those snooty women donate their castoff clothing to their second hand store in Perriwinkle Cove. Remember your poor sister's humiliation when that dreadful girl in her class yelled, "Susie. That sweater you're wearing used to be mine. My mother donated it to her club last week." Your sister will never get over that, Matthew Carter. And neither will I. Shame on you," she'd said and scowled. "Don't you have any pride? Don't you let me hear you say another good word about those uppity witches." His mother remained convinced that one's popularity in Cape Bethany hinged on the amount of one's income, one's clothing labels, and not to forget—one's family background.

"That was a crock, Mum," Matt said out loud and turned onto Lighthouse Road. Driving along, he recalled the sunny fall day when his family moved to the town of New Gloucester—far enough away from Cape Bethany to suit his mother. She couldn't wait to lock the door for the last time. Back then, he couldn't understand why she'd felt that way. He liked Cape Bethany so he was angry with his parents. But it was impossible to feel miserable in such a friendly atmosphere that prevailed their first day in New Gloucester. Their new neighbors came from miles around to welcome his family. Their kitchen table and counters were covered with homemade pies, cookies, jars of blueberry jams, and breads. His mother was in her glory when she was asked to join the garden club. The dark days she spent in Cape Bethany soon faded. She smiled more often and took an interest in her home. Soon the 1815 farm house with the four fireplaces looked fit enough to be featured in a magazine.

Eventually, an elderly lady in town taught his mother how to braid rugs, and Matt's mother had taken to braiding like a duck to water. He loved the rug he had on his living room floor, which she'd given to him for Christmas the year before she died. She'd told him that it was going to be a surprise for his sister. He'd even helped cut up old blankets, clothes, and bolts of material his mother bought on sale in woolen mill outlets. She sat in her oak rocker and braided for hours on end. And then came the last touch, which was to tie the rug together. He could see her now, seated on the floor lacing those long braids until her hands got sore and her legs kinked. Matt sighed deeply. It didn't seem possible that his mother had been dead over a year. Now he could feel a wave of homesickness washing over him.

His mother had been a sweetheart, but she was stubborn. She'd get something in her head and nobody could budge her. Like when she was dying. He remembered his father trying over and over to convince her how ridiculous it was for her to want to be buried in the old cemetery out in Cape Bethany. He reminded her over and over how much she'd hated living there. It was no use. She said she had her mind made up and that was that.

The family couldn't believe their ears when they heard her recite the epitaph she wanted on her tombstone. At first, they thought she was kidding. Not so. She had her request written into her will. Matt and his family buried her right alongside some of the wealthiest residents of quaint Cape Bethany. Her grave was situated in the very front row a few yards from an ancient, stark white church with a tall steeple. Her tombstone was light gray and it read: "I finally got used to all the money out here." Matt chuckled. He remembered the look on his aunt's face when she read it. God, Mum, he said to himself. You sure were something.

Matt glanced at the sky. As if on cue, a huge harvest moon peeked out from behind blackish wispy clouds, illuminating the stately houses. He caught passing glimpses of the shimmering, open sea, and he rolled his window down and inhaled. Fresh salty air filled his lungs and made him feel alive. He let it drift into his car until he felt even more awake.

Every house along the way was lit up. Police sirens had obviously rousted people out of their comfortable beds. "Lighthouse Road," he said out loud. "Jesus, why in hell would somebody kill a person out here?" He didn't have the answer to that, yet. But he did know that when it came morning, and the news of the murder spread, the folks in good old Cape Bethany would be mortified. "Let's hear you toss this around the country club, Auntie," Matt said out loud. "Jesus, Mum. I wish you were here for this one. It would sure brighten your day."

Matt rounded a curve and spied the flashing blue lights of the local police in the driveway up ahead. And then he saw a yellow light. This told him that the ambulance was there. "Shit," he said. "Sonofabitch. There goes the evidence. Why oh why do those volunteer rescue people always fuck it up?" He couldn't recall one murder scene that they hadn't contaminated trying to save a corpse. They would never learn.

"And what's that?" he asked himself. "Oh, no." He

56

spied scores of costumed people running to beat hell toward parked cars lining both sides of the driveway and the road. Doors slammed. Engines caught. Headlights glared. Matt felt slightly dizzy as he watched Volvo wagons, BMWs, Mercedes, and Jeep Cherokees speed away. Some people were in such a hurry that they peeled rubber and squealed tires. Matt only hoped the murderer wasn't one of them. "Jesus," he yelled, banging the steering wheel with his fist, and he pressed on the gas pedal. "How the hell are we going to find out who was at the party and who was who? Who the fuck let those people leave?" He turned into the driveway and almost ran over a fat pumpkin with a limp green stem on its head and bright green leotards on its skinny legs. The pumpkin gave him the finger and fled.

Matt parked, shut the engine off, unbuckled, and climbed out. He saw that he was blocking two police cars that had radios blaring, crackling static. He spied the medical examiner's light gray, metallic station wagon parked next to the rescue unit near the front of the house. It was going to be a nightmare. He still had no idea how he and his buddies would be able to process the scene—let alone round up everyone for questioning. Even if they were furnished with a guest list, a person could say they were invited but didn't attend or left early or . . . He doubted if they would ever find the killer.

The wind blew hard off the sea and whistled through the naked tree branches. A dense fog was spreading fast. The fog horn at Perriwinkle cove blasted—warning ships at sea. Matt looked up at the sky. The harvest moon had disappeared. A dog began to howl off in the distance, and Matt shivered. Suddenly, quaint Cape Bethany was beginning to look like a gruesome and fitting scene for a murder. He felt a headache coming on. It was so damp and raw out now that he could see his breath. He turned his collar up and hunched his shoulders. There was bound to be a heavy frost by morning.

He had no sooner locked his car door when a van pulled

into the driveway behind him. Matt waited for his colleagues Jake Thomas, Judd Stone, and Paul Reynolds to get out.

Jake was first. He had his camera in his hand. "How ya doing, Matt?" he said with a grin and didn't give him a chance to answer. "Murder at a Halloween party. Jesus." he sputtered. "To think I left my wife and got out of my warm bed for this shit." Jake was known for his bitching. He was also known to be one of the best homicide detectives around. "Damn it all to hell, Matt," he grumbled. "Just what we need—a frigging Halloween party. What in the hell is this world coming to . . ."

"Make certain you take enough shots of everything," Matt said.

"Gotcha," Jake said.

"Your photos ought to be really entertaining," Judd said. He took in the house from the roof to the cellar. "Doesn't look like the folks who live here are feeling the economic crunch. So this is how the other half lives. My, my."

Paul, a fifteen year veteran, who never seemed to get upset over anything, pointed to the mock graveyard in the front yard. "Different," he said and shook his head. "Really different. I don't know about the rest of you guys, but I've got a feeling this case is going to be a real winner." He scratched his gray head and said, "Sonofabitch. Will you look at those tombstones. I bet those are the names of all the guests. Gives me the jitters."

"Forget that stuff," Judd said. "Take a look at that angel in the back. Scares the shit out of me. Whoever made her is really twisted. Man, oh man."

"Screw the angel," Paul said. "The folks who live in this palace must be down a quart to make that thing. Crazy I tell ya. Right out of a horror book."

"What's the matter, Paul?" Judd asked and laughed. "Afraid you're going to meet the Count tonight?"

"Naw. I like to have my neck sucked. Don't you? Hey. Maybe there's a lady vampire inside. Bet she'd love to sink her teeth into this sexy old hide." Paul laughed at what he'd said but nobody else did. He scowled and said, "Sorry. I didn't mean to keep you guys up. Christ. I'm so tired I wouldn't know if anyone did actually sink their fangs into me. Haven't had much sleep the past week," he yawned. "Seems like Maine folks are in a bad temper this fall. Real bad. Did you hear about the woman up north who found out her husband was sleeping around? She waited until he was asleep and then she cut off his balls and . . ."

Matt changed the subject. "I'm tired, too. I was looking forward to getting a good night's rest."

"Oh, yeah. Who with?" Jake snickered and poked Paul in the ribs.

"None of your business, wise guy." Matt said and tried not to grin. Jake was always making jokes about sex. His reputation as the pervert in the group was overlooked because of his dedication. Jake always showed up when he was called. But, Matt thought, this was true of all the men in the division. He couldn't think of a one, when off duty, who wouldn't respond when asked . . . That wasn't true of some that he knew throughout the state. They thought that anyone who answered the phone on their free time was insane. Matt didn't understand that reasoning. He and the men under him felt they had a responsibility, even though it wasn't required in their contracts, to answer a call at any time. They were prepared to go whenever they were summoned, no matter where—day or night. Noble, he guessed. Or maybe we're just plain stupid.

Judd interrupted Matt's thoughts when he said, "I see the rescue people are here. Volunteers have done their stuff have they? Jesus. When are they going to learn that they can't save them all? Last case I was on could've been solved that night if they hadn't contaminated every damn thing in sight." Judd could feel his blood pressure soar. It was time to get on with business. "Okay, you guys," he said. "Let's get this show on the road." He glanced at the mock graveyard one more time and then he slapped his beefy hand against his forehead. "A Halloween party. I'm going to go off my fucking rocker. I can see it all now. We'll be saying, "Hey. Where did the clown go? Did the witch take her broom and fly home? I should've been a truck driver."

Matt and the rest of the men knew exactly what he meant. They laughed at Judd and then they walked up the roundabout driveway toward the massive front entrance.

They lined up on the front steps. Without expressing it, all four men felt a familiar thud hit the pit of their stomachs. Matt was first in line. He rang the bell which was immediately opened by Frankenstein.

"Evening, Frank," Paul said softly and rolled his eyes to the heavens. He tried not to laugh as he marched into the house.

The detectives found themselves standing in a wide front hallway full of unmasked, costumed people. Matt tried to do a head count but it was impossible. He wondered how many took off before the Cape Bethany police arrived—let alone the ones he'd seen running to beat hell. The murderer was probably one of them. Matt studied the faces of those around him, who in turn, were doing the same to him. Some looked pasty white. He could bet they had seen the body. Others looked wide-eyed and some trembled from fright. A witch who had her back braced against a wall for support sobbed uncontrollably. A man dressed as Count Dracula tried his best to comfort her. Every time he wiped her nose with a tissue she cried all the harder.

Matt's gaze fell on a pretty blond woman dressed like a rag doll. In her left hand she dangled what appeared to be a yellow wig. Her costume made her look like a little girl. *God*, Matt thought. *She sure is cute.* He noticed a man dressed like a doctor walk over to her and put his arm around her shoulders. Matt could tell she didn't like him touching her by the way she moved his arm and sidestepped out of his reach. The man didn't try to touch her again and he didn't move away. He kept talking and talking, but she didn't respond. She just stared into space. Matt decided to question them first.

The closer he got to the woman the prettier she became. Before he had a chance to introduce himself to her the doctor said, "I'm Steven Hadley. I live here."

"Detective Matt Carter of the State Police," Matt said and they shook hands.

"This is Piper Jordan," Steven said.

"Hi," Matt said to her. At first, she didn't look at him, and when she did she tried to smile but couldn't manage it. *Jesus, she's beautiful,* he thought. *What's the matter with me?* He started to speak to her, and once again the doctor interrupted.

"This is a nightmare," Steven said to Matt. "I still can't believe that Kelly's been murdered in my very own house. It's unbelievable!"

"Where is the body?" Matt asked and saw Piper Jordan flinch.

"In there," Steven replied and pointed at a closed door. "In the living room. The Cape Bethany police are there and so is the medical examiner and the rescue people."

Matt wasn't impressed with Steven Hadley. He'd been a detective long enough to spot a loser when he saw one. He looked at Piper Jordan, cleared his throat, and asked, "Are you okay?"

"I don't think so," she answered so softly that Matt could hardly hear her. She began to shiver. Tears welled, but she managed to hold them back. Matt saw her bottom lip quiver, and he fought an urge to take her in his arms and comfort her. "Did you know the victim?" he asked her as gently as possible.

". . . my best friend," she whispered. She noticed the puzzled look on his face and repeated what she'd just said.

"I'm sorry I have to do this at this time, but I have to ask you some questions. First I have to go into the room where the bod . . . I mean your friend is. Please don't leave the premises. I'll be back as quickly as I possibly can."

She nodded and lowered her eyes.

Steven Hadley scowled and said, "Piper's had a terrible shock. Use some sense. Does she have to answer your questions tonight?"

"Afraid so," Matt said coolly. "You do, too. So does everybody present, and then you have to leave the premises while we process the scene. It should only take us a few hours and then you can come home." That's the way, he told himself. Now I'm back to business. But when he glanced at Piper Jordan one last time he knew he'd have to watch his step or he'd make a fool out of himself. God. He wished that he'd met her any place else but at a murder scene. He wondered if she was married. The thought depressed him.

Matt headed for the living room. Before he had a chance to open the door, Jake came over and asked what he should do with all the guests. Matt answered him, but his eyes and mind were on Piper. He could hardly wait to question her. *Piper*, he said to himself. *What a terrific name. I wonder how old she is?* He shook his head as if to clear it. He'd never acted this foolish before. He excused himself from a puzzled Jake, who had just asked him another question that he hadn't answered. He opened the door and stepped into the living room to take a look at the victim.

Matt wasn't prepared for the gruesome scene that awaited him. If he hadn't known better he would've sworn he was in a real honest-to-God funeral home. All that was missing was the organ music. The medical examiner and two Cape Bethany policemen were standing next to a coffin that contained the body of a pretty dark-haired girl. Matt walked over to the coffin.

"Detective Carter. Right?" The medical examiner said to Matt.

"That's right. Have we met?"

"No. But I've seen you on the news a few times. My name is Warren Sylvester."

They shook hands and then Matt asked, "How did she die?"

"Strangled," Sylvester said. "By the looks of things she didn't even have a chance to put up a struggle."

"How long has she been dead?" Matt asked.

"Not more than an hour."

Matt turned to one of the Cape Bethany policemen and asked, "Did you find whatever was used to strangle her with?"

"Nope."

Matt frowned and said, "I hope you guys didn't touch anything with your bare hands."

There was no answer.

Fuck, Matt said to himself. *I should've known better than to ask such a dumb question.*

"This is the damndest thing I've ever come across," Warren Sylvester said. "The people who hosted this party have to be weird. I wouldn't be a bit surprised if they were into devil worshiping."

"I met the man who lives here," Matt said. "Does anyone know if he has a wife?"

"I'm his wife." The minute Mona Hadley said that everyone turned to see a half-man-half-woman come sauntering across the floor. Judd stifled a laugh and so did Paul.

Jake said sincerely, "Nice costume. Original."

Mona ignored him.

Matt introduced himself and the others. As he studied the bizarre-looking woman before him he thought that she was the weirdest-looking creature he'd ever encountered. He braced himself for what might come next.

"I'm Mona Hadley. One of your men said that my husband and I have to leave here tonight and that we have to stay until you say it's okay for us to come back. Do you know how long that is going to be?"

"You have to leave now," Matt told her. "You can probably come back in a few hours. It all depends on how long it takes us to process everything." Well, Matt said to himself. I've seen a lot of hard people in my day but this broad takes the prize. Her eyes are like rocks. Jesus. She hasn't even glanced at the body. She acts like we're a bunch of workmen come to paint the house or something. And then he said, "I'm sorry, Mrs. Hadley. But, you can't stay.

We're trying to safeguard any evidence."

"Little late for that," she said and headed for the door. "Everybody and their brother has trampled about and touched the coffin. Some of us even touched Kelly."

Jesus, Matt said to himself and looked at the body of the pretty young girl before him. Her lifeless blue eyes were half open. The asshole who had strangled her had placed a lollipop in one of her hands. A tiny teddy bear was hanging out of her apron pocket. Who hated you so much, Kelly Stewart, that he choked the life out of you like that and then stuffed you in that coffin? And if what Mrs. Hadley just told me is true, then we'll be lucky to find out who killed you. Let's hope you scratched the sonofabitch that did this to you so we can got a blood type. And let's hope you have some hair and skin underneath your nails.

"Judd," Matt yelled. "Get the lunch bags on her hands before someone screws up that evidence." Every time Matt saw brown grocery bags, he thought about what he'd learned from a session with the FBI. He'd been taught that paper was a friend and plastic the enemy. If a body had to be refrigerated, paper was used, because moisture forms in plastic and destroys evidence.

"Will do. Shit," Judd said. "I just happened to remember that we were almost out of white evidence tape. What am I going to use to secure the bags if we're out?"

"We're not out," Paul told him. "There's plenty."

"Thank God," Judd said. "I'd hate to send her off with rubber bands or dental floss."

Matt wasn't in the mood for Paul's jokes. He ignored him and said, "Be careful of the lollipop." He asked Jake if he'd taken enough photos.

"More than enough." Jake said.

Matt was about to say something else when Jake said it for him. "I know, Matt. I know. You can relax. I'll take shots of every inch of this place. I can hardly wait to see the photos of the cemetery."

"Have you called the next of kin?" Matt asked Paul.

"Yes," Paul said. "Her parents are going straight to the

hospital. I hate this part of the job. Her father was pretty shook up."

"No kidding," Matt said. "I can't imagine what it must be like to get a phone call like that. But I do know one thing for sure."

"What's that, Matt?" Judd asked him.

"We've got a real screwy killer on the loose," Matt said. "This is the damndest thing I've ever seen. Doesn't look like the victim put up much of a struggle. Poor kid. Jesus. Sometimes, I wish Maine had the death penalty. Life in prison isn't enough punishment for the asshole that did that to her.

Chapter Four

Piper Jordan

Two nights after Kelly Stewart's murder—and the clock on Piper's night stand said it was almost midnight. The brass candlestick lamp next to her bed had been on for hours and would continue to burn until daylight. Piper had gone to bed at 9:00. She was exhausted, but that wasn't the main reason she'd retired so early. Kelly's murderer was still on the loose and she was scared to death he would come after her. She felt her bedroom to be the safest place in the apartment because it was the only room other than the bathroom that had a lock. She'd tried not to think about Kelly and about the murderer. She'd watched television for about a half hour but couldn't concentrate. She'd thumbed through six magazines but her tired eyes wouldn't stay focused. The temperature had dropped during the course of the evening. The tip of her nose and her feet were ice cold. She yearned for another blanket, but the bedding was in the linen closet in the hall. There was no way she would leave her room to get one.

All Piper could think about was how depressed she was over Kelly. And then it happened. She heard a strange noise out in the hall! She held her breath. For a moment she thought she might black out from lack of air. Her tired mind tried to sum up the situation. *No*, she said to herself.

It can't be footsteps. Don't be so stupid. This is the second floor. She knew there was no way anyone could get in. She'd locked both the front and back doors and all the windows. Her eyes flew to her door. For a split second she wasn't sure she'd locked it. And then she could've sworn she heard footsteps again! "Who's out there?" she managed to ask weakly. There was no answer. Then she could see the knob turning. The door flew open. The clown from Mona and Steven's party charged. He was grinning and holding the rope in his hands. "It's your turn," he said and laughed. He dangled the rope in midair. "Look what I brought for you."

"No!" Piper cried, and a scream locked in her throat. "I don't want to die," she whimpered.

"You have to," he said and then he lunged at her. She was beyond fear now. Her body felt paralyzed. This made it so easy for him to put the rope around her neck and pull it tight. Piper began to choke and tried to cover her throat with both hands. The clown was right in her face. His laughter echoed through her brain. Everything was growing dark.

Piper sat bolt upright and opened her eyes. She had been having another nightmare—not the first she'd had. She'd been plagued by the same clown dream ever since Kelly died, and she wondered if it was an omen. She told herself to stop thinking such gruesome thoughts. Fatigue did that to a person, she told herself; once she got a good night's rest she would be able to cope better. And then she wondered if she'd ever be able to sleep peacefully again. Her body felt weak from the ordeal and she was in a cold sweat. She laid her head on her pillow and tried to calm herself. "It was only a dream," she reassured herself, but the horrifying truth nagged her. Kelly's murderer was still on the loose; that was no dream.

She stared at the brass lamp on her nightstand and thanked God for precious light. Then she turned her gaze on the rolled green window shade. When she was a kid she used to sleep with a light on and her shade up because she was afraid of the dark. Nothing had changed.

She fell asleep two more times only to have the clown return. Awake, she heard each and every noise. Her keen ears honed in on a flushing toilet in the apartment above, a passing car traveling too fast on the street below, a dog barking in the distance. And when the quiet returned, she tried in vain to prepare herself for the next wave. Every muscle in her body throbbed. She cried so much that her eyes felt as though they were filled with gritty sand. She waited all alone to die.

Finally, the morning came. Piper tried hard not to think about Kelly's funeral which was scheduled for eleven, but her efforts failed, and she sat up in bed and winced. Her neck felt so stiff that she couldn't stand another second of the pain, and she wondered for the umpteenth time about who killed Kelly. Which one at the party did it? It had to be someone they both knew. She stared at the heavy oak bureau she'd dragged across the floor to put in front of her door to stop him. But what if it didn't work? What if he was able to push it?

Piper took several deep breaths in a row; she felt her head clear and her taut muscles slacken—and then Kelly's body flashed in front of her eyes. Suddenly her throat felt bone dry. Her stomach growled. She told herself to get out of bed but she didn't make any attempt to do so. Her ears were tuned—listening, listening for those expected unfamiliar sounds. No footsteps. All she heard was the beating of her own heart and the incessant ticking of the wind-up alarm clock on her nightstand. She wanted to shove the thing underneath her pillow or stuff it into a bureau drawer. Her shoulders stiffened. She reached out, grabbed the clock, aimed it at the wall, and caught herself just in time. She put it back on the nightstand.

Her eyes found the radio that Kelly had given her last Christmas—yet another reminder of her best friend, another vision of her in death. Piper yearned for the sound of soothing music to lull her to sleep, but she was afraid if she turned on the radio she wouldn't be able to hear if the killer came after her.

She looked at her window. The sun was slowly rising, and the darkness of the sky was fast giving way to a lovely shade of blue. Pink clouds swirled. Her freshly starched, off-white curtains with the ball fringe began to flap gently from a salty breeze blowing off the ocean down over the hill. Portland was waking up. She heard the early city bus pull to a noisy stop to pick up the regulars on their way to work. A horn blared, a door slammed, footsteps. Piper reached out and turned off the lamp. Once again her gaze rested on the radio Kelly had given her. And once again she was forced to remember Kelly's funeral was this morning. Piper's brain felt scrambled. Her eyes watered but no tears fell. Who killed Kelly? Why? Oh, God! What's happening? She didn't want to think any more. The only way for her to shake loose from such torture was to get out of bed and do something constructive until it was time to leave for the funeral. She still couldn't make herself get out of bed.

"This isn't real," she cried. "I'm going crazy. God. I'm so tired." Depression was no more than tired nerves. No wonder her mind felt cluttered; she hadn't had a full night's sleep since that . . . that awful night. She knew that she had it backwards. Nightmares aren't supposed to happen when you're awake. She yearned to be able to close her eyes and drift to some precious shelter of her mind to get away from reality, even if only for a few hours. She was so afraid. Ever since they were kids, Kelly had teased her about being such a sissy. Kelly had always been the bravest one. "Dear God," Piper cried. "I'm never going to see her again."

A neighbor's dog began to bark, shattering her morbid thoughts. The barking stopped and now the quiet of her room made her feel jumpy again. The ticking of the clock seemed even louder and more annoying. She yearned for a companion and held a thought of Jeremy and found herself suddenly missing him. But she knew that it was stark terror and not love that made her feel lonely. Their relationship had always been a click off. She didn't like the way he'd made fun of her, and he hadn't liked it when she'd brought this to his attention. How long had it been since she told him she didn't love him? Four months? Six? She thought about all the pain she'd gone through over hurting him. Jeremy had said he was crushed, and he pleaded with her to try and work out their differences. She'd refused, and they had both cried. Friends told her that Jeremy was miserable and that she should go back to him. There were moments she almost relented. Kelly was the one who helped her keep her thoughts straight. It wasn't long before she discovered just how crushed Jeremy was over their split. Mona Hadley had been the one to tell her the news.

"Piper," Mona had blurted. "Did you know that Jeremy has moved in with some girl he met at Griddy McDuffs? I'm told that they have a hot thing going."

She hadn't reacted. There was no way she'd give Mona that kind of satisfaction. Underneath she knew she was more angry than hurt over Jeremy. He'd gone to such great dramatic lengths to get her to stay with him. Three weeks was all that it took him to find a new bed partner. Kelly had been right. "Screw love," she used to say.

Piper's nerves couldn't afford to allow her to think about bad things any longer. She kicked off her flannel top sheet and her mother's homemade patchwork quilt and got out of bed. The minute her bare feet touched the cold pine boards her head hurt. Her arms were like lead weights and her legs felt rubbery. She slowly made her way to the window.

The sun was shining. Piper put a hand across her brow to shield her eyes from the glare. She squinted as she looked across the way at a chocolate brown house with cream-colored vinyl shutters. The young couple who lived there with two little girls had placed two pumpkins with crooked teeth on their brick steps. The silly, soot-smudged faces were beginning to rot and cave in. In one window, a large cardboard witch with scraggly gray hair and wart-riddled nose straddled a broom. A thin black cat, with huge purple and orange eyes, that looked like it had been electrocuted, rode behind the witch. Halloween, Piper thought. It was a holiday she'd just as soon skip from now on.

The phone rang and shattered the silence. Piper jumped, turned, and quickly went to answer it.

She heard a muffled voice make garbled sounds. "I'm sorry," she said, "I can't understand you."

"Piper Jordan?" The voice was clear now but still muffled and unfamiliar.

Piper couldn't tell if the person was a man or a woman. "Yes. Who is this?"

"Me."

"Me who?" Piper snapped. It was definitely a crank call. She knew that she should hang up, but something compelled her to listen.

"Who?" the person sounded annoyed and then sighed. "Who the hell do you think? Jesus. You're so fucking stupid. I was at the Halloween party. I killed Kelly."

Piper slammed the receiver as if it were too hot to handle. She backed quickly away. The only sound that escaped from her was an anguished moan. Then, to her absolute horror, the phone began to ring again. It wouldn't stop. Five, six, seven . . . twelve . . . She fought the urge to answer and blocked her ears to try and muffle the noise. It didn't help. Finally she screamed, "Stop it. God damn you." She moved quickly toward the phone, aware that she was sweating profusely. Her breathing was ragged. Her instincts told her to unplug the cord, but morbid curiosity made her lift the receiver. She pressed it against her ear.

"Now, now, Piper," the voice scolded. "That's wasn't nice to hang up on me. I wasn't finished."

"Who is this? You're not funny." Piper's voice sounded shaky.

"I'm not trying to be funny. I'll tell you one more time. I'm the one who killed Kelly." The voice was singsong now.

Piper's ears sang. She wanted to hang up—to get rid of the evil on the other end of the line—but she couldn't. She heard a sinister chuckle, and then the person said, "Kelly's funeral is at eleven. Bet there'll be a large crowd. What a crying shame. I made a big mistake, Piper. It's your fault. You and Kelly shouldn't have gone to the party dressed like twins. I didn't want to kill her. I wanted you. Well I've got news for you. You're next. And very soon. Bye bye, Piper. I'll be in touch."

The line went dead. Piper hung up, and then with an unsteady hand she lifted the receiver and poked the numbers for the police. The night Kelly died, she'd found out from a Cape Bethany policeman that the town only had four men on their force. That's why the State Police Criminal Investigation team had been called in to the scene. One of those detectives, a man by the name of Carter, had asked Piper where she lived. When she told him Portland, he said that if she should need assistance to telephone him. If, by chance, she should run into an emergency she should call a Detective Miller in Portland because he could get to her faster. Carter had given her his own number and Miller's. She'd memorized them, but prayed that she'd never have to use them.

The phone rang a long time before Piper heard a deep, gruff voice "Detective Miller speaking. Can I help you?"

"This is Piper Jordan," she blurted. "I was a friend of Kelly Stewart. She was murdered in Cape Bethany last Saturday night. Detective Carter of the State Police told me to call you if I needed help."

"Yes, Miss Jordan," Detective Miller responded. "I know the case. I've been in touch with Detective Carter. He said that you might call. What can I do for you?"

"A man," she paused a second, gulped, "at least I think it was a man—just phoned me twice. He told me that he killed Kelly. He said he made a mistake. He said I was next.

He said he's going to kill me!" She gripped the receiver so tight her fingers ached.

Detective Miller heard hysteria in the girl's voice. "Where are you?" he asked very calmly.

"I'm home."

"Alone?"

"Yes. I live alone."

"Address?"

"5180 Pine Street. It's on the west end. One block from the Promenade. It's a three story brick house. I live on the second floor. Can you come right away?"

"Yes. I'll be there as fast as I can. Are you certain all your doors and windows are locked?"

"Yes."

"Where are you now?"

"In my bedroom," she said and then she said, more to reassure herself than him, "Ever since Kelly was murdered I've put my bureau in front of my bedroom door at night."

"Do you have a window in your bedroom?"

"Yes."

"Can you see the street from your window?"

"Yes."

"Go to it," he said firmly. "Don't answer the phone if it rings. Better yet—unplug it. Stay at the window until you see a dark blue car pull up in front of your house. You'll see me and another man get out. I'll be wearing a black overcoat and tan pants. My partner is wearing a blue coat and blue pants. Don't leave your room until you see us. Have you got that straight?"

"Yes. Please hurry," she pleaded.

"Hold on. We're leaving right away. Give us ten minutes. I'm going to hang up now. Go to the window. Remember. Unplug the phone and don't leave your room until you see us get out of the car."

Piper cradled the receiver, yanked the cord and unplugged the phone. She ran to the window and scanned the street below. Her heart raced wildly and she was dizzy.

If she didn't calm down she would collapse. Somehow she had to relax and concentrate on other things while she waited for the police. She forced herself to stare at the pumpkins on the brick steps of the brown house across the street. Her eyes traveled from building to building and from window to window. Suddenly the front door of the brown house opened wide. A slender woman with cropped, blue-tinted hair came into view. Piper concentrated on her. She wondered if she was the grandmother of the two little girls. She was very well dressed. Had she ever shopped at Tatjana's? Had she ever had to explain to that woman, as she had to all the others, how to pronounce the name of the store? She couldn't count the number of times she'd forced a smile and said, "You say it this way—Tat-yah-nahs, not Tat-john-ahs. It's Russian. The owner named it after herself."

Piper wondered if Kelly's murderer had ever come into the store. Why did the caller say he meant to kill her? Who was that? Think. Maybe I've heard that voice before? "Enough," she reprimanded herself before she became unglued again. Her eyes swiftly found the gray-haired woman walking down the street. Piper thought she radiated old Portland money. Maybe she was a doctor's wife or a lawyer's. The Promenade was sprinkled with them.

Piper wondered if that woman had grown up on the Prom with maids and a cook imported from Ireland. Perhaps she had a chauffeur-driven limo. She wondered what it must feel like now that she was reduced to walking, cooking her own meals, answering her own doorbell? It must be worse to have been rich and lose it than to have always been poor.

The gray-haired woman turned a corner and faded from Piper's sight. There was nobody to watch now, and the quiet unnerved her. She stood rigid and strained to hear unfamiliar noises behind her bedroom door, but there was only silence, deathly silence.

My God, she thought. *This can't be happening to me. It's another bad dream. Yes. That's it. I'm going to wake up and it will be okay*. But she knew better. Her mind raced. *Someone wants to murder me. But why? Who? Don't think. Don't think. Concentrate on anything—but don't think about that awful voice.* She stared out the window, but she couldn't get her mind off the caller. Whoever had phoned could be watching her that very moment from a window across the street. He could shoot her with a rifle. She could see her head exploding. Blood and brains would be everywhere.

She gasped, leaped to one side, and hid behind one panel of the curtains. Every few seconds she peeked out at the world. She saw no danger lurking in the shadows. The police should've arrived by now, she said to herself. Where are they? She could be dead by the time they got here.

Her imagination was out of control. She stared with horror at the unplugged phone as if she thought that evil person who had called could come through the line and get her. And now she had to go to the bathroom. Detective Miller told her not to leave the room, but even if he hadn't said that, she knew she'd have been too afraid to leave. She had to think about other things or she'd go mad. It was only four days ago that she'd stood in the same spot and wondered how many of the neighborhood kids would be out trick or treating. The year before only a handful had showed up at her door. That hadn't surprised her. Sometimes crazy people put razor blades in apples and poisoned popcorn balls.

She and Kelly used to spend hours putting together homemade costumes. Just like this year—she sighed. Their friend Buddy Sullivan always had the best costume. They'd never seen anything quite like the one he created out of cardboard boxes that was a replica of the lighthouse in Cape Bethany. His mother had helped him glue on real moss, perriwinkle, and clam shells, plus a few rocks plucked from the beach. His father rigged up a flashlight to be used as a beacon. All Buddy had to do was tug on a string attached to his wrist and the light came on. This also activated a tape recorder strapped to his chest, and

Buddy had walked around all night playing a tape he'd made of the fog horn blowing, sea gulls crying, and the surf crashing on the shore. His costume smelled strongly of the sea and it was heavy. Buddy didn't mind. All he cared about was winning first prize.

Piper heard a siren off in the distance. She peeked out the window and expected to see a squad car coming around the corner, squealing tires. Just like in the Clint Eastwood movies she'd seen. The siren she'd heard stopped. Her temper flared. Why had Detective Miller lied to her? He told her that he would be right over. Had he gone to the wrong house? She realized that she'd never paid any attention to sirens because there had never been a need. Did police cars sound different than ambulances? Kelly would say, "Who cares?"

"Kelly," Piper moaned. She hugged herself and cried, "Somebody please tell me what's happening?" She had a quick flash of Kelly's corpse. "Oh, no," she said and rubbed her eyes as if that would make the image disappear. Her best friend was dead. But the caller said he'd made a mistake—Kelly wasn't supposed to be the victim. *She* was. But why? What had she done to cause someone to hate her so? Who did she know that was that twisted? Jeremy? Steven? Maybe it was a stranger. A friend of the Hadleys she didn't even know. There must've been over a hundred guests there. Was the killer the clown—like in her dreams? Maybe he'd come dressed like Joker from Batman—or maybe it was Dracula or . . . Maybe there were puncture marks on Kelly's throat as well as rope burns. She was unaware that she'd covered her own throat with her hands. "Don't!" she said out loud.

She heard a car door slam and then another. She peeked out the window and looked down at the street. Two men were walking up the front steps. One wore a black overcoat, the other dark blue. Tan pants. Blue pants. It was the police. She heard her doorbell ring and suddenly realized that she was still in her nightgown. She ran to the oak rocking chair where she had placed her green robe the

76

night before, she put on the robe, tied the belt snuggly around her narrow waist, and slipped her feet into matching green slippers. She then pushed the heavy bureau out of her way, gouging the floor as she did so. She unlocked her door, pushed it open and flew down the hallway. She charged across the spacious, plant-adorned living room. She nearly tripped over a magazine basket, and the latest issues of *Greater Portland* and *Harper's* went flying. She picked them up and tossed them on top of a now lopsided pile. Standing before the door, she spoke into the old-fashioned round brass speaker that reached the vestibule downstairs. "Who is it?" she asked.

"Detectives Rooney and Miller." Miller responded.

"Turn the knob when you hear the buzzer," Piper told him and promptly pushed a black button underneath the speaker.

Down in the vestibule, Detective Miller twisted the cold brass knob. He and Rooney, his partner, stepped inside. They walked upstairs to the second floor.

Piper was so tense she jumped when she heard a knock.

"Piper Jordan?" Miller asked.

"Yes." Piper answered. She recognized Miller's voice and opened the door. She stared at the two men.

"I'm Miller," he said. "This is my partner, Detective Rooney."

"Please, come in." She studied the two. She'd guess their ages to be fortyish. They were both broad-shouldered and over six feet tall. Their height made her feel safer, but then tall men always made her feel that way. Detective Miller reminded her of her father. This comforted her. Suddenly, she felt lonely for her parents, who had died within two years of one another. She had been a change-of-life baby. Her older brothers were already out of the house when she came along. They were like strangers to her. The oldest had moved to California when she was eight and the other had married a girl from London and had lived there since the early seventies.

The two detectives followed Piper into her living room.

Rooney nudged Miller with his elbow, rolled his eyes, and blew a kiss at Piper's back. Miller looked at his partner with a scowl on his face and shook his head. Rooney never failed to make some gesture about a good-looking woman. Each man had a different opinion of what they considered pretty, but this time, Miller agreed with his partner. Piper Jordan was beautiful, in a China-doll sort of way. She had magnificent big blue eyes and those eyelashes. *Christ,* he thought. *They must be an inch long.* He wondered what it would be like to run his fingers through her hair. He wondered what it would be like to reach under that green robe and touch her soft skin . . . *Jesus,* he thought. *If I wasn't married* . . . An image of Betty, his wife of twenty-three years, flashed in his mind. Now he saw his four kids. His mind quickly erased his sensual thoughts about Piper Jordan. It was time to concentrate on the purpose of his visit.

Piper had led them to a comfortable-looking beige leather sofa. Teal and deep rose cushions adorned each end. "Please sit down," she said. "Can I get you some coffee or tea?"

"No thanks. Just finished a cup," Miller and Rooney answered in unison. They sat down. Miller hadn't realized how tired he was, but that's what happened to a guy when he stayed up all night working on a case. He dreaded the thought of having to get back on his weary feet.

"Rooney," he said smothering a yawn. "Why don't you check the rest of the apartment while I talk with Miss Jordan."

Rooney nodded, stood up, and wandered into the hallway.

Piper sat in a teal-painted wicker rocking chair with a deep pastel-yellow cushion. She folded her delicate hands in her lap.

Miller broke the silence. "Miss Jordan. I want you to repeat what happened to you this morning."

Piper needed no prodding. She quickly explained. Miller paid strict attention to her every word. He noticed that by the time she finished, her face had paled and she was trembling. Her bottom lip quivered. He expected her to cry and was surprised when she didn't.

What the fuck is coming off here, he wondered. *Jesus. We've got a lunatic on the loose.* He'd heard how the killer had stuffed the Stewart girl into a pine coffin. Sicko. And what about the jokers who thought up having a mock funeral? Fucking looneys. Piper Jordan was in big trouble.

". . . do you think I'm in danger?" Piper asked.

"Yes, I do," Miller responded seriously. "And, I think you should leave your apartment until the murderer is caught. Can you stay with family?"

"No. My parents are dead. I have two brothers but they live out of state."

"Friends then?"

"Yes, of course. But I don't know who I can trust. I . . . can't think straight right now."

"I know. This has been a terrible shock. I saw in this morning's paper that the funeral is at eleven at Watts. Are you going?"

She nodded but didn't say anything.

"Well, Miss Jordan. As soon as the funeral is over you should pack up and get out of here." He rubbed his chin with a large hair-covered hand. He noticed that his cuff was dirty. He'd been in the same shirt for a couple of days. Too many murders in a row. There hadn't been enough time to change.

"I guess you're right," Piper said. "I've been upset since Kelly di—and now tha-those awful phone calls. I guess I'm not just upset—I'm terrified."

"You have every reason to be." He knew he was probably scaring her more, but facts are facts. "Look, I'll make arrangements to have the officer who patrols this area keep an extra eye on your building." He scratched his head and said, "I suppose that's not much comfort but it's the best I can offer right now. I want you to know that you're not in this alone. Okay?"

"Okay. Thanks," Piper said. Detective Miller was right. Having an officer keep an eye on the building wasn't much comfort. But there was no use in telling him so.

Rooney came into the room. He was smiling. "Place checks out. No sign of forced entry. All is well."

"Thanks," Miller said. They made idle chitchat with Piper for another ten minutes so she wouldn't think they were in too much of a hurry. They had a lot more to do before the day was out, and they hadn't eaten. It was time to go to McDonald's down on St. John Street and get a breakfast. The two men asked Piper easy-to-answer questions about her job, her friends, and about Kelly Stewart. Then Miller stood up and said, "I guess we'd better be heading out. We have some business to take care of on St. John Street."

"Was there a murder on St. John Street?" Piper asked, wide-eyed. She dreaded his answer.

"No, no," Miller reassured her. "It's nothing like that." He and Rooney made their way to the front door. Piper followed. She didn't want them to leave her alone again. She wanted to go with them. As soon as the two detectives disappeared down over the stairs she quickly closed and locked the door. She braced her back against it. The silence of the apartment felt overpowering, and she moved toward her stereo and turned on the radio. Soft, easy listening music filled her ears and soothed her nerves. This peaceful state lasted only a few minutes because she began to relive the phone calls. *I'm the one who killed Kelly*, the voice had said. *I made a big mistake and it's your fault. I'm going to do the same to you very soon.*

That voice could belong to anyone of the people at the party. She thought she would go mad trying to place it. She was so tired. Coffee would wake her up. She went to the kitchen, made a small pot, and put it on the stove to perk. The perking reminded Piper of the sound of waves rushing to reach the shore, and her body began to relax; the ocean always brought her peace of mind. She decided she would walk on the beach as soon as she could. Now,

80

the tantalizing aroma of coffee drifted across the room and reached her nostrils. She inhaled deeply and felt more calm spread over her body. She poured herself a steaming mugful, took a sip, and wondered if it was a good idea. Coffee always did smell better than it tasted. Her already raw nerves would soon be more frayed. "Deceiving stuff," she said and sipped again.

Two cups later her heart raced and she couldn't stay still. She was wired. It didn't matter. At least she had more energy. It was going to be a long day.

She glanced at the black phone sticking out against a stark white wall. What if that one should ring? She moved quickly, lifted the receiver, and let it dangle in midair. A few seconds later she heard a crisp female voice order her to "Please hang up and try your call again. If you need assistance dial your operator. Please hang up now. This is a recording . . ."

The voice finally stopped—replaced now with an annoying beep that lasted for at least two minutes. The round clock on the wall over the stove let Piper know that she had less than an hour before she had to leave for Kelly's funeral. She shook her head. "Her funeral," she cried. "God. This isn't real. Why do I think that she's going to come through the front door any minute?" She visualized Kelly's smiling face. "Come on, Piper. Don't be a poop. Let's go spend our paychecks on clothes and then have Mexican for lunch." Piper felt like crying but her eyes remained dry. Another wave of depression washed over her. She knew that she was in for a lot more of that.

She poured herself another cup of coffee and took it with her into the bedroom while she got dressed for the funeral. What in God's name, she wondered, had she done to cause someone to hate her so much? She must be careful of everyone until the police caught the murderer. But what if they didn't? Miller had been right. She should not stay here alone. Just the thought of spending another night by herself caused her to feel nearly hysterical. But where could she go? Kelly's parents' house? No. Relatives had arrived from out of state. She couldn't imagine going to Mona and Steven's place ever again. Homesickness for her parents struck. She longed to be a child again. "Oh, stop it," she cried out loud. It was time to get ready for the funeral. She would have to wait until later to figure out where to stay. Maybe there wouldn't be a later, she thought. I might be dead by then. Suddenly she felt ice cold. She hugged herself to keep warm. What a nightmare.

And the worst thing was, she knew she was awake.

Chapter Five

The Funeral

At exactly ten-thirty, Piper Jordan and Mona and Steven Hadley climbed a steep flight of granite steps and stood before the frosted-glass, double front doors of Watts Funeral Home. Kelly's service was scheduled for eleven o'clock, but her brother Chad had phoned the day after her death to invite relatives and close friends to join his family for a few private minutes with Kelly. Piper had told Chad that she felt honored to be asked. She'd lied. The minute she'd hung up she was overcome with depression. She couldn't bear the thought of seeing Kelly in death again, but she knew that she couldn't stay away; Kelly would have made an appearance if it had been the other way around. Somehow Piper had to gather enough strength to get through the funeral.

When Piper stepped inside Watts, Steven offered his arm to help steady her but she refused his assistance. Mona gave him one of her jealous glaring stares. He ignored her and proceeded to greet Chad who was waiting just inside the vestibule. Now the four stood on a soft gray carpet in a long hallway full of marble-topped tables and brass and china lamps bearing off-white shades. Two huge paintings in gilt frames—one a seascape and the other a portrait of some long dead undertaker—hung perfectly straight on walls painted a light peach.

Piper studied Chad. He had dark smudgelike circles under his eyes that stood out against the paleness of his handsome face. He was dressed properly for a funeral, she thought, in his dark gray suit, stark white shirt, and black tie. Piper caught a scent of spicy aftershave. She couldn't tell if it was Chad's or Steven's. Now Mona's nose began to twitch, signaling a sneeze. Piper knew that Mona was allergic. She watched her struggle to hold back a sneeze, but it was no use. Steven didn't look at his wife as he automatically reached in his suitjacket pocket and brought out a crumpled tissue and handed it to her.

Steven and Chad spoke in near whispers. Mona joined in. Piper had no idea what to say. She practiced in her mind. "How are you doing? Such a shock . . . If there's anything I can do . . ." Such stupid things to say. She couldn't help Chad.

Piper heard Mona say how sorry she felt about Kelly and she heard Steven inquire about the family. Then there was silence. All eyes were upon her. She knew it was her turn. She cleared her throat and said, "Chad, I'm so . . ." and then she couldn't find her voice. A steady stream of tears streaked her cheeks.

Steven put an arm around Piper. She flinched and moved away from his grasp. "I'm okay," she told him.

"Steven," Mona said with a cold edge to her voice. "I think Piper can manage."

"I was just trying to be helpful," he said and began to talk to Chad again.

Mona admired herself in an oval Victorian-era mirror hanging over a white marble-topped table. Piper watched her quickly reach in her purse, bring out her lipstick, and quickly apply a new coat. Her lips coated, Mona brushed off the front of her beige cashmere cardigan, then fiddled with the collar on her off-white silk blouse. Her raven black hair was pulled into a neat chignon. With skill she tucked in one wispy strand that had come loose, checked the clasps on her gold earrings, and noticed that Piper was staring at her.

"Why are you looking at me like that?" Mona asked.

"No reason." Liar, Piper called herself. Why don't you ask her how she can be so vain at such a time? And then she softened. She knew that Mona must be hurting over Kelly, too. She decided to try and make her feel better. "You look lovely," she told her.

"Thanks."

Steven and Chad had moved to the end of the corridor. They stood next to an open doorway conversing with a short, rugged man, about fifty, with a balding head and a slight smile on his face.

Mona whispered in Piper's ear. "That guy talking to Steven and Chad is Charles T. Watts, the undertaker. What a lech. Can't keep it in his pants," she snickered. "Steven told me that his wife just left him. She comes into Tatjana's sometimes. You've seen her. She's really heavyset. The one that's always trying to shove her bod into a size fourteen and can't understand why it doesn't fit." Mona imagined Watts preparing Kelly's body. She said to Piper, "I wouldn't want him to put his mitts on me."

Piper couldn't take any more of Mona. She was on the verge of telling her to shut her damned mouth when Steven walked over and saved her. "Are you ready to see Kelly now?" he asked them. Mona took him by the arm.

Piper felt her body tense up again, and then her stomach churned. She was overcome with a strong urge to bolt out the front door and run home. Her mind raced. *Please God. Give me the strength to get through this.* She felt her legs move and then she found herself walking slowly behind Mona and Steven, who were headed toward the room where Kelly rested. The closer Piper got to the doorway the more she could smell the sicky-sweet scent of too many greenhouse flowers. Their perfume overwhelmed her. Her nostrils seemed to close tight and then she felt as though she couldn't breathe. She sneezed several times in a row and then Mona started to do the same. Lightheaded now and staggering slightly, Piper tried to walk in a straight line. She didn't want to be alone, so she stayed close behind Steven and Mona; as closely as she could without stepping on the back of their heels. Now they were in the same room with Kelly. Don't look at her, Piper told herself. Don't look. You'll cause a scene if you do. Pretend you're somewhere else. Do it now. She focused on the floor. The gray carpet was gone, replaced by a huge, dark red-and-gold Oriental with a thick pad underneath that softened the clicking of her heels.

Steven and Mona stopped moving. Piper knew they must be close to the front of the room now. Steven began to sidestep and inched his way past some wooden chairs. He sat and so did Mona. They stared at Piper, who looked frozen. "Sit down," Mona ordered in a hushed voice.

Piper did as commanded. Once seated, she folded her hands on her lap. Beads of perspiration covered her forehead. She was so warm. She wished that she'd chosen another dress. Mona leaned over and said softly, "Doesn't Kelly look lovely?"

Piper ignored her. To keep her attention diverted, she tried counting the tiny pink rosebuds on her dress—another reminder of the baskets of flowers in the room. Her nose caught the sicky-sweet scent. She fought urges to sneeze and she battled waves of nausea. She wanted to go home. No. Not home. She wanted to be a kid again with Kelly—at Higgins Beach out in Scarborough. Precious memories now, playing frisbee with Kelly and their boyfriends on the wet sand at the water's edge. Piper could almost feel the foamy waves splashing over her feet. Now they were on blankets, their skin slippery with suntan lotion, listening to music, planning their lives. *Oh, Kelly.*

Somebody sniffled. It was Mona. Piper saw her grope in her purse for a tissue, quickly yank one out, and then blow her nose. The honking sound she made stood out in that room. Piper knew Mona must be embarrassed over calling attention to herself in such an undignified way. She wasn't surprised when Mona nudged her and said quietly, "I have to get some water and take an allergy pill or I won't be able to stay." Piper knew what Mona said was true. She also knew that Mona smoked whenever she was nervous or upset. Piper bet she'd go outside and have a cigarette.

Organ music began. Piper hated it because it always

sounded so heavy and morbid. Someone coughed to the left of her. She peeked and caught sight of dark pants, black shoes, pantyhose, and brown Italian heels moving slowly toward the front. Once, she looked up and saw Tim, Kelly's former boyfriend. Last year they had made plans to be married. Kelly had changed her mind at the last minute, and Tim never got over her. Piper felt so sorry for him. And then she wondered if Tim had killed her! Maybe he was so depressed he . . . no, Tim couldn't have done it because he wasn't even at the party. Besides, the killer had said he made a mistake. He didn't want Kelly. *He wanted me. But why? Why would anyone want to kill me?*

The organ stopped. Piper could hear the organist ruffling paper, no doubt searching for the next hymn. She was right. Only this time, the music was accompanied by a woman singing "Amazing Grace." Piper couldn't hold back her tears. That one always made her cry. She wished Kelly's parents had chosen to have Watts play tapes of some of Kelly's favorite music.

Mona returned. She nudged Piper's shoulder signaling her to shift her legs so she could get past her. Piper stood up, but kept her eyes on the floor. No sooner had they seated themselves than the organ music and singing stopped. Piper recognized Chad's voice, which was now thick with emotion. He had to stop speaking every few seconds to gain control. "My parents," he said, "have asked me to speak for them. I want," he fell silent and then he cleared his throat and said, "I want you to know that Kelly loved each and every one of you so much." He paused again, longer than before. Finally, he gulped and then he was able to continue, "This isn't easy for any of us—seeing Kelly in death—knowing that someone has taken her life. But, my parents feel that it is important for our relatives and friends to see her at peace before her casket is closed. You may come forward now."

Piper heard Chad's soft footsteps and then they stopped. He must've sat down, she thought. Mona nudged her. Piper was frozen. Mona nudged her again, leaned over, and said with emphasis, "Get up, Piper."

Piper somehow found the strength to get to her feet but she couldn't move any further. Her eyes were shut tight. She felt like a statue. Mona and Steven waited for her to move. Mona finally gave her a little push. "Move." she said.

Piper felt her legs work as she stepped into the aisle and backed up to let Mona and Steven go ahead of her. She couldn't see Mona glaring at her and she couldn't see Steven trying to get her attention. It was obvious to him that Piper was suffering. He wanted to take her arm and escort her, regardless of what Mona thought. Piper wouldn't look his way, so he had no choice but to move on. Mona followed. There were people waiting behind Piper. A man said, "Please move. We can't get by you."

Piper felt herself unlock. Her legs carried her in slow motion. She stopped when she bumped into Mona. She knew from that that they had reached their destination. Piper peeked past Mona, keeping her gaze low. She spied a red-velvet-covered bench in front of a flower-banked white casket with three brass handles across the front. Mona knelt and bowed her head in silent prayer.

Piper felt someone beside her. It was Steven. "Piper," he said softly, "I'll kneel with you. You'll be okay. Kelly's not here. She's in heaven."

Piper took comfort in what Steven had just told her. Braced now, she took a deep breath, swallowed hard, and lifted her eyes. The body of a young girl was before her. *That's not Kelly,* she said to herself. *She doesn't part her hair that way. She doesn't like red lipstick. That girl is wearing a scarf. Kelly can't stand them.* Piper studied the corpse's folded hands, which looked as if they were made out of flesh-colored plastic. And then she noticed the ring on her finger; it was the one she bought Kelly for her birthday. Piper's eyes flew to the girl's face again—the scar Kelly got in a sledding accident when they were little was there, and Piper was faced with the painful truth: her best friend had been murdered and was laid out in front of her in a casket. *What's that noise?* she wondered. *Who's moaning like that? I feel strange. Why does Kelly look so far away?* Piper hadn't realized that she'd reached out and touched Kelly's lifeless hands until she felt her cold flesh. Suddenly the room tilted.

Piper opened her eyes. At first the room spun and then it stopped. Everything was blurry. When she could focus, she saw that she was stretched out on a hard, green velvet Victorian loveseat. Mona and Steven loomed over her. Steven looked worried. "Welcome back," Steven said. "Are you okay?"

Piper nodded and then she asked, "What happened?"

"You fainted," Mona blurted. "Seeing Kelly was too much for you and that room was dreadfully warm. I thought I was going to lose it a couple of times myself."

"Want to try your sea legs?" Steven asked.

With his help, Piper struggled to her feet. "I'm so embarrassed," she said and blushed. "Who carried me here?"

"Chad and I," Steven answered. "You bumped your head a good one on that little bench. Feel the lump?"

Piper touched the side of her head and winced. "I feel like I got hit by a truck. God. I don't want to ever do that again. What a terrible sensation. My head hurts so much. I need an aspirin."

As if on cue, Watts, the still-smiling undertaker, came into the room carrying a glass of water. He reached into his suitjacket pocket and came forth with two white pills. "Thought you might want some aspirin."

"Thanks," Piper said, took the pills from him and put them in her mouth. He handed the water to her. She took a swig and swallowed the tablets. Feeling terribly weak, she sighed deeply and laid her head against the back of the loveseat.

Mona looked at her watch. "The service will be starting in less than five minutes." She looked at Piper and asked "Are you up to going back in that room?"

"Yes. I have to."

"No you don't," Steven said firmly. "You've got a nasty lump there. Maybe we should have someone drive you home."

"I'll be okay, Steven. I want to be here."

Mona became more impatient. "Well, come on then. We're going to make a bigger spectacle if we show up after the service has started."

Once again, Piper followed closely behind Mona and Steven. This time she didn't look at the floor, but she still avoided looking at Kelly. Now the large room was filled to capacity. All of the seats had been taken. They would have to stand. Piper heard Mona swear under her breath as Steven guided them to the nearest wall. No sooner had they squeezed beside others in the same predicament when the minister began the service.

Piper stared at a floral painting across from her. She recognized the minister's voice and she smirked. It was Reverend Bartlett. Kelly couldn't stand him. She used to tell Piper that she thought he was perverted because one time he pinched her bottom. Piper tried to concentrate on what the Reverend was saying but she couldn't. Her eyes and mind wandered.

In a back row she spied Tatjana, who had flown in from New York just for the afternoon. She was dressed expensively, in black. Then she spied Mr. and Mrs. Stoll, the elderly couple who took care of Tatjana's farm out in Freeport. Piper was fond of that old couple and of their Newfoundland dog, Crutches. Seated next to the Stolls were Eric Swenson and Maggie Burke, childhood pals. Both were sobbing, and the sight of them made Piper weepy. Alongside Maggie sat Miss Freeman, Kelly's former piano teacher.

Some faces were strange. Odd, Piper thought, how one person touched so many. One elderly man dressed in an expensive blue suit kept fidgeting. At first, Piper assumed he was with the pretty young girl beside him, but she didn't act as if she knew him. A terrible thought struck. *Maybe he's the killer!* Chills raced up her spine. *Stop it,* she ordered herself. *Don't start.* But it was too late. Everyone around her became suspect. She stared at faces until she heard someone cry out, "I want Kelly! Oh no!"

Piper knew the voice belonged to Kelly's mother. Her

raw grief tore away what remained of Piper's composure. She felt warm again and then sick. Her ears began to hum. If she didn't get some fresh air, she knew she would faint. She exited just as Kelly's cousin Sarah started to sing "The Old Rugged Cross," off-key. *Kelly would've been pleased*, Piper thought. *She never did like Sarah.*

Mr. Watts stood at the far end of the corridor fussing over a Boston fern. "I don't feel well," Piper told him as she stumbled toward him. She stopped and gripped the back of a green overstuffed chair for support. "It's so stuffy in that room. I can't stand it."

He moved quickly toward Piper. "Oh, you poor thing," he said. "Here. Let me help you." He took her by the arm and led her away. Before Piper had a chance to protest he opened a door, guided her into an office, and released her arm in front a black leather wing-back chair. "Please, sit down," he said.

Piper sat and took a deep breath as Mr. Watts walked over to a window, opened it wide, and let the cold fresh air rush in. Piper inhaled deeply, and a bit of color returned to her cheeks.

"Now doesn't that feel good?" Watts asked. "Breathe deep. I can't leave the window open too long—you'll get chilled." He waited until Piper stopped inhaling heavily and then closed the window and sat down behind his walnut desk. He studied Piper carefully—especially her legs. "I'm sorry you're having such a difficult time. Was the deceased a relative?"

"No. My friend."

"Yes, well, just the same it's an awful shock. Natural death is one thing—and illness—but murder is so dreadful. Is this your first funeral?" He had assumed by her reactions that this had to be the case.

"No."

He seemed shocked. "Really?"

"No. I've been to several." She wanted to get up and leave but she was still too weak to move.

"Were you close friends?"

"Best," she said. "Since we were kids." He was too nosy.

She was getting annoyed.

"I see. Don't you think she looks beautiful? Did her myself—from a recent photograph."

"No," Piper said. "Her hair is wrong and she hated red lipstick and she never wore scarves." She couldn't believe she was party to such a conversation.

"Oh, I didn't know that. Somehow I thought she'd wear red." he started to say something about the scarf and then he changed the subject. "This is an interesting business. I see everything. You know I was going to be a teacher."

"Oh," Piper replied, uninterested. She knew that she had to find the strength to get away from him.

"Yes. My full name is Charles Timothy Watts. I was named after my father. He was an English teacher and so was his father before him. I was going to go to college in Rhode Island to become a teacher. Then my uncle died and my life changed. The funeral director was so kind to my family and to me. He touched me in such a way that I decided that I wanted to do the same for others. My father was so upset, but I stuck to my guns. So here I am." He smiled proudly at Piper.

She couldn't imagine how he—or anybody else could be touched in such a way. She shivered. He noticed but never dreamed it was because of him.

"Cold?" he inquired.

"No. I don't understand how you can spend your life with the dead." She cringed.

"Oh, I understand. My ex-wife had a problem with that, too. But just like I told her. This business is not all that bad. I have fun. I like to golf and to go to the movies. I like good food and attractive women." He looked at Piper's legs again. "I enjoy being a funeral director," he said, more to himself. He got up from his desk, and walked over to the open window to stare at passersby hustling down the street. "Little kids get to me though. And young adults, like your friend. My grandmother used to say: 'The old *must* die. The young *will* die.' Makes sense I suppose." He turned from the window and asked, "Feeling better?"

"Yes." She lied. "I'd better go back now."

"Oh, no. Not yet. I want to show you something. You see, we just renovated our preparation room. I'd like to take you downstairs so you can see it. I love the new peach tiles and the green walls. Reminds me of salmon and peas—one of my favorite dishes."

"What's a preparation room?" Piper asked, already dreading what he would tell her.

"It's where we prepare the deceased. It was rather drab but now it's all modern, what with our new sinks and tables. Most modern preparation room this side of Boston."

"I don't want to go," she almost screamed. God he's weird, she thought.

Some of his smile faded. "Not scared, are you?" He didn't wait for Piper's answer. "The preparation room is very kitchenlike. There's nobody down there—get it—*no body*." He said and winked, thinking a joke would relax her a bit. Piper sat frozen-faced.

Mr. Watts continued as if he had her undivided attention. "So many people are scared of death. Shouldn't be. It's the living we have to watch out for. Like the person who murdered your poor friend. Killing her like that. You should've seen the bruises on her throat." He didn't understand that he'd gone too far.

Piper stood up. She had heard enough. She had to get away from the man before she slapped his face.

"Oh, good." He clapped his hands and said, "You've decided to see the preparation room. Like I told you a minute ago, it's very kitchenlike."

Piper found her voice. "I'm *not* going to the preparation room. I have to go back before the service is over." She started toward the door.

Watts was disappointed but he kept silent. He was determined that she remember his name. He'd give her time to get over her grief, and then he'd call her to see if she'd like to have dinner with him. He ran to his desk, opened a drawer, and brought out a small stack of cream-colored business cards. "Wait," he said. "Please take these with you. You never know when you might need one. Give them to your friends."

Piper took the cards and shoved them deep in her purse. She opened the door and on wobbly legs walked back to the service.

The Reverend Bartlett was still talking. Piper stood just inside the doorway. She glanced at the person beside her. He smiled and nodded. She recognized him and managed a smile. It was Detective Carter of the State Police. Standing beside him was Detective Miller. Why had they come? she wondered. Then she heard Reverend Bartlett say, "The Lord has taken Kelly home to heaven. She is there—waiting for us. Grieve not. I promise you that she does not suffer. She forgives the person who took her life as should we. It is not for us to sit in judgment. It is said in Corinthians 5:10: *For we must all appear before the judgment seat of Christ; that every one may receive the things done in his body, according to that he hath done, whether it be good or bad."* Reverend Bartlett continued: *"I am the resurrection and the life, said the Lord; he that believeth in me, though he were dead, yet shall he live; and whosoever liveth and believeth in me, shall never die. Amen.* The Stewart family has asked me to invite everyone present to come to their home after leaving the cemetery. You may come forward now and pay your last respects."

Piper began to tremble again, and Detective Carter noticed. He leaned her way and whispered, "I'll go up front with you if you like."

"Please," she said and reached for his arm for support. He could feel her trembling. Two by two, they and a long line of mourners moved slowly toward the front of the room. Piper gripped Detective Carter's arm so tightly that her fingers began to ache. He stopped moving, and she knew why. She stared at Kelly. Her throat tightened as she struggled to hold back her tears.

Matt Carter felt sympathy for Piper Jordan. He didn't know what to do to comfort her other than to hold her arm and pat the top of her hand. He didn't think she was going to make it through without collapsing. He was surprised when she let go of his arm. He thought she was going to faint or run away but she didn't. Tears slid down his own cheeks as he watched her lean over the casket and lightly kiss Kelly Stewart's cheek. "I love you, Kel," she whispered, stood up, and swayed.

Matt grabbed her just in time and quickly led her away. She rested her head against his chest. He realized that he never wanted to let her go.

Outside in the hallway, Kelly's parents came to her and hugged her. Matt paid his respects and then together he and Piper stepped outside. At that moment, nothing on earth could compare to the comforting feel of the warm sun and the refreshing, crisp fall air that filled their lungs. They were alive and it felt good. Stepping out of Watts Funeral Home was like coming out of a tomb.

Detective Carter spoke first, "Look. I'm going to the cemetery, too. Are you riding with anyone special?"

"I was going with Steven and Mona Hadley."

"I was wondering if you wouldn't mind riding with me? I could use the company." He hoped she couldn't tell by the look on his face tht he was praying she'd say she'd come with him.

Piper thought for a moment and then she said softly, "Okay. I'll ride with you, but first I have to tell Mona and Steven." Just as she said that they came outside.

Piper walked over to them and explained that she was going to ride with Detective Carter. Carter could tell from such a short distance that the Hadleys looked surprised, but all they did was nod. The policeman in him took note that Steven Hadley quickly kissed Piper's cheek. He also noticed his wife's face had a look of pure jealousy written on it. Matt heard Piper say that she would see them at the Stewart house after the cemetery, and then she excused herself and came back to him. He took her by the elbow, led her to his car, unlocked her door, and held it open for her until she was seated. When he climbed behind the wheel, he noticed that she was staring trancelike at something straight ahead. He looked. The pallbearers were bringing Kelly's casket out a side door.

Matt glanced at Piper and took her hand in his and

squeezed it gently. She felt clammy to the touch. He had all he could do to keep from taking her in his arms to try and make her hurt go away.

It seemed to take a long time for Charles Timothy Watts to line up the cars. To ensure that local traffic did not break up his procession, he instructed each driver to turn on their headlights, and then on each antenna he stuck a little purple flag with white lettering that said "funeral." Matt Carter and Piper were about the fifteenth car in line, and there were at least thirty more behind them. She could see Charles Timothy Watts loading baskets of flowers into the back of a black station wagon behind the hearse. The pallbearers had disappeared. Piper had recognized all of them—Kelly's brother Chad and her little brother Eddie, her Uncles Ted, John, and Joe, and Kelly's former fiancé, Tim, who still appeared terribly shaken. Piper watched Watts climb into the hearse opposite the driver. It was time to go.

As the entourage wound through Portland to the cemetery, Matt Carter tried to converse with Piper. At first she was very quiet but she began to loosen a little not far from the South Portland bridge. She even showed a bit of temper when a green Mercedes found an opening big enough to squeeze into the procession up ahead and whizz through two red lights along with them. "Jerk," she said.

Matt smiled. "Takes all kinds," he said. His car radio began to squawk. He quickly shut it off. "Did you know Kelly long?"

"Since the first grade."

"Were you close?"

"Best friends." She exhaled deeply.

"I'm sorry. I know this must be difficult for you."

Piper didn't respond. She swallowed hard to stop her tears.

Matt Carter continued. "It's probably not the best time to bring this up," he said, "but Detective Miller told me about the phone calls you had this morning. He said that the caller said he made a mistake and that he really meant to kill you and not Kelly."

"Yes," she said and looked at him. "But why?" she asked as if she thought he knew the answer.

"I don't know," he said. "But I'm going to try and find out. Do you have any enemies?"

"No."

"Are you 100% certain?"

"Yes. I think so. God. I don't know any more."

"Take your time," he said. "Think about the people you know. Maybe something important will come to you."

"Please," she cried, "Do we have to talk about this right now?"

"Sorry. I must seem terribly coldhearted." He glanced at her to see her reaction. Jesus, he thought. She is so beautiful.

She took a deep breath and then she asked, "Why did you come to the funeral?"

"To tell you the truth, I'm working."

"Working?"

"Yes," he said. "This is all part of my job."

"You don't think the killer came to the funeral, do you?"

"Maybe. Think about the person who called you. Try to remember if you've ever heard that voice before."

"Are we back to that again?"

"Sorry," he apologized. "But I have to ask. There is a killer loose."

"No," she responded. "I don't know who called. Do you think it could have been a prank?" She prayed he would say that was the case but she knew she was fooling herself again.

"No," he said. "I think it was Kelly's killer. Can you tell me word for word what he said?"

Piper repeated what happened. Matt Carter listened intently. When she finished, she noticed he was tapping his fingers on the steering wheel.

"I really don't know why anyone would want to kill me."

"I don't know either," he said. "But like I said a minute

ago. I'm going to do my best to find out. You must be careful. Every person you know is suspect. Even family. Do you have a boyfriend?"

He felt relieved when she said no.

"Any recent breakups? Fights with friends?"

"No."

"At work?"

"Yes. But that was a long time ago."

"Time doesn't matter. Who was it with?"

"Mona Hadley."

"About something at work?"

"No. Steven, Mona's husband," Piper said and looked at Matt. "But please don't get any ideas about Mona. She wouldn't kill Kelly or me. And anyway, I'm pretty certain that whoever called was a man."

Matt decided he'd better not upset her further. She'd been through enough. He noticed that the hearse had just turned into the cemetery up ahead, and he braced himself for what was to come. He knew she must be suffering. He reached across the seat and patted her hand. "I'll be right there with you. Are you okay?"

"Yes," she said, none too sure of herself.

Matt pulled the car to a slow stop, turned off the engine, opened his door, got out, and quickly went to Piper's side and opened hers for her. He took hold of her hand, and together they walked across the soft green earth toward an awning that formed a shaded canopy over Kelly's open grave. Matt looked at Piper. She was so small and helpless. He wanted to kiss her and hold her tight. *Christ*, he thought, *what's happening to me? I'm supposed to be working, not daydreaming about that kind of stuff.* He'd never ever had this happen to him before. This girl was really getting under his skin.

Fortunately, the ceremony was brief. Kelly's Mom didn't do well. She began to sob so hard that her husband had to take her away. Piper watched them walk quickly back to the black limo that had brought them to see their daughter laid to rest. Charles Timothy Watts had seen them, too, and he quickly headed in their direction. He made it just in time to open the door for the mourning couple.

"Ashes to ashes; dust to dust," the Reverend Bartlett said somberly.

Piper couldn't take any more. She reached up on tiptoes and tried to whisper in Matt Carter's ear but she was too short. "Please. I want to leave now."

Matt Carter opened the car door for Piper. He no sooner got behind the wheel when she grabbed her handle and said, "I forgot. I'm supposed to go to Kelly's parents' house. I'll ride with Mona and Steven."

"No. Wait," he said. "I'm going there, too. I'll take you unless you want to ride with your friends." He hoped she would stay with him.

"Okay." She said, laying her head against the back of the seat, and she shut her eyes. She was silent for a few minutes as they drove along, and then she said, "I dread this. Kelly's family is so close. I just don't know how they're going to survive without her. I don't know how I'm going to either."

Matt glanced at her and saw that she'd turned her head toward the window. He heard her sobbing ever so quietly. *Damn, he thought. I've got to work fast before the killer comes after her.* The very thought made him flinch. *Why don't I do something else for a living? What am I? A masochist?* He and Piper made the rest of the trip in complete silence, each lost deep in their own dark thoughts.

Later that afternoon, Matt Carter drove Piper home from Kelly's parents' house and went into her apartment with her to make sure it was safe. Piper followed behind as he checked all the closets and even underneath the bed, which reminded her of what they did in the movies. When he finished, she offered to make him some coffee, but he said he had to get back to headquarters. Matt thought he detected a faint look of disappointment on her face. "Will you be okay?" he asked her.

"I don't like being alone, but I'll be okay. Thanks for checking everything for me."

"Don't mention it." He didn't want to leave her alone. She looked so frightened. Losing her best friend was a terrible shock, let alone having a murderer tell her that he'd made a mistake. He decided that if she agreed to it, he would come back later that night to see how she was doing and to ask her more questions. "Look," he said. "I have to ask you some more questions just as soon as possible. Can I come back later this evening—that is, if you feel up to it?"

"You could, but I won't be here."

"Where are you going?" he asked, trying not to sound alarmed.

"I'm not sure. But I'm afraid to stay here alone. The past few nights have been agony, and now these—those phone calls. I won't go far. I just need to have people around me. I'll call you and let you know just as soon as I find out where I'm going to be."

"Good. When are you leaving?"

"Hopefully this afternoon."

He nodded. "Please don't forget to let me know where you are as soon as you can. I have to be going," he said and made his way to the front door. "Don't forget to lock the door after I leave."

"I won't. I want you to know that I really appreciate your checking the apartment for me."

"Don't mention it. It's better to be safe than sorry, my mother used to say. Besides, it goes with the job. And I'm really glad you're getting out of here." He stepped into the hallway, waved, and then he disappeared down over the stairs.

Piper closed the door, locked it, and went to the kitchen to make herself some coffee. She listened carefully to every sound, expecting each minute that the killer would charge at her, and staring at the phone and praying that it wouldn't ring. "Forget the coffee," she whispered to herself. "I have to get out of here before it's too late. But where am I going? God. Who can I trust? Mona and Steven?" The thought of finding Kelly's body in their living room flashed. *I'd go crazy there.* Her mind whirled with possibilities, until finally she had an idea. Tatjana's farm! Why hadn't she thought of that before? She glanced at the clock on the wall. Tatjana would be back in New York by now.

Piper ran into her living room to her desk to get her red leatherbound book of phone numbers. She ran back to the kitchen, lifted the receiver, and dialed Tatjana's apartment in Manhattan. The phone rang no more than four times when Piper heard the familiar voice with a thick New York accent say, "Tatjana's. May I help you?"

"Tatjana. This is Piper Jordan."

"Piper, dear. I'm sorry we didn't get a chance to chat after the funeral. Are you okay?"

"Yes." She fibbed.

"Hideous thing. It must've been dreadful for you to find Kelly like that. Do the police have any idea who did it?"

"No," Piper managed to say. She sighed deeply and couldn't find her voice.

"What's wrong, Piper?"

There was total silence for several seconds and then Piper blurted, "The person who murdered Kelly phoned me this morning. He says he made a mistake," she caught her breath. "Kelly wasn't supposed to die. He said he wanted to kill me. I called the police."

"Oh, my God, Piper! Are you alone?"

"Yes. That's why I called you."

Tatjana obviously hadn't listened, because she said, "Did you tell the police?"

"Yes. They can't do anything."

"Don't be silly, Piper. Of course they can do something. They're the police. That's what their job is, for heaven's sake."

"What do you think they should do?" Piper asked, and realized that Tatjana could tell by her voice that she was getting annoyed. She hadn't called her to listen to a lecture.

"Well," Tatjana said, and then paused. "They could furnish you with a bodyguard or something." Then she quickly changed the subject. "You mentioned the voice sounded like a man. Did you recognize his voice?"

"No."

"Are you certain? Think carefully."

"No," Piper said. "I'm sure. Listen, Tatjana. I'll get right to the point. I called to ask you if I could stay at the farm until the murderer is caught. I'm afraid to be alone and I know I'll be safe at your place with Mr. and Mrs. Stoll."

"Of course you can go there. Stay as long as you need to. But don't tell anyone except Mona, Steven, and the police."

"I won't. Thanks Tatjana. I wouldn't ask but I'm so afraid."

"Don't be so silly, Piper. My farm is yours as long as you need it. As soon as we hang up, I'll call the Stolls and let them know you're coming."

"Thanks."

"Don't mention it. The Stolls will be delighted. They like you. She's been lonely ever since her children grew up and moved away. She'll dote on you. She loves to cook for people. And you know John. He'll keep you busy listening to his stories. They'll both love having you with them. You'll be safe there." Piper couldn't see that Tatjana had the fingers on her left hand crossed for luck.

"I hope so."

"Don't worry. You will be. But while we're at it, I want to tell you that I'm worried about your health. I noticed how pale and drawn you are. Losing Kelly has been a terrible shock to your system. The country will put some color in your cheeks." She paused and then she said, "I forgot to ask. When do you want to go?"

"Right away."

"No problem. And one more thing before I forget."

"What's that?"

"I insist you take time off from work."

"Thanks, but that's not necessary."

"Sorry, Piper. I'm the boss. I'll fire you if you don't do as I say," she teased.

"Okay, you win." Piper responded quickly. She was

102

relieved. She hadn't any idea how she was going to face going into the shop without Kelly being there. But she also knew there was another person to consider besides herself. "What about Mona?" she asked.

"So what about her?" Tatjana said.

"C'mon, Tatjana. Kelly was murdered in Mona's house. You know that she and Steven must be going through hell, too."

"I talked to Mona at the funeral. She's doing okay, considering. I told her that I was going to have you take some time off. She thought it was a good idea. She said she could run the shop alone."

"Are you sure she won't mind?"

"That's what she told me. You know her as well as I do—if not better. Working is her way of handling problems. She's tough as nails. Cold as a corpse." The minute Tatjana said "corpse," she wished she could have bitten off her tongue. Piper had seen enough of death lately; she didn't need to hear her making a joke out of it.

"Okay, Tatjana," Piper said. "I'll take time off. I have a week's vacation left. I'll use that."

"Nonsense. A week isn't enough. I want you to have a month off to pull yourself together. You are the best salesperson I've ever had and I want to show my appreciation. We'll call it an early Christmas bonus. Don't tell Mona that," she warned. "I want to tell her. Besides, I'm going to do the same for her later."

"I promise I won't mention it. Thanks, Tatjana."

"You're welcome, Piper. Before I forget. I just thought of two questions I want to ask you before we hang up. The first is—who was the man you were with at the funeral? And the second is—do you have a gun?"

"He is a state police detective assigned to Kelly's case. And no, I don't have a gun," Piper said all in one breath.

"Cute guy. Look, Piper. I'm going to ask Mr. Stoll to show you where I keep my pistol and I'll ask him to teach you how to use it. Don't hesitate to squeeze the trigger. Your life may depend on it someday."

"Okay, Tatjana," Piper said and sighed. "I'll learn."

Tatjana could tell that Piper was just being agreeable—she probably had no intention of learning how to handle her gun—and she was getting angry. "Don't try to snow me, Piper," she said crossly. "You'd better learn to shoot. And, if necessary, you'd better aim at the heart or the head."

"Okay, okay. I promise I'll do it." Piper would promise her anything to get her off the subject.

"Good girl," Tatjana said. "Now, we'd better hang up so I can phone the Stolls. If there is a problem about you staying there I'll call you right back."

"Thanks, Tatjana."

"Will you stop thanking me for heaven's sake," Tatjana inhaled deeply. "Look, Piper. I'm sorry. I guess I'm tired and cranky. I don't mean to sound so ugly. But about the gun. Get serious about it. I don't want you to wind up like Kelly. I couldn't bear to lose both of you."

Piper thought she heard Tatjana's voice crack and then she heard a click and the line went dead. She hung up and stood by the phone for several minutes waiting to see if Tatjana called back after she spoke with the Stolls.

Tatjana didn't call. Fifteen minutes later, Piper had changed into a pair of jeans, a red-and-white checkered shirt, and sneakers. She'd stuffed two suitcases full of clothes and an overnight bag full of cosmetics, made certain all her windows were locked, and the back door, and then she left. Halfway down the stairs, she remembered she'd told Detective Carter that she would phone him when she knew where she was going. She looked at her watch. He'd had ample time to get to his office. She went back into her apartment, dropped her luggage, picked up the phone, quite aware that she was eager to hear Detective Carter's voice. While the phone rang she admitted to herself that she found Matt Carter attractive.

"Detective Carter here."

"Hello. This is Piper Jordan."

"Hi, Piper Jordan," he said cheerfully. "What can I do for you?"

"I said I'd phone and let you know where I'm going. I'll

be staying at my employer Tatjana's farm in Freeport."

"That's a good idea. Where is it and what is the phone number?"

Piper gave him the number and then she said, "It's off the Hunter Road on Mill Pond Road on Route 89. Do you know where that is?"

"Yes. I have friends who have a farm at the end of that road. Nice area."

"Yes, it is. The place I'll be staying is an old farm house. It has a huge red barn. It's on the left, half way down the road past the railroad tracks. You can't miss it."

"I know where that is," he said. "Big ark. Looks haunted." He wished he hadn't said that. The poor woman didn't need any new scary thoughts.

"It looks haunted but they say it isn't," she responded as if it hadn't phased her.

"Who?"

"Mr. and Mrs. Stoll. They take care of the farm for Tatjana. She lives in New York. The Stolls are great. He tells jokes and she's a wonderful cook."

"Sounds like an interesting place. I still need to question you. I know you must be exhausted, but would you mind if I come out there tonight?"

"I don't mind but I'll have to ask the Stolls. Can you phone there in a couple of hours? I should know by then." She hoped the Stolls would say okay.

"I'll call you. I wouldn't ask but it's important." He knew it was more than that. He'd be disappointed if she turned him down.

"I have to hang up," Piper said. "Being alone in this apartment gives me the jitters. I keep waiting for someone to jump out of the closet."

"I know," he said. "It has to be awful for you."

She was eager to change the subject. "Look, now that I think of it, it would probably be better if I phone you instead of the other way around. Will you be in your office?"

"Yes. Unless there is a murder somewhere." He knew he wouldn't be able to relax until she reached the farm.

Maybe he should escort her? "Look. I would've stayed longer today but I had some important things to take care of for a pending court case but I'm finished now. Do you want me to come into Portland and drive you to Freeport?"

"Thanks, I think I'll be okay. Besides, I couldn't stand waiting for you. I have to get out of here or I'm going to go crazy."

"I understand. I'll be waiting for your call. Don't forget, okay?" He really wanted to tell her that he'd be hanging by the phone until he heard from her.

"I won't forget," Piper reassured him.

There was silence for a second and then he said, "Be careful. I don't want anything to happen to you."

"Thanks. I'll call you as soon as I can." She heard a click. Talking to him had taken some of her fright away. She had a flash of kissing him. *Stop that,* she said to herself. *He's not interested in you. He's a detective. It's his job.* She wondered if he had a girlfriend, and if so, she envied the woman.

Next, Piper remembered to phone Detective Miller in Portland to let him know that she was going to the farm. The person who answered said that he was out of the office for the rest of the day. She left word that she'd call him back in the morning. Then she remembered that Detective Mooney said he'd have a squad car patrol frequently, and she peeked out the window. There was no sign of the police. She felt alone again, and felt an urge to run. She picked up her luggage and moved as if the devil were chasing her.

She was halfway out the door when she thought about Mona and Steven. She came to an abrupt halt, sighed with exasperation, and went back to use the phone. If Mona and Steven phoned her and she didn't answer they would freak. They'd probably call the police—afraid that she'd been murdered, like Kelly. She lifted the receiver and dialed.

Steven answered. Piper asked to speak to Mona. He told her that she was taking a nap. He also told Piper that he was exhausted but that he was okay. Piper explained about the phone calls that she'd had that morning and that she was going to stay at Tatjana's where she'd be safe. She made Steven promise not to tell anyone except Mona where she was going.

". . . and, Steven," Piper was saying. "Will you please remind Mona that Tatjana insisted that I take some time off from work. She told me that she already spoke to Mona about this. I hope she won't mind. On second thought, don't mention it to her. When she gets up from her nap have her phone me at the farm. I'm leaving right now." She wanted to ask Steven if he had any ideas about the killer but at the last minute she decided not to.

It wasn't until after she hung up that it crossed her mind that Steven could be the murderer. Impossible, she thought—or was it? He was strange, and Matt Carter told her that everyone was suspect. But he was wrong about Steven. He might be a lech, but she knew he wasn't capable of murder. Piper glanced at her watch. It would soon be dark. There was so way she wanted to be alone on the highway when the sun went down.

Chapter Six

The Farm

Piper sat behind the wheel of her blue Tempo and headed north on I-95 toward Freeport. Every few seconds she looked in her rear view mirror. Her body was tense with fear that the murderer had watched her leave her apartment and was following her to Tatjana's farm. Every car on the highway became suspect.

Miles down the road, Piper still expected the murderer to apper alongside her car and aim a gun at her head. A black station wagon was hugging her back bumper. She tried to see the driver's face but the windshield was tinted. Piper picked up speed. The wagon followed suit. She looked at her speedometer: seventy-five and climbing. She was pushing her old car too hard. Her eyes searched the highway for the police and saw none.

Piper checked her mirror again. He was in the passing lane now. Her mind was out of control. She visualized the killer pulling alongside and blowing her head off. She slid down in the seat as far as she could and still see the road. She forgot about her car being old and drove faster. She knew she'd get a bullet in her head any second, careen down an embankment, and smash into a tree. She had a gruesome vision of Detective Carter arriving at the scene and staring at her mangled body.

The killer's car was alongside hers now. She used her

left hand to shield that side of her head from the explosion of glass and lead that she knew was coming. Suddenly, a huge green and white information sign loomed. It said that the Hunter Road exit was two miles away. She knew if she was going to live, her timing had to be perfect. The black car remained beside her. She passed another Hunter Road exit sign. It was only one mile away but it seemed like an eternity to her. "Why is it taking so long?" she whined. Finally, she saw the exit. Her heart pounded. "Please, God. Please, help me," she cried. She waited until the very last minute and then swerved to the right. Tires squealed. Gravel flew. Her car zigzagged down the ramp, but somehow she managed to bring it under control.

"I did it!" she yelled. She looked in her mirror. The wagon had pulled into the parking lane and was backing up. Her heart thumped. She went faster and ignored the yield sign at the end of the exit, pulled into the middle of traffic, and barely missed slamming into a truck. The driver honked and gave her the finger.

Piper avoided glancing in the rearview mirror. She noticed a gas station up ahead on the left. When she was almost there, she turned the wheel hard. The car shot across the highway and into the driveway. Piper's foot came down hard on the brake. Had she not had her seat belt buckled she would've been thrown against the windshield and smashed her head. She put the car in park, left the engine running, opened her door, jumped out, and raced toward the office for help.

She was out of breath but almost to the door. She heard a car. Was it him? An engine stopped. A door slammed. Footsteps now. He was coming!

The man in the office saw her and started to open the door. Before he could, she heard a voice say, "Yoo hoo. Wait up."

Piper came to a complete stop and froze. The voice was familiar. She turned her head so fast she heard crack. *Oh, no,* she thought. *God. Not him.*

But it was. There he stood. Charles Timothy Watts, the undertaker. He was smiling as he moved toward Piper. "I thought that was you," he said. "I tried to honk but nothing happened. My horn must be broken. I waved to get your attention but you wouldn't look my way. Where in the world are you going in such a hurry? You almost got into a terrible accident."

"I have an appointment," she responded coldly. Relieved, her fear turned to anger which she was barely able to contain.

The gas station attendant was outside now. "Are you okay, Miss?" he asked. "Is that man bothering you?" He glared at Watts.

"Thanks. No! I'm okay," Piper said. "I know him." The man went back inside but he stood in the window and watched just to make sure Piper was safe.

"Me, too," Charles Watts said in response to Piper saying she had an appointment.

"Me too what?" she asked.

"I mean I have an appointment. I'm on my way to a nursing home a few miles from here to pick up an old lady who passed away. I thought you might want to have a cup of coffee and some lunch first. There's a nice place just down the road. Delicious food. How about it?"

"No way," Piper snapped. She was so angry with him that she had to restrain herself from walking over and slapping his grinning face. Then she noticed that his smile had vanished.

"Oh," he said disappointed. "I hoped you'd say yes."

He sounded so sad that Piper softened. "Look. I don't mean to sound so angry. But you scared me and I lost my temper. I don't have time for coffee right now," she lied. "I'm late." She walked back to her car, climbed in behind the wheel, and buckled up.

Just before she slammed the door she saw Watts wave and heard him say, "Maybe another time?"

"Maybe."

He seized the opportunity. "How about tomorrow?" Piper noticed that he was smiling.

She shook her head and sped away. She looked in her mirror. There was no sign of Watts. Every muscle in her body throbbed, and she wondered if she would ever again have peace of mind. One thing she knew for certain; she'd make a will as soon as possible, and the first item would be to make it known that in the event of her death she did not want to be taken to Watts Funeral Home. The idea of being stretched out naked on a cold stainless steel table in Charles Timothy Watts's preparation room was chilling.

She was on Mill Pond Road now and could see Tatjana's farm ahead. She crossed the railroad tracks and turned into the long roundabout driveway. The Stolls's black-and-white cow stopped eating in the field and watched her approach. Pumpkins lined the edge of the road along the way. Cornstalks had been tied to the two pillars on the front porch and three more perfectly shaped pumpkins were on the steps.

Piper spied Crutches, the Stolls' huge black Newfoundland, stretched out on the porch. He heard her car, lifted his shaggy head, and looked her way, struggled to his feet, and limped down the steps, tail wagging, barking happily, drooling as usual.

Piper adored Crutches. He was such a friendly old boy. Not a mean bone in his gigantic body—even though he had been born with bad hips and had every right to be grumpy because of the pain. Piper had been told by the Stolls that because their dog was born with a defect, his breeder, a friend, couldn't sell him. She was going to put him to sleep, but the Stolls begged her to let them have the pup. The woman relented and said they could—if they promised to see that the dog had surgery to help correct his problem. Three years and two operations later, Crutches was able to walk a bit better, but he would always feel some pain, and he moved with a noticeable limp.

Piper pulled to a halt, turned off the engine, climbed out of the car, and locked her door. Crutches awaited, tail swishing, pink tongue hanging, whimpering and snorting his hello. She walked over to the big fellow and wrapped her arms around his powerful neck.

"Hi, Crutches. Good boy coming to meet me. I've missed you." She kissed him on top of his black head.

The dog was so big that he came up to Piper's chest. Good thing he was so good natured, she thought. If he wasn't he could do a lot of harm with those big white teeth.

Crutches sniffed at Piper's purse, expecting the huge bone-shaped dog biscuit she always brought him. Piper patted him again. "Sorry, Crutches. I didn't bring any treats. I promise I'll go to the store tomorrow and buy you a big box."

Together the two walked toward the front porch. Just before they reached the bottom step, the front door opened, and then the old-fashioned, green storm door. The Stolls came out on the porch to greet Piper. "Hi, there," they said at the same time.

Piper noticed how much older they both looked. "Hi. How are you? Did Tatjana phone?"

"Yes, dear," Mrs. Stoll answered and wiped her flour-covered hands on the front of her red apron. The air around her turned dusty white when she said, "Come in, child. It's chilly out here. You'll catch your death." Now, that was stupid, she sputtered to herself. Death was the last thing the poor girl needed to hear about.

"Need to get stuff out of your car, Missy?" Mr. Stoll asked, tweaking his gray beard.

"Yes. I brought some luggage."

"I'll fetch it for you."

"They're heavy," she warned.

"That's okay. I'm strong as an ox."

Piper reached into her pocket, came forth with her keys, and handed them over to Mr. Stoll.

"Nice key ring," he said admiring the silver disk.

"Thanks. Kelly gave it to me for my birthday."

The Stolls both felt uncomfortable at the mention of that poor girl, and they quickly changed the subject.

Mrs. Stoll led Piper into the kitchen. Piper smelled fresh perked coffee and then she and Crutches both caught a tantalizing aroma coming from the oven. Piper asked, "What's cooking?"

"That's my homemade bread, dear," Mrs. Stoll said. "And earlier I made some of those soft molasses cookies with raisins that you and Kelly . . ." she stopped and didn't finish.

Piper put her at ease. "It's okay, Mrs. Stoll. Don't worry about mentioning Kelly. I think we should speak about her. Someone told me it helps the healing process."

The old woman was relieved. "Oh, thanks, dear. John didn't think it was a good idea to talk about her because it would make you sad. I told him I thought it was okay. I think it's healthy to do that. I knew if we didn't, we'd flub. That kind of thing seems to stick out like a sore thumb. Now enough of that sad stuff. Take a seat, dear. Let me get you a glass of milk and some cookies."

Piper sat down at the far end of the table near Crutches, who was now flopped on a huge, round, red-and-black plaid dog bed. The door opened and John Stoll came into the kitchen loaded down with Piper's luggage. She noticed that he was out of breath. "Let me help you," she offered and started to get up.

"Don't you dare," he snapped. "I'm not crippled." He looked at his dog. "Sorry, no offense, Crutches." Then he said to Piper. "I have to make another trip. Couldn't handle the small one."

"Let me get it," Piper offered.

"No. Listen here, Lady Jane Mariah. I may be in my eighties but like I said I'm no crip and I don't need no help."

Crutches struggled to his feet, walked over to Mrs. Stoll, and wagged his bushy tail. He was drooling and painting heavily. "What's the matter, dear?" Mrs. Stoll asked her dog. She looked at Piper and explained, "He usually doesn't like the warmth of the house. Bothers him, what with having such a heavy fur coat and all. He likes to stretch out on the porch and watch the world go by. But when company comes or he smells something he likes cooking on my stove, he paws at the door to come in."

Piper nodded and watched Crutches. His rugged body took up a great deal of room and his huge paws had left muddy tracks, but the Stolls didn't seem to mind. The dog had always been treated like family. Piper's gaze rested on

113

his bed, which was filled with cedar shavings and took up one whole corner and then some. Tatjana had given Crutches his bed for Christmas the year before. She'd told Piper and Kelly that she'd paid $66.00 plus tax for it. She'd also threatened Crutches not to gnaw on it or she'd order the Stolls to make him sleep in the barn for the rest of his life.

Nellie had told Piper that Crutches had chewed one edge of his bed and that her husband had properly scolded the dog. He never gnawed on it again. Mrs. Stoll often carried the bed out to the porch. Crutches would plop on it and doze for hours at a time.

While Piper sipped a huge glass of fresh milk and nibbled on a warm cookie, Mrs. Stoll pulled two loaves of bread out of the oven. "Hope you're planning to stay a long spell, Piper."

"Yes. I am. That is—if you don't mind. I don't want to make any extra work for you."

"Mind. Land, child. John and I love company."

Piper smiled and then said, "Can I ask a favor?"

"Certainly, dear. What is it?"

"A state police detective asked me to find out if it's all right for him to drop by this evening to ask me some questions about Kelly. Do you mind?"

"Course not. Do you think he'd like to have some supper? I made a pot roast with carrots and potatoes. John loves that, you know. Especially my gravy. I make it very dark."

"Yes. I know. I had some before. It was delicious. How about Mr. Stoll. Do you think he'll mind?"

"Mind what?" John Stoll asked as he came through the doorway.

"Piper wants to know if it's okay for a police detective to come here tonight to ask her some questions about Kelly."

John Stoll studied Piper. "I don't know. Your face looks kind of peaked to me. You feel up to that question stuff?"

"Yes. I think so. He's a nice guy." She felt color flood her cheeks.

"Well, now. Look at that girl blush with color now, Nellie. You sweet on this fella, Piper?"

Piper laughed nervously. "No. I don't even know him."

Mr. Stoll scratched his gray head. "Okay with me if he comes over. Invite him to supper. Nellie's made her pot roast. Sinful for a man to pass that up."

"Thanks. I'll ask him. Can I use your phone? I told him I'd call."

"Sure, dear," Nellie said. "Help yourself. You're welcome to use the one on the wall over there or the one in the front parlor."

"Take your pick," John Stoll offered.

"What's his name, dear?" Nellie inquired.

"Matt," Piper said. "Detective Matthew Carter." She was blushing again.

"That's a nice name, Isn't it, John?" Nellie asked her husband.

"It's okay. Can't understand it though."

"Understand what?" Nellie asked.

"I can't understand how a person can do awful work like that. Tough job if you ask me."

"Well nobody's asking you, dear," Nellie told him nicely. "It's time for the cow to come home. Want me to help you get her settled in the barn and help you slop the pigs before I start supper?"

"Nope. You visit with Piper. Tell her the latest gossip. Say, Piper. Did I ever ask you how they get holy water?"

Piper had heard that joke a dozen times but she played along. "No. How do they get holy water?"

"They boil the devil out of it," he chuckled and slapped his hands on his thighs.

"Oh, John," Nellie said. "Get on with yourself. The cow must be getting impatient."

"Okay, okay, Nellie. I'm going." He looked at his dog. "Crutches. Don't you want to go out to the barn with me?"

The dog had flopped on his bed again. He struggled to get up and then padded out the door behind his master.

While Nellie Stoll poured herself a cup of coffee, Piper used the kitchen phone to call Detective Carter. It rang just twice. "Detective Carter." Once again, Piper relished hearing his voice.

"Hi, this is Piper. I'm at the farm now. Mr. and Mrs. Stoll said it's okay for you to stop by. They asked me to invite you to supper." Before he had a chance to respond, she continued, "The menu is pot roast with dark gravy, and homemade bread. Fresh-baked this afternoon." She gasped for air.

"And coffee, apple pie, and ice cream for dessert," Nellie chirped.

"And coffee, apple pie, and ice cream for dessert," Piper repeated.

"Sounds great. I haven't had a home-cooked meal in ages. What time?"

"I'll ask. Mrs. Stoll, he wants to know what time?"

"Call me Nellie, dear. Let's see. John has to milk the cow and feed the rest of the animals. Let's say seven."

"Nellie says seven. Is that okay with you?"

"Are you sure you don't want to wait until tomorrow night?"

"No. I'm tired, but I really don't mind. I'll do anything to help catch the murderer."

"I'll be there at seven on the button," Matt said. "See you then."

As soon as Piper cradled the receiver, John came back into the house without Crutches. Before he had a chance to say anything Nellie said, "You know, Piper, when we first came here five years ago from our home in Pennsylvania, I never in my wildest dreams thought I'd be moving into such a beautiful place. Isn't that right, John?"

"Yup," John agreed.

"I know how you feel," Piper said. "I'm so lucky I went to work for Tatjana and met you. I remember the first time Kelly and I came here. And Mona and Steven. They really—" The phone rang and shattered the moment. Nellie picked up the receiver.

Suddenly the door burst open and Crutches ambled in.

"Did you leave the door open for him?" Piper asked John.

116

"Nope. He opens it himself. Don't you, big fella?"

"But how?" Piper asked.

"Puts the knob in his mouth and opens the door with his paw. Smart dog. Best one we've ever had. Crutches. Close that damn door. What's the matter with you? Were you brought up in a barn?"

Crutches gave the door a push with his muzzle but not hard enough. He headed for his bed. "Oh, no you don't," John said. "You get back there and close that door all the way."

Crutches gave John a look, then went back to the door and whacked it with his paw. The door closed tight.

"Good boy!" John said, like he meant it. Crutches ambled over to him and rubbed up against his leg. John stroked his head.

Piper was impressed.

"Well ladies. I have to go back to the barn," John said and made his exit. Crutches obviously had decided not to follow because he went to his bed and stretched out with his big head resting between his two front paws.

Nellie shouted into the phone. "The Church fair? Land. The time goes fast. Can't believe Christmas is just around the corner. Yes, I have. Now let's see. I've made ten pair of mittens and matching caps—some are dark blue and some are red. Tuesday. At two. Okay, dear. I'll be there. Oh, Helen. Which Saturday night is the bean supper? Okay, bye." Nellie hung up, looked at Piper and explained, "Sorry I made so much noise. Helen is deaf as a mackerel. Now. Where were we, dear?"

"We were talking about the farm," Piper said. She didn't get a chance to finish because the door opened and John came in again.

"Nellie, my love," he said sweetly to his tiny wife. "I'm running late. Had a problem with one of the sheep. I need a hand slopping the pigs. Can you free up?"

"I'll help you," Piper volunteered.

"Well, now. That all depends, Missy. You might be able to feed the chickens and sheep but the pigs are a different story. First you have to pass the test."

"What test?"

"I have to hear you call suey suey."

"Suey, suey," Piper yelled.

"That's just so-so," John said. "Try it again."

Piper yelled louder.

John tugged on his beard. "Hmmm. I guess you'll do but you need a lot more practice."

"I thought I sounded pretty good." Piper pouted. She still had no idea that John was teasing her.

"He was only kidding, dear," Nellie said coming to her husband's defense.

"Nellie's right. I was just joshing." He gave Piper an impish grin and then he said, "By the way, Missy. Can't stand it when people call me Mr. Stoll. Too formal. Know what I mean?"

"Yes, John." Piper responded.

He looked down at her feet. "Missy. If you're going to slop my pigs, you'd best wear boots. I hope you brought some along. If not, Nellie's might be your size."

"I didn't bring mine. And John. I can't stand it when friends call me Missy. Sounds so little girllike. Know what I mean?"

"Gotcha, Piper," he said and saluted. "Now how about them boots?" He walked over to the door and picked up a small pair off a cotton rug near the door.

Piper tried them on. They couldn't have fit any better. She was glad that she hadn't packed hers because the only kind she owned were high fashion: totally out of character for slopping the pigs. John would never have stopped teasing her if she'd worn her high-heeled boots.

The week before, everyone had set the clocks back one hour because standard time had returned to Maine. Piper didn't enjoy the short days. Darkness had always scared her. She was deep in thought about this when she and John finished their chores. On the way out of the barn, her foot caught on something, and she fell face first onto the hay-strewn floor.

"Did you hurt yourself?" John asked, helping her to her feet.

"No," she said and brushed herself off. "What in the world did I trip on?" She kicked at the hay and uncovered a metal hoop sticking out of the floor. "That's the culprit. What is that thing?" she asked John with a puzzled look.

"Hold your horses and I'll show you," John said and went to a shelf where he grabbed a flashlight and handed it to Piper. He then kicked more hay out of the way, bent over, pulled on the metal hoop, and lifted a squeaky trap door made of wood. "I put that metal loop on there the other day. Wasn't such a good idea. I'll have to figure out something else. Flash that light down there," he ordered Piper.

She did as she was told and poked the light into the opening in the floor. A huge rat, rudely interrupted by their snooping, darted out of sight across what appeared to be a dirt floor. John noticed that Piper hadn't carried on at the sight of the rodent, as most women would.

"Wow," Piper said. "That's a big mouse."

John laughed. "That's no mouse. That was a rat. Big colony of them down there," John grumbled. "I keep setting traps and they keep multiplying. "Nasty little jerks. Stealing food from my critters. Saw a bigger one than that the other day. Had the longest and skinniest tail I've ever seen. When I was a kid I had a friend whose little sister had her throat eaten away by a rat and . . ."

Piper wasn't about to listen to John's macabre story. She interrupted him, quickly shined the light to the left, and saw a short flight of wooden, cobweb-covered steps. "Do you know what this was used for?" she asked, noticing that at the foot of the steps was a rusty lantern tipped on its side, a white pitcher and basin, a thumb-back chair with a broken rung, and a spool bed frame.

"Yep. There's a bunch of old trunks in the attic that came with the house. Tatjana asked me to go through them and throw out anything that she wouldn't want. The other day, I came across a beaut. Belonged to a woman by the name of Sophia Fredericks. Found a diary she wrote in the 1800's. She mentioned this here dugout several times."

Before Piper could ask what the woman said about the

dugout, John continued with his story. "Also found a bunch of love letters she and her husband wrote to each other when he was in the Civil War. Awful hard to read because the writing is like chicken scratch. Paper must've been scarce because they wrote on both sides and along all the edges. They folded the letters up and stuffed them into tiny envelopes."

"Can you understand any of the writing?"

"Yep. I know that Sophia and John, that was her husband's name, were abolitionists."

"I used to know what that means, but I've forgotten."

"Antislave folks. You know. Like that Harriet Beecher. Can't think of her last name right this minute."

Piper helped him recall now. "Harriet Beecher Stowe. She lived in Brunswick. She's the one who wrote *Uncle Tom's Cabin*."

"That's the one. Her house has been made into a fancy restaurant. Nellie and I ate there on her seventy-fifth birthday. Good steak. Well, anyway," John said and scratched his beard, "Sophia mentions this room we're looking at in her diary. Hid a bunch of runaway slaves that came up here on the underground railroad on their way to Canada."

"This is amazing," Piper said. "How come Tatjana never mentioned this before?"

"Tatjana doesn't know about it yet. I just found out about it a few weeks ago. I was saving it for a surprise. Intended to tell her the next time she came up from New York. I was going to tell her at the funeral but it slipped my mind in all the confusion. I'm glad I did forget. Timing wasn't good. Nellie doesn't know yet either. I'm going to tell them when Tatjana comes up at Thanksgiving. They'll be pleased. Both like history. I could care less about it. Too much changing the truth."

"What do you mean?"

"Come on, Missy. I mean Piper. Don't tell me that you really believe that George Washington never told a lie. When I was a kid my teacher had all us kids in the class write an essay about George Washington never telling a lie. A friend of mine wrote that if George Washington said he never told a lie then he was a liar. Teacher had a fit. Whacked him good with a ruler. But the more I thought about what that kid wrote—the more I knew he had something there. Think about it."

"I guess you're right, John," Piper laughed. "But I still believe there's mostly truth to historical facts."

"Some. I think Abe Lincoln walked to school every day but not twenty miles barefooted. He'd have no feet left for shoes. And General Custer. He was a butcher, but he's made out like a hero."

"Well how about Sophia's diary? Do you think she's telling the truth?"

"Sure. But that's different."

"How is it different?"

"Nobody ever read it but me, at least not that I know of. It was hidden underneath the lining in the bottom of the trunk. I hope Tatjana doesn't go giving it to some muckity-muck who'll mess around with it. Next thing we know Sophia Fredericks was really Florence Nightingale."

"Oh, John. You know that can never be. You're distorting history now. Can I read Sophia's letters and her diary?"

"Sure. Don't forget to remind me to give it to you though or you'll be up the creek without a paddle. Seems like I forget an awful lot these days. Hate to admit it but I'm getting old."

"Talk about old," Piper said and shook her head. "This farm is unbelievable. Think about the history behind it. It's seen Indian attacks and probably protected many runaway slaves. Just imagine," Piper said and paused. "But, John, I thought that people hid slaves in houses—not barns."

"They did. Maybe the Fredericks decided to be different. But you're right. A dugout in the floor of a barn isn't exactly the best place. The air would be kind of scarce and the smell of the animals would be a bit ripe on a hot day. I don't think I'd want to have stayed down there for any length of time." John noticed that Piper looked funny.

"What's the matter with you?" he asked.

"Nothing's the matter," Piper responded. "My nerves are a bit on edge." She wanted to confess that she was having a hint of a panic attack over what he said about scarce air. Once, when she was a small girl, she had been riding an elevator by herself and it had stopped between floors. She was trapped for about a half hour before being rescued. After that, she had never been able to tolerate closed-in spaces and oftentimes would walk as much as ten flights of stairs rather than take an elevator. If she did take one she always felt as if she would get hysterical or maybe faint. She'd break out in a cold sweat, and her heart would pound hard. That's what was happening to her at the moment. She knew she had to concentrate on something else before she caused a scene. Her voice cracked when she said to John, "Have you ever read *Uncle Tom's Cabin* by Harriet Beecher Stowe?"

"Nope. Saved it for a rainy day. Guess I'd better get my hands on a copy cause I'm running out of rainy days in this life."

"I read it when I was a child," Piper told him. "It's a good book. It really teaches you about the horrors of slavery. I read somewhere that Stowe was really hated in the South."

"Yep," John agreed. "I've heard folks say that she started the Civil War."

"Have you ever climbed down there?" Piper asked and looked into the dugout.

"Nope. I've been meaning to, but first I wanted to make sure that rickety ladder is safe and I wanted to get rid of those pesky rodents. Don't like rats. Like I said I had a friend whose little sister . . ."

"I know," Piper interrupted. "You already told me. Please. I can't stand that story. It gives me the creeps."

"I know what you mean," John agreed. "When I heard the part about . . ."

Piper wanted to block her ears but she didn't. Somehow she suffered through John's gory tale. When he finally finished, she asked him if she could go down into the dugout when he did.

"Maybe. But you'd better make sure you don't get panicky. I don't think there's much air down there and I wouldn't be a bit surprised if this is the only way out. I checked all around the barn and I can't find a tunnel anywhere."

Piper felt another wave of panic wash over her. She knew that she couldn't ever go down into the dugout but she didn't want to tell John because he'd think she was a sissy. It was time to leave the barn before she made a fool out of herself. "Don't you think we'd better go into the house now?" she asked. "Nellie will be wondering where we are." She hoped that she hadn't sounded too desperate. She yearned to get outdoors in the fresh air. John hadn't answered her question. "Don't you think we should go to the house now?" she repeated.

"Yep. You're right," John said and dropped the trap door. He and Piper kicked hay back over it to hide it from Nellie in case she came out to the barn for something. Piper gasped. "What's the matter?" John asked. "Awful jittery."

"I know I'm jumpy," Piper said. "Guess I'm tired." She moved fast toward the barn door. The minute she stepped outside, she filled her lungs with precious cool air and immediately felt her body relax. She noticed that it was dark out now.

John caught up to her, and side by side they walked toward the house with Crutches limping along in front of them. Piper held her wrist up in front of her face to try and see her watch.

John said, "Quit struggling. I looked at mine just before we came out of the barn. It was about five-thirty. You in a hurry?"

"No. But I thought I might have time to shower before I help Nellie get supper."

"Oh, yeah. What time is that detective fella coming over?"

"Seven."

"Don't forget perfume," he said with a grin.

"Why?"

"So you don't smell like the barn, that's why."

"Thanks for telling me. I won't forget."

"Healthy smell, if you ask me," he mumbled. "But some folks don't think so. By the way. You did a good job slopping the pigs."

"Coming from you that's a compliment. I enjoyed it. If you need help tomorrow, I'm on call."

"I get up at four. And remember. Don't you breathe a word about what you just saw in the barn. I don't want Nellie finding out about that dugout until I tell her. That's why we covered the trap door with hay."

"I didn't see a thing," Piper said, wincing at the idea of having to get up at four. She was glad he couldn't see her expression in the dark. They went up the porch steps and into the house. Crutches headed directly to his food dish. John and Piper removed their dirty boots and left them on a multicolored cotton rug next to the door. Nellie wasn't in the kitchen, but Piper could smell her homemade bread and pot roast, and her mouth watered—she could almost taste it. Crutches stopped eating, lifted his head, and sniffed. He padded over to the stove, whimpered, and looked at John. "Stop that, Crutches," he ordered. The dog obeyed, limped to his bed in the far corner of the room, lay down, and looked at John sorrowfully.

John called out, "Nellie, where in tarnation are you?"

"In the dining room, dear. Setting the table for supper."

As soon as he and Piper hung up their jackets they went into the dining room and found Nellie fussing over the table settings. "I decided we should eat in here tonight because we have company," she said and looked at Piper and smiled sweetly. "I'm using my grandmother's wedding plates." She touched one ever so gently, as if it were sacred.

"Everything looks lovely," Piper said. "Those dishes look so delicate. What a pretty shade of blue. It looks so nice against the white background. They must be very old."

"Yes, they are, dear. My grandmother brought them

from Germany. She came from Hamburg."

"What is that floral design?"

"It's called Zwiebel," Nellie said. "Still popular in Europe. Zwiebel means onion in German."

"I didn't know that," Piper said. "How nice of you to set the table so pretty for me. Thank you both for being so kind. You don't know how relieved I am to be here." She was suddenly overcome with emotion. They were such a sweet old couple.

"Don't mention it, dear," Nellie said and looked at her husband. "John, don't you think you ought to change your clothes before supper?"

"Nope. But I'll wash up. How's that?"

Nellie scowled but she didn't comment. "John, you didn't tell me how you think the table looks." She waited for him to say something—anything.

"Wonderful, wonderful," he muttered. "I'm hungry. What time do we eat?"

"I think Piper told the young man to come at seven."

"Oh, yeah. I forgot," he said.

Piper glanced at her watch. It was getting late. "Nellie, do you mind if I go upstairs and take a shower before I help you get dinner ready?"

"Land, Piper," she said. "You don't have to help me. You go fix yourself pretty." She sniffed the air. "My pot roast is catching on the bottom of the pan! It won't be fit for the pigs to eat if it gets scorched." She left the room and headed for the kitchen as fast as her ancient legs could carry her.

"Wait for me, Nellie," John said and started after her. He stopped just in the doorway, turned, and said to Piper, "I don't know if you remember that you have to let the hot water faucet run for a long time. It never does get piping hot. Nellie and I are old-fashioned. Only take a bath once a week so it's not much bother to us. But you young folks have to hop in the tub every five minutes. I've told Tatjana a hundred times we need a new heater but she won't listen. One of these days we'll have to lug kettles from the stove."

"Thanks for reminding me."

"You're welcome and you'd better get going. Won't be long until supper. And another thing. If you want to make a good impression on that fella, you'd better wear something pink. Pink's a good girlish color. Looks great on Nellie. Should look almost as good on you."

"Thanks for the advice, John. I think I brought a pink blouse with me." She smiled and quickly left the dining room. She climbed the winding staircase to the second floor. She was alone again, alone to feel fear and to realize how much she missed Kelly. Piper walked faster and felt a lump in her throat.

She opened the door to the guest room and flipped on the wall light. She noticed that John Stoll had laid her luggage on top of the double brass bed. The room hadn't changed. Her eyes took in an oak rocking chair, a homemade braided rug, lift-top oak commode, complete with a white ironstone water pitcher, and basin. The walls were painted a soft yellow and covered with needlepoints framed in black. Tatjana had told Piper that every chance she got when she visited Maine she frequented antique shops. Every room in the farm was decorated from the era in which it was built. Piper loved every inch of the place and had often wished that it belonged to her.

By the time Piper went into the bathroom, her depression had lifted. John had been right. It took a long time for the warm water to reach a comfortable temperature. When it finally was ready, Piper climbed into the old-fashioned tub with the claw feet and pulled the white plastic curtain around her. She stood underneath John Stoll's makeshift shower and let a steady stream beat her body until she felt her taut muscles relax. She couldn't remember a time when water soothed so much. As she lathered her skin with soap, she thought about Matt Carter. She wondered what it would be like to take a shower with him. And then she thought about what it would be like to make love to him. And then in an instant, Kelly flashed before her eyes. Kelly would never be able to make love again. Piper knew that she'd better think about something else or she'd get depressed. She concentrated on shampooing her hair.

It was six forty-five when she went downstairs. She found Nellie in the kitchen stirring a pan of dark gravy with a wooden spoon. John was reading the evening paper. Crutches was drinking water out of his aluminum bowl and had managed to spill half of it. A puddle had formed around his huge front paws.

"Hi, dear," Nellie said. "You look lovely in that pink blouse. Good color for you."

"Thanks, Nellie," Piper said and winked at John.

"Is your room okay?" Nellie asked. "I made the bed up fresh as soon as Tatjana phoned."

"Yes. Everything is fine. I love that room and so did Kelly. She was about to say something else when she thought she heard a car outside.

John kept an eye on Crutches, who'd obviously heard a strange noise because he was at the window, ears alert, tail wagging furiously. "Company, girls," John said to Nellie and Piper. He slowly got up from the table. Crutches went to his side. John opened the door wide before whoever it was had a chance to knock. "Hi, there," Piper and Nellie heard him say. "You must be that detective fella Piper blushes over."

Piper was so embarrassed she wanted the floor to open and swallow her.

"John's gruff, dear," Nellie said softly so he couldn't hear her, "but he has a big heart. He loves to tease folks. He doesn't mean any harm."

Piper managed to say, "I know, Nellie. I only hope Detective Carter understands."

Detective Matthew Carter stood in the doorway with a grin on his handsome face. Crutches sniffed his pant legs. "Nice dog," said Matt. "What's his name? Cujo?"

John laughed. "That's good. That's good. I like a man with a sense of humor."

"Who's Cujo?" Nellie asked.

"For crying out loud, Nellie," John said and frowned. "You remember that book about that St. Bernard. That Maine fella by the name of King wrote it. Dog was a nasty brute. Sad story. A little boy died. They made a movie out of it. Don't you remember when we saw it?"

"Yes. I recall it now," Nellie said but didn't sound too sure of herself. "But I can't think for the life of me what that has to do with Crutches. Why, he wouldn't hurt a fly. Would you dear?" She looked at her dog with a knowing smile. Crutches continued to wag his tail and sniff Matt Carter's pant leg. Matt stood there not daring to move.

"I'm sorry," he said sincerely. "I was trying to be funny. Seriously, though, I'm awful glad your dog is friendly." He reached out and patted Crutches on top of the head.

Piper caught herself staring at Matt Carter. He's good-looking, she thought. I love the way he smiles. He saw her staring. "How are you, Detective Carter?" she quickly asked him. God. She hoped she hadn't sounded like a silly school girl.

"Call me Matt," he said.

"What's this Matt stuff?" John sputtered. "Getting kind of personal if you ask me." He winked at Piper and then took Nellie by the hand and pulled her towards Matt. "Detective Carter. This is Nellie, my wife."

"How do you do, Nellie? Please call me Matt."

Before she could speak John said, "Nellie makes a mean pot roast, as you're soon to find out. Now give me your coat and have a seat. I used to know a state trooper. His name was . . . can't think just now. Religious sort. Nice fella but drank too much. Liked to sing when he was tipsy. Had a hound dog that howled when he hit a high note. Speaking of drinking. Did you ever hear how they get holy water?"

"No sir," Matt Carter said with a grin and let go of Nellie's frail hand and removed his suit jacket. He handed it over to John who was delivering the punch line to his joke.

Matt laughed. "That's a good one, Mr. Stoll. I'll have to remember to tell it at work tomorrow."

"Call me John."

Piper knew then that Matt Carter was okay in John's eyes.

Nellie noticed that the young man hadn't taken his eyes off Piper, and that she was watching him. *Something brewing here,* she thought. *And what a fine looking couple they'd make. Their babies would be a sight for sore eyes. Folks used to say that about me and John.* She sighed deeply. *That was so long ago. Sometimes I can't remember what we looked like. One of these days I'll dig out the photo album and refresh my memory.*

Matt started to sit down at the table, but Nellie stopped him.

"Don't sit there, dear. We're going in the dining room. And if we don't eat my pot roast pretty quick it's going to be tougher than shoe leather. Piper. You take Matthew in the dining room and John and I will bring the food."

"I don't mind helping you, Nellie," Piper offered. "John can take Detective Carter into the dining room if it's okay with you."

"No. I want John to help me. Now go on with you. Take Matthew into the dining room."

"Call me Matt," he reminded her again.

"Do I have to, dear?" Nellie asked. "Matthew is one of my favorite names." She smiled warmly at him. "Our oldest boy was named Matthew. He died in Vietnam." She tried not to act sad but her eyes watered and gave her away.

Matt felt like a heel. "I'm sorry, Mrs. Stoll. You can call me Matthew. It's fine with me."

"Thanks, dear."

"Piper's offer to help sounds awful good to me," John said, interrupting Nellie before she started blubbering and spoiled supper after all the effort she'd put into fixing it. "Cooking is a woman's job," he grumbled. "Isn't that right, young fella?" To Matt's relief, John didn't give him a chance to answer. "Nellie's fixed a fancy table tonight," he continued. "Used her grandmother's best dishes. Trying to make a good impression for Piper's sake. You know how that is?" He chuckled and slapped Matt on the back.

Piper wanted to smack him.

"Get on with you, John Stoll," Nellie said. "Come on,

Piper. Don't you pay any attention to that husband of mine. You can pour the gravy. And be careful, dear. I wouldn't want my gravy boat to get chipped. It's very old." And then she said to Matt. "Make yourself comfortable in the dining room. Pick any seat except the one at the head of the table. John insists he sit there. Old-fashioned, you know. Breadwinner and all of that. But we like things that way, don't we John?"

John didn't answer, because he and Crutches had already disappeared into the dining room. Piper could hear him call out, "Say young fella. Did you ever hear the one about the traveling salesman who had a flat tire and went to a farm house . . ."

Matt winked at Piper and then he went into the dining room to catch the punch line. Nellie laughed. "That John. He never quits." Piper shook her head and poured the dark gravy, taking care not to chip Nellie's fragile boat. *God,* she thought. *He's so nice.*

John Stoll had been absolutely correct as far as Matt was concerned—Nellie did fix a terrific pot roast. It was so tasty that he had three huge servings. He felt so full he could hardly move and he wished that he could unbuckle his belt a notch or two. "Mrs. Stoll," he said and sighed deeply. "I haven't eaten anything that tasted as good as this since my mother died. She used to fix pot roast for dinner every Sunday."

"Oh, that's kind of you to say, dear," Nellie said. "But I'm awful sorry about your poor mother. Was it sudden?"

"No. She had cancer and she suffered a long time."

"Miserable stuff eats you up," John added. "I knew a fella that had cancer of the intestines . . ."

"John," Nellie scolded. "Dear heaven. Don't talk about that stuff while we're eating. Mind your manners."

"Okay, okay, Nellie. Say young fella. Did you ever hear the one about the Russian ballerina?"

"John Stoll," Nellie blurted just in time. "Don't you dare tell dirty jokes at my dinner table. Behave yourself or so help me I will wash your mouth the way your mother used to do when you were a kid."

"Darn it, Nellie. What can I say?"

Before Nellie had a chance to answer, Piper changed the subject. "Where do you live, Detective Carter?"

"Please. Call me Matt," he said again and smiled. "I rent a log cabin on Soudahook Lake in Gray. It's right on the water. I like it there."

Before Piper had a chance to comment, John said, "You ought to show it to her. Buy a bottle of wine. If you have a fireplace, burn a couple of birch logs. Cozy up a little. Know what I mean?" John winked at Matt.

Piper tried not to show her anger and she hoped her cheeks weren't too flushed when she said, "John. Please. You're embarrassing me and I'm sure you're doing the same to Matt."

"Piper's right, John," Nellie said. "I told you to behave. Land. You're worse than the seven year itch."

"I'm not embarrassed," Matt said and looked at Piper. "Really I'm not and don't you be. Actually, I was thinking of asking you to go for a drive after supper. I'd like to show you my place—that is—if you want to go?" He didn't know what he was going to do if she turned him down.

"I'd like that," she said, forgetting that she was angry at John and now concerned that she hadn't sounded too eager.

"Great," he smiled. "But I have to warn you. I'm a typical bachelor so it's not the neatest place. Although I do wash my dishes and make my bed every day."

"Well, there," Nellie said and looked at Piper. "If you were to ask me, it looks like this young man was brought up right."

"Watch it young fella," John warned. "Don't want Piper to know that you do that housework stuff. You'll be at the altar before you know what hits you if she gets down wind of too much."

Piper gasped.

Matt laughed and winked at her. She shook her head in disbelief. If she didn't change the subject right away, John was bound to have Matt believing he should run for his life. "How about dessert?" Piper asked.

"That's a grand idea," Nellie said and got up slowly from the table. "Piper, dear, how about you making the coffee while I cut the pie."

Piper got up from the table. She dreaded leaving John Stoll alone with Matt Carter. There was no telling what he'd say to him if she and Nellie were out of sight. But there was no need for her to fret because Matt Carter got on his feet, too, and picked up his dishes.

"Oh, my," Nellie said. "Will you look at that, John Stoll? You'd best take note of what that young man is doing. Maybe you can learn something from him."

"Oh, no," John said and slapped a hand on his head. "Look what you're doing. Now my life is never gonna be the same. I can see it all now. I'm going to have to get off my haunches and help Nellie clear the table from now on or I'll be in trouble. Being in hot water with my missus puts the fear of God in this old body." He slowly got to his feet, moaned, groaned, and picked up his plate and silverware off the table.

"Don't strain yourself, John," Nellie said and chuckled.

"Nope," he said and started toward the kitchen door. "I'm awful tired tonight, Nellie . . . What do you say? Let's you and me go up to bed right after dessert and the dishes." He gave Nellie a high sign.

Nellie got the message and immediately gave an exaggerated yawn. "I'm tired too, dear. Been up since the break of dawn."

Piper, still unaware that the Stolls's plot was thickening, said, "I'll do the dishes."

"I'll help," Matt offered.

"Heavens no," Nellie said. "I can't allow company to clean up my mess."

"Please, Nellie," Piper said. "I want to do them for you. I have to earn my keep somehow."

"Well, okay, Piper," Nellie gave in easily. "Remember though. Like I told you earlier, you must take care with my dishes. Sentimental and all that."

"I know, Nellie," Piper said. "I promise I'll be careful."

"Now that that's settled," John grumbled, "can we have our pie? Think I'll have vanilla ice cream on mine. I love it that way."

A half hour later John and Nellie said goodnight to Matt and Piper and slowly made their way upstairs to their bedroom. While Nellie turned down the covers on their old fashioned spool bed, John said, "Bet you a dollar he kisses her. What do you bet, Nellie?"

"I bet he does, too, John. My, my. You're a romantic old fool underneath that tough hide."

"Paul Newman ain't got nothing on me," he said and winked. "You'd better watch your step," he warned and gave Nellie a bear hug. "I've got a hunch about that young couple. Looks like they'd go well together. Hope they see it."

"They will dear," Nellie reassured him and then pecked his cheek. "I watched Piper closely. She has that glow about her. And that Matthew couldn't take his eyes off her." She sighed. "Wouldn't they make a nice couple? I was thinking earlier that their babies would turn out to be beauts. A cute little girl like her and a handsome boy like him."

"Jesus, Nellie. You've seen too many of them Rock Hudson and Doris Day lovey-dovey movies," John chuckled. "These two kids just met and you've already got them married off and changing diapers. Work fast, don't you?"

"I know. I know. But you should talk. You're the one who brought up the subject," she reminded him. She was silent for a minute and then she blurted, "You know what I'm thinking?"

"What?"

"I think love is grand." Nellie looked up at John with a twinkle in her faded watery eyes.

He smiled down at her and then he kissed her wrinkled brow. "Nothing quite like it. Best move I ever made was marrying you."

"Really, John?"

"Yep. I wouldn't joke about something as serious as that. And besides, you make the best pot roast I ever tasted. I'd have been one stupid fool to pass up that kind of home cooking. My other girlfriends couldn't boil an egg right. Remember Florence? Her cakes were like cement. Took one bite of her chocolate layer cake and broke a tooth. That's the one that has the gold filling." He opened wide so Nellie could take a peek.

"I'm not looking at that gold filling again, John Stoll. And I'm not falling for you saying that you only married me for my cooking." She playfully pushed him away and tried to sound stern when she said, "I knew there had to be a catch to that mushy song and dance you just gave me. Remember. What's good for the goose is good for the gander. Do you want me to talk about that handsome Tom Wilkie that wanted me to marry him? His family was loaded with money. His mother was in the Social Register. To think I could've been sipping cocktails at the country club instead of slaving over a hot stove."

"Poor woman," John said and yawned. "You'd have been some bored if you'd tied up with Wilkie. He was such a sissy. Scared of his own shadow. You made the right choice marrying a brave guy like me." He patted Nellie on the bottom. "Time for bed, Nellie. We need some sleep before the rooster crows. Four o'clock comes early. C'mon, woman. Let's turn on the television and cuddle up under the covers."

Chapter Seven

Just a Sip of Wine

Piper had no idea what she was going to say to Matt.
Every time she glanced his way, she had a vision of him
holding her in his arms. *This is ridiculous,* she thought.
To get her mind off the subject, she gave Crutches a dog
biscuit, and then she filled the sink full of hot soapy water
for the dishes. Matt took the cue and grabbed a red-and-
white checked dish towel that Nellie had hung on a brass
hook next to the sink. Piper carefully scraped food off
Nellie's favorite plates and put them gently into the hot
sudsy water.

"John and Nellie are a couple of characters aren't they?"
he said, thinking how much he liked the natural way
Piper acted and the sound of her laughter and her silky
hair—he wanted to run his fingers through it. He wanted
to . . . He knew that he'd better watch his step or she'd
throw him out.

"Yes they're characters," Piper said. "John is a devil. I
don't know how many times he's told that holy water joke.
They are so opposite. He's gruff and she's as gentle as a
lamb. She's so proud of these dishes. They belonged to her
grandmother, but I guess she told you that." She felt so
stupid that she couldn't think of anything intelligent to
say.

"What a treat it is," he said, "to see a couple together

135

that long and still act like they're in love."

"Oh, I don't think it's an act," Piper said. "They really do care for one another. I think John acts gruff on purpose. Nellie says that he's really a teddy bear underneath that tough hide."

Matt laughed. "He's a funny guy. Gets right to the point—that's for sure. My grandfather was like that—only worse. He used to embarrass me in front of my girlfriends. Nothing would stop him. The more people protested, the more he did it. He was the biggest tease I've ever met in my life."

"At least John stops when Nellie gets after him," Piper said. "She has more control over him than people think. I love it when Nellie calls people dear. They are a cute couple." Piper laughed.

"I agree. Funny, five minutes after I met them I forgot their age. Probably because they act so young. Maybe they should be observed to see just what their secret of a long lasting marriage is all about. Maybe they have the answer to divorce."

"I think you may be right," Piper laughed. "I really respect them—even if I have to be prepared for what might pop out of that mouth of John's. He really embarrassed me tonight." Even now her cheeks were flushed thinking about some of the things he'd said.

"Really?" Matt said. "Well, I thought he was a big help."

"How do you mean?" she asked.

"I wanted to ask you to go out with me tonight but I didn't know how I'd get around to it."

"Why can't you question me here?"

"I can. But I thought you might want to get some fresh air and a change of scene." How could he possibly tell her that he wanted to be alone with her?

"Thanks. That's nice of you. And speaking about Nellie and John. I worry about them because I don't think she feels well."

"What's wrong with her?"

"I don't know, and she hasn't said anything, but sometimes she looks like she's in pain."

"Maybe you should ask her what's wrong."

"I will. You know, I don't think John would want to live if anything happened to Nellie and vice versa. I had an aunt that lost her will to live right after my uncle died. Within months she died, too. I don't think I'd want to live if my husband died."

"That's a nice thing to say," he told her. "But let's hope that John and Nellie have many more years together. I only hope that I find someone as dedicated as they are someday." He wanted to kiss the tip of that cute nose of hers.

"Do you have a girlfriend?" Piper asked knowing that she was being too forward.

"Nope. No one steady, that is. I don't have much free time. Just when I think I can go out for an evening my phone rings and I have to go to work."

She tried not to act too relieved that he was available. "You make your job sound so routine," she said. "It amazes me how casual you sound when you speak about it. One would think that you were talking about going to the office—not off solving gruesome murders." Piper had another vision of finding Kelly in that pine coffin. She didn't envy Matt Carter.

"I know. I guess I do make it sound like it's pretty common. You're shivering. Are you cold?"

"No. I was just thinking about finding Kelly," she said. Her face took on an anguished look and her eyes watered but she didn't cry. She knew she had to stop thinking about Kelly before she lost control. "I don't mean to sound rude," she said softly. "But I don't know how you can stand to do what you do. It must be very difficult most of the time—I mean seeing life snuffed out so unnecessarily, and all that gore. Why did you choose homicide?"

"Because it's so interesting," he responded with enthusiasm. "Every case is unique. Even beyond that, they are the most complex cases and are defended so vigorously by defense attorneys. No cases go to trial as often." He was out of breath. "I'm sorry," he said. "I guess I got carried away."

"No. Please don't apologize. What you're saying is very interesting. Tell me more."

"Are you sure I'm not boring you?"

"Positive," she said. "What kind of person commits murder?" Thoughts of Kelly came to mind, and the threatening phone calls she'd received.

"Well," he said in answer to her question. "I've met a lot of different types. Most of the people I've arrested were indigent. They can't afford an attorney."

"What happens to a person like that?"

"Well the state furnishes them with a court-appointed lawyer and they usually plead not guilty."

"Why?"

"If you'd killed someone and were about to face a minimum of twenty-five years incarceration, and maybe more than that just because of the type of crime you committed, and you know it's not costing you anything in legal fees, why would you plead guilty?" Matt didn't wait for Piper to answer. "I wouldn't," he said. "A person would be pretty stupid not to want a trial. There's always a chance of getting off—with a jury. You just never know. I've seen many cases that I thought were airtight and the accused was found innocent. I've even sat with the Attorney General who had said that we had enough solid evidence to indict a guy; that we should go ahead with the case because it was a sure thing. But the jury came back quickly and with a not guilty verdict." He shook his head and looked frustrated. "I'm sorry. I shouldn't have rattled on that way."

"That's okay," she said. "It must be very difficult for you at times. I don't know if I'd have the fortitude to continue. How do you cope with knowing that someone has taken a life and is now roaming free?"

"It's very difficult. I've thought of quitting."

"I know what you mean," Piper said and sighed deeply.

"It hurts me so much to think about Kelly. I don't know how I'm going to go back to work knowing that she won't be there." Her throat tightened at the thought.

"I felt that way when my mother died," Matt said.

"Really?" She was relieved he understood the same pain. "I guess I did, too, when my parents died," she said. "I didn't think I could go on but as the months passed I began to feel a bit better." She paused and then she said, "Ever since the phone calls this morning, I've felt guilty."

"Why?"

"Because the person said that Kelly was a mistake. I was the one who was supposed to die. But why? Who could be so mad at me that they want to murder me?"

"I don't know," he said. "But I promise I'm going to try to find out." He could tell that she was on the verge of crying. The look in her eyes made him want to take her in his arms. He quickly reached for another plate to dry before he made a fool of himself.

"Do you think the person who killed Kelly will get caught?"

"I'm going to do everything I possibly can to see that happen."

"God. I hope you catch him before . . ." She stopped talking and turned her face away.

"Before what?" he asked, softly.

"Before he kills me." She turned her head and looked up at him with such fright in her eyes that he couldn't bear to look at her.

Piper's throat tightened again and she swallowed hard before she spoke. "I, I—" she couldn't seem to get the words out. "I'm sorry," she managed to croak. "But if I talk about this I'll cry." She turned so Matt couldn't see her face. She pulled herself together and then she said, "I'm so afraid. Maybe I should run away before it's too late."

The very mention of her leaving put him on the edge of panic. Before he realized what he was doing, he plunked the sopping wet dish towel on the counter and took her in his arms. She didn't resist and laid her head against his chest. The solidness of him felt so comforting. He stroked her long, silky blond hair. She felt so damned good to the touch. He hugged her tighter for a few seconds and then he pushed her gently away, put his finger under her chin, and tilted her face upward. He leaned down and put his lips on hers and kissed her tenderly. She didn't resist. He stopped kissing her and pulled away. "I'm sorry," he said huskily. "I had no right to do that." His handsome face was flushed.

"No," she said. "Don't apologize. It's okay." She stepped toward him, stood on tiptoes, twined her arms around his neck, and kissed him.

He responded. Piper felt quivery from the top of her head to her feet. Matt was the one who again shattered the moment when he pulled away. "I think we'd better stop," he said. "Let's finish the dishes so we can get some fresh air." He wondered if she thought he came on to other women he met on his job. He decided that he'd better clear that up straight away in case she had the wrong idea about him. "Piper," he said. "I hope you don't think that I kiss all the women I have to question. This is the first time I've ever done that. I hope you believe me."

"Yes," she said. "I believe you. The same goes for me. I hope you don't think that I go around kissing every man I meet."

"That never even entered my head."

Piper smiled at him and then she turned on the hot water faucet to rinse the dishes. She told herself to move cautiously. Matt Carter's kiss had undone her. If they did that again they might not be able to stop. It had been a long time since she'd responded so passionately. She glanced at Matt. Talking to herself wouldn't help. She had to be honest about the situation. She didn't care about restraints. She wanted very much for Matt Carter to make love to her. Kelly flashed—guilt struck. Piper couldn't believe she was thinking about making love at such a sad time.

"There," Matt said as he dried the last dish. "Nellie will

be pleased that we didn't chip any of her plates." He hung the dish towel on the brass hook, looked at Piper, and said, "Well. What do you say? Do you want to go out for a bit?"

"Sure," she smiled. "Just let me go upstairs for a minute. I'll be back in a second." She made a quick exit and raced upstairs to her room, grabbed her coat and purse, glanced at herself in her bureau mirror, and stopped in her tracks. Her hair was a sight and her lipstick was smudged on her chin from kissing Matt. Very quickly she pulled a tissue out of her pocket and wiped her face. She stole one last glimpse at herself in the mirror to make certain she looked okay and went back downstairs to find Matt. On the way, Kelly crept into her mind. Twinges of guilt returned. Stronger than before. Her best friend had been buried just a few hours ago and here she was, eager to go for a ride with the detective assigned to the murder. Piper knew that she should be ashamed of herself, but the truth was she wasn't. She was so upset over Kelly and all that had happened that she craved a change of scene. Oh, Kelly, she said to herself. If you were here you'd understand. But Kelly wasn't there. She was dead. Piper wasn't sure at all that Kelly Stewart would understand. This can't be real, she thought. She could feel another wave of depression sweeping over her.

Piper walked into the kitchen and saw Matt Carter seated at the table petting Crutches, who had his massive head in his lap. The dog heard her come into the room, lifted his head to see who it was, and then ignored her. Matt had to wiggle free. "It's a good thing this fellow is so gentle. Did you ever notice the size of his teeth?"

"Sure have," she said. "But I don't think he'd bite. He's one of the gentlest dogs I've ever seen."

Matt stood up. They both said goodbye to Crutches and went outside. He held the car door open for Piper and watched her buckle up. He climbed in his side and shoved the key into the ignition. Seconds later they drove out of the driveway into the dark of night. Piper didn't talk. She was deep in thought about their kissing in the kitchen. He struggled not to take hold of her hand. "Are you feeling better?" he asked.

"Yes," she fibbed. "Thanks for asking. This is quite the car. I didn't notice. Does it have any official markings on the doors?"

"No. We don't carry the state police logo like patrol cars." He was quiet for a second and then he tried to create some conversation between them. "I was a road trooper for three years. You have to do patrol before you can make detective." He waited for her to respond.

"Did you cover a big territory?" she finally asked.

"Yes," he said. "But after a few months, I got so I didn't pay any attention to the miles." Their conversation stopped again.

She stared out the window at the passing homes. In seconds her mind returned to dwelling on Kelly and the funeral. She thought of Mona. Piper had no idea what Mona would think when she told her that she wouldn't be going back to work at Tatjana's until she felt better. And then she decided she didn't give a damn about what Mona might think. There was no way she could face going to the shop knowing that Kelly wouldn't be there. She toyed with quitting. But then she knew that she couldn't do that. Tatjana had been too good to her. She would play the martyr and stay—at least until Tatjana could find replacements for both her and Kelly. She decided that she'd phone Mona from Matt's house and let her know her plans. She braced herself for Mona's reaction. She prayed it wouldn't be another performance like the one at Mona's dinner party when she accused her of flirting with Steven. She lifted a hand to her face and unconsciously rubbed her cheek where Mona had slapped her. She could almost feel the sting.

The moon had been out in full view when Matt and Piper left the farm. Now, it had disappeared behind fluffy rolling clouds. Rain drops began to pelt the windshield, and Matt turned on the wipers. They had driven about ten miles when Piper turned away from the window and asked Matt, "Where are we going?"

"Actually, I don't know. Any ideas?"

"No. Not really."

"Well, John had a good one. You can say no if you want, but I'll ask anyway. Would you like to see my cabin?"

"I thought you were supposed to be working," she teased.

"I am. But I thought you might like to see the place. I don't get a chance to show it off very often."

"Do you take all the women that you have to question home with you?"

"No," he said, seriously. "You're the first. Well—what do you say?"

"About my being the first?" she asked, teasing him.

He laughed. "No. Not that. You know. About going to the cabin? You have to make a decision now before I have to change directions."

"Okay, Matt Carter. How could I resist seeing it after your vivid description? My answer is yes. I want very much to go to your place."

"You won't be disappointed," he promised. "The owner said he might sell it in the spring and if he does, I'm going to buy it."

Piper glanced out her window again as Matt clipped along the highway towards Soudahook Lake in Gray. She became aware that the stars had vanished along with the moon and it was raining. The night was totally black, except for the reflections from the car lights. The motion of the car made her sleepy. She intended to only shut her eyes for a few seconds to rest. Exhaustion overtook her.

Piper didn't wake up until she felt Matt nudge her. "We're here," he said. She looked out the window and could tell that Matt had turned onto a dirt road by the crunching sound the tires made rolling over the bare ground. They were in the woods. Tall pine trees lined both sides of the narrow way and brushed against the car. Piper calculated that they must have gone about a half mile when he said, "Here we are," and then drove as close as he could possibly get to the cabin. Piper didn't comment. He shut off the engine. Both climbed out of the car at the same time. He walked quickly to her side, closed her door for her, took her by the arm, and guided her toward the front door so she wouldn't stumble in the dark. When they were on the porch he pulled his key out of his pants pocket but he couldn't see well enough to slip it into the lock. After he finally succeeded, he opened the door wide and they stepped inside. He flipped a light switch on the wall. Piper squinted from the glare. When she could focus she discovered that they were in the living room. On a table next to her rested a huge bowl full of candy. "Want a piece?" Matt asked her.

"No thanks. Maybe later." She fell in love with the place at first glance, especially the large fieldstone fireplace that covered one wall. She looked up. The ceiling had thick handhewn beams that stretched from one end of the room to the other. The floor was made out of wide, pine-pegged planks and were stained a handsome shade of pumpkin pine. The room was extremely cozy. But Matt's furniture confirmed that he was a bachelor. A black, leather, three-cushioned sofa and a matching recliner filled the room. A pair of sneakers sat pigeon-toed on the floor in front of the hearth. A blue and green plaid shirt, a black leather belt, and a pair of faded jeans were draped over one end of the sofa. Matt noticed his clothes, ran to them, quickly scooped them up, and carried them into another room which Piper assumed was a bedroom.

"Sorry to run off like that," Matt apologized when he returned. "I'm not usually this messy. Been working long hours."

"You don't have to apologize," she said. "I think the place is pretty tidy—for a bachelor. Oops. I hope you don't take offense at that feminine statement."

He laughed. "No. You're right. I guess I do a pretty decent job of it most of the time. Now, what can I get for you? How about some wine or coffee?"

"I've had too much coffee. Just a sip of wine would be great."

"Okay. Follow me to the kitchen." *Christ,* he thought. *I hope I did the dishes.* He hadn't. "Darn," he said to Piper.

"I guess you think I fibbed to Nellie Stoll when I told her I make my bed and wash the dishes every day?"

"No. Not at all." Piper pretended not to notice the clutter. The table was covered with old newspapers, a few magazines, a jar of grape jelly, and a box of crackers. She could tell though, that when the things were in order, the kitchen would look terrific. The walls were white as were the major appliances. The floor was covered with huge black and white checkerboard tiles. A pewter chandelier with black and white swirled stained-glass shade hovered over the wide oak table with claw feet.

Matt moved fast to clear away a coffee cup, saucer, a basket with a partial loaf of skinny French bread, and a small pile of change, mostly pennies, off the counter. There was no way he could hide the dirty dishes in the sink. He went to the table and cleared a spot big enough for them to use. Then he went to one of cabinets and brought out a bottle of red wine and two glasses. He held them up to the light by the stems to see if they were clean. Next, he found a corkscrew in a drawer and unscrewed the cork from the bottle. As soon as he finished, he noticed that Piper was standing in the middle of the room. "I'm sorry," he apologized. "Talk about rude. Why don't you sit down? I think I've cleared a wide enough space so you don't get lost in my junk."

Piper smiled nervously, removed her coat, and draped it on the back of a ladder back chair with a cane seat and then sat down. She watched Matt stop what he was doing and remove his suitcoat. Piper noticed his black leather holster strapped to his belt. "Do you always carry a gun?" she asked and grimaced, remembering that Tatjana had insisted that she learn how to use one.

"Always," he said and took off his belt and stuffed the holster into a kitchen cabinet, out of sight. "You're making a terrible face. I can see that you don't approve of guns. Right?"

"Right. Have you ever had to use it?" She didn't want to hear his answer.

"A couple of times."

"Are you a good shot?"

"They don't call me deadeye for nothing." He laughed and noticed that she didn't.

"Was it difficult to pull the trigger?" she asked.

"I didn't have time to think about that. It was a matter of life and death."

"I suppose you've been asked this a hundred times. But here comes a hundred and one. Have you ever killed anyone?" She knew that she was getting far too personal but she wanted to know.

"No," Matt answered. "Just wounded them. Why do you ask?"

"Because my boss, Tatjana, insists that John Stoll teach me how to shoot her gun. She said I should shoot to kill. I lied and told her I'd learn. I really do hate guns. I'm for gun control. Why can't America be like England? English policemen don't carry guns."

"I think it's a bit late for us to go that route," he said. "About Tatjana's wanting you to learn how to shoot. Under the circumstances, I have to say that I agree with her all the way. If it's any consolation, I'd be happy to take you target shooting."

"Thanks." she said and then shook her head. "God. I can't believe I said that."

"What do you mean?"

"I never thought I'd thank someone for saying that they would teach me how to kill a human being." She paused a minute and then she asked, "How do you think you would have felt if the people you wounded had died?"

"It was either them or me. Look, Piper. I know it would cause you a lot of pain to have to shoot someone but you have to face some hard cold facts. Your best friend was murdered. The killer told you he made a mistake. He said he was after you and that he's going to get you. You're not dealing with a sane person. You have to be able to defend yourself. You could take judo or karate but I suggest you think about using a gun. If it comes right down to it, you'd better be able to pull the trigger." He saw her flinch. *Now you've done it*, he said to himself. *Look at her. She's pale as death. Apologize, you idiot.* "I'm sorry. I didn't mean to upset you anymore than you already are. Guess I got carried away. I can't help myself. I don't want anything to happen to you. I hope you understand?"

"Yes, I do," Piper said. "I'll call you and let you know so you can take me target shooting and teach me. But it really makes me angry that my life has to come down to that."

"I know," Matt agreed. "But that's the way it is. I don't want to sound like a broken record, but I think it's necessary for you to learn to handle a gun." He knew he'd gone too far again. It was time to change the subject. "Now," he said. "Let's stop talking about guns and have that wine." He grabbed the bottle and poured them each a glass.

Piper thanked him and immediately took a huge gulp. She took another. Before he was halfway through his first glass, he refilled hers. After several more sips, she knew she was on her way to feeling mellow. She could always tell when that happened because her lips began to feel numb. The best part, though, was her outlook. Too much wine always made her feel like everything was going to be okay. Even the pain of losing Kelly dulled. She was quite aware that Matt Carter was watching her. When her glass was drained to the last drop she pushed it across the table until it clanked hard against the bottle. She laughed and said, "Do you mi-mind if I have just a little bit more?" She didn't care that she was slurring her words.

Matt made certain that he poured her only half a glass. "You drank that stuff pretty fast," he said. "Don't you think you should take it a little easy?"

"Nope. And don't think I'm a drunk. Okay? Just need to lighten up. Everything has been so heav-heavy." She clanked her glass against the bottle again and gave Matt an understanding look. "Do—don't worry. All is well that . . ." She downed the wine. "Can I please have some mo-ore?"

"Nope. I think I'll make you some coffee." *Well, dummy,* he said to himself. *You just shot down being able to question her tonight. Christ. That was stupid.* He got

147

up from the table and went to make a strong pot of coffee.

Piper's eyes had glazed over. When she put her elbow on the table to support her chin, she misjudged and whacked her funny bone. Pain soared through her arm. She winced. The blow, along with her overindulgence in wine, made her want to cry. That was another thing drinking did to her. She tried unsuccessfully to hold back her tears. Black mascara smudged her cheeks. It was as if her eyes had turned into two open faucets. Her nose dripped.

Matt felt guilty. He should never have let her drink so much. "Please don't cry," he said. She didn't act as if she'd heard him. He wanted to take her in his arms and comfort her but he didn't know what she'd do if he did.

Piper sobbed. Matt couldn't stand it any longer. She didn't even notice when he got up from the table. And she didn't see him leave the room to go get a wet face cloth and some tissues out of the bathroom.

When Matt returned, he found that Piper had stopped crying. Now she was staring blankly at the wall. He went to comfort her. "You poor little thing." He washed her face with the still-warm cloth. Piper sat statue still. He couldn't stand seeing her in such a stupor. "Oh, honey, please don't. What can I do to make you feel better?"

She tried to answer but instead she hiccuped.

Matt thought about getting a paper bag for her to breathe into to stop her hiccups, but he knew she was too far gone to concentrate. "I need to," she paused and hiccuped again. "I n-eed the bathroom."

Matt helped her to her feet. When he let go of her she tipped backwards and fell into her seat. He helped her again—successfully this time, and then he guided her into the bathroom and turned on the light. "Will you be okay by yourself?" He didn't know what he was going to do if she said no.

"Yup. Thanks."

Matt closed the door and went back to the kitchen and got the coffee ready. He was halfway through a cup when he realized that Piper should've been out by now. He debated whether to see if she was okay but he didn't want to embarrass her, just in case. Women took their time, he knew that. He took his coffee mug and began to pace the floor and watch the clock. Approximately twenty minutes had passed and still no sign of Piper. "It's been far too long," he muttered. "Christ. She could've fallen and hit her head. She could be bleeding to death for all I know. That's it. I'm going in there after her." He dropped his coffee mug on the counter and ran, leaving a trail of coffee running down the middle of a cabinet door onto the floor.

Matt rapped on the bathroom door. "Piper are you okay?"

Silence.

He knocked again. No answer. He was really scared now. It was time to open the door. He turned the knob and pushed it wide open. "Oh, no," he said and ran to her side. Piper was in a heap on the cold floor. He quickly knelt, lifted her limp arm, and felt for a pulse in her wrist. He found a strong beat, and then she groaned and said weakly, "I'm okay." She lifted her head with great effort and tried to smile at him. "I feel better now."

A grin spread across his face. Before he could stop himself he kissed her lips and ran a finger lightly across her cheek. She responded and wrapped her arms around his neck.

He pulled away and whispered in her ear, "You're going to catch cold on this floor."

She yawned and mumbled something that sounded like, "So tired. I must be a sight."

Matt told her he thought she was beautiful, even if she did smell like a wino. He touched the end of her nose, her lips, her chin, and throat. He pulled his fingers away when they began to travel in the direction of her breasts. His lips found hers again. When they separated, she moaned and stretched her curvy body like a kitten. Her head hurt. "Ugh," she said. "I guess the wine won. My head kills." She rubbed her forehead.

"No wonder," Matt said. "Your back is going to hurt worse if you don't get up. This floor isn't the most comfortable spot. What happened to you?"

"I got sick, then I felt so weak and exhausted I couldn't move. I wanted to yell to you but I couldn't find the strength." She began to shiver. "I'm freezing."

"Here, let me help you up."

"Thanks."

Matt got to his feet and lifted Piper into his arms. She laid her weary head against his broad chest.

"I'm taking you into my bedroom," Matt told her. "You're in no shape to leave here tonight. I'll phone the Stolls so they won't worry."

She didn't object. She was worried that he must think she was a screwball. How in the world was she ever going to explain that this had never happened to her before? Matt laid her down on his bed and threw a patchwork quilt over her to keep her warm. He turned on the lamp next to the bed, and Piper winced from the glare. "What can I do for you now?" he asked.

"Nothing," she said and looked up at him with an embarrassed look on her face. "Matt," she said.

"What?"

"I, I hope you don't think I drink like that all the time. The wine crept up on me. The only other time I got drunk was when I was sixteen. Kelly and I went to a birthday party and got smashed. I fell into a bathtub and couldn't get out. I made a vow never to get that drunk again because I was sick for days afterwards."

"I know the feeling," Matt said and laughed. "It was my fault. I should've known better. You've had a rough time. You're overtired. Feel like having some coffee now?"

"Yes. But it wasn't your fault. God. I'm so embarrassed. It's a good thing I didn't lock your bathroom door or I'd still be there."

"No you wouldn't. Trust me. I'd have gotten you out somehow. You had me worried for a second. I thought you'd hurt yourself. It's a wonder you didn't, you know. Will you be okay while I go get the coffee?"

"Yes. I'm fine. Just cream in mine. Please."

"Gotcha. I'll be right back. Want the light on or off?"

"On."

When he left the room, Piper lay on the bed with her eyes closed. When she opened them the room spun for a few seconds and then it finally stopped. She was relieved that her crying jag was over. Her cheeks felt flushed. What must Matt think? She was angry with herself for drinking so much. She worked her body further under the quilt and buried her face in the pillow. It smelled of him. She hugged the pillow tighter and found herself impatient for him to come back. She was so sleepy. A few seconds later she drifted off.

When Matt returned carrying two cups of coffee, he found Piper asleep. He put the coffee on the nightstand and sat on the edge of the bed beside her. She looked like a little kid. He stroked her hair ever so gently, and she stirred but didn't wake. He leaned over and kissed her ear, the nape of her neck, her cheek. She woke up and looked at him with those wonderful blue eyes of hers. He kissed her mouth. Passion swept over both of them when he took her in his arms. She snuggled against him. He put both hands underneath her shirt and gently lifted her bra. His warm fingers caressed her firm breasts and now-erect nipples, and his hands moved slowly down her taut belly and unbuttoned her jeans. The zipper moved with ease. He pulled her jeans off, then her black silk panties. While he did this, she unbuttoned her shirt and unhooked her bra. The sight of her body made him catch his breath. "You're so beautiful," he told her, huskily. She smiled up at him.

It only took him a few seconds to undress. Piper watched him remove his shoes and socks, his pants and shirt, and then his underwear. She inhaled deeply. There was no question that he was ready to make love to her. He climbed into bed beside her and then he reached for the light switch on the lamp beside the bed. Piper pulled her body hard against his and lifted her face to kiss his lips. They kissed and kissed again. He ran his hands gently up and down her back and across her buttocks. When he touched her between her legs, she gasped, gripping him tighter, and pressed her body firmly against his. When he entered her she cried out with pleasure. He buried his face in her silky hair and inhaled the sweet scent of her. At first, he moved with a slow, steady rhythm, trying to be as gentle with her as possible. Piper couldn't seem to get enough of him. She sighed with pleasure and nibbled his ear. She could feel him shudder and then he moved faster and plunged deeper into her. Their passion quickened and then they both cried out at the same time. He wanted the feeling to last forever.

She pulled the quilt over them and then she snuggled close to him. He whispered in her ear. "That was terrific."

Piper kissed him and stayed wrapped in his strong arms. Making love had made the hurt of losing Kelly fade for the moment. She reached up and kissed Matt's cheek. At that moment she never wanted to get out of that bed. Seconds later she fell into a deep sleep.

The phone rang for a long time before Matt came out of a sound sleep. Piper woke and slowly sat up in bed. At first, she didn't know where she was. And then Matt turned on the lamp and groped for the phone on the nightstand and finally found the receiver. "Hello," he said and sounded none too pleased over being disturbed.

"Matt. This is Jake Thomas."

"What's up?"

"Just got a call. Seems another body has turned up in Cape Bethany."

"No way. Not again."

"Yup. And get this. It's the same address as before. It's Steven Hadley. Cape Bethany Police think it was an accidental suicide but they want to make sure before they rule out homicide since the Stewart girl was murdered there."

Matt was wide awake now. He looked at Piper and gave her a smile. Then he looked at the clock on the nightstand. It was already seven in the morning.

Piper was still so tired she couldn't hold her eyes open. While she listened to Matt's conversation, she put her thumbs on her temples and rubbed. Her body felt as if she had been beaten. She could tell from what Matt was saying that there had been a murder. Kelly came to mind, and

Piper shuddered and moved closer to Matt. He held the receiver in one hand, stroking her hair with the other. She stopped rubbing her temples, grabbed his arm, and kissed the palm of his hand.

"Okay, Jake. I'll be there just as fast as I can. Have you called the other guys? Good. See you there." He hung up and looked down at Piper. He decided he would wait until he came back from Cape Bethany before he told her that Steven Hadley was dead. She couldn't take any more bad news right away. "Piper," he said.

"Yes, Matt."

"I have to leave for a while."

"I know. I heard."

"Do you mind staying here for a few hours until I can come back to take you to the farm? Or do you want me to call the Stolls and see if John will come for you?" He didn't know how he was going to convince her to stay if she said she wanted to leave.

"No. I'll wait. That is if it's okay?"

"Sure it is." He was so relieved. "But I might be gone most of the day."

"That's no problem. I'll phone the Stolls and tell them that I'm okay."

"Good," he said. "And by the way. When you get hungry help yourself to anything in the fridge."

"Thanks."

"You're welcome."

Even without makeup he found her beautiful. He loved her tousled hair and pink cheeks. He couldn't resist the urge to take her in his arms and kiss her. Warm memories stirred, and he wanted her again, but there was no time. "I think I love you," he whispered in her ear.

"I think I love you, too," she blurted and then blushed.

He had to get out of bed before he became completely unstrung. He kissed her on the forehead. "I have to get up before I get carried away," he said. He yanked the covers off, climbed out of bed, grabbed his clothes and dirty socks off the floor, and piled them on a chair on the other side of the room. He opened his closet and brought out a clean pair of pants and shirt, went to his oak bureau and found some socks and underwear, grabbed his shoes off the floor, and disappeared into the bathroom to take a shower.

Piper pulled the covers up to her chin. Her thoughts were full of Matt Carter. The memory of their lovemaking made her feel warm all over. She knew that she wanted to marry Matt someday, and she only hoped he felt the same way. She wanted to spend every morning for the rest of her life in bed with him. Such haste, she thought. But that was okay. Her parents had only known each other a scant three months before they got married, and they'd often told her that they never regretted one moment. Her mother used to say that she knew that she wanted to marry Piper's father the first night they went out together.

She wished that Matt didn't have to go to work so they could make love all day. "Work," she said out loud and sat upright. Her mind raced. What if Tatjana didn't phone Mona to tell her she wasn't going to the shop? What if Steven didn't tell Mona she called? She reached for the phone. At the last minute, she changed her mind. She didn't want to talk to Mona. She knew that if she did, Mona would lay a guilt trip on her. She decided to wait until Matt left; then she'd phone her. She rested her head on her pillow and closed her eyes. She was almost asleep when Matt came out of the bathroom. He sat down on the edge of the bed. She raised herself and leaned on an elbow for support, and waited for his kiss. He was the one who broke away. "I'd better go," he said and stood up. She blew him a kiss, and then she closed her eyes and drifted off.

Matt took the phone off the hook so she wouldn't be disturbed. He tiptoed out of the bedroom and went into the kitchen to get his holster out of the cabinet, hoping Piper could sleep undisturbed all day. Rest was bound to make a significant difference in her outlook, he thought, smiling to himself as he remembered how he'd found her curled into a ball on the bathroom floor. She must be somewhat hungover from guzzling all that wine. The poor thing had been through the mill, and now there was more to come. His thoughts shifted to Cape Bethany. *I wonder what the hell has happened on Lighthouse Road now?* Steven Hadley. Two bodies in one week in the same house. Cape Bethany would never live it down. Matt thought about his mother and smiled. She sure would've loved to have been around to see his aunt's face. He could bet she'd be putting a FOR SALE sign up before the day was out.

Chapter Eight

Steven

Upon leaving Kelly's parents' house after the funeral, Steven and Mona drove straight home to Cape Bethany. She was tired and could hardly wait to shower and change her clothes. He brooded over how much he hated her. *Heart of stone,* he said to himself. The bitch. Fuck diabetes—he needed a couple of good stiff drinks. He tucked his promise to take care of his health in the back of his mind. Then he glanced at Mona and felt an urge to strangle her. The thought sent ripples of excitement through him.

They were not far from Lighthouse road now. He yearned to get home. He felt as though they'd been gone for months instead of just a few hours. He kept glancing out of the corner of his eye at Mona. He wondered what was rattling around in her head.

She caught him looking at her. "Why are you looking at me that way?" she asked, glaring at him.

"No reason," he lied, and concentrated on his driving.

"Step on it will you, Steven?" she said. "I'm very tired. I need a nap. I hope the cleaning lady came this morning. When I called her yesterday she said she was quitting because she was scared to death to go into our house because of the murder. I had to promise her more money so she would stay on."

"Can you blame her, Mona? Kelly's killer is still loose."
She didn't respond. The memory of what happened when he first woke up this morning came to his mind. He'd opened his eyes to see Mona fussing with her dyed hair and makeup. She didn't waste any time complaining about him drinking again. *Nag. Nag. Nag,* he mumbled to himself. After he hopped out of the shower and wrapped a towel around his waist, he went into the bedroom just in time to see her hanging up the phone. "Who were you talking to?" he asked her.

"None of your business," she snapped.

"You're bitchier than usual this morning," he accused.

"What do you mean?" she asked.

"I mean just what I said."

"You're crazy."

"No. I'm not crazy, Steven. You are."

"Sure, Mona, sure."

"Shut up, Steven."

"Are you going to tell me who you were talking to or not?" He really didn't give a damn. Now it was just the principle of the thing.

"Jesus," she said.

Her tone sounded softer when she asked, "Did you give yourself your insulin injection?"

"No but I will before we leave. What are you up to? It's not like you to be so sweet."

Her face flushed. "I'm not up to a goddamned thing. You know, Steven. I was trying to be nice to you, but it's hard being that way when you act like such a prick." She was so angry the veins in her neck popped out and her face turned red. "Look," she said more calmly and stood up. "I'm hungry and it's getting late. I'm going out to get some breakfast before the funeral. Are you coming or not?"

"Okay," he agreed.

"You'd better not have syrup on your pancakes or you'll go into a coma at the table."

"Oh for Christ's sake, Mona. Shut up. Jesus, how long are you going to keep this shit up? I've told you a hundred times my diabetes is my business."

"You'd better stop shaking your head, Steven. One would think you have palsy instead of diabetes."

"So help me I'm going to . . ."

"Flattery will get you nowhere," she laughed. "By the way, Steven. Did I tell you that I overheard some of your guests at the party discussing your drinking habits? Everyone knows you're a lush."

"Fuck you, Mona." He raised his fist as if he was going to strike her.

She backed away but didn't know how to keep her mouth still. "Steven, you're such a jerk. You're going to kill yourself yet. When are you going to admit that you have a serious illness and a drinking problem? You can't get it up half the time. Brother, if I ever saw a man that was still in denial, it's you." She knew that she'd wounded him by saying that.

He knew it was time to change the subject before he slugged her. If she arrived at Kelly's funeral with a fat lip and a black eye he'd be in trouble. He shoved both fists into his pant pockets for safekeeping. But if she said anything else he'd wring her neck.

Mona, having picked up her purse and wool sweater, had opened the door, turned, and asked, "Are you coming with me to get some breakfast or not?" She left before he had a chance to answer. He remembered that he had been so angry he slammed the bedroom door and followed her downstairs and out the door to the car. He'd had the shakes and it had been too early to down a couple of shots. But it wasn't too early now, he thought. He glanced at Mona again and scowled. She made him sick. He was going to have a couple of stiff ones the minute he got home. Finally he broke the silence and blurted, "Who do you think killed Kelly?" He looked to see her reaction, but her facial expression didn't change.

Mona sighed deeply. When she finally answered she said, "How many times are you going to ask me that, Steven? I've told you a hundred times since Saturday night that I don't have the slightest idea."

He was shocked—and puzzled. She said he'd asked her about Kelly a hundred times. Was she telling the truth? Good God. He was afraid he was losing his mind. Ever since he'd developed diabetes he couldn't remember a thing. He really needed a drink now so he could relax a bit and think about what was truth and what was fiction. Suddenly he didn't feel well. His mouth felt dry and he began to shiver from chills.

Mona took note of Steven's discomfort. "What's the matter? Catching cold? Or is it your diabetes?"

"None of your fucking business," he snarled. He didn't see her stick out her tongue at him and give him the finger. He felt terribly weak by the time he turned into their driveway and came to a halt in front of their three car garage. He shut the engine off and sat there feeling dizzy again. It must be getting time for me to take my insulin, he said to himself. He must not forget to take his shot. He noticed that Mona had already unbuckled her seatbelt. She opened the door and climbed out. Steven watched her walk to the front door. He got out slowly and followed her into the house. It wouldn't be long until he was free of that miserable bitch.

Steven stood in the front hallway, removed his jacket, and loosened his black tie. The house felt cold and it was terribly quiet. He could tell the cleaning lady had been there. There wasn't one balloon, pumpkin, streamer, or any other Halloween decoration in sight. The living room door was wide open. He had a flash of seeing Kelly in the coffin, and then he spied Mona, her shoes off, stretched out on the sofa as if nothing had ever happened in that room. His eyes took in the surroundings. No wooden chairs, candles, or flowers. The shades were up in the bay window area. The pine coffin had disappeared, and he remembered that Detective Carter had told him that it would be taken to the State Police Lab to be used as evidence. He stared at Mona, who had her head tilted back and her eyes shut. He was about to go to the kitchen for a drink when she said, "I'm going upstairs to take a shower and a nap." She yawned, stretched, and stood up. He didn't say a word to her when she marched past him. Now he could go have that drink.

He ran to the kitchen and he looked at his watch. He still had a few minutes before he would take his insulin shot. He made his way to the old-fashioned sideboard where Mona stored their liquor. He selected a nearly full bottle of vodka, poured himself one tall glass, and then another. The next one he decided to enjoy on the rocks. Before he had a chance to open the freezer door to get some ice cubes the phone rang. He lifted the receiver and said hello in a cold tone of voice, annoyed at the interruption.

It was Piper calling to say that she hadn't had a chance to tell him at the funeral that she'd had a couple of threatening phone calls earlier in the morning. ". . . and Steven there's one more thing I have to tell you before I hang up. Tatjana told me to take some time off. She said she already spoke to Mona about me. I've decided to take Tatjana up on the offer." She had to catch her breath. "I'm too afraid to stay home alone. I'm going to the farm. I hope Mona won't mind me not coming to work." She waited for Steven's response.

"I'll have her call you back," he said. He wanted to tell her that he didn't give a flying fuck what she did. His infatuation for her was over. She was no different than the rest. The miserable bitch.

"Thanks, Steven," Piper said. "Tell Mona that I'll be waiting for her call."

"No problem," he said. Before he put the receiver on the hook he heard a definite click. He knew then that Mona had listened to his conversation. "Jesus fucking Christ," he mumbled as he opened the freezer door and pulled out a tray of cubes, dropped two in his glass, made his way to the kitchen table and sat down. "That miserable nosy witch." He poured a shot of vodka, downed it, and did it again.

Steven sat at the kitchen table, thinking about Kelly. He remembered that just before her body was found Mona had come to him and said that the bar was out of club soda and ginger ale.

"I'm going to the store to get some more," she'd told him.

"Why don't you have the caterers take care of it?" He'd asked, puzzled. Mona wasn't the type to run errands. He usually did all the grocery shopping. The only stores she liked to go in were expensive dress shops.

"I need some fresh air," she'd said. "I have a terrible headache from all the cigarette smoke. I won't be long."

"Are you going dressed like that?" He stared at her half man-half woman costume. "If the cops see you, they'll take you to the nut house."

"Steven. It's Halloween. Remember?"

"No kidding."

"No kidding," she'd aped him. "Steven. You'd better lay off the sauce. Your eyes have that glassy look."

"Okay," he'd lied, deliberately poured himself another glass of vodka, and downed the whole thing in front of her.

"You asshole," she'd muttered under her breath and left the room.

Steven hadn't argued about her going to the store. Having her out of the way for a few minutes was blissful. This also gave him time to corner Piper alone. He left the kitchen and went in search of her. He found her in the dining room. He stole a kiss on her ear and asked her to step into the living room with him for a minute so he could ask her an important question. He knew that Mona would never suspect that he'd go in there where the surprise waited. With the living room door locked he could screw Piper and ask her to leave town with him.

Piper had just shoved him aside and started talking to someone else. He wasn't disturbed. He would ask her again in a few minutes.

But before he could ask Piper again, a cute redhead dressed like Dorothy from *The Wizard of Oz* came over to him and said, "Hi, Doctor. I took one look at you and felt my temperature go up. Do you want to check my pulse?" She lifted her wrist.

"I like your red shoes," he said and kissed her neck. He

ignored her outstretched hand. "I'd rather check your heart." He pushed up against her and fondled a breast.

Dorothy didn't struggle. He was pleased to feel a long-awaited erection coming on. He knew that he couldn't pass up such a rare moment. Piper could wait. First he would diddle Dorothy. He had to hurry before Mona came home. "Why don't we go up to my bedroom?" he asked and took her by the hand and pulled her in the direction of the stairs.

"What about your wife?" Dorothy asked.

"What about your husband?"

"He's busy with a scarecrow."

"Well. My wife is busy with some friends of hers called Stella and Joe. We have time. Trust me."

Up in the bedroom, Steven turned and faced the redhead. "Now, Dorothy. How would you like to meet the wizard? But first, what's your real name?"

"Dorothy," she teased.

"C'mon," he slurred. "Really?"

"Really."

He knew she was lying but he didn't argue the point. Names didn't matter. All that mattered was getting her onto the bed. "Why don't you take off those red shoes and I'll take off the rest."

Steven recalled that he and the redhead had been dressed and back downstairs a good fifteen minutes before Mona returned. He'd never been so embarrassed. Dorothy said she understood and had tried to comfort him. "It's the booze," she'd said. "Lots of men can't do it if they've had too much to drink."

When Steven came back downstairs he'd been in a foul mood. He immediately went to the kitchen to get a new bottle of vodka. Mona was back from the store, stuffing a plastic container into the freezer compartment. "What's that?" he'd asked.

"Chili," she said. "I was going to serve it but changed my mind. Cathy brought so much food with her we don't need it."

162

"I thought you went to the store for some club soda and ginger ale."

"I did."

"Really. Where is it?"

"I already took it to the bar." Mona had said, closing the freezer compartment, and she'd swept past him and left the room.

Steven had followed Mona into the dining room. As soon as he saw that she was busy talking to friends he went in search of Piper, but before he could find her, a tall thin ghost came over to him and gushed about what a wonderful Halloween party it was. And as soon as the ghost wandered away, a rag doll appeared in front of him. He could tell by the voice that it was Piper. "Have you seen Kelly? I can't find her anywhere."

Before Steven had a chance to answer, Mona appeared. She took him by the arm and said loudly enough for all to hear, "Okay everybody. Line up. It's time to go into the living room for the big surprise."

The rest was history.

Now, seated there at his kitchen table, Steven felt depressed and extremely tense. And then he felt dizzy. He remembered that it must be time to eat and to take his insulin. Or did he already do that? He couldn't remember. "Who the fu-fuck ca-cares. Need a another drink," he slobbered.

He poured another vodka and staggered to the freezer to get himself some ice cubes. As he fumbled with the tray he happened to see a burrito, which again reminded him he should eat something because of his diabetes, and he pulled the burrito out and stuffed it into his suit jacket pocket. That's when he remembered Mona's chili. He decided to have some of that, too. He finally found the large plastic container on the middle shelf behind several bags of frozen vegetables, a half-gallon of chocolate ice cream, and two loaves of Victory Deli molasses oatmeal bread. The container bore a white label in Mona's handwriting that said "Chili by Mona," and the date. He pulled it out, swayed, and then he zigzagged across the kitchen to the microwave oven.

Steven had to hold onto the counter for support. He opened the door of the microwave, removed the lid on the chili, placed it on the middle of the turntable, and closed the door. He made his way to the table to rest while it thawed. He'd completely forgotten about the burrito in his jacket pocket.

When the microwave buzzer went off, Steven struggled to his feet to get the chili. The minute he opened the microwave door he began to swear. The chili had spattered. Sauce, chunks of tomato, onions, and beans coated the top and sides of the oven. He grabbed a pot holder, lifted the hot, bubbly container, pulled it out, and sat it on a hot mat on the counter. That's when something in the chili caught his eye. "What the fuck," he mumbled and got a fork out of the drawer. He plunged the fork into the chili and held up what it was he'd seen. When it dawned on him what he had in his hand he dropped the fork and recoiled as if he'd been bitten by a rattlesnake.

"Je-Jesus!" he yelled. He looked into the chili again. There was something else there! He fumbled about and finally managed to open the utility drawer next to him to get a pair of tongs. He put his fingers in the holes and quickly pinched what was submerged in the chili. "Sonofabitch," he said, gave a yank, and pulled two red-soaked gloves up and out. He laid them on the counter. He looked down at the mess on the floor, tottered, and finally was able to bend over and pick up the fork and the length of once white cord now saturated in red. He tried to whistle and failed. *Mona*, he thought. *Jesus! Mona killed Kelly! She wore those gloves and strangled her with that rope.* He knew then that she hadn't gone after any ginger ale the night of the party. She must've killed Kelly while he was upstairs in their bedroom with Dorothy. *Damn*, he said to himself. *She was putting the chili in the freezer when I came into the kitchen to get a drink.* And then he thought he heard a noise in the hall. Cold, stark fear washed over him. He stood perfectly still and listened, as beads of sweat covered his brow, and finally he exhaled with relief. For a second he'd thought he'd heard Mona's footsteps out in the hall. He shoved the rope and gloves back into the chili, put the lid on, and put it back into the freezer. He had to clean up the mess before she came into the kitchen and caught him!

He staggered over to the sink, wet a sponge, and cleaned the microwave, the counter, and the floor. The red stain wouldn't budge so he had to use a scouring pad. He scrubbed and scrubbed until there wasn't a trace of chili left. His mind whirled.

He heard a thumping overhead, jumped, and glanced upward. Footsteps paced overhead. He knew then that Mona was still upstairs and that she was still awake. He had to do something before it was too late!

Steven visualized Mona in their bedroom looking wild-eyed—wringing her hands, plotting a way to kill Piper. Then it hit him that she might be planning to kill him, too! "Jesus fucking Christ, Mona," he said out loud. "You've turned into a psychopath. I have to call the police." He moved toward the wall phone and stopped midway. He couldn't call yet, because Mona might listen in and come after him. *I know*, he thought. *I'll go upstairs and tie her up so she can't hurt me. Then I'll call. Yes, that's the best way. Tread carefully, old boy. One mistake and you're a goner.*

Steven started upstairs. By the time he reached the landing on the second floor he didn't feel well at all. With each step his stomach lurched, his ears hummed, and his vision blurred. He'd forgotten to take his insulin. He stopped for a second and debated whether or not he should go back to the kitchen and take his shot. He decided not to and kept one hand on the wall to support himself as he made his way to the bedroom. He was totally oblivious of the fact that his blood sugar had soared to a near-lethal level. Now his thoughts were really fuzzy. Unable to remember where he was going or why, he stopped and winced from the pain that ripped through his head. The next second he remembered his plan, and teetered and stumbled down the corridor toward the bedroom; if he didn't hurry he'd be too weak to tie Mona. It never dawned on him that he hadn't brought any rope along.

He fell against the bedroom door, twisted the knob, and burst into the room, startling Mona. "Jesus! Steven," she yelled. "You scared me." She was dressed in her pink terry-cloth robe, seated at the kidney-shaped dressing table, brushing her hair. She observed Steven through her oval, white, wicker-framed mirror. "You're drunk," she snarled. "How many have you had?"

"'Nough," he slurred.

She frowned. "Why are you looking at me like that? What's that thing sticking out of your pocket? Do you have a problem?"

"Do I have a pr-prob-lem?" he repeated and looked at his pocket. The burrito was still there and thawing fast. For an instant he couldn't remember what she'd just asked him. And then it came to him and he blurted, "You killed Kelly." He was drooling and he lost his balance and nearly fell. "Chili." He said and squinted as he tried to keep Mona in focus. God, his head hurt.

Mona laughed at him. "So you found it. Steven," she said coldly. "This creates a problem. Yes, I killed Kelly. But it was a mistake. I really meant to kill your girlfriend . . . and then kill you."

Her voice echoed in Steven's ears. "Kill you—kill you." Don't pass out, he told himself.

"Steven," Mona said and laughed. "You must understand that I had to hide those things in a safe place after I killed Kelly. I did it right after the caterers went out of the kitchen. Then you came in. That was a close call. The chili was supposed to be for the party. Remember I told you that we didn't need it because Cathy brought so much food?" Mona didn't wait for Steven to answer. "I assumed that the police would never look in the freezer. I was right," she said proudly and smiled. She wasn't aware that Steven's eyes had blurred so badly that he couldn't make out her face well enough to see her. She didn't know that he hadn't heard her because he was on the verge of passing out.

"Mo—Mona," he managed to cry, weakly. "Help. My insu . . ." He staggered toward the bed and fell face first onto it. The room spun. Everything went black.

Mona ignored Steven and kept right on talking as if he were giving her his undivided attention. "I was going to burn the evidence in the fireplace after the police left but they made us go to that damned hotel." She frowned and brushed her hair some more. "I was going to dispose of those things and you tonight after you went to bed." She put the brush on the vanity, turned around, looked at Steven who wasn't moving a muscle, and said, "But now it's too late. Steven. Pay attention. Do you understand what I'm telling you?" She stopped chattering and heard only silence.

"Get up, Steven," Mona demanded. "What's the matter with you? Too much booze? Blood sugar sky high? Don't worry. I'll go downstairs and get your insulin for you in a minute." She crossed her heart and hoped to die. "First I want to let you know that sometimes I think you're stupid." She shook her head, scowled, and said, "Like I told you a minute ago, I made a mistake when I killed Kelly. I told Piper that very same thing when I phoned her this morning. Disgusting bitch that she is. Husband stealer. I'll fix her. It was those damned twin rag doll costumes that confused me."

The very image of Piper made Mona so mad she picked up her hair brush and threw it across the room, where it bounced off the wall and landed on the floor next to the bed. "I'm going to make her suffer big time for all this extra aggravation she's caused," she said and pouted like a five year old. She stopped talking and stared at Steven. "But first, my dear husband, I have to take care of you." She glanced at him in her mirror and waited for his reaction. He gave none.

"Oh, you poor thing," Mona said. "I know you must be shocked. But don't be. It will all make sense if you think

167

about it. I have to kill you because you know about Kelly. I have to kill Piper because she wanted to steal you from me. Well. She can't have you. You belong to me. But pretty soon you won't belong to anybody. That's what I did to my former husband and his girlfriend in St. Louis." She laughed and then her face took on a sad look. She said, "I don't have any choice, Steven. You have to die, too. Then I don't have to worry that you'll tell on me. So you see there is no other way around this." She got up from her dressing table and walked gracefully to Steven's bedside, got down on her knees, and laid her head on his back. "You understand don't you?" Mona waited for Steven to answer her and when he didn't she lifted her head. "Steven," she said sharply. "Turn over so I can see your face. Say something, for God's sake."

Silence. She poked his ribs. He didn't flinch. She knew then that he must be unconscious. He hadn't taken his insulin and he'd had too much to drink. Steven had lapsed into a coma. It was too good to be true. She clapped her hands and then she got on her feet. She flipped Steven onto his back. His face was chalk-white and his body was limp. He hadn't even moaned. She stood up and walked over to her dressing table and took a pair of black, fleece-lined leather gloves out of the top drawer and put them on. She returned to Steven's bedside and poked his arm. He didn't move. She jabbed him again. Nothing.

In order to carry out her plan, it was important for her to know that Steven had been drinking a lot. She charged out of the bedroom and raced downstairs to the kitchen. The first thing she noticed was an almost empty bottle of vodka and a glass on the table. *The stupid bastard,* she thought. *He's finally drunk himself to death.* It was too good to be true! She began to hum a catchy tune, as she always did when she was very pleased with herself. Steven had made her job so easy. How thoughtful of him to go into a coma. The props were ready made. What could be better, she thought, than to have an empty vodka bottle and a glass on the table covered with his fingerprints! She was so excited she completely forgot about the chili in the freezer, and it was still the furthest thing from her mind when she took Steven's insulin bottle out of the refrigerator. Kelly's death was history. Steven was now foremost in her mind. She dropped the insulin bottle into her robe pocket and took a couple of cotton swabs and a syringe out of the drawer next to the sink.

Back upstairs now, Mona dashed to Steven's bedside and laid the insulin bottle, the syringe, and the alcohol swabs on the nightstand. Then she took hold of Steven's arm and felt a weak pulse in his wrist. She was reassured that he was definitely in a diabetic coma and that he was certain to be dead by morning. She picked up the insulin bottle and Steven's right hand and smeared his fingerprints over it. She did the same to the swabs and syringe and placed all on the nightstand again. "This is too perfect," she cried.

Mona stared at Steven's chest to see if she could see him breathing. It barely moved. She leaned over his pale face and pecked his cheek. Ever so softly she said, "Sleep well, my darling. Have a nice trip. Hope it's not too hot where you're going." She laughed and kissed him again, this time on the lips. Next, she gently propped two pillows underneath his head. "Just want to make sure you're comfy. I'll be back in a couple of minutes. I have to run downstairs and take care of a few last minute details." She laughed again and then she did a little dance on the way out the door.

She charged downstairs to Steven's study and found some paper in the right hand top drawer of his desk. She inserted a sheet into his typewriter and then she hit the keyboard with a passion. Minutes later she read what she'd written: *I killed Kelly Stewart by mistake. I really wanted to kill Piper Jordan so nobody else could have her. I can't live knowing what I've done. Steven.*

Mona got up from the typewriter, yanked the paper out, and waved it in the air. In a singsong voice she chanted, "Now Piper can't have you. Now Piper can't have you." And then she thought about what she was saying. "Not that I give a damn you understand."

When Mona went back upstairs to the bedroom she

looked to see if Steven had moved. He hadn't. She put the note on the nightstand beside the rest of the paraphernalia. She crossed the room to her vanity table, picked up the white wicker chair, and set it next to the bed. Seated, she pulled off her gloves and shoved them into her robe pocket. She then folded her hands in her lap and stared at Steven. She had the best time seated there thinking about what had just happened. Steven had been such an asshole. Soon she yawned, laid her weary head on Steven's chest, and thought about killing her first husband and that redheaded bitch girlfriend of his. Now that had been a messy event. She had been so upset because she couldn't go to their funerals. Still, she had to consider herself fortunate to have been able to skip town without getting caught. Now she remembered the Halloween party and Kelly. It had been easy to kill her, but lifting her dead-weight body into that coffin had been totally exhausting. Steven had been much easier. She was thankful to him for flopping onto the bed. She only hoped Piper's death turned out to be as simple. Suddenly Mona's eyes felt heavy. In seconds she was fast asleep. Her snores filled the bedroom.

The Cape Bethany fog horn bellowed warning ships at sea, and the noise woke Mona up. She yawned, wincing from the pain of a stiff neck that had developed during the night from having slept with her head on Steven's chest, sat up straight, rubbed her neck gently, and yawned again. When she could focus she poked Steven's cold body.

"Dead as a doornail. I'm so clever," she praised herself and then went to lift the receiver off the phone on the nightstand beside her to call the police. In doing so, she knocked the insulin bottle and syringe onto the rug. She quickly picked everything up and arranged it carefully on the nightstand. And then, just as she went to phone the police, she happened to remember that if she was going to tell them that she spent the night in the guest room she'd better mess up the bed. She ran out of the room to do so. When she was finished she decided that she'd take a nice hot shower, put on her makeup, and get dressed; she wasn't going to greet the police or anyone else looking like a frump. She would pack a suitcase for herself in case the police made her leave again, and she'd pack the clothes she wanted Steven to be buried in. She would go to the garage, put the suitcase in the Jag and cover it with her coat or a blanket. Her eyes flew to Steven again. She would have his body sent to Watts Funeral Home: he deserved that. As for his casket, she decided that he must have one of the best. She'd arrange for a cemetery plot and order a headstone, of course—she had no idea what to put on his epitaph. She would ask Watts about that and about flowers.

She felt so happy.

As she studied Steven's lifeless form, she thought he looked ridiculous in death. It was time to think about his clothes. She opened his closet to find his best dark blue, wool suit for him to wear for eternity. Should she put mothballs in the pockets? Next, she took a freshly laundered and stiffly starched white shirt out of his bureau and clean socks and underwear. She chose a pair of baby blue boxer shorts printed with little golfers swinging clubs.

And, now, came the crucial part of Steven's outfit—the tie. He was never any good at picking the right one; she always had to do it for him. Back to the closet again. Steven had at least fifteen silk ties, and she had bought them all. They dangled from a wooden rack on the back of the closet door. Mona finally chose Steven's least favorite, dark blue and sprinkled with little red lobsters. "Serves you right, you jerk," she said and laughed. "Now let's see. What have I forgotten? Oh, yes, his belt." She found a dark blue leather belt hanging from a hook and then she searched the closet floor for the right shoes. There were none that would go well with his suit. She would have to buy him a new pair and then she wondered: did dead people wear shoes? She would have to ask Watts about that one. If not, then Steven could wear his socks.

Next, Mona went into the bathroom and took Steven's black leather shaving bag off the top shelf of the linen closet. She filled it with his aftershave, razor, tooth brush, paste, dental floss, deodorant, shampoo and conditioner.

She knew that dead people were dolled up for their final appearance. She assumed that Watts would ask her to furnish such items. Or would he? she wondered. No matter. She wouldn't give him a choice. Steven would have to be groomed with his own toiletries. And then she laughed again. "I love it," she said out loud. "I just know Watts is going to put makeup on Steven's face. Jesus. He'd have a fit."

"Speaking of makeup," she said and went to her dresser to get what she needed. When she finally finished packing for herself her mind was so jumbled that she couldn't remember half of what she'd put in the suitcase, and she was too tired to check. Whatever she had stuffed in there would have to do. She reminded herself that later, she should call Cathy and ask her to cater the food for after the funeral. There was so much to do.

Suddenly, Piper flashed in her mind. She could hardly wait to phone that slut and give her the news about her precious Steven. Piper was going to be so sad when she heard that her lover boy was dead, and Mona wanted to tell her that there was nothing to worry about because she would join him very soon. "The undertaking business is certainly booming," Mona said and laughed. "Yes, indeedy. Just you wait, Piper. Your turn is coming."

Next, she lifted the heavy suitcase and carried it downstairs to the kitchen and then out to the garage. She put it in the back seat of the Jag and covered it with a wool, red plaid lap robe she'd given Steven for Christmas. Then she went back into the house, lifted the receiver on the phone in the kitchen, and poked the numbers for the Cape Bethany Police Department.

The phone rang no more than twice. "Cape Bethany Police," a man's deep voice said.

"Help! My husband," Mona cried and made certain she gasped for breath. "I think he's dead." She faked her sobs. She remembered that when she was a kid her mother must've told her a hundred times that she should be an actress when she grew up. "You're the Betty Davis of the family," she'd said with motherly pride.

172

After she hung up the phone, Mona raced into the living room and stood in front of the bay window waiting for the police to come. A few minutes later she heard the faint whine of a siren. "The neighbors are going to be livid again," she said out loud. "Oh, well. There is no way around it."

Two police cars pulled into the driveway and came to a halt. Mona ran out of the living room to answer the door. She stopped and glanced at herself in the hall mirror. Her cheeks were flushed from all the excitement. She loved that; pink cheeks gave her a wholesome look that all men seemed to admire.

Just before Mona opened the door she made certain that she wiped any trace of a smile off her face. A somber look was the order of the day. She knew that she wouldn't make herself cry. If she did her eyes would be bloodshot and puffy. There was no way she'd be seen at Steven's funeral looking a sight. Besides that, in her opinion, the asshole wasn't worth shedding tears over—even if he had been so considerate as to check out of this life on his own. She took a deep breath, opened the door wide, stepped to one side, and said to the first policeman that charged up the steps, "He's up in the bedroom at the top of the stairs."

He and three others brushed past her, tracking her rug. "You should have wiped your feet," she complained, slammed the door, and stomped into the living room. "Damn it," she sputtered. "It's going to cost a fortune to have this place cleaned after they're finished making a mess." She sat down on the sofa, grabbed *Yankee* magazine off the coffee table, and started to thumb through the pages. She didn't have the slightest idea that the police might be curious as to why she hadn't taken them upstairs to her husband.

Chapter Nine

He Did It

When Matt opened the front door to leave for the Hadleys' house in Cape Bethany he felt the fall chill. It was drizzling and the landscape looked bleak. He knew that the temperature only needed to drop a few degrees to turn into snow. It was going to be an early winter, he decided, and dashed to his car to get out of the raw dampness.

Taking the same shortcuts to Cape Bethany as he had done on Halloween night, he tried not to think too much about what awaited him. Instead he concentrated on Piper. He'd never felt so strongly about a woman before. It made no difference that he had just met her because he felt as if he'd always known her. He thought about how great it was having her body next to his—the way she caught her breath when he entered her, the feel of her lips on his. He wanted to have lots of children with her. "You'd better stop," he warned himself and fought a strong desire to turn the car around to go back home and crawl into bed with her.

A half hour later, Matt turned onto Lighthouse Road out on Cape Bethany. He could barely see the ocean because of a fog bank that hovered over the white-capped swells. When a fishing boat suddenly appeared out of the mist, Matt glanced at its foamy wake and wondered how fishermen could stand such a harsh life. He knew several, men whose faces and hands were weather-beaten from too much exposure to sun, wind, and salt water, and he wondered if fishermen ever gave any thought as to how someone like himself could do *his* job? To each his own. He stepped on the gas.

Steven and Mona Hadley's house loomed. As he approached the place, he counted three Cape Bethany Police cars parked in the driveway. He also spied the station wagon belonging to Dr. Sylvester, the medical examiner. He was the same one who was called to the scene the night Kelly Stewart was murdered. Just before Matt turned into the driveway he glanced in his rearview mirror. Jake Thomas was behind him. And behind Jake came Judd Stone and Paul Reynolds.

Matt parked his car and climbed out. The others did the same. "Morning," Matt said none too cheerfully.

"Morning," the three said to him almost in unison.

Matt asked, "Do you know for certain it's the husband?"

"That's what I was told," Judd responded. "I spoke with Officer Konan on the phone just before I left the house. He thinks the Hadley guy accidentally killed himself. But since the Stewart girl was murdered here the other night, he thought he'd better call us just to make certain there was no foul play. But it sounds to me like he did it himself."

"How did he die?" Paul Reynolds wanted to know.

"Well," Judd answered. "Hadley was a diabetic. Didn't take his insulin. Drank. Shit like that. Heard he left an interesting note for the wee wife. If I was to bet, I'd stake my money that it was suicide."

"Come on you guys," Paul Reynolds said. "It's too wet out here. Let's go inside before we get soaked. I'm getting over one hell of a cold and I don't want another. Christ. I could catch my death if we stay out here."

"C'mon, Reynolds," Jake Thomas said and slapped Paul on the back. "Little water won't hurt you. Say, Matt. Have you had a chance to question that Jordan girl? I can't remember her name. Isn't it the same as some kind of bird?"

"Piper." Matt said.

"That's it. I knew it was the same as a bird. Sand Piper. Anyways. I thought you were going to drive up to that farm in Freeport last night. Didn't you say that's where she's staying from now on?"

"Yes. I went." Matt didn't offer any other comments.

"And?" Paul asked impatiently.

"And what?" Matt responded gruffly.

"Jesus Christ, Matt," Judd snapped. "I've never seen you so grumpy. What the fuck is the matter with you this morning?"

"Nothing."

"Nothing," Paul imitated. "Get that will you, guys. Bull shit, Matt. Judd's right. You're a grump. Anyway, that's one cute girl. Nice jugs. If I were single I'd . . ."

Matt interrupted Paul before he could finish, "Knock it off," he said coldly. He had to overcome an urge to belt Paul in the mouth.

"Sorry, Matt," Paul said as though he really meant it. "God. You're crabby this morning. What the hell is eating you?"

"Nothing," Matt answered far too quickly. "Look. I didn't mean to take your head off. I'm tired. Didn't get much sleep last night. Let's forget the whole thing."

"Oh, yeah," Judd said. "How come you want to forget, Matt? You been getting into mischief?"

Matt just shook his head. He should've known better than to try and get these guys to quit their teasing. Still, he tried one more time. "Let's change the subject, okay?"

Obviously the men were ready, too, because they started to walk silently toward the front entrance of the Hadley home. Each was quiet and held his own thoughts as to what they were going to find inside. And then they all heard a man's voice say, "It's unlocked." Matt opened the door and stepped inside. One by one the others followed.

Standing in the front hallway, Matt could see Mona Hadley and two Cape Bethany Policemen in the living room. They stopped talking to her and came into the hall to greet Matt and the other detectives. The older of the two men introduced himself as Warren Todd, Cape Bethany's one and only investigator. "Who called you guys?" he asked.

"Officer Konan," Judd told him.

"Well," Todd said, frowning. "I don't think there was any need to call you. But while you're here you might as well take a look and see what you think. The guy is upstairs on the bed. Looks like he killed himself. He left a note confessing he killed the Stewart girl. You'll find it on a nightstand next to the bed. Dr. Sylvester is up there now checking out the stiff. Like I said, it looks pretty clean cut to me. I didn't think there was any need to process the scene so I didn't make the wife leave . . ."

While Todd talked, Matt kept his eyes on Mona, who was seated on a pale yellow wing-back fireside chair staring out the bay windows at the sea. It was obvious to Matt that she'd found time to get dressed—unless she'd never gone to bed at all. No, he thought. She looks too rested. She slept. He was willing to bet his next paycheck that she'd showered and changed her clothes. He excused himself from the others and went to speak to her.

Mona heard his footsteps, turned to face him, and did not acknowledge his presence. There was no sadness on her face, and the icy look in her hazel eyes sent chills racing up his spine. And there was something else—her eyes weren't red and puffed. Maybe she'd used some kind of drops to take the redness out. But he knew that stuff couldn't work that well. Mona Hadley hadn't shed one tear over poor Steven. He also noticed that her hands didn't shake. She held no tissues to wipe her nose. Not one strand of hair was out of place. She wore bright red lipstick and her makeup looked fresh and flawless. Matt wondered if her long black eyelashes were false.

She was a fashion plate, he couldn't deny that. There she sat, clad in an obviously expensive olive-green silk blouse, tan slacks, and camel-colored heels. He could bet that the three bangle bracelets that dangled from her wrist were solid gold. They matched her two chain necklaces and her large hoop earrings. She looked like a Fifth Avenue store-window mannequin.

"Hello, Mrs. Hadley," he said coolly. "Remember me? I'm Detective Carter of the State Police. I was here the other night when the Stewart girl was murdered."

"Yes. I remember you. How could I forget?" she said snidely, and didn't utter another word.

Matt ignored her flippant response. "I'm sorry about your husband." He watched for her reaction.

"Thanks." She still showed no outward emotion.

"Do you feel up to answering a few questions?"

"If I have to," she sighed. "I probably don't have any choice about the matter, do I?"

"No. You don't." He had to force himself not to tell her to take a flying leap.

"Well. Hurry up then. I have a lot to do. So many people to call. And then there's the funeral arrangements to be made."

Jesus, Matt thought. *You'd think she was going to hold a party instead of a wake.* He frowned and said, "I'll have to put you on hold for a few minutes. First, I have to go upstairs. I'll get back to you as soon as I can. We'll make this as easy on you as possible," he said, just in case he was wrong about her. He'd been on the job long enough to realize that everyone has his own way of handling death. "Have you called anyone?" he asked her.

"Call who? Who do you mean?" She snapped and gave him a puzzled look.

"Relatives, your minister, priest, or friends to come and be with you." Her cold answer had been interesting, if nothing else. He'd seen all kinds, but she took first prize for being the most callous widow he'd ever met. He wondered if she'd tried to reach Piper but he didn't ask if she had. If he mentioned Piper to her she was bound to phone her. Then she'd discover that she'd spent the night at his house. And that wasn't any of Mona Hadley's damned business.

". . . Steven has no family but me," Mona was saying. Matt deliberately acted like he hadn't heard her. "Are you listening to me? I'm talking to you," she said.

"Sorry. I was thinking about something else. What did you say?"

"I said Steven doesn't have any family but me. Why are you here anyway? I thought you only investigated murders?"

"That and child abuse cases," he offered. "But since Kelly Stewart was found strangled in your house, we have to make certain that your husband wasn't murdered, too."

"He did it," she blurted.

"Excuse me?" Matt wasn't certain he had heard her right.

"I said he did it. He killed Kelly and then he accidentally did himself in. The bastard. He was going to commit suicide. He said so in the note he left. But I know better."

"How do you know that?"

"If you knew Steven the way I did, you'd understand that he didn't have the guts to kill himself. He was a diabetic. He drank too much last night and by the looks of things he neglected to take his insulin. He's been warned a hundred times."

"Meaning what?"

"Meaning," she snarled, "that he could die if he wasn't careful. His doctor and I were constantly after him to watch his blood-sugar. As usual, he chose not to listen. Last night he goofed big time. You'll find out when you go upstairs. That sonofabitch killed Kelly. I was going to divorce him but now I won't have to go to the trouble. Good riddance to bad rubbish."

Matt was quiet. Jesus, he thought. I'd never want to be on the bad side of her. He felt cold at the sight of her and hunched his shoulders. Mona noticed.

"Cold?" she asked. She didn't give Matt a chance to answer. She kept right on ranting about Steven. "He seemed depressed after we came home from the funeral yesterday afternoon. I thought he was upset over Kelly. When I asked him if that was what was wrong he told me to mind my own business. I got mad and went to our bedroom and got some of my things. I spent the night in the guest room. I didn't find Steven until after I got up, took a shower, and got dressed," she caught her breath. "It seems I was right," she said.

"About what?" Matt asked and smothered an urge to tell her that she was a heartless bitch.

"I mean I was right about Steven. He was upset over Kelly," she laughed, knowingly. "I guess upset isn't the word for it. Afraid is more like it. I tried a hundred times to get him to talk about who could've killed Kelly. He always acted uncomfortable at the mention of her and he always changed the subject. Now I know that he must've been scared out of his wits that he'd be caught and sent to prison for the rest of his life. Sniveling coward. It's all in the note he left. Go read it. You'll see." She folded her arms across her chest and glared at Matt.

Matt had had enough of Mona Hadley for the time being. "Excuse me," he said abruptly. "I have to go upstairs now." He turned and made his exit. He could feel her hazel eyes boring into his back. A passage from one of Shakespeare's works came to him. He couldn't remember which piece it came from or the exact words. He only knew that it said something about someone protesting too much.

Matt was told by a Cape Bethany policeman standing in the hall that the others were upstairs. On his way up, he thought about Mona Hadley. He had a gut feeling that she was in some way party to her husband's death. She was sick enough to kill. He thought about Piper, and he realized that he'd have to move on his intuition before it was too late.

When Matt entered the bedroom he spied his buddies, Todd, and the medical examiner, Dr. Sylvester, and the corpse. If he hadn't known better, he'd have thought that Steven Hadley was sleeping peacefully. He hadn't seen a body look so natural in a long time.

Dr. Sylvester said to Matt, "You look a little pale. Feel okay?"

"I'm fine."

"This death was an accident," Sylvester said firmly to

180

Matt. "The guy was a full blown diabetic. Look," he said and pointed at the nightstand beside the bed. "He had his insulin ready. That syringe is all set to be used. He must've lapsed into a coma before he had a chance to inject himself. Too bad. Not very old by the looks of him. Probably in his late thirties or early forties."

"He left a note, Matt," Judd Stone interjected soberly and pointed to the nightstand next to the bed.

Matt looked. He saw the syringe, the insulin bottle, and the note. He pulled some disposable gloves out of his pocket and put them on. Then he picked up the note and read. At first, he was stunned when he read that Steven Hadley said he'd been in love with Piper. But once he collected his thoughts he was certain this infatuation was one-sided. There was no way that Piper would take up with Hadley. Furthermore, he just wasn't convinced that Steven had typed the confession. "Why would a person leave a note if he died accidentally?" he asked everyone present. He only hoped that his question would push Sylvester and the others in a different direction.

"Maybe he intended to kill himself," Sylvester said crossly. "But it looks like he'd changed his mind at the last minute because he filled that syringe with his insulin. I believe he slipped into a coma before he had a chance to inject himself. As far as I'm concerned this is an accidental death. I don't see much point in discussing this any further."

When Todd was out of earshot Judd whispered to Matt, "The Cape Bethany police blew it big time. They've touched everything so much that they should be arrested. Dumb sonsofbitches. Didn't even wear gloves when they handled that needle. How the hell do they know the guy didn't have AIDS?" He shook his head, sighed deeply, and frowned.

Matt scowled and said, "That figures. Dumb idiots. Damn." He dropped Steven's confession into a plastic evidence bag that Jake held open for him. Then he turned and faced Sylvester and said, "Look. I want you to think about this situation. Where there was a murder here a few days ago, we shouldn't rule out homicide. I think that it makes sense to have an autopsy."

"I told you that there is no need for one," Sylvester said too loudly. "In my opinion, there is no question about the cause of death. He did himself in. An autopsy isn't going to turn up anything other than what he had for supper. And I'm not too certain he ate. Take a look at the burrito stuck in his jacket pocket. Lighten up, Carter. Relax and enjoy the fact that you've killed two birds with one stone."

"What do you mean?" Matt asked.

"Jesus Christ," Sylvester blurted and rolled his eyes. "It's pretty simple. This guy killed Kelly Stewart and then he accidentally killed himself."

Matt didn't buy it. But, at the moment there was no way he could prove otherwise.

"Looks that way to me," Paul Reynolds timidly agreed with Sylvester. "Steven Hadley doesn't know it, but he saved us taxpayers a lot of money. We don't have to go through a trial to get him convicted of the Stewart girl's murder. And think of the money that's been saved by not having to keep him in prison for the rest of his life. He could've lived until he was a hundred. Jesus, Matt. This is a clear-cut case if I ever saw one. You ought to be celebrating—not complaining."

"Don't be too sure of that, Paul," Matt cautioned. "You'd better think carefully about what's happened here. If this guy's death is an accident, then why did he go to the trouble to leave that note? It's too clean."

"C'mon, Matt," Paul said. "Hadley is guilty. He confessed in the note that he killed the Stewart girl by accident and that he couldn't live with himself. His diabetes killed him before he could do it himself."

Matt ignored Paul. He faced Sylvester and asked, "Are you going to order an autopsy on this guy or not?"

"No. For God's sake. I already told you that I don't see any need for one."

"Jesus," Matt said. He was getting very angry now. "I'll repeat myself one more time to see if I can get it to sink into your thick skull. I'm sorry," he quickly apologized. "I shouldn't have said that. But it's like this: Kelly Stewart was murdered here last Saturday night. Now we have another body right in front of our noses. Don't you think that's suspicious?" He hoped they'd come to their senses. If not, he'd have to go over their heads.

"No! I don't think it's suspicious," Sylvester half yelled and felt his round face flush. He took a deep breath to calm himself but it didn't work. "Now," he half shouted. "It's my turn to repeat the facts. It's like this: There is no need to hold anything up pending further study. The deceased was a diabetic. He drank. He confessed to killing the Stewart girl. He couldn't live with his guilt and so he decided to kill himself. At the last minute he changed his mind. He filled a syringe with insulin but he passed out before he could inject himself. No. This was no murder." He had to stop a second to catch his breath. "Look at that stuff on the nightstand," he continued. "What's the matter with you, Carter? I'm firmly convinced Steven Hadley had every intention of injecting himself with his insulin. He waited a click too long. Accidental death is what I'm going to call this one. It's over. The end. Period. Now. Is there anything else I can do for you before I wind this up and go home?" He hoped Carter got the message. He was so damned tired. He'd about decided that the lousy fifty dollars he was paid for this job wasn't worth the trouble. Especially with guys like Carter on duty.

It was the end of their conversation as far as Matt was concerned. He turned and started for the door. Just before he made his exit he stopped and turned to Paul Reynolds and said, "Don't let anyone touch that body. I'm going downstairs to call the Attorney General's office and try to get someone to give me permission to have an autopsy performed on Hadley."

Matt left. Out in the hallway he could hear Sylvester raving. "Matt Carter doesn't quit. Stubborn sonofabitch. Well, I'm sticking to my guns. There was no foul play here. Carter's mind is working overtime. He acts like he's losing it. I think he needs a vacation."

Ten minutes later, Matt was back upstairs. He walked

into the bedroom and said to all present, "I just spoke with Jim Green, an assistant attorney general." He glared at Sylvester and said, "I have permission to have an autopsy performed. Until we are certain that there was no foul play here this case is under investigation. I'm going downstairs and ask Mrs. Hadley what funeral director she wants called, and to tell her that she has to leave the premises right now." Matt didn't say anything else. He waited for the others to respond. Nobody talked. Dr. Sylvester's face turned scarlet as he gathered his equipment together and stomped out of the room, down the stairs, and out the front door.

Matt was anxious to go tell Mona that she had to leave so they could process the scene. On his way out the door, he said to Paul, "Make sure you take enough photos and comb this room. Since an autopsy is going to be performed, make sure you put Hadley in one of our body bags because you know that undertakers use the same ones over and over. Talk about screwing up evidence." He paused for a second and then he said, "And one more thing. As soon as we finish up here, I want you to start checking into the wife's background. Trace her all the way back to the womb. I want to know everything about her—I mean everything."

"Gotcha," Paul said and got busy.

"Want me to go downstairs with you?" Todd asked.

"No thanks. I'll do it. You guys take care of matters here." He left the room and went down to the living room, where he found Mona still seated where he'd left her. This time she was shaping her nails with an emery board.

Mona looked up at Matt and scowled. "Well, well. So you're back. While you were gone, I made an interesting phone call." She waited for him to react. When he didn't say anything, she slapped the emery board on the table beside her and said, "Well. Aren't you the least bit curious about who I called?"

"Should I be?"

"If you're smart, you'll inquire." She laughed pleased with her game.

"What's that supposed to mean?" he asked.

"Well," she sighed. "I suppose I'd better tell you before you get too worked up." She laughed again and then she glared at Matt. He noticed that her eyes had lost their hard look and now radiated excitement. She inhaled and then she gushed, "Well, I called Tatjana to tell her about Steven. She asked if I'd told Piper. I told her I hadn't seen or spoken with her since Kelly's funeral." She smiled at Matt. He couldn't possibly have any way of knowing that she had listened in on the phone conversation Steven had with Piper when she called to say that she was going to be staying at the farm. "Tatjana," she continued, "told me that Piper is at her place in Freeport. She told me that I could reach her there. After I hung up, I called the farm and guess what I found out?" She stopped talking and waited for Matt to take the bait.

But Matt fooled Mona. He didn't say one word. Rage mounted in her and it was difficult not to scream at him. He was supposed to have lost his temper. Had he done so, she might have been able to get him suspended—perhaps removed from the case. He was too controlled and way too nosy. Watts was going to have more business. But first things first. Before she could kill Carter she had to concentrate on getting rid of Piper. Life was becoming too complicated.

". . . and," Mona continued, "John Stoll told me on the phone that Piper is supposed to be staying there but that she had left with you last night. He said that you didn't bring her back." She paused and raised an eyebrow. "Naughty, naughty," she taunted. And then her eyes turned hard again. "John Stoll told me he thinks that Piper spent the night at your place. Is it commonplace for detectives to screw their witnesses? Is she still there?" She already knew the answers to both questions but she wanted to ask to see him squirm.

"That's none of your business," Matt said and ignored her remark about screwing.

"Maybe so," Mona agreed. "But I'm the curious type. I think it's interesting if nothing else Piper seems to be good at seducing men. You're not the first and you won't be the last she racks out with." Well maybe you will be, she thought and smirked.

She was pushing all of his buttons, and Matt had to restrain himself from reaching out and grabbing her by the throat. He knew that if his superiors found out that he'd taken Piper home he'd be in serious trouble; he also knew that if he so much as tapped Mona Hadley with his index finger, she'd jump at the chance to report him. For a second, he fought another strong urge to wring her neck. He took a few deep breaths to calm down and then he was able to gain his composure. The ball was in Mona Hadley's court. He stood rigid as he waited for her to make the next move. "Did you get a chance to read the confession Steven left on the nightstand?" she asked and looked at him curiously.

"Yes. I read it," he told her.

Mona shook her head and said, "I don't know how I'm going to live this down."

"Live what down?"

"The embarrassment, of course. I'll have to sell this house and move. But who will want to buy it after all the junk that's gone on here this past week."

"You call your friend's murder and your husband's death junk?"

"What do you want me to do? Cry?"

"It's not for me to tell you how to act. That's not my job. My job is to find out what happened to Kelly Stewart and to your husband." Damn, he thought. Why was he arguing with her? Get back on an even keel. Do it now. "Look. Mrs. Hadley. The medical examiner has said that he believes your husband died accidentally. But, due to the fact that Kelly Stewart was murdered here a few days ago, I've called the Attorney General's office to get permission to have the body taken to the Maine General Hospital for an autopsy. Do you have any idea what funeral home you're going to use to handle the burial?"

"Watts," she told him. "The same place that handled Kelly's. Why do you ask?"

"Because Watts will have to transport the body. I'll call him."

"No. Don't. I will because I have some arrangements I need to discuss."

"Sorry," Matt said. "No more phone calls. You have to leave right now so we can process the scene. I'll call Watts."

"Help yourself," she snapped. "But I want you to know that I'm very upset."

"Over what?" Matt inquired and moved toward the phone.

"Over making such a fuss out of this. Making me leave. And ordering an autopsy is a waste of time and money. I told you that Steven had diabetes. He killed Kelly and then he killed himself."

"How can you be so sure of that?" Matt asked.

"I already told you," she said snidely. "If you knew Steven the way I did you'd know he must've suffered over killing Kelly. He was a sissy. He wouldn't even use a fly swatter. I'm convinced that he was going to kill himself—chickened out—didn't take his shot and so he died. Ask Piper Jordan. She knew Steven *very well.*" She said with deliberate emphasis.

Matt wanted to tell her to shut up but instead he picked up the phone, dialed information, and asked for the telephone number of the Watts Funeral Home. Mona made no attempt to leave. He wanted to tell her to get the hell out but instead he dialed the funeral home. A woman answered right away. Matt asked for Watts and was told that he was out and wouldn't be back for an hour. After he explained what he wanted, the woman said that she would have two attendants come right away. Matt thanked her and hung up.

He looked at Mona and said, "Mr. Watts wasn't in. He'll be back in an hour if you want to phone him from wherever you will be. Two of his assistants will be coming for Steven. By the way, where are you going?"

"Tatjana said that I can go to her farm in Freeport," she answered. "But I don't want to—not just yet. Maybe I'll go there after the funeral." She had to catch her breath. "I'm probably going to the Danforth Hotel in Portland. The Stolls gave me your phone number. I tried to call Piper but the line was busy. She is going to be upset when she finds out that Steven is dead and that he killed Kelly. I suppose you're going to tell her when you get back to your place or have you told her already?"

He wasn't about to answer that, so he changed the subject. "I told you," he said. "You have to leave now."

"No problem," she said coldly. "I'm very tired and there's still so much to do to prepare for Steven's funeral. And like I said, I'll probably go to the Danforth Hotel. That's where Steven and I stayed the night Kelly was murdered when *you* made us leave. You wouldn't even allow us to pack our toothbrushes." She glared at him.

"Sorry, but that's how it goes when there is a murder. Besides, you were able to return the next morning. And, I'm fairly certain that you can come back home in about four hours. So you really don't need to stay at a hotel."

"No," she said. "I'm going to be at the Danforth tonight because I don't want to be here all alone. Unless, of course, I can reach Piper and ask her to spend the night."

Matt knew that he was going to try and prevent that from happening. And he was aware that he had one hell of a headache. But still, he wanted to find out the answers to a few things before he let Mona go. "Before you leave," he said. "Would you answer a couple of questions?"

"It all depends on what they are," she said.

Matt rubbed his aching temples and got right to the point. "Your husband mentioned in his note that he was in love with Piper. Do you know anything about this?"

"Yes," Mona said. "I've known for a long time that Steven was in love with her. I caught them once." Mona tried not to let her face show her rage. She must be careful; Detective Carter must not find out how much she hated Piper. One slip and she'd fall under suspicion. She hated playing his cat and mouse game but she had no choice.

"What do you mean you caught them?" Matt asked.

"It was at a dinner party Steven and I held a few months

ago," Mona said. "Piper went to get her coat, and Kelly's, out of the bedroom. Steven must've followed her. When I walked in, Piper was struggling to get away from him. At first I blamed her. When I calmed down, I realized it was Steven's fault. Piper is my friend and she has strict morals. Steven was a pig. He was so damned fickle. This year he loved Piper. Last year it was some silly secretary. If he'd lived another month he'd be trying to hit on someone else."

"Why didn't you leave him?"

"I told you earlier that I was going to, but now he's dead." She pouted.

"I see," he said. But his thoughts registered something else. No court battles. No legal fees. Piece of cake. Plus— he probably had a lot of insurance. No doubt she was going to be a rich widow. He wasn't certain but it looked like her eyes were filling with tears. *Give me a break, lady.* "Don't be too sad," Matt blurted and knew that he sounded facetious, but he couldn't help himself.

"Don't worry. I won't, Mr. Smart Ass," she snapped and rolled her eyes.

Matt let that one pass, knowing he was responsible for her reaction. He was tired of their bickering back and forth.

"I used to love him," she said as if Matt cared to hear about her feelings.

Matt had detected a note of tenderness in her voice. He couldn't resist asking, "When did you stop loving him? Was it when you caught him with Piper Jordan?"

"No. It started when I found out he'd been sleeping with a secretary."

"Did you dislike him enough to kill him?"

Mona laughed, nervously. "Oh, no you don't," she said. "I'm not falling in your trap. You don't give up do you, Detective Carter?"

"No, Mrs. Hadley. Not when something doesn't feel right." *Careful,* he warned himself. *Don't go too far. Play it cool.*

"Well, now. Aren't we dedicated? How noble. But this

189

time you're barking up the wrong tree."

"Why is that?"

"What does it take to get through to you? I told you that I'm certain Steven killed Kelly and then he accidentally killed himself. I don't want to discuss the matter with you again. The end."

"You might think it's the end," he said. "But I'm not so sure."

Mona stood up and moved gracefully toward the door. Just before she made her exit she turned and said snidely, "I feel sorry for you, Mr. Detective."

"Why is that, Mrs. Hadley?"

"Because you're wasting your time. Like I said. Steven did himself in."

"I don't think so," Matt said.

"What do you mean?" she asked.

"I mean," Matt told her, "that I don't think so. I'm going to try and get to the bottom of this case one way or the other." *File that, you bitch.*

"How stupid to waste such precious time," she said and left the room.

Matt heard the front door slam. He immediately left to go back upstairs. On his way, he summed up the situation. He began to develop a scenario, and he talked to himself. Mona is obviously insanely jealous over Piper because Steven was in love with her. She planned to kill her at the party. In her frenzy she mistook Kelly for Piper. Steven found out and so Mona had to get rid of him. But how did he find out? Did he find the weapon? She strangled Kelly but with what? *Jesus. She is so sly. If she is guilty, I only hope that she's made a mistake.* But right at that moment that didn't look promising. He and his men had carefully gone over every inch of the house after Kelly was murdered. His headache was much worse.

He was upstairs now. "He did it," he muttered, aping Mona's words. "Bull," he grumbled. "I bet you did it lady. And I'm going to prove it somehow. You can bet on that."

He entered the bedroom to see that Judd, Jake, Paul, and Todd and one of his men were busy processing everything in sight. He noticed that Steven was in one of their body bags. Matt told them that Watts Funeral Home was on the way. Nobody said anything.

Matt scanned the room and came to rest on Mona Hadley's dressing table. He walked over to it and studied each item. He became particularly interested in her hair brush. There seemed to be several variously colored strands tangled in the bristles. "Hey, Paul," he said. "Bring me something to put this brush in, will you? I want to send it to the lab."

"Sure thing," Paul said and came over to Matt and picked up the brush and dropped it into a bag. Paul watched as Matt started rummaging through a white jewelry box. Several earrings and a rhinestone bracelet rested on a bed of red velvet. Matt recognized the bracelet as the one that Mona had worn the night Kelly Stewart was murdered. He also remembered that she'd worn a matching bow in her hair, but he couldn't find it anywhere. "What are you looking for now?" Paul asked him.

"Mona Hadley wore this rhinestone bracelet the night the Stewart girl was killed. She also wore a matching hair bow. It's not here. Don't women usually keep these things together?"

"My wife does," Paul said. "Maybe she put it in one of the drawers. You look in the ones on the left and I'll take the right." Paul opened the top drawer on his side and began to search through Mona's things. "Damn," he said. "I've never seen so many lipsticks and makeup junk. Good thing my wife isn't here to get any ideas or I'd go broke."

Matt was the one who found the bow underneath a pile of silk scarves in the bottom drawer. "Here it is," he said to Paul. "Seems to me she was trying to hide it." He noticed there was a stone missing. He shook everything vigorously and searched the bottom of the drawer carefully to see if he could find the stone. It wasn't there. Paul searched the top of the vanity, the jewelry box, and the floor. Then Judd asked him to help with something and he left Matt to search alone, without any luck. Matt wondered if Mona had lost the stone before the party. It seemed unlikely; she wasn't the type to wear broken jewelry; it had to have fallen out when she murdered Kelly. But unless that tiny thing turned up there was no way to prove her guilt. And then he realized that it would be impossible to prove she killed her even if they did find the stone. He felt defeated. But he rallied when he realized that Mona had to have screwed up somehow—some way. But how?

Matt again wondered where she'd stashed the weapon she'd used to strangle Kelly. She'd probably burned it or threw it in the ocean. Damn. The hair brush wouldn't help, either, because Mona and Steven had both been hanging over Kelly's body and that coffin. So had Piper and had every Goddamned guest, the Cape Bethany police, the rescue people . . . unbelievable.

Matt put the bow back where he found it and wandered about the bedroom, looking carefully for anything out of the ordinary. He went into the bathroom and then into the guest room where Mona said she'd spent the night, but there was nothing unusual to be seen. He wandered back to the bedroom and searched some more.

Before long there was a knock on the door and Jake opened it to see two men wheeling a gurney. "We're from Watts Funeral Home," one said. "I understand you have a customer for us."

A few minutes later, the Cape Bethany Police, Matt, and the other detectives stood outside in the driveway and watched the two men from Watts bring out the gurney, now loaded with Steven Hadley's body bag, and lift it into a shiny black hearse.

As soon as the hearse drove away, Matt decided that he would leave and go home to tell Piper about Steven before Mona had a chance to reach her. He'd tried to call her on the phone several times but it had kept ringing busy. He was relieved to know that so far it was still off the hook, the way he'd left it. He told the other men that he was leaving and that he would call them later. Paul said they were almost finished and would be going soon.

Matt climbed into his car, waved, and drove away,

knowing that if all went well he should have Steven's autopsy results in three or four hours. He also knew that this depended on the medical examiner not being behind schedule or it could take much longer.

Suddenly, he felt so tired. On top of everything else he craved sleep, and he could hardly wait to get home. He would take Piper in his arms, kiss her and then . . . But he had no idea how he was going to break the news that Steven was dead. He hoped that Piper hadn't discovered the phone off the hook and called Mona. Not knowing what he'd do if Mona had reached her already, he stepped on the gas and drove over the speed limit all the way to Lake Soudahook.

By the time Matt turned into his driveway it was already dark. The temperature had dropped and he could see puffs of smoke billowing out of his chimney—Piper had obviously built a fire. The minute he stepped out of his car he caught a whiff of pine-scented air. Just as he was about to turn the knob on the front door, Piper beat him to it. She stood there smiling. Once again he was struck by how beautiful she was, even with red, puffy eyes from all her crying the night before.

"Hi," she said and smiled warmly. "I hope you don't mind but I built a fire and I found some chicken in the freezer so I made dinner. I hope you like rice and green beans." She had to catch her breath. He couldn't tell from the way she sounded that she was a nervous wreck, worrying that he might be annoyed that she had poked around his kitchen, fearing that he might not feel the same toward her as he had that morning.

"I love the stuff," he said, and he reached out and gently touched her hair. She didn't pull away. "Did you sleep?"

"Yes. Until three. I didn't realize that you took the phone off the hook."

"I didn't want anybody to disturb you," he said, relieved to learn that Mona Hadley hadn't been able to contact her. "I knew you were exhausted and that you would probably have a hangover. Do you?"

"Not now. When I first got up I did. But I felt better after

I showered. I borrowed some of your shampoo and I used your washer and dryer, too. Is that okay?" She hoped he wouldn't think her too bold for making herself so much at home.

"Of course it's okay," he laughed, and he kissed her on the lips. When they parted she said, "Dinner is ready whenever you are," Piper knew that she sounded wifely. She enjoyed the role.

"I'm starving," he said. He debated whether to tell her right then about Steven. He was about to blurt the news when he looked at her smiling face. There was no way he was going to spoil the effort she'd put into making dinner. Steven would have to wait until later.

"What happened today?" Piper probed, then said, "I'm sorry. Maybe you aren't allowed to talk about it." She hoped that this wasn't the case. Her curiosity about what took place in Cape Bethany had the best of her. "If you want to talk I'm a good listener."

Matt almost weakened. Then he glanced through the doorway into the kitchen. Candles flickered. Wine glasses and plates. The smell of chicken drifted through the air. "I'll tell you after we eat, okay?" he said.

"Sure," she said and smiled. "Besides, we'd better sit down at the table before everything gets cold." She took him by the hand and led him into the kitchen.

Matt poured the wine while she served the chicken. The food was delicious, but he found he didn't have as much appetite as he thought he had. He didn't talk much.

Piper was disappointed over his silence. She noticed how long it took him to finish everything on his plate, and she finally mustered the courage to ask him what was wrong. "Matt. If you didn't like my cooking you didn't have to eat. I'm not that sensitive."

"No. It's not that. It was delicious," he said sincerely. "I'm sorry I've been so quiet. I'm really tired." He smiled warmly at her. "I consider myself lucky."

"Why is that?" she asked.

"Nellie Stoll's pot roast last night and your chicken tonight. Who taught you to cook like that?"

"My mother," she said and paused. "You told me last night that your mom died of cancer. Is your dad alive?"

"Yes. He lives with my sister and her family in New Gloucester. He likes it there, but he misses my mother and being in his own house. The place got too much for him. My sister says that he looks at his family albums several times a day. Kisses my mother's photo."

"Oh, that's so sad," Piper said and felt her eyes water. "He must have loved her very much."

"Yes he did," Matt said. "We all did." He felt a lump in his throat.

"I know. I feel that way over my parents and now Kelly." She gulped and suddenly lost her appetite. "I can't eat any more. I guess I'm still pretty shaken over this whole thing. Nothing seems real. It's like I'm having a nightmare." Her bottom lip quivered. *Damn*, she thought. *If I cry he's bound to think that I'm a stupid, blubbering idiot.* But she didn't cry. Instead, she hiccuped. She couldn't stop. She tried holding her breath until she was almost blue in the face.

Matt grinned, got up from the table, pulled her to her feet, and held her in his arms. "Hold your breath," he said. "That always makes mine go away." She tried it and it didn't work. He leaned down and kissed the top of her head. He could tell by the fragrance that she had indeed used some of his lemon shampoo. She started to hiccup again, and he held her tighter and wished that he'd never have to let her go.

Piper finally stopped hiccuping. "I'm okay now," she laughed, looking up at Matt. He smiled and kissed her.

When they stopped he cleared his throat and said, "Piper. I have bad news. I put off telling you until now because the timing was so lousy. Let's go into the living room and sit." Before she had a chance to ask what was wrong he took her by the hand.

Piper could tell from his face that something was dreadfully wrong, and her heart began to beat faster. Her legs felt weak.

They were in the living room now. Piper wondered if it

195

was the heat radiating from the fireplace that caused her to feel warm. Matt led her over to the black leather sofa and they sank deep into the soft cushions. He wanted to smile to help ease the tension, but he couldn't seem to manage one and kept the worried frown on his face. Piper sat rigid and waited for him to speak to her while he rubbed his palms together, and she knew that whatever it was he had to say must be awful.

Finally Matt took hold of her hand and blurted, "Piper. Steven is dead."

Chapter Ten

A Blue Lining

After Matt Carter left, Mona grabbed her purse and coat out of the hall closet, stomped out of the house, yanked open the garage door, and climbed behind the wheel of Steven's Jag. The engine caught right away. She threw the car into reverse, backed out of the driveway, and peeled rubber.

Just out of sight of the house, she luxuriated in the knowledge that Steven's precious Jag now belonged to her. She shuddered with excitement. The house was all hers, too, no Steven to share the pie with anymore. She laughed. It was going to be fun being a rich widow again. How clever she was to have picked two husbands with elegant taste in material objects. Thank God they had both believed in having joint bank accounts. Their taste in mistresses stank, however. God, how she hated that Piper.

Oh, well, she said to herself. *My husbands are history.* It wouldn't take her long to find a new one. As soon as Steven was buried, she'd close up the house and move to California or Hawaii. She'd never been to either place. But first she had to take care of some unfinished business. Piper had to die. She'd make her suffer like she had that redhead in St. Louis.

She wondered if Detective Carter had told Piper about Steven yet. She decided to call her and find out as soon as she got settled in her hotel room. As for that snoopy Detective Carter, there had to be a way to get him out of the picture before he screwed up her plans; she would have to think of a way to kill both of them pretty soon. And they had to die in a special way, that was for sure.

As soon as Mona was settled in her room at the Danforth Hotel she decided to phone Watts. She was so tired she couldn't possibly go there to make the funeral arrangements; those would have to wait until the first thing in the morning. In addition, she hadn't the slightest idea how long it took to do an autopsy. She hoped that the medical examiner at the hospital wouldn't keep Steven's body too long. If they did, she wondered if they would put him in a freezer to keep him fresh. *Oh, well,* she said to herself. *I always told Steven that he'd be late for his own funeral.* It only took her a few seconds to find the number of Watts Funeral Home in the yellow pages of the Portland phone book.

The phone rang once. Mona recognized the somber voice that answered. "Watts Funeral Home. Charles Timothy Watts speaking. How may I help you?"

"Mr. Watts. This is Mona Hadley. I met you at Kelly Stewart's funeral yesterday. My husband Steven used to golf with you at the country club."

"Hello, Mrs. Hadley," Watts replied. "I was told that the Police called," he said. "I was so sorry to hear about Steven. When did it happen?"

"During the night."

"Oh, I'm sorry, Mrs. Hadley," he repeated. What she didn't know was that he was more shocked over the obvious lack of emotion in her voice; he'd dealt with enough relatives of the dead to know when there was no grief involved. He'd observed Mona Hadley at the country club and at the Stewart girl's service. He'd found her to be as cold as one of his corpses then, and now, when the deceased was her husband, she sounded devoid of emotion. Sometimes he wondered what it was he liked about women.

". . . Steven had mentioned that if anything ever

happened to him, he wanted you to handle his funeral. He trusted you with his soul." She grinned and wondered if he got the joke.

"How nice of Steven to have said that," Watts said and puffed with pride. "Steven was such a nice man. Good golfer, too. He beat my ass." Oh dear, he said to himself. He shouldn't have said that. He cleared his throat and said, "Excuse me. I meant to say that he beat me. You can rest assured that he'll be missed at the club."

Mona didn't say a word.

Watts cleared his throat again and said, "Steven looked the picture of health when I saw him yesterday, Mrs. Hadley. What happened to him? Was it an accident?" He knew he was being nosy, but he couldn't resist.

"Sort of. He was a diabetic who drank heavily and didn't take his insulin. He went into a coma."

"How awful. Why, I just can't believe it! My heavens," he said and exhaled into receiver. "He did die at home, didn't he?"

"Yes, in his own bed."

"Oh that's wonderful. So natural. More and more people are leaving us that way. Not sterile like a hospital or nursing home. Don't you agree?"

"Yes. I suppose you're right," Mona said. "Your men were here and took Steven's body to the—" She didn't get a chance to finish because Watts interrupted her.

"I know. Marjorie, the lady attendant who works here told me. Don't worry. It's routine to check to make certain there was no . . ." he didn't finish his sentence for fear of insulting her.

"Say it," she demanded.

"Say what?" he asked, and wondered what was making her so rude.

"Say what you were going to say. I can't stand it when people beat around the bush."

"Oh, I wasn't doing that," he said defensively. "I didn't want to insult you."

"By saying that Steven was hauled away to the Maine General morgue because the police suspect foul play?

C'mon Mr. Watts. Don't act so damned wishy-washy."

"I'm sorry, Mrs. Hadley. I was going to say because of foul play and also because Kelly Stewart was murdered in your house."

"That's better," Mona said. "Nothing like getting right to the point. You're right on both counts. They want to make dead sure Steven died naturally because of Kelly's final performance."

He thought she sounded as if the Stewart girl was in a stage play in her living room—not murdered and shoved into a pine coffin for God's sake. He knew he should never have lent Steven that container and those chairs for his Halloween party. Darn. If word leaked out, his business would suffer. "Did the police say that they have any new leads as to who killed the Stewart girl?" he asked to take his mind off his troubles.

"Yes. Steven did it," Mona blurted. She heard Watts gasp. Another smile spread across her face. Oh, how she loved to shock people. She could see that prick's face turning whiter than it already was.

"You can't be serious, Mrs. Hadley. I can't believe Steven could ever do such a dreadful thing."

"Well, believe it," Mona said. "The asshole left a note saying he killed her."

"I'm so sorry," Watts said ignoring her crude remarks. He couldn't believe that Steven Hadley's wife could sound so coarse, so matter-of-fact about it. But it took all kinds.

"Listen, Mr. Watts," Mona said. "I have a lot to do so I have to get off the phone. A detective by the name of Carter insisted that an autopsy be performed on Steven. The medical examiner and I tried to tell him that there was no need. Steven drank too much yesterday after Kelly's funeral, and like I already told you, he didn't take his insulin. He slipped into a coma."

"Yes. You told me that." He wondered why she kept repeating herself. Was there something fishy here?

". . . Steven never took care of his health. It was a constant battle to get him to follow his diet and to take his shots twice a day." She knew that she'd better get on with what she wanted so she could hang up. "Anyway, as I said before, Detective Carter insisted that an autopsy be performed on Steven's body."

"I guess I agree with Detective Carter, Mrs. Hadley." Watts was used to explaining the value of the procedure to his clients, many of whom cringed at the thought of having their loved ones autopsied.

"I didn't ask for your opinion, Mr. Watts," Mona said. "My intent in phoning you was to ask that Steven's funeral be held at your establishment. I never dreamed you'd interject your personal views. If you want this funeral, you'd better keep your thoughts to yourself. Is that clear, Mr. Watts? Or shall I call your competition? I'm sure Truman's would welcome the business."

"I'm sorry, Mrs. Hadley. I didn't mean to upset you. I shouldn't have added my two cents worth." Watts was stunned. He'd never expected her to react in such a way, and he was good and angry now. For her to even suggest that she would take her business to Truman's was unforgiveable. He wanted to tell her to go chase herself, but somehow he regained his composure. She was by far the rudest, coldest person he'd ever spoken to. He was beginning to think that Steven Hadley was lucky to be dead.

"How is he going to get back to your place?" she asked.

"I will personally pick the body up after the autopsy is finished," Watts said. That was the least he could do for the poor fellow.

"Do you have any idea how long it takes to carve up a body?"

"No more than a few hours, depending on the medical examiner's schedule or any complications that might arise." He couldn't believe he was hearing such talk. The woman acted as if her husband was a hunk of meat in a butcher shop. She didn't sound at all normal.

Thinking this unnerved him even more, and it took a great deal of effort on his part to speak to her calmly. "When I get word that he's going to be released I'll call you. In the meantime, when do you want to come here to make the necessary funeral arrangements and to pick out a container for Steven?"

"Container?" Mona said loudly. "I thought you called those things caskets."

"We do. But I also call them containers because that's what they are."

"I don't want to come until tomorrow morning," Mona interrupted again. "I'm tired and I had to leave home until the police are finished with their snooping. I suppose I could go home tonight but I'm not. I'm staying at the Danforth. I have to do my hair and nails. Then I have to go shopping for a hat and veil. Steven is going to wear a blue suit so I should buy something that will complement that color. I have to call our friends and let them know what's happened. And I'm so tired," she whined. "This has been an exhausting day. I'm going to go to bed early tonight. If I don't get some decent rest I'm going to look a fright at the funeral."

"Tomorrow morning is fine," Watts said. "How about nine?" *Vain bitch,* he thought. *How the hell did Steven ever wind up with the likes of her?*

"Okay. I'll be there."

"Well then," Watts said. "I guess we can hang up now, unless there is anything else you care to ask me?"

"No. Nothing," she said.

Mona was about to hang up when Mr. Watts interjected. "Wait. You didn't tell me what your room number is in case I need to reach you."

"Room 270," she said.

"Thanks." Watts tried to sound pleasant. "They say the Danforth is a fantastic place to stay. Their food is good, too. I had a steak there the other night that was cooked perfectly. I like mine almost raw."

"It's a fleabag," Mona said and hung up. Watts stared at the receiver, made a sour face, and stuck out his tongue.

Before Mona unpacked, she phoned room service and ordered a steak, medium rare, a baked potato and sour cream, a salad with French dressing, and a bottle of white wine. When the waiter came to the door and wheeled in her food, she gave him a fifty-cent tip. The man scowled at the two quarters in the palm of his hand, but Mona didn't give a damn. "Well," she said. "Just don't stand there. Please leave."

The waiter left, but not without muttering something that sounded like "cheap bitch" under his breath.

Mona slammed the door. She was famished. But when she uncovered her dishes she was disappointed. The food looked like a typical hotel meal. The steak was well done and as tough as could be. The salad was wilted, the potato shriveled, and there was no sour cream. It took her less than ten minutes to eat everything, and then she poured herself a second full glass of wine and gulped it down.

Minutes later she felt mellow enough to phone a few friends. But first she would try to reach Piper. She dialed Detective Carter's number. It was busy. Mona's temper flared. She slammed the receiver on the hook, poured another glass of wine, sipped, and dialed again. The annoying busy signal buzzed in her ear. She tried the Stolls.

Nellie answered. "Hello," she said sweetly.

"This is Mona. Has Piper come back there yet?"

"No dear. Not yet. I was sorry to hear about Steven. John and I tried to phone Piper several times, but the line rang busy. Maybe it's off the hook. What a terrible shock. How are you doing dear?"

"I'm fine," Mona said, curtly. "Look. If Piper comes back, or if she calls, tell her I'm at The Danforth Hotel in Portland."

"Really?" Nellie asked. "Why are you there?"

"The police made me leave the house until they're satisfied Steven wasn't murdered."

Nellie gasped. "Murdered! Like Kelly? Lord have mercy. I thought he died from his diabetes?"

"He did," Mona told her and yawned.

"Well," Nellie sighed. "That doesn't sound like murder to me. Maybe the police are wrong."

"They're wrong all right. Look, I have to hang up now. Don't you forget to tell Piper where she can reach me."

"I won't." Nellie hung up, turned to John, and said, "That was Mona Hadley."

"I gathered that, Nellie. What's up?"

"That Hadley woman," she said. "Her husband is dead and all she seems to care about is getting hold of Piper. She said the police think Steven might've been murdered. You know, John, that woman didn't sound upset over that poor man. Land, if that was you that was dead, I'd be beside myself."

"Well that's a comfort," John said. "Murdered, huh? Well, I'll be damned."

Nellie looked puzzled. "I think it's odd that Mona isn't upset over Steven. But maybe she's no different than . . ."

"Than what?" John interrupted.

"Oh, John," Nellie sighed. "You made me forget what I wanted to say. Oh, well it will come to me. Seems like my memory fails me lately." She paused for a few seconds and then she said, "Some people can't open the lid and let their true feelings show. Remember my Aunt Lucinda?"

"How could I forget her? Mean old coot."

"Now, John. She had her good points, too."

"In her little toe."

"John! Stop that kind of talk."

"Truth hurts. Old bag couldn't say a kind word to anybody. I'll never forget those eyes of hers. Funny color blue. Awful light. Like one of them husky dogs that pull sleds."

"Well, John, before we get too far off the subject, I just remembered what it was I wanted to say in the first place. Mona is no different than the rest of us. I'd bet she's grieving on the inside."

"You can bet, Nellie. Not me," John said. "I don't think that woman gave a damn about Kelly or Steven. Kelly was a sweetheart so she should've shed a few tears. He wasn't any prize, I'll grant her that, but he was her husband. Liked to chase after women so Tatjana told me."

"That's gossip and you know it, John Stoll."

"Okay, okay, Nellie. I'll change the subject if you will. Say, we have another funeral coming up. Is my suit too wrinkled to wear?"

"Yes it is, dear." Nellie told him. "I'll have to press it for you later." She looked at the clock. "I wonder where Piper is? Times sure have changed. My father would've had the shotgun ready if you hadn't brought me home when you were supposed to."

"That's why we did our fooling around during business hours," John said with a wink. "Boy oh boy, those were the days. Remember the time your father almost caught us up in his hayloft?"

"Okay, John. That's enough," Nellie said and felt her cheeks flame. "I get embarrassed whenever I think about how close we came. Isn't it about time for you to milk the cow and slop the pigs before they starve to death. Don't forget to give them some fresh water."

"I'm going. I'm going, Nellie. Don't want to get you too worked up. You might attack me or something."

Nellie threw a dish towel at him as he started for the door. Just when he was reaching for the knob the phone rang again. This time he answered instead of Nellie. It was Piper. "Well, now," he said. "Good to hear from you. Have you had a nice trip?" Nellie scowled at him.

"John," Piper said. "Matt told me that Steven Hadley died last night."

John could hear the sadness in her voice. He decided he'd better not tease her further.

"I know. He's dead." John said.

"How did you find out?" Piper asked.

"Mona's phoned here several times. She's been looking for you all day. I gave her the number where you are but she said the line's been busy. Nellie's tried to get you, too, but she ran into the same problem. Have you had that cussed phone off the hook all this time?"

"Yes. But not intentionally. Matt took it off and I didn't know it. I slept most of the day." Piper caught her breath and then she said, "John. Matt told me that Steven left a note confessing that he was the one who killed Kelly."

"No kidding," John said flippantly.

Nellie was at his side now. "What's wrong. Tell me.

Tell me." She tugged on his shirt and he kept swatting her away.

"When?" Piper asked.

"When what?" John was confused. "You mean when did Mona phone? Nellie, quit tugging on my shirt before you rip it to shreds."

"Yes," Piper said.

"About ten minutes ago," Nellie prompted.

"Nellie says it was about ten minutes ago. Mona said she's staying at a hotel in Portland."

"The Danforth?" Piper asked.

"Yep. That the one. She didn't leave the number."

"That's okay. I have it. I'll call her now. I'll let you two know what's happening."

"For starters, are you coming home tonight?" John asked in a fatherly tone.

"No. Tomorrow."

"Hmmm," he said. "I don't know about this situation. Maybe I'd better ask that young man what his intentions are."

"Tell Nellie I said hello," Piper said, ignoring John's last statement. "I'll see you in the morning." After she hung up, she turned, faced Matt, and said, "I guess Mona's been trying to reach me." Just as Piper started to dial her number the phone rang. She answered.

"Piper?" Mona said sharply.

"Yes, it's me."

"Well it's about time I got ahold of you. I've been trying for hours. Did that Detective Carter tell you that Steven is dead?"

"Yes, he did," Piper said softly. "I'm sorry, Mona." She thought that Mona's voice lacked emotion. She couldn't tell if she was upset over Steven or not.

"It was an accident." Mona sounded defensive now.

"How did it happen?" Piper asked.

"His diabetes finally caught up with him." Mona paused and then said, "Piper?"

"What?"

"Steven killed Kelly." Her voice sounded cold and hard.

"I know," Piper responded. "I still can't believe it." Inside, she was glad that Steven was dead after what he'd done to Kelly. And she was relieved for herself. To think that he really wanted to kill her. That sick bastard. She didn't have to worry about being murdered now. And she wouldn't have to put up with Mona's jealousy. Maybe life could get back to normal.

"How did you find out about Steven?" Mona asked. She knew the answer to that, but she thought she'd make her squirm. That's what you got for shacking up with someone you just met.

"Detective Carter told me," Piper answered quickly, hoping that Mona wouldn't ask her any more questions.

"Did Carter also tell you that he had Steven's body hauled off to the Maine General Hospital for an autopsy?" She seemed angry now. "I tried to tell him there was no need, but he wanted to be certain that Steven wasn't murdered."

"He's only doing his job," Piper said defensively. "You should understand that, considering what happened to Kelly at your house." Now she was getting mad.

Mona let that one go. "Look. I've asked Watts to handle Steven's funeral. I have to go there in the morning and pick out a casket and all of that. I'll let you know when the funeral is going to be."

"Okay." Piper so wanted to confess to her that she hated Steven and that she wasn't up for going to his funeral, especially at Watts, but she didn't have the heart. It wasn't Mona's fault that her husband was a murderer. "Do you want me to go with you to the funeral home?" she asked dreading that Mona would say that she did.

"No. I want to go alone."

"Are you certain?" Piper said and breathed a sigh of relief though she couldn't understand why Mona wanted to do something like that by herself. "I would want someone to go with me if it were the other way around."

"Well, you're not me," Mona said and then caught herself. She knew that she was being too cool about Steven. "I'm sorry, Piper. I don't mean to sound so coldhearted. I guess I'm in shock. This has been the longest night of my life." She made certain that her voice cracked and that she sniffled loud and clear into Piper's ear.

"Oh, Mona, you poor thing. Of course you're upset. Are you okay by yourself? Do you want me to come to the hotel and stay with you?"

". . . I want to be alone," Mona said. "I have a lot to think about. It isn't easy for me knowing that Steven had a thing for you. He meant to kill you—not Kelly. I think he must've been mentally ill, don't you, Piper?"

"Yes, Mona." *Poor woman*, she thought. *How awful it must be for her.*

". . . he never would have attempted such a dreadful thing if he'd been in his right mind. I know he really loved me. It must've been his diabetes that made his mind go. Oh, it's so awful! Poor Kelly. I should've paid more attention. Maybe I could've prevented all of this. I should've seen to it that he got some help." Mona was pleased with her performance.

"It's going to be okay, Mona," Piper soothed. "Look. You're tired. Let's hang up now. You should try to get some sleep. Believe me. Rest makes a difference." She felt sorry for Mona now, and she decided that somehow she would find it within her to attend Steven's funeral—for Mona's sake.

"I am tired," Mona whined. "I feel like somebody whipped me. I'll call you just as soon as I find out what's what. And Piper," she said and paused.

"What?"

"Thanks for being such a good friend. I know that I don't deserve such kindness after—after I accused you of carrying on with Steven. I'm sorry I slapped you." She paused and then she said, "I can't believe that Steven wanted to kill you!"

Piper couldn't take any more. "Don't be so hard on yourself Mona," she said. "Get some rest. I'll talk to you later. Don't you forget to call me after you find out when Steven's funeral is going to be." She didn't give Mona a chance to say another word. After she cradled the phone she turned and faced Matt. He had a worried expression on his face. "I don't want to go to Steven's funeral," she confessed.

"Don't go," he said. "You've been through a lot. Mona should understand."

"I can't leave her in the lurch. She doesn't have any family that I know of, at least she's never mentioned any."

Matt wanted to tell her that was understandable but he remained silent. He wanted to warn Piper that he suspected that Mona killed both Kelly and Steven, but he was afraid that she couldn't face it right now. He'd wait until the facts came in from the lab.

". . . you're so quiet," Piper said. "Do you feel okay?"

"I'm fine," he said. "Just tired. It's been a long day. How is Mona?"

"She's holding up. I feel so sorry for her. It can't be easy knowing that your husband is a murderer." A look of confusion covered her pretty face. "I can't believe Steven was in love with me and that he actually wanted to kill me because he couldn't have me." She shook her head and continued. "It's too weird."

"Mona told me this morning that she caught Steven hitting on you at a dinner party some months back."

Piper looked surprised. "Yes, yes he did. But Steven was always doing things like that. Not just to me but to lots of other women. Mona walked in on us that night. It was awful. At first, she blamed me but when she came to her senses she knew that I didn't have anything to do with it. Did she tell you about that?"

"Yes. She also said that she apologized to you."

"That's right. She called me later that night. She slapped me, you know?" Piper automatically lifted her hand and touched her cheek. "Left the print of her hand on my face. She was so mad I thought she might . . ."

"Might what?"

"I don't know. I guess that I was going to say kill me."

"Do you think that Mona could kill someone?"

"I don't know," Piper said and frowned. "Why do you ask?" She didn't give Matt a chance to answer. "You don't suspect Mona of killing Kelly and Steven do you?"

"Maybe." He had finally said it. Screw waiting for the autopsy report. She might not believe what he was about to say, but at least she would be put on her guard.

"But, Matt," Piper said. "I thought you said that Steven left a note confessing that he was going to kill me and that he accidentally killed Kelly."

"I did say that. But who's to say that Mona didn't kill both Kelly and Steven. Maybe she typed that note."

"Did Steven sign it?"

"Yes, yes he typed it."

"Well, there. That's proof isn't it?" She wanted to believe Steven was the killer, and she knew why she felt that way. It wasn't because she was fond of Mona. The truth was that she wanted the danger to be over. She didn't want to live in constant terror. A vision of Kelly in that pine coffin flashed in her mind. She tried to make the grisly image go away and failed.

"Look, Piper," Matt said. "I'm not saying that Mona is the killer, not yet. Maybe it was Steven. But that remains to be seen until all the facts are in. In the meantime, you should be cautious. Everyone is suspect." He could tell by the look on her face and in her eyes that she was getting scared. He went to her and took her in his arms. "I'm sorry, honey. I don't mean to frighten you. Let's stop all this murder talk and enjoy the evening. Why don't I make us some hot chocolate?"

"Great," she said and already began to feel better.

"Want to sit in front of the fire and talk?"

"Okay," she said. Inside, she agonized. *Mona. No. It can't be. Matt is wrong. Or is he?* Suddenly she felt beyond fear. Her body went numb all over.

After they had their cocoa, they showered together and then crawled into bed. The touch of the cold sheets gave Piper the chills, and she cuddled closer to Matt to get warm. She laid her head against his chest while her fingers lightly massaged his chest and taut belly and he caressed her breasts and throat. He kissed her neck and ear and felt her shudder. He found her lips; they kissed passionately, and she could feel his maleness against her. She kissed him again and pulled him on top of her. He buried his face in the softness of her hair. The very smell of her drove him wild. They kissed again just as he entered her. After their lovemaking they fell fast asleep in each other's arms.

The next morning at nine, Mona arrived at Watts Funeral Home carrying her suitcase, which now contained Steven's shirt, tie, underwear and socks. His blue suit was draped over her free arm. With great difficulty, she opened the oak front door, stepped into the hallway, and bumped into a smiling Watts. He told her he'd seen her coming up the granite steps from his office window. Mona noticed that he had his hands clasped. He was impeccably dressed in a black wool suit and tie, offset by the whitest shirt she'd ever seen. She looked down at his feet. His shoes were so highly polished she could almost make out her reflection. She must remember to ask him if Steven needed his shoes.

"Good morning, Mrs. Hadley," Watts said. "Here let me take those for you." She handed over Steven's things. "Please follow me into my office," he said. "Can I get you a cup of coffee or tea?"

"No thanks. Can we get on with this? I have a lot to do today."

"Yes, of course you do," he agreed. "Please be seated." He hung Steven's suit on an oak coat tree with brass hooks and plunked the suitcase on the floor beside it. He turned, faced Mona and said, "I found out that Steven's body is going to be released early this afternoon. I'll be picking him up," he said cheerfully. "My attendants, who drove him to the hospital, offered to go for me, but I said I wanted to do it. That's the least I can do for a friend."

"Did they do an autopsy?"

"Yes, they did."

"That didn't take long." She wondered if she sounded as relieved as she felt.

"No. Unless there are complications it can be done in a

211

couple of hours."

"Did they cut him up?"

She had taken him by surprise again. "Yes," he said, trying not to sound shocked. "But I prefer to use a different term. I prefer to call it a surgical procedure."

"Well good for you. I don't. Anyway, it doesn't really matter what he looks like because I want a closed coffin, I mean casket," she corrected herself.

Watts nodded. He didn't tell her that he knew she was going to have a closed casket. Well-to-do people didn't go for open ones. Funerals were social affairs. Everything had to be just so. Bodies were considered blights. He could also bet that he knew what kind of a container she would pick out for Steven. He cleared his throat and said, "Before we take care of any other details, would you like to go upstairs with me to the selection room and choose a container for Steven?"

"Okay," she said. They both stood up at the same time.

"Shall we take the elevator or walk? I must warn you that the elevator is old-fashioned. It has an iron scissor type door, it makes a terrible grinding noise, and it thumps when it starts and stops. It's also very slow but adequate. I hope you don't mind."

"Let's go," she said impatiently.

Minutes later, Mona and Watts opened a door on the second floor. Having anticipated her arrival, he'd already turned on the lights in the selection room to create the best effect. Everywhere she looked she saw caskets of all shapes, sizes, and colors. Watts observed her with silent confidence. She didn't even wait for him to lead the way. She swept past him and halted in front of his most expensive container. He walked over to her with a smile on his face.

"I want this one," she told him.

No kidding, he said to himself. "You have wonderful taste," he praised. "This is our finest container." He gently touched the lid.

"What kind of wood is that?" Mona asked.

"African mahogany," Watts said with pride. "Hand-rubbed finish. Very expensive."

212

"The price doesn't matter," she said. "I'll take it."

He knew that. He just wanted to hear her say it. "The beige velvet lining will complement Steven," he told her. "Actually, it's called silver beige."

"His dark blue suit will clash," she said.

"No it won't," he said and then he saw the look on her face and knew that he should've kept his mouth shut. "I'm sorry. You're right. Blue would clash." He knew that a dark brown one would look much better, but her kind never dreamed of having their loved ones dressed in brown. That color was considered cheap and suited common people.

"No," she said more to herself than to him. "His blue suit won't look right. I want a container with a light blue lining."

"But we don't have one. We only have the tan velvet."

"Don't you have someone who can redo it?" she asked icily.

"Yes, although I must warn you that it will be very expensive."

"Do it," she ordered and walked to the door.

"I'll take care of it right away," he said to her and forced a smile. He could hardly wait to jack up the price. That would fix her. "Steven will look wonderful with a light blue lining." *Whatever makes you happy*, he thought.

"I want you to know that I'm not at all pleased," Mona said sharply.

"Excuse me?" Watts said. He was shocked that she would say such a thing. His mind did a fast evaluation of the situation. So far he'd done everything he could for this ungrateful widow, and now she had the nerve to complain about the service. If she spread the news to her friends that she was unhappy with him he would lose a lot of wealthy clientele to Truman's. He'd better smooth her feathers fast. "I'm so sorry," he apologized. "Please. Tell me what's wrong and I'll make it right."

Mona frowned and then lashed out at him. "You'd think you'd have a better selection of containers. I really don't like that African whatever you call it."

Now Watts looked hurt. "I thought the African would be perfect for Steven. We've never had any complaints about it—until now," he said that a bit too accusingly. He knew that he should stick to the customer always being right routine, but he just couldn't resist. "And it's quite inexpensive for the quality. I haven't told you the cost." That ought to fix her.

"I already told you that price doesn't matter." She had raised her voice an octave. "How much is it?"

"Four thousand seven seventy plus tax." Watts watched her, but she never even flinched. He seized the opportunity to lock up a big sale. "That's very reasonable," he reassured her. "Other states have caskets that cost as much as $60,000 or $70,000—or more. Some are beautifully handcarved and silverplated. So ornate." He loved telling customers about such containers. But he knew that most of his clients couldn't imagine or appreciate such beauty.

"Why don't you carry that kind?" Mona asked him.

"I did but they never sold," Watts said, looking disappointed. "I could order one for you," he said more hopefully. "There is enough time for one to get here before the visiting hours." His eyes glittered, and he mentally crossed his fingers for luck. What a spectacle that would be! What a profit! Maybe a new hearse wasn't so far off.

"No," Mona said. "Forget it. I don't want to chance it not making it here on time for hubby poo." She glanced at her watch. "I told you I'm in a hurry. Let's go back to your office and make the arrangements for the rest of this mess."

Hubby poo, he thought. And how dare she call Steven's funeral preparations a mess! What a horror she was. It took all of his reserve to smile sweetly and say, "Of course. I realize you're in a hurry. Follow me." *Steven doesn't know how fortunate he is to have passed on. Hell would be better than living with her. Ungrateful, cold-hearted twit.*

After they came back downstairs on the elevator, Watts took Mona to his office. He asked her to sit down and he did the same. When they were settled he asked her what she wanted written in the newspaper obituary. Again, he already had an idea about what she'd tell him—he always

214

knew. When Mona finished answering all his questions he puffed with pride. *Chalk up another one Charlie old boy.* He knew the answer she'd give to his next question, too. "You do want a private funeral service don't you?"

"How did you know?" she asked.

"I didn't," he lied. "I was just guessing. Do you want flowers or do you want Steven's friends to donate the money they would've spent on them to Steven's favorite charity?"

Charity begins at home, stupid, Mona said to herself. *Send checks.* "No. I don't want people sending cheap bouquets of flowers. I'll order something special."

"I can do that for you," Watts interjected eagerly. "And I'll mention your wishes in the obituary. But you didn't tell me if you want any donations made to a charity?"

"Just give me the money. I'll pick one. And as for the flowers, I don't want anything mundane." She frowned, visualizing some of the floral displays that people had ordered for Kelly's funeral. "I don't want carnations or daisies or any other cheap fill."

Watts silently sputtered to himself like an old fuss-budget. *Your type wouldn't be caught dead with carnations or daisies. And they're not cheap, dummy. But you're an orchid person if I ever saw one.* "What kind of flowers do you want?" he asked.

"I want orchids," Mona responded.

"They are lovely," Watts grinned. "There is a florist in town that has the prettiest I've ever seen. What color would you like?"

"Purple and white."

"Wonderful choice," he said sincerely. He dearly loved orchids no matter what the color. "Now, Mrs. Hadley. It's time to discuss a cemetery plot. Perhaps you and Steven have already purchased yours?"

"No."

"Well then," he said and rubbed his palms together. "May I suggest Memory Gardens. It's the prettiest setting around. I just did a funeral for the Somerset family." *That ought to get you.* Anybody who knew anybody, knew that the Somersets were among the wealthiest people in Maine. "Gorgeous lot," he told her. "Overlooks the White Mountains in New Hampshire. And when the sun sets it's breathtaking. I almost bought it for myself, but I waited too long. I bought the one across from it," he pouted and sighed. "I believe there is a beauty available a few yards away. But I must tell you that it's not quite the same view as the other and it will be expensive." He could tell by the look on her face that he'd just made another sale.

"Okay," she said. "I'll take that one."

"A wise choice," he told her. "I'll make the arrangements just as soon as you leave." He could hardly wait to discuss Steven's headstone. He just knew that his friend who owned the monument business would have another order before the morning was out. Gray marble would suit Steven.

"No matter. I'll take it," Mona said without any deliberation. "Now how about a gravestone?"

Watts smiled. "You're one step ahead of me. Headstones are so important. There is a company on the other end of the city. They do the best work. Family business. I've seen stones from them that go back to the early 1800's. The engraving is still easy to read. Wonderful craftsmen."

"You order one," Mona commanded. "I don't want to be bothered with that kind of thing."

"But what about an epitaph?"

"I'll think of something and call you." She stood up and made her way to the door. "I have to go now. There is so much to do."

"I know, I know," Watts clucked. "Thank you for bringing Steven here. We'll do well by him. And let me know if there is anything you need." He stood up and went to open the door for her.

"Just make certain you take care of the most important detail."

"What's that?" he asked.

"Why, the blue lining for his casket. Did you forget?"

"No, no. I wasn't thinking straight." *God*, he thought. *I'll be glad when she leaves. She's such a demanding, mean bitch. Look at those eyes. They're like two stones.*

". . . think straight before you screw up the whole thing," she said and made her exit.

Watts heard the front door slam. He went to his window and watched Mona Hadley go down the steep flight of granite steps. "You bitch," he sputtered. "You and your fucking blue lining. I'd like to be able to do your funeral one of these days. That would be like a dream come true."

Chapter Eleven

All Alone

As soon as Mona left Watts she drove back to the Danforth Hotel. The minute she reached her room she kicked off her heels, sat on the freshly made bed, and phoned Piper at the farm.

John Stoll answered. "Hello," he said gruffly.

"This is Mona."

"I know. I can tell your voice." He wanted to say he could feel the chill through the line.

"Is Piper there?"

"Nope."

"Is she still with that detective?"

"Don't know. Any messages if she calls here?"

"Yes. You can tell her that Steven's funeral is tomorrow at eleven at Watts."

"Alrighty. Kinda quick don't you think?"

"What's quick?" she snapped.

"The funeral. Back when, we waked them longer. Kept them at home. Laid em out in the front parlor. I want Nellie to have my wake here at the farm."

Mona cut him off. "I don't have time to discuss your demise," she said coldly. "Tell Piper I'll be staying at the Danforth Hotel until after the funeral. I just can't stand being home alone after all that's happened." She tried to sound depressed. There she thought. That ought to make the old coot think I'm really grief-stricken.

"Okay," John said. He wasn't about to fall for her sad tone of voice. "I'll give Piper the message if she calls. Say, I have an idea. Why don't you call her at that detective's house?"

"Not now. I can't be bothered chasing after her all day. I have to hang up." She didn't even say goodbye.

John Stoll hung up the receiver. He sputtered to Crutches who was stretched out on his bed, "Nobody ever taught that snip manners. She needs her hide tanned."

Nellie came into the kitchen carrying a laundry basket full of ironing. "What in tarnation are you mumbling about, dear?" she asked.

"Mona," he said. "She just phoned looking for Piper. I swear that woman is the rudest person I've ever met. She wants us to tell Piper to call her when we hear from her. And she said that Steven's funeral is at Watts at eleven tomorrow morning. I told her I thought it was pretty quick."

"Tomorrow! Land. You're right, John. What's the matter with people these days. Never saw folks buried so fast." Her wrinkled face took on a worried look. "John," she said. "If I should die first will you promise not to bury me that fast?"

"I won't, Nellie. I won't. That is, if you'll promise not to plant me in a hurry."

"I won't, dear. And I want you to keep me at home like in the old days. I can see it all now. The whole church will camp out in our living room to keep me company. The minister will talk for a half hour or better. Mabel Place will sing "Onward Christian Soldiers." Everyone will cry. The women will cook up a storm. My heavens, John. You'll have enough food to last a year. Be sure you freeze it in time. Sarah Congdon's chocolate cake is awful good. Makes it from scratch and her own boiled frosting, too." She rolled her eyes and said, "I'd like to have a slice of that right now. And Penny Dean's homemade baked beans are delicious. She always adds an apple to keep them nice and moist. Make sure you set the table with my Zwiebal plates." She had a vision of John being rough and chipping them. "On second thought, dear. I think you'd better die first. Do you think I should leave my dishes to Piper or to our daughter-in-law?"

"Give them to Piper. Connie is a tart. Leave her your everyday plates. That will serve her right for not writing or calling."

"Now, John," Nellie scolded. "Don't you think you're being too hard on Connie?"

"Not hard enough. When's the last time she wrote to us or came for a visit."

"Well, John. It's your son's fault as much as it is hers. Maybe more."

"That's different."

Nellie knew it was no use trying to convince him that their only living son was at fault. John's children could do no wrong. She sighed and went to get her ironing board. Just as she plugged the iron into the socket Piper came through the door with Matt Carter. Nellie noticed that Piper had more color in her cheeks and her eyes had lost that sad look. "Well, well," she said. "Look at what the cat dragged in. It's about time you came back home, Piper. I made you some beef stew and an apple pie. I thought it might spoil before you came back."

"Sorry." Piper apologized. "I had a little too much wine the other night. Last night we had a late dinner and . . ."

"And what?" John probed.

Piper was speechless. She dreaded what John might say next.

"And," he continued on like an angry parent. "What did you do after dinner that was so all fired important that you couldn't come home?"

Piper's face flushed. Matt came to her rescue. "We watched a movie on television and then we got to talking and before you know it it was long after midnight."

"Hmmm," John said. "I'll buy that. But I'm old-fashioned. I want to ask you an important question."

"Shoot," Matt said.

"What are your intentions?"

"John," Piper half yelled. "Please. You're embarrassing Matt and me."

"Yes, John," Nellie said. "Piper's quite right. Cut that stuff out right this minute. It's not your business what these kids do."

"I'm not embarrassed," Matt said. "And don't you be, Piper."

"That's right," John said to Piper. "You don't have any folks to look out for you. I think it's proper for me to find out what's going to happen."

"I think I want to mar—" Matt couldn't finish because Nellie interrupted.

"Oh, mercy, Piper. We forgot to tell you Mona phoned. She wants you to call her."

"At home?" Piper asked.

"At The Danforth Hotel," John said. "Crabby thing. Worst disposition of any woman I ever met. And burying that poor husband of hers so fast his head would spin, if it could."

"Did she tell you when and where the funeral is going to be held?" Piper asked.

"Yep," John said. "Tomorrow morning at eleven at Watts's. That guy is doing a booming business if you ask me. Maybe I should've been an undertaker. More money in that than farming. And you don't have to worry about the crop after it's planted."

"John!" Nellie said loudly for her. "Stop that talk right now."

"Okay, Nellie, okay." John said and went to the stove to pour himself a cup of coffee. He offered Piper and Matt one but they refused.

Piper sat down at the kitchen table and exhaled deeply. "I don't know if I can do it," she said to no one special.

"Do what?" Matt asked.

"I don't think I can go to Steven's funeral after what he did to Kelly. Poor Kelly," she said so sadly that Nellie walked over to her and placed a frail hand on her shoulder and began to massage her ever so gently.

"There, there, dear. We understand. Don't we, men?"

221

"Yes," Matt responded quickly. "I don't think you should go either. Enough is enough."

"That's right," John added. He was alarmed by the chalky color that had just spread over Piper's face. He scratched his beard and said, "Steven won't know the difference. And Frosty doesn't deserve all this attention."

Everyone was quiet for a few minutes, and then Piper said, "I don't want to sound like a martyr, but I suppose I should go to the funeral for Mona's sake."

"Why?" Matt asked.

"Yeah. Why?" John aped.

"Leave the poor child alone," Nellie clucked. "I think I'll make us a pot of fresh coffee and we'll all sit down at the table and talk this thing over. How's that sound?"

"Good idea," John agreed. "This coffee I'm drinking tastes like the bottom of a bird cage."

Piper made a face at John and then she said, "I think I'll go to Steven's funeral. And I think I'll go upstairs and change my clothes while the coffee perks. I can't stand this outfit any longer."

"Serves you right for not coming home," John scolded.

"I'll go to Steven's funeral with you," Matt said. He hoped his face didn't reveal how worried he was. And he hoped that the lab hurried up with Steven's autopsy. If they didn't come up with something to link Mona to his death, Piper was going to be in serious trouble as soon as Steven's funeral was over.

". . . thanks Matt," Piper said. "I'd feel much better with you there."

"And we're going," Nellie said with a sweet smile. "Right, John?"

"Sure." John answered, and then tugged on his beard. "Lately, funerals seem to be an important part of our social life. I guess that's what happens when old age sets in."

"But Kelly and Steven weren't old," Nellie reminded him.

"I guess you're right," John said and looked at Matt. "You know, young fella. When I was a youngster I could work from sunup til sundown. Now it seems I wear out at high noon."

"Me, too," Matt said.

"You don't say," John said and straightened his shoulders. "Well maybe it's not old age. I'm awful glad you told me that. I feel better already. Sometimes I think it's just me that's wearing out. Maybe it's something in the air."

Piper got up from the table and started to walk out of the kitchen to go upstairs to take a shower. She stopped halfway and said to Nellie, "I'm starving. I don't suppose you have any of those wonderful molasses cookies for me to munch on do you?"

"Yes, I have plenty. I made a fresh batch early this morning. They turned out real well. Didn't burn on the bottoms like they've been doing." She went to the cookie jar, lifted the lid, and pulled out a plump cookie. "Here's one to take upstairs with you while you change your clothes."

"Thanks," Piper said, took the cookie, and a big bite. She rolled her eyes. "Mmmm, Nellie. You are a great baker."

"Thanks, dear," Nellie said and then she pouted. "I just had a thought about Mona. The last time she came up to the farm with Steven, he ate about a dozen of my cookies. Mona took one little tiny bite and spit it out in the trash. She told me it was the worst cookie she'd ever tasted."

"Oh, Nellie," John warned. "Don't start that stuff again or you're bound to start blubbering. What did you expect that icicle to say? Doesn't surprise me none. She wouldn't know a good thing if she saw it."

Piper blew Matt a kiss as she left to go upstairs. Passing through the dining room she heard John say to Matt, "Say young fella. Did I tell you the one about the traveling salesman and the farmer's daughter?"

Later, after Nellie, John, Matt, and Piper had their coffee and cookies, Matt said that he had to be going.

"What's up?" John asked. "Got another grisly murder you're working on?"

"No. Things are pretty quiet right now. Keep your fingers crossed it stays that way. If it doesn't, I might not be able to go to Steven's funeral tomorrow." He looked at Piper and asked, "Want to walk me to my car?"

"Sure," she said and got up from the table.

"Thanks for the coffee and cookies, Nellie," Matt said.

"Oh, you're welcome, Matthew. Drive carefully now."

"I will."

Matt and Piper left with Crutches trailing behind.

As soon as the door closed, Nellie ran to the window and peeked.

"What the heck are you doing?" John asked. "Nellie. Quit that. How'd you like it if Piper spied on us?"

"Just a second, John. I want to see if he kisses her goodbye."

John got up from the table, took Nellie by the hand, and pulled her away from the window. "If it's kissing you want then I'll give you a smooch."

Nellie struggled free. She straightened her hair and said, "You're such a loverboy underneath that tough hide of yours, John Stoll."

"That's what all the girls say," he teased.

Outside, Matt had just kissed Piper for the second time. "My bed is going to be pretty lonely tonight," he told her. "Sure you don't want to come along?"

"Don't tempt me," she said.

"C'mon. Why don't you pack your suitcase?"

"I can't."

"Why not?"

"Because."

"Because why?"

"Gee, Matt. I don't think I should until I know in what direction you and I are headed." She couldn't believe that she said that. What must he think of her being so pushy? She fully expected him to get in his car and speed away.

"Is that all?" he said. "Well now, I have the answer to that. Want to hear it?"

"Yes."

"Well I was thinking it would be a good idea if we got married one of these days."

Piper looked up at him and asked, "You're not kidding are you?"

"Nope. I wouldn't joke about something that important. Now, how about it? Do you think you'd like to marry me? We could make beautiful babies together."

Piper's serious expression vanished and was instantly replaced with a radiant smile. "Yes. I would like very much to marry you."

He took her in his arms and kissed her. When they finished he said, "Maybe I'd better go back into the house and tell John my intentions."

"No," Piper said. "Please. Not yet. I want to keep this a secret until after Steven's funeral. I don't think it's right to be spreading the news about such a happy occasion for at least a week or so. What do you think?"

"I think it's none of Mona's business what we do. And I have to say that she didn't seem too shook up over Steven's death."

"You really don't like Mona do you, Matt?"

"Nope. And I think . . ." He decided not to go any further. If only the lab would come up with some solid evidence. . . .

"I guess I don't like her either," Piper said, "but at the same time I feel sorry for her. Like I said before. It can't be easy finding out your husband is a murderer. Anyway, let's not tell Mona and the Stolls that we're going to get married. Let's wait a week. I don't think it would be right to spring such happy news on people at such a sad time. Okay?"

"Okay for Mona and the Stolls," he agreed. "Do you mind if I call my father and tell him?"

"No, of course not."

"Good. I was thinking we should pay him and my sister and her family a visit this weekend. What do you say?"

"That would be great," she said. "I hate to repeat myself. But please promise me you won't tell the Stolls or

Mona about our engagement."

"I promise." He took her in his arms and kissed her again. When they stopped he said that he really had to go. "I'll call you tomorrow morning. Do you want me to pick you up to go to the funeral?"

"No. I can ride with John and Nellie and meet you at Watts's."

"What time?"

"How about quarter to eleven in the parking lot?"

"Fine. I'll see you then. And I'll call you tonight to make certain you haven't changed your mind about marrying me."

"I won't change my mind," she said firmly. "I think I should go inside now." She blew him a kiss and went up the porch steps. Crutches waited on the landing, tail wagging, ready to go inside to his bed.

Matt climbed in his car and drove away. He couldn't believe that Piper said that she would marry him. The very idea of her becoming his wife made his pulse quicken. As soon as he could, he'd drive into Portland and buy her an engagement ring. He wanted something different than the traditional diamonds. Jade would be nice. He wondered if she'd like that. . . .

John heard commotion on the porch. He opened the door and saw Piper and the dog. "C'mon in, you two," he said. He looked closely at Piper. "Your cheeks are pretty pink. Looks like you've been up to mischief."

"How can you tell?" she asked.

"I have my ways. What's happened? That young fella pop the big question?"

"That's for me to know and for you to find out," she teased and when John wasn't looking she winked at Crutches. She couldn't believe John had guessed her secret. "Nellie," John said. "I'll bet you five bucks that Piper's going to marry that detective fella one of these days. Just look at her face."

Nellie came over to Piper and said, "Well, now. I don't

think she looks any different than she did when she went out the door. She has rosy cheeks from the crisp air is all. Isn't that right, Piper?"

Piper didn't have the heart to lie to them. She decided to let them share in her joy. She hoped Matt wouldn't get angry, especially since she'd made him promise not to tell. "You're right, John," she blurted. "We're getting married. But you're not to tell Mona. I'll do that after Steven's funeral."

Nellie was delighted with the news. She kissed Piper and promised not to tell a living soul until she got the okay from her. John did a little jig. "I knew I was right," he said. "Sonofagun. I can always tell. When's the big day?"

"We don't know yet. We haven't had time to set a date."

"I asked John to marry me," Nellie said with a grin. "Didn't I dear?"

"That's right. Couldn't believe it. She was always such a shy girl. We were sitting on her parents' porch swing one summer night. Drinking lemonade. All of a sudden out she pops with the big question. Unbelieveable."

"Didn't take you long to say yes, did it dear?"

"Nope," John responded and then he said, "Awful quick. Don't know what this world is coming to? We've been burying 'em faster than we can shake a stick and now we're gonna marry 'em off the same." He looked at Piper with suspicion. "You're not in the family way are you?"

"John!" Nellie half-screamed. "Now you quit that. That's none of our business. How would you like it if someone asked me that question?"

"That's okay, Nellie," Piper said. "No, John. I'm not in the family way as you put it." And then she looked puzzled. She'd just remembered that she and Matt hadn't taken any precautions.

"Well that's good to hear. Not healthy to start with a shotgun wedding. Couples should have a chance to get to know each other before they have kids. Kids are nice but they can be a pain in the ass—I mean rear."

"That's better," Nellie said. "I don't like it when you swear."

Suddenly, Piper felt her stomach churn. She thought she might be sick. Nellie noticed. "What's the matter, dear? You look a bit green at the gills?"

"I don't know," Piper said. "All of a sudden I feel sick to my stomach."

"Oh no!" John said. "Maybe you are in the family way. Nellie always got sick to her stomach the first week. Your lower back doesn't ache does it?"

"No," Piper fibbed. She would never admit to John that her back had been bothering her all day. That's crazy, she thought. This is all in my head. Too much has happened. It's impossible to feel pregnant so soon. Or is it? She really hadn't the foggiest what being pregnant felt like. Her stomach knotted again. "I have to go upstairs to the bathroom," she said and ran out of the kitchen.

Nellie and John looked at each other and shook their gray heads. "John," she said. "You don't suppose . . ."

"Time will tell, Nellie old girl. Time will tell. But that's no way to start out," he fussed.

"That's not what I meant, dear. I was about to remind you that I had the twenty-four hour flu the day before Kelly's funeral. Piper probably caught my germ. And besides. We did just fine with a baby, didn't we?"

"Yep. But we were married a good two years before our first one came along."

"Never you mind, dear. Piper and Matthew have good heads on their shoulders, too. They'll be fine with or without a baby."

"I suppose you're right, Nellie." He looked at the clock on the wall. "I have to go out to the barn and take care of the animals. What time is supper?"

"In about an hour. I'm going to peel the potatoes right now or do you want baked?"

"Mashed. With lots of butter and salt and pepper."

"Salt's no good for you and you know it. We have to use that substitute stuff like my doctor said."

"That old horse doctor," John sputtered. "What does he know about salt?"

"He knows plenty. Now get going out to the barn before the animals starve to death."

John had no sooner gone out the door when the phone rang. "Hello," Nellie said sweetly.

It was Mona, and she didn't even say hello. "Is Piper back yet?"

"Yes she is. But I don't think she can come to the phone right now."

"Why the hell not?"

"Because her stomach is upset and she's upstairs in the bathroom."

"Call her anyway. She probably wants to talk to me. Did John tell her that I phoned earlier?"

"Yes, he did. But I still don't think I should disturb her right now."

"Get her. I need to talk to her right now."

Nellie inhaled deeply and said, "All right. I don't want to, but I will. Hang on while I go to the stairs and yell to her." She let the receiver dangle in midair and left the kitchen. Out in the front hallway she yelled up the stairs to Piper as loudly as she could.

Piper came out of the bathroom more white-faced than before. "What is it, Nellie?"

"Mona's on the phone. I told her you don't feel too good but she insists on speaking to you. Do you want me to tell her you're not up to talking?"

"No. I'll talk. I feel awful. I must have a touch of stomach flu."

"Then I'll tell her you're sleeping, dear. That's only a little white lie."

"No, that's okay, Nellie. I'll talk to her. Is there a phone up here?"

"In my bedroom. Help yourself."

By the time Piper lifted the receiver to her ear Mona was livid from having waited so long.

"Jesus, Piper," she said coldly. "What the hell took you so long?"

"I'm sorry, Mona. I don't feel so hot." Mona's voice was

so irritating it made her aching head throb worse.

"I called to see if you would come and spend the night with me."

"I would, but I feel so awful all I want to do is go to bed. Is there anyone else you can call? How about your friend Lucy?"

"She's not my friend. I couldn't spend a minute with her, let alone a whole night. Besides, she's under a doctor's care for her nerves. She's tranquilized out of her mind."

"Oh, that's too bad," Piper said.

"Lots of things are too bad. Look. I have to go. I'm really disappointed that you won't come and spend the night. I had a surprise for you. I was going to give it to you at my Halloween party but then Kelly was murdered."

Piper didn't hear the part about the surprise, because her stomach churned again. She said, "I have to hang up now." She cradled the receiver and ran to the bathroom, making it just in time. After she felt better she went to her room and flopped on her bed. Every muscle ached. Minutes later she was sound asleep. She didn't even hear Nellie come in to check on her. An hour later she was awake and back in the bathroom again. If she didn't feel better by morning she wouldn't be able to make it to Steven's funeral.

Matt called around nine and Nellie answered. She congratulated him on being engaged. He laughed because Piper couldn't keep it a secret after all. Nellie told him that Piper had come down with her flu bug and was now sound asleep.

"Shall I come over and take care of her?"

"You can if you want," Nellie told him. "But you won't do her much good. She's sleeping soundly now."

"I won't bother her, then." He didn't tell Nellie that he'd called Piper to tell her that he'd talked to his father about getting married, and about how happy his father was. The news would have to wait until tomorrow.

"You need your rest, too, Matthew," Nellie said and proceeded to tell him that if Piper had the twenty-four hour bug then he was apt to come down with it soon. "It hits fast and leaves as quick," she cautioned. "Piper will feel better by tomorrow, but she won't be up to going to Steven's funeral."

"Will you tell her that I called?"

"I surely will, dear. Now you take care of yourself. Like I said, those germs spread like wildfire. Goes through everyone in sight. Go to bed. Get plenty of rest. That's the best thing."

"Thanks for the advice, Nellie. I am exhausted. I'm going to grab a sandwich and hit the hay."

"Don't eat a sandwich, Matthew. Chicken soup. Best thing for you. Do you have any fresh cloves of garlic?"

"Yes. Why?"

"Cleans your germs out. Chop up a couple of cloves and lace your soup with it. I'll bet you a dollar you won't catch any flu if you do what I tell you."

"You're the doctor, Nellie. Tell Piper that I'll call her in the morning to see how she feels. Good night."

"Night dear. Sweet dreams."

The next morning, Piper woke up feeling like she'd been hit by a truck. Her stomach was no longer sick, but her head throbbed from the slightest movement and when she got up she felt so weak she didn't think she could make it to the bathroom. When she came out she went right back to her bed. There was no way she could attend Steven's funeral. She dozed and awoke when she heard someone tapping on her door. "Who is it?" she asked weakly.

"Nellie. May I come in?"

"Please," Piper told her.

Nellie opened the door. "How are you feeling, dear?" Piper opened her eyes and noticed that Nellie was dressed up.

"Terrible. My head is killing me."

"What a shame. Can I get you some aspirin?"

"No thanks. What time is it?"

"Almost ten. John and I are leaving for Steven's funeral now."

"Oh, God. The funeral," Piper said, trying to sit up. The room spun and pain ripped through her head. "Ouch," she cried and laid her head back on the pillow. "I guess I can't go. Has Matt phoned?"

"Several times, dear. Once last night and four times this morning. He's so worried about you. I keep telling him you'll be fine. We're going to meet him at the funeral home. Any messages?"

"Yes. Please ask him to call me this afternoon around two. Maybe by then I'll feel better and can talk."

"I'll tell him. Do you want me to get you some ginger ale before I leave?"

"No thanks. I don't feel like putting anything on my stomach yet. Nellie?" she said and sighed.

"What is it, dear?"

"Please explain to Mona why I couldn't come to the funeral. She may not understand. But it doesn't hurt to try."

"I'll tell her. Now you get some more sleep. That's the best thing. You'll be fit as a fiddle by night. That nasty bug leaves as fast as it hit."

"I sure hope so," Piper said sleepily as Nellie quietly made her exit.

Piper slept until Crutches barked and woke her. When she sat up in bed she discovered that she felt better, although her head still ached a little. Standing up, she still felt weak, but better than earlier that morning.

She made her way to the window and looked outside. Nellie and John were walking up the porch steps. Piper glanced at the clock on the bureau and saw it was after one. The funeral was over. *Thank God*, she thought. *I really didn't want to go.* She stared at seemingly nothing outside, her thoughts full of Kelly and Steven. She still couldn't believe they were dead.

Someone knocked on her door and brought her out of her stupor. "Piper, dear. It's me, Nellie. Are you awake?"

"Come in, Nellie."

Nellie was pleased to see Piper out of bed. "You look better," she said. "Not quite so pale. Feel like eating some chicken soup now?"

"Yes. I think that would give me some strength. I'm still weak as a dishrag."

"I'd be happy to bring you a tray. How about some nice dark toast and butter?"

The thought of food made Piper feel ill again. "No thanks, Nellie. How did the funeral go?"

"It was nice. Lovely casket. Mona picked it out. The undertaker, Mr. Watts, told John that she had him hire someone to change the lining."

"What do you mean?"

"Well, it was beige and she wanted light blue. Mr. Watts said it cost a lot of money for her to do that."

Piper didn't want to hear another word. "Did you ask Matt to call me this afternoon?"

"Yes. He's such a nice boy. Fretting something terrible because you're sick. He's going to make a wonderful husband and father."

Piper hugged herself and said, "I know."

"Well," Nellie said. "I'd better go downstairs and get your soup ready. Are you coming down with me?"

"No. I think I need to take a shower and change my clothes. I'll be down shortly."

Piper felt almost normal after she showered and dressed in fresh clothes. She even felt hungry. After she finished her soup she said, "You know what, Nellie?"

"What, dear?"

"I think I'll go back to work tomorrow. I need something constructive to do. Besides, Tatjana is losing money with the shop closed."

"Are you sure you feel up to snuff enough to go back?"

"Yes. I have to. Mona is in no shape to go. The more I think about it, the more I look forward to it."

"That's good, dear. Tatjana will appreciate it." The phone rang and Nellie answered. "Yes, Matthew. She's feeling much better. She's right here."

Piper got up from the table and took the receiver from

Nellie. "Hi, Matt. Sorry I wasn't able to talk to you when you called."

"That's okay. Are you feeling better?"

"Much. I hope you don't get it."

"I think I have it."

"Oh, no. You poor thing. Do you want me to come over to your place and take care of you?"

"I would love it but you're not well enough yet. I want you to get a good night's rest."

He was right; she still felt rocky. "I have to admit it. I really don't feel all that great. But I will come if you need me."

"Nope. I can manage. I love you."

"I love you, too."

"I told my father about our getting married."

"You did. What did he say?"

"He was thrilled. He can hardly wait to meet you. We're going to dinner there on Saturday night. Is that okay with you?"

"Fine," Piper said and paused. "How was the funeral?"

"Different. Mona was very composed. She acted like she was hostessing a party. She sure has expensive taste. One of Mr. Watt's assistants told me that she paid a lot of money for Steven's casket. Not many flowers. Just orchids. They aren't cheap," he said and felt his stomach rumble. "I think I'd better hang up. I'll call you tomorrow. I love you."

"I love you," she said. After she cradled the receiver she turned and faced Nellie. "Matt's sick."

"Doesn't surprise me any," Nellie said. "You should go back to bed and get some more rest." The phone rang again. Nellie answered.

It was Mona. "I want to speak to Piper," she demanded. Nellie handed Piper the phone. "It's Mona," she whispered.

"Hello, Mona." Piper said. "How are you doing?"

"I'm okay. Were you really too ill to come to the funeral?"

"Yes. Otherwise I would've been there. Why do you ask?"

"I was just wondering."

"Where are you?"

"I'm home."

"All alone?"

"Of course."

"Can't you get somebody to spend the night?"

"That's why I called you."

"I would but I can't. I'm too sick. Why don't you come here? I'm sure Nellie and John won't mind. Do you want me to ask? Nellie is right here."

"No. I'm too tired to drive all that distance. I can make it through the night. How about coming tomorrow?"

"I can't. I've decided to go back to work."

"Why so soon?"

"Because I think it would be good for me. Besides, Tatjana is losing money with the shop closed."

"Will you spend the night with me tomorrow night?"

"I can't. I promised to spend the evening with Matt."

"You mean the night," Mona snapped. "Some friend you are. I've just lost Steven and I'm all alone. A lot you care."

"That's not true, Mona. I do care. But to be perfectly honest I don't think I can come to your house again." She knew she sounded as angry as she felt.

"Why for God's sake?"

"Because Kelly was murdered there. I don't think I could stand to see your living room." There, I said it, she said to herself. "I hope you understand." She really didn't care if she didn't.

"Well I don't."

"Mona, please. It's been difficult for both of us. I don't want to fight. Look. I have to hang up now. I'm not feeling well. I'll talk to you later." Piper didn't give her a chance to say anything before she hung up.

"Did she give you a hard time?" Nellie asked.

"Sort of. She's such a strange person. I really don't

understand her."

"I know, dear. She is peculiar, but it takes all kinds. She'll come around as soon as she gets over the shock of losing both Kelly and Steven."

Mona was in a rage over Piper hanging up on her. She had no idea that she was becoming more deranged by the hour. Her plan to kill Piper had been spoiled. How was she going to get at her? She paced the living room floor for a solid half hour trying to think.

Just as she was about to go out to the kitchen to pour herself a glass of white wine to calm her nerves, she thought of an idea so wonderful that she clapped her hands and did a little dance. "Piper," she said out loud. "That stupid bitch had the right idea! If she won't come here to me—then I'll go to the farm and get her! I'll kill the Stolls, too. And that fucking dog. Who knows maybe Detective Carter will drop by." She laughed until she almost cried and then said, "And now for that glass of wine."

Chapter Twelve

So Cold

Mona arrived unexpectedly at the farm, along with frigid winds that rushed in from Canada. At Memory Gardens, flowers on Steven's grave were lifted in the gusts and scattered across the frozen ground. There was snow coming, and Maine would soon be dusted in virginal white.

At the farm in Freeport, Gertie, John's cow was in the barn, ready to be milked. Crutches, delighted with the weather, trotted briskly at John's side as they made their way from the warmth of the cozy house out to the barn so John could do his chores. John was well aware of his dog's energy. "Whoa," he said. "Where do you get your pep? You're not a young pup, you know. Quit that kid stuff." Crutches stopped in his tracks, snorted, and wagged his bushy tail. He trotted on as if all the more energized. John had all he could do to keep up with his four-footed pal.

Upstairs, Piper stirred and snuggled deeper under the covers. There were four quilts piled on top of her, yet her feet were cold. She exhaled and the vapor made her look like she was smoking. As the days grew shorter and colder, it was harder for her to get out of her bed in the morning. Just the thought of her feet hitting that cold floor made her shiver. She lay there and wondered if Tatjana was ever going to break down and pay to have the upstairs heated.

After that her thoughts shifted to Matt. She stretched her lithe body, remembering how wonderful it was when they made love. She wished he was there beside her right now so she could cuddle against him.

The alarm clock on the old-fashioned smoking stand next to her bed said that it was time for Piper to get ready for her first day back at Tatjana's since Kelly's death. She dreaded the confrontation with the fact of her friend's absence. *Enough morbid thoughts,* she said to herself.

"One, two, three, four, five," she counted, then bravely tossed the covers aside and leaped out of bed, shivering when her bare feet connected with the cold pine boards. She quickly threw on her green robe and stepped into her tan leather fleece-lined slippers, but her feet and hands took a long time to warm up. *Cold hands—warm heart,* she said to herself. That was what John Stoll says to Nellie every morning when they go downstairs to breakfast. Blowing her breath on her hands to keep them warm, Piper went to her window and tugged on the green shade until she let go of it and it rolled with a snap. It made so much noise that she was afraid she'd wake Mona, who was asleep in the next room. Piper expected to see daylight breaking over the hillside, but the window was coated with a thick layer of frost. It was a pretty sight, and it made her remember when she and Kelly used their fingernails to make lacey designs on windowpanes. "Kelly," she whispered and felt a terrible churning sensation deep in her stomach.

A door opened and closed out in the hallway. Mona must be awake. Piper knew that she should do everything possible to help her get through this dark time. With that benevolent thought in mind she opened her bedroom door and peeked out to see if she could see Mona.

The hallway was empty, but she could hear the sound of running water in the bathroom. Mona was in the shower. Piper debated whether or not to go downstairs and help Nellie fix breakfast while she waited to use the bathroom. She decided not to because she knew that John and Nellie enjoyed having the early morning hours to themselves.

She decided to read the latest issue of *Down East* magazine. The real estate ads fascinated her. Soon she would be able to live with Matt on Soudahook Lake. She sighed happily and began to flip the pages.

After chores, John and Crutches returned to the house to enjoy Nellie's usual farmer's breakfast of bacon, eggs, toast, homemade apple jelly, coffee, and juice. John told Nellie that seeing Crutches romp made him aware of his own age. "Getting to be an old rascal, right," he complained.

"Speak for yourself, dear," she replied.

"Well," John said. "Like they say. There may be snow on the roof but that doesn't mean the fire is out in the furnace." He winked and patted Nellie on the bottom.

"John," she mildly protested. "Quit that. How do you expect me to be able to fix your breakfast with you acting so lovey-dovey."

"Okay, Nellie, I'll behave," he promised and sat down at the table. Crutches sat next to him. He patted the dog's head. He noticed that Nellie was moving rather slowly for her. She kept putting a hand on her chest as if she hurt. "What's the matter?" he asked. "Your condition acting up?" He tried not to sound too concerned.

"Yes, John. My bones ache this morning. And my chest hurts," she said and winced. "Must've pulled a muscle somehow. Darn this old age stuff," she moaned. "I hurt more and more each winter. Maybe we should go south like other folks do until spring." The minute she said that she knew that she'd caused John's blood to boil.

"Jesus, Nellie," he grumbled. "Have you lost your reason? Go down there with them creepy-crawling things. You think you hurt now? Well I'll tell you, you'd be in worse shape if one of them alligators got hold of your toes. Makes me shudder to think about it. I'd have to nickname you Stubby."

Nellie laughed, put her hands on her hips, and said, "Oh, John. It's civilized down there. Besides, when's the last time you heard of anyone getting chewed up by a 'gator?"

"Never you mind, Nellie. I'd rather be planted six foot under than spend a winter stretched out in one of them fancy lawn chairs. Next you'll suggest we get ourselves one of those camper rigs. What do they call them? Can't remember." He scowled at the thought.

"RV's," Nellie said as she put a cookie sheet full of her butter-brushed biscuits into the oven. She wiped her hands on her apron and said, "Never mind about going south. We've got enough to do around here this winter. I love having Piper here, but that other one gives me a bad feeling."

"I know what you mean," John agreed. "She's a pip. Cold as ice. Hasn't shed one tear over that husband of hers." The very mention of Steven brought tears to Nellie's faded eyes. She pulled a hankie out of her apron pocket and blew her nose.

"Now, now, Nellie. Don't start blubbering all over the place. Too early for that stuff. Your eyes will get all puffy. Next thing you know you'll have to put those drops in them to see straight." John stood up and walked over to his wife and put his arm around her shoulder. "Would you cry over me if I was a murderer?"

"Yes, John. I would. But don't be so silly. Sometimes you sound awful bad but you wouldn't harm a fly."

He tugged on his beard and said seriously, "If it's any comfort, I really do understand what you just said about Mona. Cold as a witch's tit. Must've been some kind of chilly underneath the sheets with her."

"John," Nellie said. "Stop that nasty talk."

"No other words to say it, Nellie. She's more frigid than poor Steven's corpse."

"That's enough, John. She might hear you. Old men can't say such things and get away with it. Heavens. They'll call you senile."

"You're right about that. If a younger fella like Matt said it folks would think it was a funny joke. An old fella like me pops it out and they'd call me gone in the head."

"Matthew wouldn't talk nasty and you know it, John." And then Nellie's voice softened when she said, "Oh,

John. Sometimes you're so difficult. Be good and go fill the dog's water bowl. He's almost out and I think he needs some food in his other dish. Poor thing would starve if I didn't remind you to take care of his needs."

Mona came through the door, unsmiling, dressed in a wool red-and-black plaid bathrobe, with dark red slippers on her feet. "I'm going to freeze to death upstairs," she complained. "And it took forever for the hot water. It never did get warm enough. Breakfast ready yet?"

"Not quite," Nellie told her and took her in from head to toe. She could tell that Mona had her makeup on. "Nice robe. Slippers match just right. But you should wear long stockings. It's awful cold this morning. If you go outside you'd best bundle up. Wear a warm hat, scarf, and mittens or Jack Frost will get you."

"He already has," John mumbled and sipped his coffee.

"What did you say, dear?" Nellie asked him. She smiled and Mona glared straight at him as they waited for him to repeat what he'd mumbled.

"I said it's almost half past," he fibbed. "Is breakfast about ready?" He had his eye on Crutches. Usually the dog wanted to be petted by guests, but he didn't go near Mona. *Good judge of character,* John thought. *Had that girl been born in the right century, in Salem, Massachusetts, she'd have been burned at the stake, and I'd have lit the match. Warm her up a bit.*

"John. Are you listening to me?" Nellie asked. "I said I was waiting for Piper so we could all sit down at the table together." Then she turned and said to Mona, "Really, dear. You should pay attention to what I said about dressing warm today."

"Thanks," Mona said coldly. "But I think I'm quite old enough to know how to take care of myself."

John couldn't resist. He scowled and said, "Well that's true enough. I'd guess you must be pushing forty or better. Right?" He knew she was only in her early thirties but that would teach her to be so mean to Nellie. It didn't take long for him to see that he'd got her good. Her cheeks had turned almost as red as her slippers.

241

Mona's voice trembled with rage when she snapped, "My age is my business."

Nellie saved the moment when she said sweetly to Mona, "I think I'll cook up some scrambled eggs, laid fresh this morning. John brought them in from the hen house a little while ago. But before I tackle that, why don't I get you a cup of nice hot coffee, a piece of toast, and some of my homemade strawberry jam? I made the bread, too."

"Please," Mona said coolly and picked up the morning paper off the table.

"Nellie's right," John said unconcerned that Mona wasn't paying any attention. "Miserable outside. Windy and spitting snow. I heard the weather report on the radio earlier. We might be in for some freezing rain. And the temperature is supposed to drop way down tonight." Mona didn't pay any attention to his weather report, so he said to Nellie, "Think I'll go check on the pigs. Be back for one of those terrific biscuits of yours in a jiffy." Crutches started to follow him. "Stay put, old boy. I'll be back in a few minutes."

John had no sooner stepped out the door when Piper came bounding into the kitchen, already showered and dressed for work. "Morning you two," she said to Mona and Nellie.

Mona mumbled something that sounded like a greeting and continued reading the paper.

"Piper," Nellie said with a smile. "Land, child. Aren't you a ray of sunshine on this dismal morning. Bet it has something to do with that nice boy, Matthew. There's a glow about you. I had the same thing when I met John."

Mona looked up from the paper and snickered. "How could you possibly remember that far back?"

Nellie looked stunned.

"Mona. That's not nice," Piper said sternly.

"Wasn't meant to be," Mona replied and went back to reading the paper.

Piper had to bite her tongue to keep from giving her hell. "Are you working this morning?" she asked determined to get things on an even keel.

Mona didn't answer.

Piper repeated the question. She was losing patience.

Mona sighed deeply and said, "No. If you must know, I'm not going to work. I don't feel up to it yet."

Piper tried to reason with her. "Look, Mona," she said softly. "I know it's none of my business but I think I might've been wrong. The idle mind is the devil's workshop, so they say. Anyway, because of Kelly, I thought going back to Tatjana's would be the worst thing for me, but I was wrong. I wish that you'd change your mind and come with me today. How about it?"

"You're right, Piper," Mona agreed. "It's none of your business. I'm getting sick of this shit. If it's not Nellie telling me how to dress, what to eat, how to wipe my ass— then you're on my case. Just mind your own business—all of you."

Color tinted Piper's cheeks. She was about to really let Mona have it, but she didn't get a chance because Nellie had reached her limit, too. "Look here young lady," she said sharply to Mona. "I've had just about enough of your snippy ways. If you're going to be so miserable I think you'd better pack up and leave."

Mona laughed. "You can't be serious."

"Well I am." Nellie said, standing her ground.

"Give me a break. Who died and left you boss?" Mona had spoken so loud that she couldn't hear Crutches growling at her. And she paid no attention to the hackles that had risen on his neck. Piper noticed. She walked over to the dog and patted him on top of the head.

"Easy, big boy," she crooned. "It's okay." She turned and faced Mona. "Stop it, Mona. The dog is upset. Look. We all know that you've been through a lot losing Steven and Kelly. But we're hurting, too. Stop taking your frustrations out on us."

"Yes," Nellie agreed. "Piper's right. I won't make you leave if you do."

Mona stood up and laughed in Nellie's face. "Piper's

right. Piper's right. Jesus. I can't take any more of this shit. I'm going upstairs to my room." She stomped out of the kitchen.

Awkward silence filled the room. Piper had a headache. She rubbed her temples and debated whether or not to take some Aspirin. It was Nellie who spoke first. "Land. That woman is awful. If you were to ask me I'd say that she needs a good swig of Castor Oil. That's what my mother used to give me when I was cranky. She always said that when I was in a grumpy mood that I must be constipated."

Piper couldn't help but laugh. "Good idea, Nellie. Maybe I'll give Mona a dose of that stuff myself. God. I don't know about that woman. I wish she'd leave." And then Piper looked at Nellie and wondered if all the commotion was too much on her and John. "Nellie. Would you prefer that we both leave?" She prayed that she would say she wanted them to stay.

"No, no, dear. We like having *you* here. And as far as that other one, once she has a good bowel movement her disposition will improve. You'll see. Maybe a bowl of bran cereal . . ."

The door opened and John came into the house along with a blast of cold air. "Wind is blowing pretty strong out there. Snowing. Don't know if you should drive into the city," he said to Piper. "Have a feeling the weatherman made a mistake. I think it's going to snow to beat the band and the roads are gonna be slicker than pig snot."

"I'll be okay," Piper said cringing over his choice of words. "I don't think it's going to be that bad."

"Yes it is. I've been around enough winters to get the feel of what's coming."

"Breakfast is ready," Nellie interrupted, plunking a heaping basket of hot biscuits on the table. Next she brought eggs, bacon, juice, and coffee. All three sat down, but Piper had to force herself to eat so she wouldn't hurt Nellie's feelings. The tiff she'd had with Mona had killed her appetite. *Mona*, she thought. *She's not just crabby. There's something different about her. Her eyes looked so wild. And that look on her face.* Piper couldn't erase the image. She took a bite of her eggs and swallowed with difficulty. She didn't think she could eat another bite. Then the phone rang and saved her. John got up and answered.

"Hi there," he said. Nellie and Piper stared at him, waiting for him to say who it was he was speaking to. "Yes. She's here. Hold the line a second. Piper. It's Matt."

Piper got up from the table and rushed to the phone. "Hi, Matt."

"Hi, honey. I called to tell you that you should keep an eye on the weather. One of the guys just told me that he heard over the radio that there is a possibility of a severe ice storm later this afternoon. Take your time going to work. Been a lot of accidents already."

"I'll be careful. Thanks for the warning," she said and then she whispered into the receiver, "I love you."

"I love you, too. I'll see you tonight."

"What time?"

"Probably around seven."

"Seven is fine."

"Tell him to come to supper, dear," Nellie interjected.

"I heard," Matt said before Piper had a chance to tell him. "Tell her thanks and that I'd love to have supper."

She repeated what Matt said. Nellie beamed. "Bye, Matt," Piper said and blew a kiss into the receiver and hung up. It wasn't until she was seated at the table that she remembered that she'd forgotten to tell Matt that Mona had arrived last night.

"Heard you whispering to that young fella," John said as he spread butter on a hot biscuit.

"Snoop," Piper said with a grin. "Know what, John?"

"What?"

"I love Matt Carter."

"You don't say," John teased. "Hear that, Nellie? Piper's in love. When's the wedding?"

"I don't know," Piper said. "We haven't had time to set a date yet." She got up from the table. "I'm going to be late for work if I don't hurry." She braced herself against the kitchen wall for support as she pulled on her boots. She lifted her dark green wool coat, beige angora tam, and shoulder-length brown leather purse off a brass hook on the oak tree stand and put them on. "I'll call you later. Good luck with Mona today."

"Thanks," John said. "We'll need it. That woman depresses me so much I think I'll go down cellar and jump out the window." He laughed and slapped his thigh.

Piper tried not to laugh at John's joke when she opened the door and said, "Have a nice day you two."

"You too, dear," Nellie said.

Piper stepped outside. It was snowing heavily now. She could see her breath as she dashed to her car. She looked up. By the looks of the sky the sun wasn't about to come out. Maybe John had been right about the weather and Matt had said . . . Oh, well. But she'd be careful.

It turned out that there was no need to be concerned, because the roads weren't slippery. The salt trucks had obviously been out. She caught 295 to Portland. Once there, she took the Washington Avenue exit and shot across the Eastern Promenade to the old waterfront district to Tatjana's shop. Piper enjoyed the view from the promenade as it overlooked some of the cottage-studded islands out in Casco Bay. There was always something to see—and right that minute an island ferry clipped along leaving a foamy wake as it transported year-round residents to the mainland. Piper and Kelly had often brought their lunch to the Prom in good weather. But this morning the view was dismal. The white-capped choppy water appeared quite menacing with the island ferry struggling to keep an even keel and several fishing boats bobbing wildly. And worse, Kelly wasn't there. Piper had no idea how she was going to feel when she walked into Tatjana's. She felt tears coming. It was time to think about something else.

Back at the farm, Mona was still upstairs in her room. John and Nellie were still in the kitchen. He was reading the paper and she was washing the breakfast dishes. Every so often she stopped and clutched at her chest.

John happened to see her, "What's the matter, Nellie?" he asked with concern. "That pulled muscle still bothering?"

"Yes. It's getting worse. And my left arm hurts. John, you don't suppose it's my heart, do you?"

"Nope. And I don't think you pulled a muscle. It's gas. Drink some warm water. That will make you burp and then you'll feel better."

Nellie drank a full glass of warm water. She burped as John predicted and felt better for a few minutes, but the pain continued. John got up from the table and peeked out the window over the sink. "Look at that," he said and shook his gray head. "Crazy weather people. This one is going to be a beaut if you ask me."

"I think you're right, dear," Nellie agreed. "I think I'll go upstairs now and make our bed. Then I'll rest a bit and see if this ache won't go away. Maybe I should use some of that horse liniment?"

"Nope. Don't do that yet," John answered. "Stuff smells to high heaven and it might burn your skin. I'm going out to the barn and work on the tractor for a spell. Need anything before I go?"

"No. I'm all set. Watch yourself with that tractor. Last winter you nearly cut your thumb off."

"I will. You stay out of Frosty's way."

"Frosty?"

"Mona."

"I'll try to avoid her, dear. You missed her performance before breakfast. She was awful to Piper. I told her she had to leave if she didn't stop it."

"What did she say to that?"

"She laughed. And you know what else she said, John?"

"What?"

"Well, I was telling Piper that she had the same kind of look on her face as I had when I met you and Mona asked me how I could remember . . ."

John's temper flared. "Nobody talks to you that way and gets away with it, Nellie. When I come in from the

247

barn I'm gonna tell her to pack up and get out."

"You could set a fire underneath her and I bet she wouldn't budge, John."

"She'll go. I'll make her, even if I have to drag her by the hair. Miserable woman," John sputtered as he put on his boots, coat, hat, and gloves, and went outside to the barn.

Mona paced her bedroom floor. Every so often she talked out loud to herself. Her mind was full of hatred. She knew that she couldn't take much more of Piper and those two ancient assholes. She would kill all of them and she would do it now. But how? And she must hurry before Piper left for work. She paced and paced until she came up with a solution to her dilemma. Strangling was out—shooting was no good. She wanted something messy. Stabbing was the answer. Yes! That was the way to go. She would go down to the kitchen and get a butcher knife and cut their throats from ear to ear. What a thrill it was going to be to see them bleed to death. Mona laughed and then she pouted. Watts was going to be disappointed. There wasn't going to be enough blood left for him to embalm Piper when she was through with her. What a pity.

And then she heard a noise in the driveway. She ran to her bedroom window, peeked out, and saw Piper driving off. "Sonofabitch," she cried and kicked the wall. "I'll have to wait until she comes back from work." Then her eyes lit up and she said out loud. "But I can kill John and Nellie." She started for the door and stopped. Now she had second thoughts. It would be better if she waited until dark when everybody slept. Sneaking up on them was the way to do it. Instead of stabbing, she decided it would be more fun to bash their heads in with John's hammer—if she could find it. If not, Nellie's rolling pin would do. Now what about that fucking dog? She was at a loss as to how to get rid of him.

She went to her bed and flopped on it. She was tired of thinking. She would rest all day to save her strength. What she was going to do would be exhausting, especially if anyone put up a fight. The thought of Piper doing so thrilled her. She would like nothing better than to beat

248

that bitch senseless before she finished her off. That's when it hit her that she should write down everything so as not to forget anything. She opened her purse and took out a small pad of paper. Minutes later, Mona was deeply engrossed in writing a synopsis. She enjoyed putting her thoughts down and even wrote about how she murdered Kelly and about what had happened to Steven. Then she wrote about the redhead and her first husband. When she was finished she read every page over and over. She thought it was so good it should be published. There was no question in her mind. She was a brilliant writer.

An hour later, John and Crutches came in from the barn. Snow clung to their eyelashes and John's beard. He stomped his boots before he pulled them off. A puddle formed on the floor around them. He removed his gloves, coat, and hat. Nellie wasn't in the kitchen. He assumed she was still resting upstairs. He went up there to check on her. In the hallway, he could hear talking coming from Mona's room. He assumed she had her television on or her radio. And then he thought that perhaps Nellie was in there with her. But when he opened his bedroom door, he saw Nellie seated on the edge of their bed, holding onto her chest. He was alarmed over the pasty-white color of her face. "Nellie," John said. "What's wrong?"

"John, the pain is getting worse. I don't think it's gas that ails me. You'd better call Dr. Garside."

John was scared but he tried not to show it. He knew that Nellie wouldn't mention the doctor unless she was in big trouble. "Okay, I'll call him," he said. He lifted the receiver off the phone on the nightstand next to their bed and dialed information. Seconds later the doctor's answering service informed him that they would contact Dr. Garside right away. John hung up and put his arm around Nellie. "You're gonna be just fine, sweetie pie. Hold tight to the rigging. The girl said that she'd get hold of the doctor. He'll probably prescribe some of that milky stuff to get the gas up."

The phone rang. John answered. It was the doctor. John described Nellie's symptoms. The doctor told him not to let Nellie exert herself and that he was to bring her to the Maine General Hospital as quickly as possible. He said that he would meet them in the emergency room.

When John hung up, he tried to act normal when he told Nellie what they had to do. She started to get off the bed.

"You sit right there," John ordered. "Dr. Garside said you're not to exert yourself."

"But I need my knee-high nylons and my good black shoes. I can't go to the hospital in these old things." She looked at the worn blue flowered slippers on her tiny feet.

"Relax, Nellie. I'll get your stuff for you."

"And . . . and I need," she paused and gripped her chest.

"What do you need?" John asked softly. "Tell me, honey bun. I'll get it for you."

"I need my pink bloomers," she said. "There are several pair in the top drawer of my dresser."

"Now that's a job I know I'll enjoy," John teased.

Ten minutes later, John had Nellie dressed and ready to leave. He helped her to her feet. She leaned her frail body against him for support. She was perspiring. Out in the hallway, they heard music coming from Mona's room. "Stop a minute, Nellie," John said. "We'd better tell Frosty where we're headed." He knocked on the door.

"Who is it?" Mona asked.

"It's John Stoll. Open the door a minute."

"No. I'm not dressed. What do you want?"

"Nellie's not feeling good. I called the doctor I'm taking her to the Maine General Hospital in Portland. We're leaving now. Don't know when we'll be back. Keep an eye on the place and on Crutches will you?"

Mona didn't answer.

John and Nellie started on their way downstairs. He wanted to rave over Mona not having the decency to answer him or to open the door and offer help. But he kept his thoughts to himself for fear of upsetting Nellie. His thoughts were black. Never in all his born days had he met a person as unfeeling as that Hadley woman. He decided that as soon as Nellie and he got back home that he'd ask her to leave. They didn't need her kind hanging around.

Crutches greeted them with a wagging tail when they reached the kitchen. John had Nellie sit on a chair while he got her boots and coat for her. The dog was in the way every second when he tried to dress Nellie. "Good boy," Nellie said while she patted his neck with her frail hand.

"You know something is wrong with our Nellie, don't you?" John said to the dog. "Well, we have to go out for a couple of hours but don't you worry. We'll be back in time to fix your supper. You be good while we're gone. I'd stay out of Frosty's way if I were you," he warned Crutches. He hugged the dog and then he helped Nellie up and they left.

Nellie was quiet in the car. John kept glancing her way to see if she was still okay. A couple of times he heard her moan, and he saw her continually grab her chest. She asked him to hurry. That worried him even more, because Nellie hated speed. When he noticed that she was perspiring again he laid a heavy foot on the gas. His old eyes showed him that the speedometer was on eighty. He was near the town of Falmouth when he spied a blue flashing light in his rearview mirror. He pulled into the parking lane and eventually crawled to a stop. "Sonofabitch," he muttered.

"What's happening?" Nellie asked weakly.

"I was speeding. Coppers are after me. Don't worry, Nellie. This shouldn't take long."

"Hurry, John. It hurts me to breathe."

John rolled down his window and came face to face with a rugged, round-faced, young State Trooper with a thin black mustache. John smiled and said in his most pleasant voice, "How ya doing, young fella?"

"Going a little fast there wouldn't you say?" the trooper asked.

"Yup. I was doing eighty or better. Give me my ticket. I haven't got time to make small talk."

"Is that so. Well, now. Would you mind telling me what's your hurry."

"My wife's ailing. I'm taking her to the hospital."

The trooper glanced at Nellie. She managed to smile at him as she clutched at her chest. A ton of bricks didn't have to fall on the trooper to know that the woman was probably having a heart attack. There was no time to waste. She could die any second. "Look," he said to John. "You get in my car and I'll carry your wife. I can get you to the hospital a lot faster and in one piece."

John didn't argue. He climbed out of his seat, pushed the button down on the lock, and slammed the door. He walked quickly to the trooper's car.

The trooper, who when standing straight, towered well over six feet tall, opened Nellie's door. "Hello, Ma'am," he said. "Relax now. I'm going to lift you into my arms and carry you to my car. Just let me do the work."

"Okay," Nellie said. "What's your name?"

"Frank Nelson," he said and lifted her into his arms without effort because she was as light as a feather. He freed one hand, pushed the button and then he closed the door.

"This is nice of you, Frank." Nellie said sweetly.

"Glad to help," Frank said and gently put her down on the front seat. He ran to his side and climbed behind the wheel. "What's your name?" he asked her.

"Nellie Stoll. My husband's name is John. We live on a farm in Freeport. Do you know Matthew Carter?"

"Yes. How do you know him?" He reached across her and buckled her safety belt. He told John to do the same.

"Nope," John said. "Never used one before and I'm not about to start now."

"I'm afraid you'll have to if you're going to ride with me." John could tell the fellow meant business and he buckled his belt.

"How do you folks know Matt Carter?" Frank asked again.

"He's sweet on a girl we know," John explained.

Nellie started to say something. "Mrs. Stoll," Frank Nelson interrupted, "please don't talk. You shouldn't exert yourself. Hang on. We'll be at the hospital in just a couple of minutes."

Frank Nelson radioed ahead to make certain that the Maine General Hospital knew that Nellie Stoll was on the way. She was very quiet now and had closed her eyes. John had to fight the urge to get out of his safety belt and pat her shoulder for moral support. Instead he kept saying, "It's gonna be okay, Nellie. We're almost there . . ." Finally he stopped saying that and he looked at the back of the trooper's head and asked, "Say, what's going to become of my car?"

"No problem. I'll make arrangements for someone to drive it to the hospital for you if you'll trust me with your keys."

"Remind me to give them to you at the hospital," John said.

"No. You'd better do it now or we're apt to forget."

John reached deep into his coat and brought forth his black leather key case. He tossed it over the front seat. Frank Nelson groped until he found it and then he put it on the dash.

Nellie was in more pain now. She sat hunched over. She couldn't remember ever hurting so bad—not even when the children were born. She wasn't so sure it wasn't her heart acting up. She said a silent prayer. *Dear God. If it's my time please don't let me linger. John hasn't got enough money to keep me in a nursing home. Take care of him, Lord. He doesn't know how to cook anything but lumpy tomato soup. And please don't let him chip any of my good dishes.*

By the time they arrived at the emergency room parking lot the snow had changed to freezing rain. Frank Nelson parked as close to the double doors as he could get. John unbuckled and climbed out right away. He tried to open Nellie's door and remembered that it was locked. "Open up," he said and tapped on the window.

Nellie didn't have a chance to do anything because Frank Nelson said, "Don't move." He unbuckled his seat belt. "I'll do everything for you." He unbuckled her and then he reached across her and pulled her door handle and pushed it open. He looked up at a hovering John and said, "She shouldn't walk. Don't you touch her. I'll carry her." Frank opened his door and climbed out and quickly ran to Nellie before John changed his mind and tried to lift her. When Frank picked her up he noticed that her skin felt clammy. He tried not to jostle her too much as he ran towards the double doors that swung open the minute he faced them. "Are you okay, Mrs. Stoll?" he asked out of breath.

"Yes, dear," she said in a whisper. She paused a second and then she said, "If I should die, will you tell John that I love him. I left a note and some money for him in the sugar bowl, in the kitchen on the shelf over the stove." She couldn't seem to catch her breath.

"I promise I'll tell him," Frank said. "You're going to be just fine." He only hoped he'd told that frail little woman the truth. She was such a sweetheart.

John followed. Things were happening too fast for him, and he felt dizzy. They were inside the emergency room now. Two nurses and Frank placed Nellie on a gurney and whisked her through a pair of double swinging doors. John tried to follow. He was stopped by a heavyset nurse who pointed at three cubicles, complete with chairs, desks, computers, and female receptionists. Two cubicles were occupied—one by a young man and the other by an old man about John's age.

The nurse said to John, "You have to go over there and give one of those receptionists the necessary information they need. After that you may see your sister."

"She's not my sister. She's my wife," he grumbled.

"I'm sorry. Your wife?"

"Yes and I don't want to sit behind any desk and talk to any girl. I'm going with Nellie."

"I'm sorry. But you have to see one of those women first. Then you can go to Nellie."

"That's the craziest thing I've ever heard," John yelled. "Get out of my way. I'm going in there right now and nobody's gonna stop me if they know what's good for them." He'd doubled his fists as if he were going to belt that nurse. She noticed and backed up a few steps.

Frank Nelson was across the room talking to an orderly that he knew. He'd heard John yell at the nurse. He excused himself and walked over to them. "You have to do what she says, Mr. Stoll. How long has it been since you've been in a hospital?"

"About forty years," he sputtered.

"Well, times have changed," Frank Nelson said. "They have new rules these days. It's hospital policy that you have to provide them with the necessary information about Nellie and about insurance matters. It will only take a few minutes and then you can see her. Do you want me to help you with the information they need to get from you?"

"Sonofabitch," John grumbled. "They'll hold me for ransom next. Of all the low-down dirty tricks in the world this has to take the cake. Having to stop and give stupid information at a time like this." But John didn't argue further. There was no way he'd disagree with that nice young trooper after he'd been so good to Nellie. He'd do what that nurse had told him to do. He went to the empty cubicle and sat down.

The young woman behind the desk was busy typing and didn't acknowledge his presence. She was wearing a lime-green smock and a white name tag with black lettering on her breast pocket that said Judi Baker. John stared at her as he waited patiently for her to finish. When after a few minutes, she continued to ignore him he reached the end of his patience. He cleared his throat and began to tap his fingers on the desk. She got the message and without looking at him said, "I'll be with you in a minute."

John decided he'd waited long enough. He stood up. Judi stopped typing. "Where are you going?" she asked.

"To see my wife," John responded sharply. "I'm already an old man and I'm getting older every minute. I haven't got time to waste waiting for you to finish fiddling with that contraption."

"I'm all done now," Judi Baker said. "Please be seated. It won't take but a couple of minutes to fill out these forms and then you can go. I'll get in trouble if you don't." There was a pathetic tone to her voice.

John relented and sat back down because he didn't want the girl to get in trouble because of him. Ten minutes later, after he suffered through endless questions, he was free to go to Nellie. He didn't bother to thank Judi Baker because he really didn't think she deserved it. Besides he wasn't sure she was a real person. The only emotion she'd showed was when she said she'd get in trouble. What a robot, John thought. Her face was so damned rigid. He wouldn't be at all surprised if she was a mechanical doll.

Behind the double doors that John passed through was a large room with a long counter on the left and several curtained cubicles on the right. The place was filled with all sorts of strange-looking equipment, as well as doctors of all ages and sizes clad in white coats, pants, and polished shoes. A young nurse darted behind a curtained cubicle, came out, and went into another. Three more nurses were seated behind the counter. One was writing on a chart. Another was on the phone. The third, whom John found to be a pretty little thing, appeared to be making eyes at a strapping young doctor. Nobody paid any attention to John, although the nurse on the phone stared at him while she talked. John was the one who finally grabbed hold of a young doctor's arm and stopped him before he had a chance to get away. "Listen, Sonny. I'm looking for my wife. Her name is Nellie Stoll. Do you know what they've done with her?"

"No," the doctor said, "but if you wait just a minute I'll find out for you." Leaving John in the middle of the room, he went behind the counter and spoke to the nurse who had been writing on a chart. He looked at John and said, "Cubicle four. It's right behind you." He pointed in that direction.

John thanked him, pulled the white pleated curtain aside, and saw Nellie resting on a wheeled table that was covered with a white sheet. Her eyes were closed. A young nurse, who had just finished taking her blood pressure, smiled sweetly at John. He let the curtain go and he walked over to Nellie and poked her arm gently. "Hey," he said softly. "How are you doing?"

Nellie's eyes fluttered open. "Hi, dear. I'm doing better. Doesn't hurt quite as much as it did. Awful tired though. How about you?"

"I'm fine. Don't worry about me. Are they treating you okay?" He couldn't remember ever being as relieved as he was at that moment. Nellie had more natural color in her cheeks and she wasn't sweating. He laid a hand on her no longer clammy forehead. Maybe it wasn't her heart. Maybe it was a rip-roaring case of indigestion—just like he'd thought. Doctors. He wondered how many specialists racked up big bills for heart attacks when the poor sonsofbitches in their clutches had a bad case of gas.

"Are you her husband?" the nurse asked and interrupted John's thoughts.

"Well, she's not my sister," John replied and offered no more conversation. The girl was a nuisance. Didn't she know that he and Nellie needed some privacy? Did he have to tell her to get the hell out of the way?

"The doctor has been in and checked her," the nurse told him. "He had to leave to tend to another emergency. I'm sure he'll be back in a few minutes." She looked at John and said, "I know he'll want to talk to you."

"Hope he moves a little faster than that woman who's got her fanny plunked behind that electronic contraption in the other room."

The nurse ignored his comment and so did Nellie. She didn't have enough strength left in her tired body to get after him. "Why don't you drag that chair out of the corner and sit beside your wife?" the nurse asked. "Don't you think that would be more comfortable while you wait for Dr. Garside?"

John didn't answer. He simply dragged the chair across the floor to Nellie's bedside. The minute he sat he was aware that he felt tired. His feet ached and so did his back. He and Nellie couldn't ride with such excitement at their age.

The curtain was pulled back, and in walked Dr. Garside. "Hello John," he said in his deep voice, nodding to the nurse, and walked quickly to the other side of the table next to Nellie. "Well, now. How's my favorite patient?"

While Nellie explained her symptoms, Dr. Garside began to feel her abdomen with his fingers. That was enough for John. He wasn't about to watch his Nellie poked and probed. He stood, quickly pecked Nellie's cheek, and said, "I'll be just outside the curtain if you need me."

Nellie nodded. Dr. Garside said, "This shouldn't take long. I'll speak with you as soon as I'm finished. Don't go too far away."

"Nope." And then he remembered Piper. He knew he should phone her and let her know what had happened. "I will be in the hallway if you're looking for me," he said to the doctor. "I have to make a call. Going to phone Piper," he said to Nellie.

"Don't you upset her, John," Nellie cautioned. "I'm going to be okay. Isn't that right, Doctor Garside?"

"That's right, Nellie. Now you have to be quiet so I can listen to your heart."

"Okay," she said sweetly. "But can you please give me a blanket? I'm so cold."

Chapter Thirteen

Stormy Weather

When John found a payphone, he reached deep in his pant pocket and came out with a quarter, lifted the receiver, and dropped the coin into the slot. His index finger felt stiff as he poked the buttons.

Piper answered after the first ring. "Tatjana's."

"Piper. This is John Stoll."

"John," she said with concern because his voice sounded unusually serious. "Is everything okay?"

"'Fraid not. Nellie's had some sort of attack and I brought her to the Maine General."

"Oh, no. What sort of attack?"

"Dr. Garside doesn't know yet. Could be her heart. Could be indigestion. Personally, I think it's gas. The doctor is checking her now."

"How did you get to the hospital? Did Mona drive you? Did you take an ambulance?"

"I drove her. Was doing all right until I started stomping on the gas pedal. Trooper pulled me over. He was awful nice. Brought us the rest of the way to the hospital in his car. Must've been doing ninety. Fast bastard."

"Where's Mona?"

"She stayed at the farm." He was about to tell her that Mona hadn't acted like she gave a damn about Nellie, but he decided not to waste his breath. Besides, Dr. Garside might show up any minute and he didn't want to be caught gossiping like an old lady on the phone. "I have to get going," he said abruptly, cutting the conversation short. "I told Nellie I'd be right back."

"Wait, John. I'm going to close the shop and come to the hospital right away."

"Nope," John said. "No need to do that. Wait until the doctor finishes and tells me what's wrong. I'll call you back just as soon as I find out. Nellie might go home with me." He wished that were true.

"I'm coming," Piper said firmly. "Do you want me to phone Tatjana?"

"Nope. No need to alarm her yet." And then he cautioned, "I hope Tatjana doesn't find out you're closing up shop. I won't tell. Nellie won't either. But Mona will. Think you ought to ride it out until we know for sure what's wrong?"

"No. I could care less what Mona and Tatjana say. I'm coming to the hospital right away and that's final. Besides, business is very slow today because of the bad weather. It's still snowing. Now, where shall I meet you?"

"Stubborn as all get out aren't you? Well, have it your way. I'll wait for you in the emergency room hallway." In fact he was touched by Piper's concern over Nellie. She was an awful good girl. Not at all like that other thing at the farm.

". . . and, John?" Piper was saying.

"What?" he asked.

"Nellie will be okay. She's tough and Dr. Garside is one of the best around."

"I hope so. Doctors bury their mistakes, you know? I'm going to hang up. I have to get back to Nellie."

"I'll be there as quickly as I can," Piper said in one breath while there was time, and then she cradled the receiver. She grabbed her purse and coat out of the back room, turned off the lights, and locked the door on her way out.

The snow was beginning to turn into freezing rain, and

the minute she took a step outside she slipped and almost fell. When she drove out of the parking garage next to Tatjana's she skidded in the direction of a slate-gray Mercedes sedan. She held her breath and at the last second managed to gain control of her car. Piper drove slowly across nearly empty Congress Street, passing by the poet Longfellow's brick home, then Raffles Book Store, the State Theater, Joe's Smoke Shop, and the Good Egg Cafe. Finally, she reached Benedict Street where the hospital was located. She turned right and continued to creep to her destination. Ordinarily it would have taken her no more than five minutes to reach the hospital from the waterfront. This time it took her over twenty.

She drove into the emergency area parking lot. The place was nearly full and she had to circle three times before she found a space. When she had finally parked, she climbed out of her car, skated across the lot, walked through a set of double doors, and bumped right into John. "Hi," she said cheerfully. "How's Nellie's doing? Do they know what's wrong with her yet?" She had to catch her breath.

"No," John answered soberly. "The doctor is still poking and probing her. Using all kinds of contraptions. Got wires everywhere but in her ears. Never saw the likes of it. Poor Nellie. I wish that horse doctor would come out and tell me what's wrong with her so we can go home."

"Can I get you anything? Some coffee from the cafeteria? A sandwich?"

"Nope. Thanks. I don't have much of an appetite right now."

"Is there a pay phone close by?" Piper asked. "I'm going to call Matt and tell him what's happened."

"Good idea," John told her. "The trooper that brought us said he knows him. His name is Frank Nelson. He must've left because I haven't seen him around. Be sure and tell Matt that Nellie and I ran into him." John pointed her in the direction of a pay phone which was right around the corner. "You can't miss it," he yelled. "See it? It's just behind that guy with the bloody face on that stretcher over there. That poor sonofabitch has been there ever since Nellie and I arrived. He'll bleed to death before they get around to him." He shook his head and faced Piper. "Hope you have a quarter. I used my last one to call you." He slapped his hands against both pant pockets. "If you don't have any you'd better go to the cafeteria and get some change. These folks that work here won't pay attention to your needs. Hell could freeze over first," he said louder than before.

"I have some quarters," Piper said softly, hoping John would take the hint and lower his own voice. "I'll be right back. Why don't you sit down and rest? Pacing doesn't solve anything. All it does it make you more tired." She noticed that his cheeks were flushed. His blood pressure must have soared over Nellie being sick, she thought. She was afraid that if he didn't calm down he'd wind up in a hospital bed along with Nellie.

"Hell, no. I'm not sitting," John hollered. "Can't sit my ass on a chair at a time like this. Where is that damned doctor? Slow as snails. That crazy sonofabitch better hurry up." Heads turned John's way. A middle-aged lady seated in the waiting room reading a magazine looked straight at John and scowled. Another woman giggled. John made a face at her. He knew that Nellie would give him what for if she found out he was acting up. But he couldn't help it. Hospitals always brought the worst out in him.

Piper cringed and walked quickly away to find the phone. The bloody-faced man on the stretcher tried to laugh as she squeezed past him. "I get a kick out of that old fella. He doesn't take any guff from anyone. Is he your grandfather?"

"No, a friend," Piper said and smiled. "And you're right. He doesn't take any crap. He's concerned about his wife. They've been together for years." Piper didn't tell him that she wouldn't put it past John to start throwing things. She visualized computers sailing through the air, stethoscopes, chairs.

She slipped a quarter into the coin slot of the phone, waited for the signal, and dialed Matt's number. He answered after three rings. "Detective Carter," Matt said.

"Hi. This is Piper."

"Hi, yourself."

"Matt. I'm in the emergency room at the Maine General. Nellie Stoll is having some sort of attack."

"Oh, no. What kind of an attack? Is she going to be okay?"

"I just got here. John doesn't know what's wrong with her yet. I think it's her heart. John is having an absolute fit," she sighed. "Calling people sonsofbitches—bastards. And he's not exactly whispering. I don't know what he'll do if the doctor doesn't tell him what's wrong with Nellie pretty soon." She took a deep breath and then she exhaled.

Matt laughed. "I'm sorry. I shouldn't do that," he apologized. "He's an old rascal. Can't you get him to calm down?"

"I've tried. I asked him to sit down and he got madder. Poor old man is beside himself. His face is beet-red. I'm worried he's going to have a stroke or a heart attack himself."

"I know," Matt said. "Look, honey, I can't come to the hospital. There's been a murder up near Bath. I have to leave right away. I have no idea when I'll be finished. I'll give you a number where you can reach me if Nellie gets worse." He gave Piper the number and then he said, "If they admit her are you going to stay all night or go back to the farm?"

"I'll be here until I know how she is. After I find out, I'll go back to the farm." She paused and then she said, "Matt."

"What is it honey?"

"The roads are very icy. Be careful driving. I don't want anything to happen to you."

"I'll be careful and you do the same. I'll talk to you later. Better yet, maybe I'll get finished early. If I do, I'll stop at the farm and see if you're there. If not, I'll call and see if you're at the hospital and I'll come there." He paused for a second and then he said, "Piper."

"What Matt?"

"I love you."

"I love you, too, Matt."

"Tell Nellie and John that I'm praying for them."

"I will." Piper hung up and started to walk back to where she'd left John. She'd only taken about five steps when she remembered that once again she'd forgotten to tell Matt that Mona came to the farm the night before. Oh, well, she told herself. She'd tell him the next time they talked. She dreaded finding out if John's behavior had worsened. She knew that she'd better think of something pretty fast to keep him in line. The man on the stretcher was still there. "How long have you been here?" Piper asked.

"About two hours now. Guess they have some other emergencies more critical than me."

"Guess so," Piper said and hoped that that was the case. She'd heard stories about people who had to wait eight hours to be treated.

To her relief, Piper found John talking to a doctor. John saw her approaching. "Excuse me," she said. The two men stopped and looked at her. John said, "This is Piper Jordan. She's a good friend who's been staying with us at the farm."

"How do you do, Miss Jordan. My name is Dr. Garside." Piper nodded and remained quiet as the men continued with their conversation. "As I was saying, John. I don't think it's Nellie's heart. She said it was indigestion and I think she might be right. Her cardiogram looks fine. Her blood pressure is high, but not bad for her age. She's out of pain and seems to be resting comfortably. She wants to go home but I told her no. To be on the safe side, I want to keep her in here for a couple of days. The nurses are getting her ready to go upstairs to her room. You're welcome to stay with her all day—all night if you choose. Now, if you'll excuse me I have another emergency." He looked at Piper and smiled and then he said to John, "I'll drop by Nellie's room later this afternoon to see how she's doing. If you're not there, where can I reach you?"

"I'll be right here," John said firmly, and then his face fell. "I'll have to leave for a couple of hours because I have to take care of my animals."

"No you don't, John," Piper interjected. "I'll do it."

"Oh, I don't know if that's a good idea, Piper."

Dr. Garside said, "I have to go. I'll leave you two to settle who's going to do what. John, if you're not going to be here then leave a number where you can be reached at the nurse's station and I'll call you there."

"He'll be here," Piper said firmly. "He taught me how to slop the pigs. I'm an expert now." But Dr. Garside hadn't heard her because he was already on his way out the door.

"Okay, okay, you win, Piper," John said. "I appreciate your offering to help out." He was acting very sweet all of a sudden. "Frosty didn't offer to lift one finger. Just as soon as Nellie's feeling better and we go home I'm going to ask her to leave bag and baggage."

"Now, John. Tatjana told Mona that she could stay at the farm as long as she wants."

"Tough. I'll tell Tatjana that she can let that woman stay if she wants to, but if she does Nellie and I are moving."

Piper visualized what was certain to come. She knew that Mona wouldn't leave the farm on her own accord. She wondered if she should warn her that John planned on asking her to leave, to put it politely. Maybe we should both leave, she said to herself. He and Nellie have been working too hard ever since we arrived.

". . . Piper," John said. "Are you listening? I'm talking to you."

"I'm sorry John. I was daydreaming and didn't catch what you said."

"I said let's find out what room Nellie is going to be in and we'll go upstairs and wait for her."

"Okay. But do you think I should see her? Don't you think she needs her rest?"

"Sure she does," John said. "But she's gonna be awful upset if she finds out that you were here and she didn't see

265

you. Just stay a couple of minutes."

"Okay. I was hoping you'd say that, because I want to see her."

"Well, let's go then. I can't stand this waiting around." John shook his head as he made his way to the same cubicle as before. Judi was typing. "Excuse me," John said. "Can you find out what room my wife is going to be in?"

"One second," Judi said and continued to type.

"No way," John said. "I'm not waiting. If you don't find out right now I'll break that computer."

Piper wanted the floor to open up and swallow her.

Judi stopped typing. She glared at John, picked up a phone next to her, picked up a pen, and used it to poke three numbers. It didn't take long before she said to someone on the other end of the line, "This is Judi out front. Do you know what room Nellie Stoll is going to be in? Her husband wants—I mean demands to know." She glared at John again. "Thanks," Judi said, hung up, and said to John, "Fifth floor. The nurse at the desk up there will give you her room number because they're not certain which one they're going to put her in."

Piper and John left. She had never been so glad to get away from a person. They got on the elevator and got off on the fifth floor. They stopped at the head desk. John asked a plump nurse with round glasses, rosy cheeks, and a friendly smile which room was Nellie's.

"Go down that corridor over there," the nurse said, pointing to a wide hallway off to the left. "Room 526. She's already tucked into bed. Don't let her talk too much, though. She's pretty tired."

Piper and John found Nellie propped up in bed. Her face looked a bit pale to Piper, but her eyes were still bright and alert. "Hi, dear," she said to John as he bent to kiss her on the forehead. "Hi, Piper, dear. How sweet of you to come. But aren't you supposed to be at work?"

"Yes, but that's okay. You're more important than selling dresses. Besides, the weather is getting worse and there wasn't any business. How are you feeling?"

"Better, dear. I don't know what all the fuss is about. John thought it was a good case of indigestion and so do I. Dr. Garside is a worrywart. He thinks I should spend a couple of days in here to make sure it's not my heart."

"I think he's right," Piper said. "This is a good hospital, you know."

"Look, Nellie," John said. "You have a television hanging overhead. Want to watch something?"

"No, dear. It doesn't work. Guess you have to promise to pay money before they'll turn it on."

"Jesus Christ Almighty." John sputtered. "What's this world coming to? What kind of a place is this? It would've been cheaper for you to stay at a fancy hotel with a swimming pool." The minute he said that he regretted it. Nellie mustn't get excited. He tried to backtrack. "Doesn't matter I suppose. I'll find out at the nurse's station and have it turned on for you."

"No, no, John," Nellie protested. "I'd rather read. They have a gift shop. Nurse told me that they sell books there. I'd like one of those romantic suspense mysteries. Will you get one for me?"

"Yup. I'll go right away."

"I'll go with you, John," Piper offered and then she said to Nellie, "I'm going out to the farm and feed the animals for John. Going to milk the cow, too. How about that?"

"Well, now. Aren't you the good girl. Where's Mona? Maybe she'll help."

"Don't bet on that," John said and caught himself before he said anything else to upset Nellie.

Piper spied a phone on a metal table next to Nellie's bed. She said, "I think I'll call Mona and let her know that everything is okay. I'm sure she's wondering what's happening." Inside, she knew that what she'd just said sounded more like a question than a statement. Both Nellie and John watched her every move—expecting any moment for her to say hello to Mona. The phone rang and rang and rang.

*   *   *

Mona heard the phone ringing in John and Nellie's room, but she didn't bother to go answer because she was in too much of a dither waiting for the Stolls and Piper to come back. By now, her mind was so twisted she wasn't thinking straight, and it never occurred to her that it might be the Stolls or Piper calling. The incessant ringing became annoying. With butcher knife in hand, Mona stomped out of her room and flew across the hallway to Nellie and John's room. She flipped on the light and saw the phone on a nightstand next to the bed. She charged, oblivious to the fact that it had already stopped ringing, cut the cord, then stomped back to her room to stand in front of the window and wait for someone to come home. She was ready to kill.

Piper cradled the receiver, "She's not there. That's odd. Where would she go in this weather?"

"Maybe she decided to leave after our tiff this morning," Nellie said.

"I sure hope that's the case," John said and crossed his fingers for luck.

"I agree," Nellie said. "Mona may be having a tough time over poor dear Steven and Kelly, too, but that's no excuse. I hope she's not on her way here to see me."

"No," Piper said. "I don't think she'll show up here, Nellie. She was pretty angry this morning. Knowing her as well as I do, I can tell you that she hasn't forgiven us yet. I bet she went home. I don't think she'll drive back to the farm in this weather." She actually hoped that Mona never ever returned to the farm, but she didn't say that. Instead she said, "Nellie, if you need anything, have John call me at the farm and I'll bring it right away unless the weather gets worse. If it does I won't be able to come back here until tomorrow."

"That's okay, dear. I don't want you to be traveling about in that mess. But if it's cleared up by tomorrow, I would like my own nightie, bathrobe, and slippers, toothpaste and brush, but I can wait. The nurse said there's a bunch of stuff like that in the top drawer of this nightstand. She said this hospital Johnny will do for now and she gave me a pair of paper slippers, too. See them on the floor there underneath my bed?"

Both Piper and John looked. Piper knew that such flimsy things wouldn't last more than a day, if that.

"Where's Matthew?" Nellie asked.

"He had to go out to Bath," Piper told her. "He won't be back until later. I phoned him and told him about you. He said to tell you that he hopes you feel better very soon."

"That's sweet of him. Why is he going to Bath, dear?"

"There was a murder there," Piper said.

"Oh, what a shame."

"There's going to be one here, too, if they don't take good care of you in this place," John sputtered.

"But they are taking good care of me, dear," Nellie said softly to John. "Besides, I'm okay. All this fuss because I put too much baking soda in my biscuits this morning. That's the culprit."

Piper leaned over and kissed Nellie on the forehead and said, "Bye. I'll see you later. Try and get some rest."

"I will, thanks for everything Piper."

Piper and John left. She noticed that his step was a bit more energetic. He was obviously relieved over Nellie. Piper realized that staying alive at their age was like playing Russian roulette.

John said, "I think I'll stop at the front desk and see about getting Nellie's television set turned on. She'll want to watch her programs tonight, even if she said she doesn't. Can't miss Wheel of Fortune. She gets most all of the puzzles right. We'd have been rich a hundred times over if Nellie had been on that show."

The same nurse as before was still seated in the same spot. She looked up at John and Piper and smiled in a motherly way. "How's your wife doing?"

"Better," John said. "How do I go about getting her television turned on?"

"There was a card in her room explaining how to do that but I can take care of having it turned on, if you'd like.

It costs ten dollars a day. You have to make a deposit and then you pay the rest when your wife is released."

"Jesus," John said. "Ten dollars a day. Highway robbery. I'm not paying that. I'll bring our portable from home."

"Sorry. You can't do that."

"I can do that."

"No you can't." Piper noticed the nurse had lost her smile. Now her lips were tight; her face a bit flushed.

"Who the hell are you to tell me that I can't bring my own television for my wife?"

"I, sir, am the head nurse. And I'll tell you one more time that you cannot bring your television. Now, if you'll excuse me, I have a lot of reports to fill out." The conversation was over as far as she was concerned. John looked at Piper and shook his head. "We could stay at a hotel cheaper than the cost of this place," he grumbled. "We'd have a better time, too. I'll order the television turned on when I get back to Nellie's room."

Piper let John rave. "Like I said, Nellie could've gone to a hotel . . ." He was still ranting when they caught the elevator to the lobby. She interrupted him as soon as the door opened and they stepped into the front lobby. "John," she said, "I'm going now. Why don't you try and relax a little. Hospitals have their rules, you know."

John grumbled. "I know. I'm sorry. I don't mean to be so crabby. Listen. If you have any trouble feeding the animals or milking the cow give me a call. I'll be in Nellie's room."

"Will you come home if I run into trouble?" She hoped that he'd say yes because she was already dreading the idea of being alone. She was also worried that Mona might come back and be in worse temper than she was earlier.

"No. I'm staying here all night. You and Frosty will be okay together won't you?"

"She isn't there, remember?" She really didn't want him to leave Nellie. She managed a smile and said, "I'll be fine by myself. What about your car?"

"That state trooper said he'd have it brought here for

270

me. I gave him the keys. He sure was a nice fella. Have to have him come to supper when Nellie gets back on her feet. He'd love her pot roast and gravy."

Piper leaned over and kissed John's cheek. His beard tickled her. "I'll call you later," she told him. "Behave. Don't go picking on that poor head nurse, okay?"

"Okay," he said. "Now get going. Crutches must be missing us. He's never been alone this long. He usually goes everywhere we go. Tell him Nellie and I will be home as quick as we can. Make sure he has enough food and water. Don't forget to give him a couple of biscuits."

"Don't worry. I'll tell him," Piper said and walked away. She was tired and yearned to be able to go to bed. She hoped that Matt would come back early so he could spend the night with her. The very idea made her feel better.

The moment Piper stepped outside the hospital into the parking lot she couldn't believe how dark the night was and how much the weather had deteriorated. Sheets of freezing rain pelted her. The wind was blowing so hard it almost knocked her over. The roads were going to be bad, she knew, and she would have to be extra careful driving to the farm.

When she reached her car she saw that it was covered with ice and she had to force the key into the frozen lock. She expected the engine to catch right away, but all it did was turn over two or three times and then she heard a clicking sound. She waited a few seconds and gave the key another twist. Fortunately, the engine sputtered and then caught. "Thank heavens," Piper muttered. "That's all I needed in this weather." She turned on the defroster, searched underneath the front seat for her scraper, climbed back out, and started to scrape her windows. All the while she shivered from the chill and silently prayed that Mona had gone back to Cape Bethany. Being alone was going to be bad enough—but it was better than having to put up with that crabby bitch. It would be too good to be true to find her gone bag and baggage. She really didn't give a damn if she ever saw her again.

Finally, the car windows were cleared. Piper climbed

behind the wheel again, said a quick prayer that she wouldn't slide on the ice, and slowly backed out of her parking place. In a moment she saw her prayer had gone unanswered, for she was sliding in the direction of a pickup truck with a sticker on the back window that said in bold white letters: LIFE'S A BITCH AND THEN YOU DIE. She managed to gain control of her car just in time. But the episode had shaken her. Now she was really scared about making the long trek to the farm. "Christ!" she griped. And then she admonished herself for swearing.

Piper inched her way out of the lot and drove fifteen miles an hour across the almost empty Portland streets. "Damn. I won't get home until midnight," she sputtered. She hoped that Matt didn't show up and then leave before she got there. The very idea made her go faster. Suddenly the wind seemed much stronger. Violent gusts rocked the car. She struggled to keep in the correct lane. She could bet the ocean was wild. *Poor, poor fishermen,* she thought. No way would she want to be out to sea in this mess. The screaming wind frightened her. She conjured up images of horror movies that she'd seen. Visions of vampires danced through her head. And then she saw Kelly in that pine coffin. It was time to concentrate on her driving.

Piper tried to see some beauty in the ice-coated tree branches along the way. Electrical wires swayed furiously overhead. The faces of buildings glistened. Portland looked as though it were made out of the finest crystal. Several ice-coated tree limbs and twigs that had succumbed to the wind were scattered across the sidewalks and roads. She maneuvered the car around the big limbs and the rest crunched underneath her wheels.

Piper glanced at the little round clock with the sticky-tape back that she'd stuck on her dashboard. Where had the day gone? She glanced at passing houses and didn't see any lights. She was back on Congress Street now, near Longfellow Square. That's when the lights went out. The whole area was plunged in darkness. She wondered about electricity at the farm and didn't know how worried her face looked as she imagined herself all alone in dark in that

272

old house. For an instant she thought about turning back and spending the night at the hospital with Nellie and John. And then she remembered that she couldn't do that because she'd promised John that she'd take care of the animals. "Don't be such a sissy," she chided herself. "You have Crutches to keep you company." Still, she didn't relish the dark.

Piper held her breath as she crept down High Street hill, afraid that she wouldn't be able to stop at the bottom. She could see herself sliding into the middle of the intersection near Deering Oaks Park. But there was no need to fret because the car came to a graceful stop. She must've fought fifty urges to stomp on the brakes as she navigated that hill.

Finally, Piper made it to the expressway entrance ramp. Although it had been salted, it seemed slick in spots. Fortunately there was little traffic for her to have to worry about crashing into. After she traveled four miles, she noticed several cars skewed in all directions on her side of the road. She soon found out what had caused their disarray, because she skidded on one of the same patches of ice and nearly careened off the road herself.

Still shaken, a mile later Piper came upon a jackknifed truck. A wrecker and the police were on the scene. She hoped that the driver wasn't injured. She didn't see an ambulance so she assumed he was okay. She flipped on her radio, and after a few minutes the WPOR announcer said that the speed limit on the turnpike had been reduced to 35. She looked at her speedometer, was shocked to see that she was traveling at fifty, and eased up on her speed. Her eyes darted to the dashboard clock again. She had been on the road for over an hour.

At long last, the Hunter Road exit sign said that Piper was only two miles from the farm. Her body relaxed a bit. The instant she turned onto the exit ramp she had another flash of being alone, but then she remembered that Matt said he'd come by after he finished in Bath. Besides, Crutches and the other animals would keep her company. That made her feel better.

She glanced at passing houses and noticed they were lit up. The power hadn't gone out in Freeport, not yet anyway. She decided that she could stand anything as long as she had electricity.

She might've changed her mind about that, had she known that Mona awaited her arrival at the farm.

Chapter Fourteen

It's So Dark

At last Piper spied the farmhouse. When she turned into the driveway the headlights of her car illuminated the dark house. The place looked spooky. She bit her bottom lip and tapped the steering wheel. "And where is Crutches?" she muttered. She assumed Mona had let him stay inside the warm kitchen out of the storm. But that couldn't be, she realized, because Mona despised him; he had to be outside. Piper wasn't too worried because she knew that he enjoyed wet weather, but it soon became apparent that he wasn't around. Had he been, he would've come to greet her. Maybe he's inside the house, she said to herself. Or in the barn? She glanced in that direction. The barn doors were wide open.

Piper pulled her key out of the ignition and climbed out. The driveway was a glare of ice. If she had worn skates she could have glided gracefully to the front steps. As it was, she moved awkwardly, inch by inch. The wind was gusting so hard that it almost knocked her over, and freezing rain pelted her. She pitied the poor animals in their cold stalls, who were probably starving. She thought she heard the cow bellowing to be milked, but she knew that she wouldn't tend them until she changed her clothes and found Crutches.

Piper spied the shed where John kept his truck and

tractor. She wondered if Mona had shut Crutches in there because he had gotten too wet and smelly to be in the house. The minute she opened the double shed doors she saw that there was no dog to greet her, she spied Mona's Jag parked alongside John's tractor. "Oh! She's back," she said with disappointment. She flicked the light switch on the wall and the room lit up. The power was still on in Freeport. Piper turned off the light, stepped outside, and closed the doors.

She stood in the driveway, stared at the house, and dreaded going inside. She turned to look at the barn. It, too, was in total darkness. Something was wrong. For some reason a vision of Kelly stretched out in that pine coffin came to mind. Piper knew that fright was getting the best of her, but she couldn't help it. But of what was she so frightened? she wondered. Of the dark, she answered. Damn Mona, why doesn't she have any lights on? Where the hell *is* she?

As she approached the front porch, she noticed that the steps weren't shoveled. She was annoyed with Mona for not cleaning them off, but she knew that she didn't dare say anything to her because of the bad mood she'd been in earlier. Piper made her way across the porch to the door. If Crutches heard her approaching he didn't act like it. There was no sound of padding feet, whimpering, or barking. "Something is wrong," she said softly. "Don't say that," she chastised herself.

Her heart raced when she put her hand on the storm door knob, gave it a twist, and pushed it open. Hinges screamed as the wind caught the door and banged it against the clapboards. Piper grabbed it, opened the other door, and stepped into the kitchen. She reached for the light switch on the left hand side of the wall, and her body sagged with relief when the room lit up.

Again she wondered why Mona was in the dark. She tried to convince herself that the reason was that she was napping. And then she wondered if perhaps the power had been out and had just come back on. Yes, she said to herself. That had to be it. Mona fell asleep before it got

276

dark. Piper glanced at the electric clock on the wall and then at her watch. The time matched. The power had not gone out. And then the lights flickered. "Oh, no," she said. "Please stay on. I don't want to be in the dark."

Piper still half-expected Crutches to come bounding in. She noticed that his food and water bowls were full. He had usually licked them dry by this hour. She wondered if maybe he was upstairs with Mona. *No*, she thought. *That can't be. She hates him. Maybe he has a girlfriend in the neighborhood.* She didn't really believe that. She knew that she should've checked to see if he was in the barn, but she remembered that the doors were wide open, if he was in there he would've barked and come running. She wondered if Mona had hurt him. No, she wasn't that mean. She finally concluded that Crutches was out roaming.

Now she became aware that her feet were freezing, and she looked down; her shoes and panty hose were soaked. She kicked her shoes off and decided that she'd brave going upstairs to her room to change into a sweater and jeans. She'd put some warm wool socks on her feet and Nellie's boots, and then she'd go out to the barn and feed the animals.

The deathly silence frightened Piper. She dreaded going upstairs not knowing if Mona was really up there. She made her way to the dining room doorway that led to the front hall and stairs. She yelled as loud as she could, "Mona. I'm home. Are you up there?" She waited for her to answer. All she heard was the windows rattling from the howling wind. "Mona," she called louder. "Why don't you come down here and say hello?" There was no answer. She called again. Nothing.

Piper reached for the light switch on the wall and flicked it. The room filled with fluttery light as the power struggled to stay on, and the leaves on Nellie's plants were wiggling from a strong draft coming through the windows. The old house creaked and groaned. The noises made Piper even more jittery. There was a kerosene lamp on the buffet and she decided that she'd better light it in case the power went out. She thought she'd seen Nellie take some matches out of the top drawer the night she'd moved in. She opened the drawer and sure enough there was a book of matches and several candles, some new, others burned to stubs. She took a couple of the long tapers just in case the lamp didn't have enough oil. She noticed that the matches had bold black writing that said, "Monty's Electrical Supply. We'll light up your life." I hope so, she said to herself, carefully removing the fragile glass chimney from the lamp, setting it on the buffet, striking a match and lighting the inch-wide wick. It caught before the match had burned all the way. A tiny puff of blackish smoke rose along with the flame, and Piper placed the chimney back on the lamp, immediately smelling a pleasant pine aroma. Then the lights flickered wildly and went out.

She picked up the lamp and started toward the kitchen. That's when she thought she heard a noise in the front hall. She was trembling all over, which made it difficult for her to stand perfectly still so she could listen. *Maybe it's Mona,* she reassured herself. *Damn her.* She called to her again—louder this time. "Mona. I'm home." There was no answer.

Piper started to move toward the kitchen door, and the sudden movement caused the lamp to flicker and dim. She had to stop walking to allow the flame to grow stronger. That's when she heard a noise behind her and glanced to her left. Two shadows loomed tall on the wall. Piper screamed. When she stopped she heard cackling laughter and then Mona's voice. "Did I scare you, Piper?" she asked.

Piper whirled around; the flame dimmed again, then caught. Somehow she found her voice. "Mona. What's the matter with you? Why did you sneak up on me like that?"

Mona cackled again. The lamplight illuminated her chalky face. A picture of insanity stared back at Piper. She was wild-eyed. Her hair was uncombed and tangled.

"Are you okay, Mona?" Piper managed to ask her. "You don't look like you feel too well."

"I'm fine," Mona answered. She smiled, revealing her white, even teeth. "As a matter of fact I feel wonderful."

"How come?" Piper asked with a puzzled look on her face. She really didn't want to hear why she was so elated. She only wanted to get away from her as fast as possible.

"Because," Mona teased.

Piper was getting annoyed. "Mona. For heaven's sake we're not children. What is this game you're playing?"

"I can't tell you just yet," Mona pouted.

"Why?"

"Because it's a little too soon. Give me a few minutes. Then I will. Besides. It's not a game."

"You're not making sense, Mona. Have you been drinking?" That's it, Piper said to comfort herself. She's been into John and Nellie's liquor.

"No," Mona said. "I haven't had a drop. I've been in my room all day, planning."

"Planning what?"

"I already told you, stupid," Mona shouted. "You have to wait a few minutes before I tell." Her voice sounded hard and angry now. She doubled her fists.

Piper started to move slowly toward the kitchen door. "Have you seen Crutches?" she asked trying to keep Mona distracted.

"Yes, I have," Mona responded and scratched her head. "I forgot. I did come downstairs once to put my car in the shed out of the storm and to get a cup of coffee. That damned dog followed me outside. He wouldn't stop growling at me so I . . ."

"You what?" Piper asked, too quickly. She was afraid of what Mona was going to tell her.

". . . So I left him outside. Haven't seen him since."

There was something about the way Mona looked when she said that that made Piper not believe her. A terrible wave of fear for Crutches washed over her as she continued to move in slow motion so the lamp wouldn't go out. She really had no idea how she was going to escape.

At last she made it to the kitchen with Mona right behind her. Piper tried to seem casual when she moved

Nellie's fruit bowl and placed the lamp on the middle of the table. She avoided Mona's face and failed to sound calm when she said in a shaky voice, "I have to go out to the barn and feed the animals for John. Nellie has to be in the hospital for a couple of days. John is going to stay with her tonight." How could she be so stupid? she thought. Now she'd let Mona know they were all alone. She had to think of something to cover her tracks. Now it was going to be tough to convince Mona that Matt was coming.

Mona grinned. It was all too perfect. John, Nellie and that fucking dog were out of the way. The detective, too. She had Piper all to herself. Excitement charged through her. She hugged her chest tightly.

"Did Matt call?" Piper asked.

"How the hell would I know?" Mona snapped. "I told you I didn't answer the phone. The fucking thing rang several times. I finally went into Nellie and John's room and cut the cord with a butcher knife." She paused and then she said, "That knife is in my room. In a few minutes, I'm going to go to the kitchen and find one to use on you. You see, Piper. That's my plan. I'm going to kill you." She laughed and laughed.

Piper pretended that she hadn't heard what Mona just said. She had to keep her cool if she was going to survive. But she knew her voice trembled with fright when she said, "Ma-Matt probably tried to reach me to tell me what time he's coming here." She made an exaggerated point of looking at her watch. "He, he should be here any minute."

"You're a liar," Mona yelled. But, she wasn't exactly certain that what Piper had told her wasn't true. If that goddamned detective was coming she had to move faster. She relished the thought of his discovering his lover girl's body. Then she would kill him, but first she would try and seduce him. The idea made her quiver. "Is he good in bed?" she asked Piper, dreamily.

Piper pretended she didn't hear that. "Matt should be here. He had to go to Bath, but he's going to stop here on his way back."

"Who cares?" Mona grumbled and then her eyes lit up.

"I care," she contradicted herself. "If you had plans to sleep with your lover boy tonight you'd better forget it. Want to know why?"

Piper didn't respond.

"If you know what's good for you, you'll answer me."

"Why?" Piper asked meekly.

"That's better. Now I'll tell you why." She rubbed the palms of her hands together and licked her lips. "Because I'm going to fuck him. That's what you get for sleeping with Steven. What goes around comes around."

"But I didn't."

"Shut up," Mona yelled. "I can't stand your lying ways."

Piper started to move toward the door. She knew she had to talk calmly so as not to rile Mona further. "I didn't sleep with Steven. I've told you before that I would never take up with a married man. Why won't you believe me?"

Mona raised one eyebrow. "You're sick. How can you stand there and tell bald-faced lies like that? You're just like all the others."

"I'm telling the truth," Piper said. The door seemed an eternity away now.

Mona laughed and said, "Getting under your skin, am I? Well, not to fret. In a few minutes you won't have a thing to worry about."

"Wha—what are you going to do?" Piper asked.

Mona walked quickly over to Piper and stood so close to her that she could feel her breath on her face. Piper backed up slowly and bumped into the door. She put a hand behind her and groped for the knob. Before she could twist it Mona saw what she was trying to do.

"Where do you think you're going? Silly girl. I haven't told you my plan yet." Her voice sounded singsong. "Want me to tell you my surprise now?"

"Later, Mona. I ha-have to go to the barn and feed the animals." She could tell by the look on Mona's face that hadn't worked. She swallowed. Her throat felt like she had a bone caught in it.

"You aren't going to the barn, Piper." Mona told her.

Now her laughter sounded almost hysterical.

"Why not?" Piper asked. "What are you talking about, Mona? I haven't got time for your silly games."

Mona frowned and then she slapped Piper's face hard. "Games! Games!" she yelled. "Here we go again. When is it going to dawn on you that we're playing for keeps." She doubled up her fist and hit Piper in the mouth.

Mona's diamond ring split Piper's bottom lip. She felt it puff and tasted blood. She was growing more terrified, but somehow she managed to conceal her fear. A strong instinct to survive surfaced. "Mona," she said calmly. "Steven's death has been too much for you. Please. Let me help you." She prayed that using sympathy would work.

Piper's concern only infuriated Mona. "Help me," she screamed. "The only way you can help me is by being dead!" A look of sheer hatred covered her face.

Piper knew then that nothing she said or did was going to stop Mona. "Did you . . . kill Kelly and Steven?" she asked, already knowing the answer.

"Of course, silly girl," Mona responded with a grin and clapped her hands. Then without warning she screwed up her face, reached out, and yanked Piper's hair, making her scream. Mona enjoyed inflicting pain and pulled harder. When she finally let go a fist full of blond hair floated to the floor.

"Stupid Kelly," Mona said. "If she hadn't come up with the idea of you two dressing like twin rag dolls then she wouldn't be dead." She became so riled thinking about those costumes that she pulled Piper's hair again. This time, Piper reacted and kicked her hard on the ankle.

"Ouch! Stop it," Mona snarled, slapping her across the face. "Your such a twit. Do you think I'm that stupid that I'd let you go?" And then her voice changed and she sounded as if she was talking to another person in the room. "That Piper is so dumb, isn't she? She thinks I need help." Her voice turned icy. "Ignorant bitch. Just wait until I kill her."

Piper was frozen with terror. Her feet felt rooted to the floor.

"Yes," Mona continued to say to her imaginary friend. "I know that's messy. But it's worth it. What? What? No, boiling alive is too much of a struggle. It is," she said with wonder. "You don't say. Wait just a sec and I'll ask her?" Mona faced Piper. She got so close to her that their noses almost touched. "How does strangulation sound to you?"

Piper didn't answer. Somewhere, from deep inside herself, she felt a surge of strength. It started in her toes, worked its way up and up, and finally flowed into her arms and her hands. She doubled her left fist and quickly punched Mona in the jaw. Mona was stunned. Piper seized the opportunity and continued punching her. Mona tried to shield herself with her hands. When she did Piper quickly hit her several times in the stomach. Mona moaned, doubled over and fell against Piper, grabbing at her to try and stop her. Piper quickly shoved her to one side. The door that led to the outside was now blocked with Mona's body, so Piper couldn't get away. She had to move her, then try and reach her car. Oh, no, she said to herself. The keys are in my purse. Her eyes flew to the oak coat tree next to Mona. Her brown leather purse dangled by the shoulder strap.

Mona instantly saw what Piper was looking at. It was as if she knew what she was thinking, because she reached out, lifted the flap, and shoved her left hand deep inside the purse. Without looking, she felt a lipstick, comb, wallet, and then she touched a round disk attached to several keys. She pulled them out and held them high in the air. "Just in case you think you can get away." She shoved the keys into her blouse pocket, and said coldly, "Now, I'm going to kill you." She smiled and revealed a film of bloody red on her snow-white teeth. Her left eye was beginning to swell shut from Piper's blows.

"But why do you want to kill me, Mona?" Piper cried. "For God's sake. I never did anything to you."

"Don't play dumb with me, slut."

"I'm not playing dumb. Tell me what I've done to cause you to hate me so much."

"YOU TRIED TO TAKE STEVEN AWAY FROM

ME," Mona screamed.

"That's not true and you know it," Piper said. She knew her options were running out.

"Liar. I caught you in our bedroom. Remember?"

"But, Mona. Steven was the one who cornered me. You know that. Remember you phoned me later that evening and apologized?"

"That was an act," Mona said.

"What do you mean?"

"Just what I said. I lied to you so that I could plan how to get rid of you. Just like I did to that redhead."

"What redhead? What are you talking about?" Piper couldn't believe what she was hearing.

"You know. My first husband's mistress. And look what happened to him."

"You're not making sense, Mona. What husband? I didn't know you were married before."

"Nobody did. Not even Steven," Mona told her with pride. A look of triumph covered her face.

"Matt knows that you killed Kelly and Steven."

"Matt who?" Mona asked. Her face looked blank.

"Detective Carter."

"So what? He can't prove it. Besides. After I kill you and fuck him—he's going to die."

"Mona. Please. I was never interested in Steven. You and I work together. You know me. I wouldn't do anything to hurt you."

"You wouldn't?" Mona asked her wide-eyed. Her voice had changed. Now she sounded like a little girl.

"No, I wouldn't." Piper said and started to move slowly toward the dining room. She knew now that her only hope of escape was to go out the front door and hide somewhere. For every step that she took, Mona followed. Piper turned her head to one side and glanced out of the corner of her eye. She could tell that she wasn't on course. She stepped to the right, but she hadn't looked soon enough, and that was when Mona charged. Piper bolted and smacked into the refrigerator. Mona reached out and grabbed her by the throat with both hands in a viselike grip. Piper gagged, slapped at her hands, and tried to kick her, but Mona squeezed all the harder. Soon Piper couldn't breathe, her eyes were beginning to bulge, her face was turning red, and little black specks floated in front of her eyes. Next came visions of her parents and then Kelly—even her dog, Topper. It was as if she were watching a movie on fast forward. She could feel her energy being drained. She stopped fighting.

Suddenly, Piper felt a rush of cold wet air hit her face, and Mona's grip loosened. Piper automatically inhaled and could feel her head clear somewhat. She hadn't realized that her eyes were closed so tight until she opened them. Mona had her back to her.

"You fucking beast," Mona screamed. "Get going. Get out of here now or so help me I'll kill you."

Piper spied Crutches. Her heart quickened. The dog had pushed the door open and let himself in. His teeth were bared, a menacing growl came from deep in his throat. He moved cautiously toward Mona.

Mona now stood right next to Piper. "Piper," she said sharply. "Tell that sonofabitch to get out of here. Do it now or so help me I'll clobber him." She reached beside her, picked up a cast iron frying pan off the stove, and held it high in the air.

Piper didn't say a word. She left Mona and darted across the room to stand beside Crutches. She gripped his red leather collar and tried to hold him back, but it was a struggle. The dog was intent on attacking Mona. Piper knew that he was her only hope of surviving and she wasn't about to let go of him if she could help it. She found her voice. "So help me, Mona. If you make one move I'll let go of Crutches. I know I wouldn't want his teeth sinking into me."

Piper's warning worked. Mona froze. Piper could reach the wall phone from where she stood. She didn't even have to change hands to hold the dog's collar. She reached out with her left hand and carefully lifted the receiver off the hook. Cradling it under her chin she used her shoulder for a brace and with her index finger poked

911. She listened, but heard absolute silence.

Mona laughed. "You're so fucking numb, Piper. I'd have thought you would've guessed by now that I cut that cord, too. You can't talk to anyone but me." She reached into her pocket and brought out Piper's keys. "I still have these." She put them in her pocket again. "There. Now you can't call anyone and you can't go anywhere."

"Shut up, Mona," Piper blurted. She regretted the words the minute they came out of her mouth.

"Make me."

Piper ignored her and started to back up. Crutches moved with her. Piper kept her eyes on Mona as she moved. She was at the back door now. She put her free hand out and tried to grab hold of the knob, but the dog was so close his rear end was butted against it. Piper knew that she had no other choice than to take the dog and walk forward a few steps in order to open the door and make a run for it. Her timing had to be perfect. Before she had a chance to lose her nerve she let go of the dog's collar, turned, twisted the knob, and opened the door. She and Crutches ran out onto the ice-coated porch and down the slick steps. Once her feet touched the ground she let go of the dog. He didn't make any attempt to leave her. Piper started to run and kept turning her head to see if Mona was coming. The last time she looked she fell and landed on her tailbone. Pain soared. Both hands were scraped, her left wrist felt sprained, and her spine hurt so badly she wondered if she'd be able to get up. She looked at her feet and saw that her pantyhose had ripped, revealing bare toes.

As Piper struggled to get up she thought she heard Mona's laughter. Her eyes darted to the porch. Mona stood on the landing dangling Piper's car keys in the air. She held her other hand behind her back as if she were hiding something. She looked down at Piper with a sly grin. "Hey, Piper," she shouted above the wind. "What a shame you fell. Now you can't get away from me." Piper watched horrified as Mona slowly made her way down the steps.

Crutches started to growl again. Piper started to run,

took two steps, and fell again. This time she landed on her face and scraped her nose. Beads of blood formed. She snapped her head around and saw that Mona was getting closer. "Mona," Piper managed to yell. "If you take another step toward me I'll let Crutches attack you."

"He won't, you dumb slut," Mona snarled. Then she looked at the dog and said sweetly, "That's a good boy, Crutches. Don't you move. If you do I won't give you a biscuit."

The minute Crutches heard the word biscuit he stopped growling. He kept his dark eyes on Mona.

Piper watched as Mona brought her hand out from behind her back. She was holding a huge soup bone. Crutches saw it, too. He sniffed the air. His bushy tail started wagging. "Come and get it big boy," Mona enticed him.

"No, Crutches. Don't." Piper pleaded and knew that her voice had lacked authority. The dog's loyalty had vanished. He limped towards Mona. She began to slowly back up the porch steps, dangling the bone in front of the dog's nose every step of the way.

"Crutches, no!" Piper yelled.

The dog stopped moving. He turned his head and looked at Piper. "Come here now," she commanded. Crutches started her way with a confused look on his face.

"No," Mona yelled. "Come get your treat, Crutches." The dog stopped again. He looked at Mona. She waved the bone to entice him. He started to go after it. Before Piper could call him again, Mona had him inside the kitchen doorway. When she had him far enough inside she dropped the bone on the floor. Then she quickly ran outside onto the porch, slammed the door, and breathed a deep sigh of relief. Crutches picked up his treat, carried it to his bed, and flopped. Defending Piper was now the last thing on his mind.

Mona saw that Piper had almost made her way to the entrance of the barn. She also noticed that she kept falling on the ice. She went down the steps after her and almost fell several times herself. Sheer determination to kill Piper kept her on her feet.

Piper saw Mona coming. She tried to run. Mona pushed her from behind. Piper fell face first onto the hard ground and cut her left cheek. With great difficulty, she managed to flip over onto her back. Mona quickly jumped onto her stomach, knocking the wind out of her. Piper groaned and gasped for air that wouldn't come. When she could inhale she wasn't able to take in enough to fill her lungs because Mona's weight crushed her. She was dizzy.

Piper knew that if she was going to live she had to do something fast. Mustering what strength she had, she used her index finger to poke Mona's left eye, where now there were snowflakes clinging to the fake black eyelashes.

Mona cried out in pain and immediately let go of Piper to protect herself. Piper quickly jabbed Mona in her right eye. Mona covered her face with both hands. Piper took advantage of the moment. With all her might, she pushed Mona off her and scrambled to her feet. Mona lay on her back moaning and frantically rubbing her blurry eyes. Piper grabbed her by her tangled, ice clumped hair, yanking so hard Mona's head jerked back. Piper doubled up her fist and punched her so hard in the jaw that one of her prefectly shaped front teeth flew out of her mouth. Blood oozed and ran down her chin, her throat, and onto the collar of her shirt. Although stunned, she still tried to get on her feet. Piper was ready for her. She smashed her in the face again. Mona clung to consciousness.

Piper thrust her hand deep into Mona's blouse pocket to get her car keys. They weren't there. She grabbed Mona by her shoulders and shook her vigorously. "Where are my keys?" she yelled in her face. "Tell me. What did you do with my keys?"

Mona couldn't see Piper, but she grinned, totally unaware that she now had a bloody gap in her mouth. "Threw them away," she said with a lisp.

"Where? Where did you throw them?" Piper demanded.

"I, I'll never tell."

Piper slapped her face hard. "Tell me," she demanded. "Tell me now or so help me . . ." She had never experienced such rage. If Mona didn't tell her she might strangle her with her bare hands.

Mona clamped her mouth shut. There was no way for Piper to know that Mona had just felt a tremendous surge of energy charge through her body. Her pulse quickened and her fingers flexed. The sound of a battle cry escaped from deep within her throat. She looked up at Piper with an evil, bloody grin spread wide across her face.

Piper hadn't been prepared for Mona to make such a quick comeback, and she knew that she had to get away before it was too late. She wondered frantically where she could hide, her eyes darting from the house to the shed and then to the barn. She ran toward the barn, slipped and fell again. She glanced over her shoulder and saw that Mona was now standing on her feet, staggering in circles. Then she heard what sounded like a loud bang and her eyes found the house. Crutches stood on the porch. He'd obviously opened the door with his teeth to let himself out. The wind had caught the storm door and smashed it against the clapboards. Piper looked again. Mona was coming after her!

The dog stood on the porch and surveyed the scene. He saw Piper making her way to the barn. He growled when he spied Mona chasing after her cursing and waving her arms wildly. "You no good whore," she yelled. "You pig. Wait until I get my hands around your throat!"

Crutches began to growl low in his throat. He bared his teeth and snarled. He limped quickly down the steps after Mona. She saw him coming and tried to run. Suddenly, her feet went out from underneath her and she fell on her back. Crutches loomed over her, teeth still bared, his black wet nose just a fraction of an inch away from her face.

For the first time in her life, Mona knew real fear. She couldn't take her eyes off the dog's teeth. She had a vision of them sinking deep into her face, maiming her beyond repair. Her mind told her to remain calm and not to move.

Piper was at the entrance of the barn now. She glanced over her shoulder and saw that Crutches had Mona pinned, but for how long she didn't know. There was no time to waste. She ran as fast as she could toward the metal loop sticking out of the floor. In a flash, she wondered if the slaves who hid there had ever experienced the same kind of terror that she was now feeling. Every noise raked her jangled nerves. She jumped when the cow stomped her feet and bellowed. She did the same when the pigs snorted and grunted. Piper misjudged the location of the trap door and darted past the metal loop. She quickly got down on all fours and backtracked. Trembling, and with tears streaking her cheeks, she felt her way across the hay-covered wooden floor. Finally her shaky fingers grasped the ice-cold metal loop. She yanked hard and could feel a muscle pull in her lower back. She struggled to get on her feet while at the same time pulling on the trap door until she had it open enough to climb down onto the ladder.

Her fingers itched as they touched spider webs. With rubbery legs she moved down the creaky rungs one by one. When she reached the third she stopped. She managed to grasp the trap door and close it, but not without feeling some splinters slip into her fingers. Everything was pitch black and she heard squeaking and scurrying on the ground below. "Oh, nooo," she whimpered.

Something make her forehead tickle. She let go of the ladder with one hand to scratch. The minute she did, whatever it was ran into her hair and crawled rapidly across her scalp. She swatted her head in a frenzy. The itching stopped and then her fingers felt something juicy.

The squeaking and scurrying noises grew much louder. There was no way she would go down that ladder any further. Then, to her absolute horror, she heard a snapping noise, followed by a splintering crunch. The ladder was rotted; her weight was too much for it! The next thing she knew Piper found herself sprawled on the hard ground with half of the broken ladder on top of her. She didn't dare move. The room was ice-cold and reeked of ammoniated rodent urine. Her mouth felt dry. She could feel a scream rise and then die in her throat. She'd stifled her urge to cry out for help because she knew that Mona would be the only one to come to her; then she would surely die. It took everything in her not to become hysterical. Her wounds stung, and her feet and hands throbbed from the cold. She wondered if she was going to freeze to death. She tried to take a deep breath and succeeded, but the overpowering odors made her stomach heave. Waves of nausea overtook her and made her gag until she was spent. She'd never felt so ill. Suddenly, the thought of dying wasn't so terrifying. She wondered if she'd sealed herself in her own grave.

Mona was still playing dead; Crutches was still hovering over her, although he wasn't acting quite as menacing. She decided he was calm enough for her to speak to him. "Good boy, Crutches," she crooned, softly. "How about a biscuit for the goody-good fellow?"

The minute Crutches heard the word biscuit he backed up a few steps, his tail wagged, and he pranced toward the house. Mona got slowly onto her feet, talking constantly. "Just a minute you sonofabitch," she said sweetly. "I'll give you a treat, you can bet on that. C'mon. Let's go into the house so I get the kerosene lamp and then I'll take care of you."

Crutches limped up the porch steps and walked into the kitchen. Mona followed, picked up the kerosene lamp off the table, then stared at the dog. She intended to lock him inside so he couldn't follow her but then she had a better idea. "You love Piper don't you, Crutches? Well, now. I'm going to give you a biscuit like I promised. Then you and I are going out to the barn. I just know you'll sniff out Piper's hiding place for me." She smiled at the dog; then she went to the cupboard and found a box of dog biscuits. She pulled one out of the box and tossed it into the air. Crutches quickly opened his mouth wide, caught it, and wolfed it down in two bites. Mona took four or five more biscuits out of the box and shoved them into her pockets. She knew if that beast turned on her again she'd need all the help she could get to keep him occupied.

"C'mon, good boy," Mona coaxed. "Let's go to the barn

now. I don't want to keep precious Piper waiting too long. She really has to be on her way to meet Kelly and Steven. Now let's see," she said, and made her way across the kitchen and stopped just before she reached the door. "How shall I kill her? Shall I strangle her? Or do you think I should cut off her head with a knife?" Crutches cocked his head to one side and whimpered. Mona glared at him and said, "Why am I asking you, you idiot. Hmmm," she pondered. "I like the knife idea." She chuckled, visualizing Piper's head stuck on a fence post.

Mona walked across the kitchen and opened a drawer next to the sink. She was delighted to find several sharp knives from which to choose. She finally selected one with a serrated edge. "Oh, good," she said happily. "This will make a fancy cut," Crutches black face looked perplexed as he watched Mona. He cocked his head to one side again when she said, "Yes, indeed. I can see that bitch's head plunked on a post. Now wouldn't that be a pretty sight to greet her detective lover when he comes to call?" She laughed and with the lamp in one hand and the knife in her other, she left the house with Crutches. They made their way inch by inch across the slick, icy path to the barn. Mona almost fell four times but eventually she made it safely.

The animals heard their arrival. The cow bellowed; chickens clucked, and the pigs grunted. Crutches limped over to the cow's stall. Mona thought Piper might be hiding there so she opened the gate and lifted the lamp overhead to see. There wasn't a sign of her. Crutches went in, came right back out, and sniffed his way to the pigpen. Mona came out of the cow's stall, forgetting to close the gate.

She opened the pigpen and stepped carefully inside. The frightened pigs scrambled out of the stall and out of the barn, and the cow followed. Mona was too interested in finding Piper to pay any attention to what was happening. Her patience was wearing thin and her anger was building to a fever pitch.

She charged into the chicken coop. The flighty poultry

292

flew off their roosts, squawking in protest and pacing about nervously. Some tried to fly, only to be hindered by clipped wings. Several followed behind the protective rooster who strutted proudly. Crutches chased after him as he and his hens raced out of the coop and headed for the barnyard. The dog pursued them, but he soon tired of this game and returned to the barn.

The only stall left for Mona to search was the one where the sheep were kept. She unlatched the gate and opened it wide. One wooly ewe with a black muzzle stared boldly at her and pawed the floor. She wasn't at all happy with Mona's rude visit and began to rock back and forth as if she might charge. When the ewe saw Crutches come bounding, she and the two others in the pen charged past Mona and made their way to the outdoors and freedom. Mona was furious that she couldn't find a trace of Piper. She mumbled under her breath and tried to figure out where she might be. She finally looked overhead at the hayloft. "People always hide in those things," she said out loud.

Mona ran out of the sheep pen and climbed the rickety ladder that led to the loft. She was on the fourth rung when she heard a loud snorting sound. She held the lantern out away from her so she could see. The noises were coming from Crutches. He was frantically sniffing and scratching at something on the floor.

"What do you have there?" Mona asked excitedly. The dog paid no attention to her and kept right on scratching. Curious, Mona climbed down the ladder and went to see what Crutches was after.

Chapter Fifteen

Underground

Mona reached Crutches, who was frantically digging and barking. As she drew closer, the dog stopped what he was doing and growled. "Shut up," Mona commanded. She tried not to show her fear. The dog didn't obey. He continued snarling deep in his throat. "Shut up you dumb idiot," Mona screamed again. Crutches started to dig the floor again. Curious, Mona got down on her knees and brushed hay out of his way and saw a metal hoop and what looked to be the outline of a trap door. She smiled knowingly, and carefully placed the kerosene lamp on the floor on top of some dried hay. She rubbed her palms together and unconsciously began to hum the funeral march, but the minute her fingers touched the metal hoop Crutches began to snarl at her. He started to rock back and forth and Mona wasn't sure if he was going to attack her. She stood up, quickly shoved her hand into her pocket, and brought out a dog biscuit.

"Here, Crutches," she said sweetly. "Here's a treat for the goody-good fellow." She hoped she'd been able to mimic Nellie's sugary, singsong voice. The dog stopped and cocked his head, first to one side and then to the other. Mona tossed the biscuit into the air. She had no idea where it landed and she didn't care. Crutches limped after his treat. "That's a good sweetie pie," Mona said. "Go and get your cookie, you dumb sonofabitch."

She gripped the metal loop and pulled hard. The trap door opened. A strong odor of ammonia stung her nostrils and made her gag. She picked up the lamp and held it overhead, squinting as she strained to see what was below. She caught sight of a broken ladder, and then her eyes adjusted to the dark and she began to make out what was on the floor. She heard a squeaking sound. For a second she thought she saw something scurry. Then her gaze fell on Piper huddled in the corner, and Mona laughed insanely. "Well, well," she said. "Look who's down there." Piper looked up at her, horror etched on her face.

Her obvious fright only excited Mona further. "So you thought you could hide from me, did you? Silly girl. Wasn't it nice of Crutches to find you for me." She laughed louder, and drool slid down her chin. "That ought to teach you. That dumb sonofabitching dog who loves you so frigging much just gave you away and sealed your fate." She laughed witchlike, again. "Do a friend a favor and you get screwed each and every time."

Piper didn't respond. Despair was setting in. Her struggle was over and she knew it. A numbness crept over her body. Her heavy breathing eased, taut muscles went slack, and a vision of Matt and what might have been came to mind. She wanted to cry, but tears wouldn't come. She stared vacantly up at Mona. How haglike and pale her face seemed in the flickering lamp light.

It was time to get on with it. She tried to speak and somehow managed to find her voice. "Mona. What are you going to do to me?" And then she regretted the question. She really didn't want to know.

Mona relished toying with her underground captive. She giggled and drooled some more. "What am I going to do to you?" she said. "Why I'm going to kill you, stupid." She clapped her hands. "I can't believe how easy getting rid of you is going to be. You've all been so easy to dispose of—especially Steven. He did it for me. Diabetes does that, you know. That stupid dog," she said. "Now that's a real pal giving you away like that. Not to worry, Piper, because you won't last long in that hole. You'll probably die of exposure or starve to death." Mona paused for a second and then she said, "Maybe I should push Crutches over the edge so he can keep you company. Maybe one of you will wind up eating the other. If I send him down there with you—then I'll have killed two birds with one stone."

"No!" Piper cried. "Oh, please, Mona. Let me out. I don't want to die."

Crutches heard Piper cry out. He came running and stood next to Mona. He looked down in the hole and spied Piper. He began to whimper and wag his bushy tail which kept hitting Mona in the face. "Stop that," she demanded. Crutches growled at her. It was time to distract him with a biscuit so she could push him into the pit with Piper. She reached into her pocket, grabbed one, and held it in front of the dog's black wet nose. But Crutches was no longer interested in treats. He looked right in Mona's face and then he looked down at Piper. It was as if the dog was sizing up the situation. Protective instincts took over. This increased when Piper began to sob uncontrollably.

"Take your cookie, you dumb jerk," Mona commanded. Crutches ignored her. "Shithead," she said and spat in the dog's face. He blinked and then his massive body tensed. Mona was oblivious to the dog's actions. She was having too much fun tormenting Piper to give a damn about anything else. "I've decided not to let Crutches join you," she yelled down into the dugout. "All I have to do now is close this trap door and you'll be all alone." She smiled as her evil mind conjured up an image of Piper's panic when the door slammed shut forever.

"My, my, Piper," Mona taunted. "You sure are lucky to wind up in such an offbeat grave," she mused. "Charles Timothy Watts will be so disappointed that he doesn't get to put you in one of his *containers*. No blue lining for you. Remember I picked out light blue for Steven? But that isn't your color, is it?" she said and wrinkled her brow. "I think blood red would suit you." She stared at the trap door and said, "Well. I think I'll close this now and get on about my business. I have to leave town before someone comes here and butts in."

Just as Mona was about to close the trap door, she saw a fat rat scurry across Piper's feet. Piper screamed and quickly drew her legs underneath her.

"Piper. Stop all that whimpering." Mona said and sounded disgusted. "For heaven's sake, you should be grateful that you aren't down there all alone. That rat acts like he enjoys your company. Maybe he's hungry! Yes. That's it. He wants a snack. I read a horror book once that described in detail how much rats like to munch on humans. Damnedest thing I ever read. Made me want to throw up. I bet your friend will nibble your toes first and then he'll try your fingers. I suppose it's like gnawing on a bunch of chicken wings. Your blood will be like barbecue sauce." She paused for a second and then she said, "I don't imagine there are any worms down there. Now, if it were spring or summer that would be a different story. Did you know that worms like to slither in and out of noses, eyeballs, ears, and other places? Oh, Piper. You're in for such a trip."

Piper's horrified facial expression and her whimpering continued to thrill Mona. She decided to tease her a bit more before she finished with her. When she started to close the trap door, Piper screamed. Crutches managed to get his head out of the way just in time. He began to run around in circles, barking and snarling. Mona could hear Piper's muffled pleas coming from behind the door. She opened the lid halfway, yelled, "Peekaboo," and then slammed it shut. The next time she lifted it and lowered the lamp, she saw that Piper had her head down on her knees. She could see that her body trembled violently. "Ohhh, Piper. I'm sorry," she said sincerely. "I've changed my mind. I'm not going to kill you. C'mon give me a hand and I'll help you out."

Piper looked up at her with distrust. "Please, Mona. Don't tease me," she pleaded.

"C'mon, Piper," Mona said impatiently. "Hurry up before I change my mind."

Piper struggled to her feet. She kept her eye on the rat

that was in an opposite corner watching her. Piper knew that they attacked if cornered. She took tiny, slow steps so as not to threaten him. He moved once and made a noise in his throat. Piper froze and held her breath.

Mona laughed. "What's the matter down there? Is your flea-riddled friend with the long skinny tail getting nervous? Mind your manners, Piper or he'll leap at your throat. God. That would be messy. I don't think Watts could patch you up if that happened."

Piper covered her throat with one hand and with her other she grabbed the side of the ladder and quickly hopped onto the bottom rung. The rat moved. Piper screamed and banged her head against the ladder trying to shield her throat, but the rodent scurried past her into a hole in another corner. His tail was the last to disappear.

"What a grand show that was," Mona chirped. "I thought he had you for a second. Now c'mon Piper," she said impatiently. "I'm getting tired of you being so slow."

Piper stepped onto the second rung and then the third, where the ladder was broken in half. She looked up at Mona's smiling face. Mona reached down into the hole and put her hand so close to Piper's that their fingers touched. Piper stretched as far as she could. She felt something tear in her shoulder. Just as she was about to grab Mona's hand she pulled it back out of her reach. Piper tried to stretch more and in doing so lost her balance and fell backward. She landed with a thud on the hard floor.

Mona laughed. "Oh, well. I can see this isn't going to work. I'm tired of waiting for you, Piper." She sighed deeply. "Have a nice trip, darling," she cooed. "I hope it's not too hot where you'll be going. Give my love to Kelly, Steven . . . and Satan." She slammed the lid.

Piper scrambled to her feet and tried in vain to jump up to reach the trap door. "Nooo, Mona!" She hollered at the top of her lungs. "Don't! Let me out. Oh, God, no! Please. Let me out." She yelled until she had no voice left. Her heart pounded so hard she thought it might burst. Her mouth was dry and her legs felt weak. She leaned her weak body against the damp, earthen walls. And then to her absolute terror she felt something tickle her toes and then the top of her right foot. Piper knew what it was and then a cool, damp, thin spaghettilike thing swished against her skin. Claws dug into her; the rodent scurried up her leg. She tried to scream and couldn't. Her stomach churned, she struggled not to vomit, and her throat was burned by stomach acid. The rat was on her thigh now. She could tell it had slowed its pace. Piper's reflexes worked, and she doubled her fist and whacked the rat, knocking it onto the floor. She blocked her ears so she didn't have to listen to it squeal. She stood rigid, tried not to breathe hard, and shielded her throat with her hands. Her eyes were shut tight so she didn't have to watch the rat gnaw her throat when he jumped. Her ears hummed loudly.

What Piper couldn't possibly realize at that moment, was that the rat, defeated and a bit bruised, had crawled away and into its hole.

Overhead, Mona was so happy that she did a little dance on top of the trap door. Every two or three steps she stomped her feet for Piper's benefit. Once or twice she kicked at Crutches, but never connected. He finally backed away out of her reach. "What's the matter with you, stupid?" Mona asked. "Think I'm going to kick you in the face? Miss your pal? You dumb sonofabitch." She laughed insanely.

Mona was so far removed from reality, trying to be Ginger Rogers, that she wasn't aware that Crutches had bared his teeth and started after her. Just when she finally noticed it, the dog leaped, knocked her backwards, and pinned her against the hard floor. Her flailing left arm collided with the kerosene lamp and tipped it over. The fragile glass globe shattered. Oil leaked, the flaming wick ignited more hay, and a blazing trail started across the barn floor, igniting dried hay and Mona's clothes. Crutches' instincts took over. He jumped off Mona, and limped as fast as his lame legs would carry him for the safety of the barnyard.

Frenzied, Mona tried to make her way to the outside.

Once there, she knew that she could roll her body on the ground and put out the fire. The barn was rapidly filling with smoke. Her eyes smarted and watered, her air felt shut off, and she started to choke. The barn was fast becoming a roaring inferno. Flames shot across the floor and licked at the bottom of the animal stalls. In seconds the fire climbed up. Overhead, the hayloft ignited. Flames shot through the old roof. The angry wind fanned the blaze. Smoke poured out of every opening. The dark, stormy sky lit up.

A neighbor down the road happened to glance out his window to see a red glow in the sky and immediately phoned the fire department. "Jesus Christ, almighty," he said to his wife and two children as they all dashed about putting on boots and coats to lend a hand to their neighbors. "I bet it's Stolls's barn. No way in hell will the firemen be able to put out that inferno. God. I hope John and Nellie were able to save the animals. Jesus, I hope that old couple is okay."

Mona was inches away from the open barn doorway. She was just about to stumble through it when another strong gust of wind raced across the open fields, caught the barn doors, and slammed them shut. Fumbling, she tried to push them open but they wouldn't budge. *"No!"* she screamed. She kicked them with all her might, and then a large clump of burning hay fell from above and landed on top of her. Her hair sizzled and disappeared. She used her hands to try and put out the fire. Still damp, kerosene soaked, her shirt sleeves ignited, and soon Mona's blouse, bra, slacks, and underwear were flaming. She'd hidden Piper's car keys inside her bra, and they fell to the floor as her clothing disintegrated. She cried out in agony; then she couldn't do that anymore because her throat and lungs were seared. Her breasts, and stomach were scorched from the intense heat. She fell to the ground and lay in a fetal position on her funeral pyre.

Outside, the barn animals ran as fast as they could away from the inferno. Crutches watched, trembling, from the front porch. He began to howl as the fire trucks turned into the driveway. They wasted no time fighting the blaze.

The seasoned fire fighters knew that the barn was beyond hope. The best that could be done was to make certain that the house and shed didn't catch. Fortunately, the wind was beginning to die, so it couldn't fan the blaze. The police and neighbors arrived. Tatjana's farm was alive with people trying to put out the fire and save the barn, but it was no use.

Shortly, two sides of the barn had burned to the ground. The doors were scorched, but standing. The roof caved in. What was once the barn floor was no more. There was nothing left of the interior but a pile of smouldering rubble.

When it was safe to do so, one of the fireman opened the doors. He stepped back and gasped when he saw the charred form on the floor in front of him. At first, he thought it was the remains of a dog or a pig. But when he studied it more carefully he saw teeth with fillings and knew it was a baked human being.

"Jesus!" he said and ran away from the grisly sight. "I found a body!" he yelled to his buddies. "Someone send for the medical examiner."

Two others came running and stared at the mass on the floor. They quickly turned away. Whoever it had been had burned on the outside and boiled on the inside. Only a few patches of skin remained, looking like grilled chicken that had been cooked too long—horribly blistered, red, black, and swollen. They seeped and hung from the bone. Stubs of what were once arms and legs were bent because the muscles had contracted. Mona would've been mortified if she could've seen the looks of revulsion that covered the faces of the firemen, and now the rescue people, who gawked with horror at what was before them.

One of the firemen covered the remains with a blanket. Another automatically began to stomp out the flames. "Quit that!" yelled the one who'd covered Mona with the blanket. "For Christ's sake. That might be one of the people who live here. Nice old couple. We go to the same church. But if that's one of them—where is the other? They're never apart. Go call the state Fire Marshal. I think he'd better come and take a look to make certain there wasn't any arson or weird stuff involved here."

One of the policemen nearby overheard the fireman say to call the marshal. He took it upon himself to go to his squad car and call the state police. The dispatcher said he'd have a detective come to the scene as soon as possible.

Matt Carter had finished processing the murder scene in Bath, having stopped at the crime lab in Augusta. He'd had no trouble driving because the snow had stopped and the plows and trucks had been out and cleared, salted, and sanded the roads. Matt felt fortunate that the freezing rain hadn't reached as far north as he'd been. And he was relieved that he'd been able to drive at a normal speed to get back to Piper and to see how Nellie was doing. He kept trying to call Piper on his phone, but nobody answered. He was worried about her safety. The lab in Augusta hadn't helped. The evidence guys hadn't turned up anything on Kelly Stewart to pin her murder on Mona. And the pathologist who performed the autopsy on Steven told Matt that he hadn't met with any foul play.

Matt shifted his thoughts. Now he was reliving Mona's performance at Steven's funeral. "What an actress." he grumbled. His head ached and his stomach growled. He knew that one of these days he'd get an ulcer. Now his mind held a vision of what had happened earlier that afternoon at the crime lab. His colleagues couldn't believe the rage he'd gone into after Jake phoned him and told him that the Cape Bethany Police had called and said that they had questioned a few more of the Hadleys' party guests and had come up with one with a record. "He went to the party dressed like a clown," Jake said. "Striped suit and all. Guess what he did time for, Matt?"

"What?"

"Rape and assault. And, our Bozo the clown has skipped town. Maybe he joined the circus," Jake joked, but Matt didn't laugh. "We put out an all points on him."

"Good," Matt said. "But I don't think he did it. I think Mo . . ."

"I think he might be our man," Jake interrupted. "I bet he intended to rape the Stewart girl and he had to keep her quiet. He strangled her in the process."

"Could be," Matt said. "Still, I think . . ." Matt didn't finish. What was the use? He had no evidence to link Mona to Kelly's death. And poor Steven conveniently died before she could kill him. Matt became so frustrated that he began to rave about the party guests, the rescue people, and the Cape Bethany police and how they'd fucked up all the evidence the night Kelly Stewart was murdered. He recalled that he went on to vent his rage at what happened when the police put their mitts all over the insulin bottle and syringe. He couldn't remember which one of his men had said that the Cape Bethany cops should've been arrested for handling everything in sight. Matt was embarrassed after his anger subsided. He'd apologized to everyone that had witnessed his tirade. All present told him to forget it. He knew that they were probably thinking that he should be removed from the case. And he knew that if he didn't tread carefully he'd be suspended.

About the time Matt passed by the town of Topsham he felt sleepy. When he reached Brunswick he took the first possible exit, stopped at a restaurant, and bought himself a cup of coffee to help keep him awake. He also ordered a ham and cheese sandwich on rye, heavy on the mustard, and another cup of coffee to go. He spied a pay phone and decided to try and call Piper again to let him know that he would soon be at the farm, barring icy roads. He dialed the Stolls's number. There was still no answer. After trying three more times he gave up. He thought about calling the hospital and changed his mind because he didn't want to disturb the Stolls. He assumed Piper would be at the farm by the time he got there.

Shortly thereafter, driving down the highway, Matt noticed a red glow illuminating the sky. The closer he got to the farm the more concerned he became. He picked up speed. When he turned into the driveway he immediately saw that it was the barn that was on fire. He took note of all the people milling about. He didn't see Piper, but he saw her car, and a little alarm went off in his head. If she was there, she would've seen him drive in and come over to him. He glanced at the house and saw that it was pitch black. When he pulled to a halt he was in such a state that he forgot about the icy conditions and put too much pressure on the brake. The car didn't stop until it slid into the side of Piper's and crushed the door on the driver's side.

The rescue crew came running and yanked open Matt's door to see if he was injured. Because he was buckled up he only suffered a slight wrenching of his neck. He was in such a hurry to find Piper that he didn't even acknowledge anyone else's presence. He quickly unbuckled his safety belt and threw the car into park, not bothering to shut it off. He climbed out and ran. He slipped on the ice and fell face first, skinned his nose, and gave himself a fat lip. Once again, the rescue people came running. One of them handed Matt his car keys. He took them, shoved them deep into his coat pocket, and quickly got to his feet.

He noticed a group of firemen in a huddle around something on the ground in front of the barn doors. "Did you call the medical examiner?" a fireman asked one of the rescue people. Matt's insides twisted. He felt dizzy. "Piper," he managed to yell. All the while he ran he said a silent prayer, God. Please don't let it be her. Please. His eyes darted from one person to another, searching in vain for her. He was totally unaware that the rescue people were right behind him every step of the way. All he cared about was Piper.

Matt stood over the blanketed form and took a deep breath to keep from breathing in the odor. The rescue people stood beside him and tried not to gag. He pulled the blanket back and gasped. He'd seen a few burn victims before and he'd seen plenty of photos, but nothing could compare to what was on the ground in front of him. And then he caught sight of something shining on the ground near the entrance of the barn. He walked over and picked up a set of keys. He instantly recognized the silver disk. "Oh, God. Piper," he backed away, turned, closed his eyes, and moaned.

Someone came over to Matt and said, "I'm the State Fire Marshal. Do you know who that is?"

"I th-, I think it's Pi-Piper Jordan."

"Does she live here?"

"No. Sh-she was visiting."

"Do you know the family that lives here?"

"Yes. Their name is Stoll."

"Where are they?"

"At the hospital. The woman is sick. Her husband is probably spending the night with her. Piper offered to feed the animals for him."

"I see. Say, I've seen you before," the marshal said.

"I'm a State Police Detective."

"Sure. Now I recognize you. We worked on the Roberts case last year. Remember?"

Matt didn't say anything.

"What are you doing here?"

"I, I was eng-engaged to, to the victim."

"Jesus, I'm sorry. Damn." The marshal was silent for a second and then he said, "What a shame. . . . These old barns go up like tinder boxes once they catch."

Matt was about to tell him to shut his mouth when he felt something lick his hand and then he heard whimpering. He looked down. Crutches looked up at him. Before Matt could pat him, the dog took hold of his jacket sleeve and tugged. Matt ignored him. Suddenly, the impact of what had happened hit him. He screamed *"Nooooo."* His cry was carried across the open fields by the wind. He tried to fight the marshal and two rescue people who tried to comfort him. They finally convinced him to climb into the back of the ambulance so he could have some privacy until he could get control of himself. It took several minutes for him to stop crying. When he was okay he asked to be left alone for a few minutes. Everyone made a quick exit.

Matt sat on the edge of a cot in a stupor. Nothing seemed

real. He tried to stand and fell back. His brow felt cool and clammy. His arms and legs felt as limp as noodles, his head throbbed, and guilt consumed him. If he hadn't stopped in Brunswick to get something to eat he might've been able to save Piper. Reality hit again. Piper was dead. *Piper, oh, Piper,* he cried inside, and then he went numb all over.

Matt couldn't hear Crutches whimpering outside the ambulance. The poor dog frantically paced back and forth waiting for Matt to appear. Finally, he plunked his wide haunches on the icy ground and began to howl. A fireman came over and crooned, "There, there old buddy. It's gonna be okay. Hush now." Crutches stopped and began to whimper again. The fireman had to leave to help the others continue to wet down the smouldering mess that used to be a barn.

"What was wrong with the dog?" a buddy asked.

"He knows," he replied.

"He knows what?"

"He knows that someone died here."

"C'mon. He's a dog—not a fortune teller."

"Oh, yeah. Well I've got news for you. My grandmother used to say that when a dog howls like that it means someone just died or is going to. I used to think she was off her rocker. But you know what?"

"What?"

"She was right."

"Give me a break. You've been reading too many of those weird books."

"No way. Honest to God. She was right. I bet I've heard a dog howl like that six or seven times. I'd get the shivers—like now." He debated with himself whether to show his buddy the goose-bumps on his arms and decided against it.

"Jesus. Now you've done it," the skeptic said.

"What do you mean?"

"You and your damned stories. Now I'll never have another minute's peace when I hear a howling dog. Jesus."

Headlights beamed in the driveway. One car belonged to Paul Reynolds of the State Police. The other was a station wagon belonging to the local medical examiner. Both climbed out of their vehicles at the same time and took a look around. Paul recognized Matt's dented car. Why was he here? He's supposed to be in Bath. He stared at the damage to both cars, whistled, and said out loud to himself, "Jesus, it looks like he wrecked his front end."

"You think that's bad," said a fireman passing by with an axe. "The guy lost it when he saw the body. They had to almost carry him to the ambulance."

"Where is he now?" Paul asked.

"I think he's still in there," the fireman told him and pointed at the ambulance. "He wanted to be alone. The way he acts you'd think he knew whoever that is." He pointed across the way at a blanket covered form on the ground. "I haven't seen one that bad in a long time. Guess I'll never get used to that awful smell."

Paul went over to the ambulance to find Matt. He opened the back door and climbed in. Matt looked up. Paul was shocked to see his friend in such a state. "Jesus, Matt. What happened? What are you doing here? I thought you were in Augusta."

"I was," Matt said and paused. He wiped his brow and took a deep breath. "I finished up early. Piper was staying here. The place belongs to Tatjana, her boss. She was going to feed the animals for the caretakers because the woman is in the hospital. Her husband is with her." Matt looked down at his hands and watched them tremble. Then he became aware that he was shaking all over and he felt ice cold. He wondered if he was in shock.

". . . how do you know it's her?" Paul asked. "That body is charred so badly you can't tell."

"It's her. I found her keys near the body," he snapped.

"I know, but maybe that guy, the caretaker borrowed her car to come home to feed the animals. Maybe Piper stayed at the hospital with the wife. Did you call to see?"

"There's no need. I know it's Piper."

"I'll call the hospital to make certain," Paul said.

"Don't talk to the Stolls," Matt cautioned. "If it is Piper, I want to break the news to them."

Paul nodded and left to phone the hospital from his car. He was back in a few minutes. Matt could tell he had bad news by the look on his face.

"It's her isn't it?"

Paul nodded. "Looks that way. I spoke with the head nurse. Mr. Stoll is with his wife. Did you look in the house to see if you could find anything more to prove that it's her?"

"No."

"Well, you stay here and I'll go."

"No, wait. I'm coming with you," Matt said and stood up. The room spun and then straightened out. His legs felt rubbery but he had to go with Paul just in case he was wrong. Inside, he remained certain that the body was that of Piper.

When the two men climbed out of the ambulance, Crutches came over to Matt and took hold of his sleeve again. Matt patted his head. Crutches whimpered and looked in the direction of the barn. "Dog's really undone," Paul said. "If I didn't know better I'd say he was trying to tell us something."

Matt wasn't listening. He was too preoccupied with what he was going to find inside the house. Crutches started to bark, but Matt and Paul ignored him and walked up the porch steps. Still whining, Crutches followed the two men into the kitchen. Paul flipped a light switch on the wall just as a strong gust of wind rattled the windowpanes, and the copper chandelier over the kitchen table came on, flickered, and went out. Matt and Paul stood perfectly still, waiting to see what was going to happen. The bulb flickered, came back on, and stayed on. The men scanned the kitchen. Matt flinched when he spied Piper's purse and coat on the oak tree beside him. His agony returned, stronger than before. He was about to show Paul what he'd discovered when he noticed that he'd disappeared into the dining room. Matt was too distraught to call him. He leaned against the kitchen wall and just stared blankly at Nellie's stove.

Paul went from the dining room to the living room and saw nothing. It was time to go upstairs. Once he reached the top, he realized how quiet it was. He went into the first bedroom in his path, turned on the light, and could tell right away that this belonged to the old caretakers. A pair of farmer jeans and a red flannel shirt were draped over a rocking chair. A basket full of knitting rested beside the chair. Paul exited and went into the next bedroom and groped for the light switch. A lovely scent of perfume drifted past his nostrils, and when he could see, he noticed a pair of woman's shoes on the floor next to the bed and a pink blouse folded neatly on top of a dresser. *This must be Piper's room,* he thought. He hated to go downstairs and tell Matt that he now felt Piper was dead. He wasn't sure that Matt could take much more. The guy was ready to snap. Paul opened the door and stepped into the hall.

He was about to go back downstairs when he noticed three more doors. He opened the one that was closest to him, flipped the light switch, and saw that it was the bathroom. He closed that door and opened the last door. Pretty soon, Matt heard Paul yelling to him all the way down in the kitchen. "Jesus, Matt! Come quick. Well I'll be damned."

Matt, now oblivious to how weak he felt, ran through the house, and took the stairs two at a time to the second floor. Paul heard him and called out, "I'm in here."

Matt charged into the room to see Paul standing next to an open suitcase on a chair. He was holding a pad of paper. Matt also noticed a familiar looking pair of tan slacks and an olive shirt. It was the same outfit that Mona Hadley wore when he'd questioned her after Steven died. God! he said to himself. She's been here! Jesus! She burned Piper!

"You'd better have a look at this, Matt," Paul said and handed him the pad.

Matt took it, quickly read the pages, and his face turned the color of the paper. He was aware that he was now perspiring profusely. When he finished reading, he handed the pad back to Paul. He didn't say a word as he turned and walked out of the room into the hallway. He braced his body against the wall and in doing so bumped into a picture that crashed to the floor with a sound of shattering glass. Paul came running to see what was wrong and found Matt with his head against the wall. Matt tried to speak to him but he couldn't get any words out. It became impossible for him to stop the tears that fell from his eyes.

"God. I'm sorry, Matt," Paul said and felt like crying himself. Inside he recalled what he'd just read. The Hadley woman said she killed Kelly Stewart, her husband, and now Piper Jordan. And she said that Matt and Piper were fu . . . *Christ. No wonder he's so upset.* He knew he had to get him out of there right away. "C'mon, Matt," he said. "Let's go. Can you walk?"

"I'm okay," Matt lied.

"I'm sorry. I didn't know about you and the Jordan woman." Paul said and started down the stairs. Matt slowly followed.

Crutches waited for them in the kitchen. He came limping over to Matt. He took hold of his red collar and led him outside. The crowd of curious neighbors was still gathered. Only the firemen, the marshal, and medical examiner remained. They all watched Crutches, Matt, and Paul come down the porch steps, and then everybody's gaze turned toward the entrance to the driveway. Headlights beamed and then a black hearse pulled up next to the medical examiner. The driver shut the engine off and climbed out. He was a local man, tall, gray-haired, fatherly-looking, and well-respected in the Freeport area. His clothing and shoes were black. The medical examiner started to talk to him. The man nodded and went to the rear of the hearse, opened the door, and brought out a black body bag. Matt couldn't bear to watch what he knew was about to happen. He tugged on the dog's collar and they went back into the house.

The undertaker asked a fireman if he could borrow a shovel. He was given one and then he walked over to the

310

remains and laid the unzipped body bag on the ground. "I need someone with a shovel to help me," he called out. A fireman with a strong stomach came to his aid. In unison they lifted the body onto their shovels and placed it on top of the body bag. The undertaker knelt down, and with gloved hands zipped the bag, and then he and the fireman carried it over and loaded it into the hearse.

The undertaker closed the rear door. Then he walked over to the medical examiner who said, "Take the remains to the Maine General morgue in Portland. I called them. They know you're on the way." The undertaker nodded, went back to his hearse, climbed behind the driver's seat, and drove away.

Matt had come outside with the dog. He'd watched the hearse disappear into the dark of night. Paul started to go to him and stopped. He knew that there was nothing he could do for Matt. Only time would heal.

Matt stood on the porch, wishing that his own life was over. Then a strong wave of anger swooped over him, and he had to find Mona Hadley. When he did he'd kill her. Then he remembered the Stolls. He and Crutches went down the steps and went towards his car. "Put an all points out on the Hadley woman," he ordered Paul.

"Where are you going, Matt?" Paul asked.

"I'm going to the hospital and tell the Stolls what happened." Poor Nellie, he thought. The shock could kill her. "C'mon, Crutches, old boy, I'm taking you home with me tonight. Let's go. I can't stand to stay here any longer." Just before Matt climbed in his car, the neighbor and his family, who had seen the blaze from his house, appeared with his wife and children herding John's livestock. One of the kids opened the shed doors and the animals were put inside. When the doors were slammed shut the neighbor man said, "I don't know if we got 'em all cause I don't know how many John had. They'll be all right in there for the time being. Tell John me and my family will help make different arrangements whenever he's ready." Matt nodded. "Well, I guess I'll take my family and go home now. Nothing else we can do here tonight." He put his arm around his wife's shoulder and they left, their kids trailing behind.

Paul watched Matt help Crutches get into his car. The dog had great difficulty lifting his lame rear quarters onto the back seat. Paul wasn't certain that the car could still be driven, being so smashed up. But the engine caught right away. Matt waved at him as he went past. Paul watched until he faded from sight. *God,* he said to himself. *He was in love with her. Jesus, that poor sonofabitch will never be the same.* He kicked the icy ground, told the others that he was leaving, climbed into his car, and left the farm behind. He never wanted to see that sad place again.

While the barn burned above, underground Piper could hear noise and smell smoke. She had her back plastered against the dirt wall, not daring to move for fear that the rat would come after her again. She was so cold. She tried to think of pleasant things—anything—but dying.

Her eyes had grown accustomed to the dark, and overhead she could see flickering light that illuminated her tomb through the cracks between the boards. "Fire!" she screamed. "The barn must be on fire. I'm going to burn to death! There has to be another way out of here!" She looked down and caught sight of the old kerosene lamp she'd spied when John first showed her the place. "Now I know what slaves must've felt like," she muttered, praying that the room had only been used in times of danger. She wondered if the rat was part of a family tree that dated back to the Civil War. Her gaze rested on the lamp again. And then she remembered. She felt a bulge in her pocket. "Thank God," she cried. How could she have been so stupid. She thrust a trembling hand deep into her pocket and pulled out the matches she'd taken from Nellie's buffet. Her hopes soared when she saw that they were still dry.

She got down on all fours and reached for the lamp. When she finally found it, she picked it up and cringed over the itchy feel of webs that clung to her fingers. While lifting the fragile globe she pretended she didn't feel the light tickling as a tiny body scurried up her arm. She tore off a match and struck it. But before the wick could catch the match went out. Fumbling, she tore another from the book, struck it, and held it against the top of the wick. That one burned out, too. She lit more. Soon she was down to the last one. She watched as that dancing orange flame flickered wildly and died. She picked up the lamp, held it next to her ear, shook it, and heard nothing. There was no oil. She was so angry that she shoved the lamp out of her way; she heard the globe shatter. Death loomed. *Don't think about dying,* she told herself over and over. *Think about Matt. Think of a way to get out.*

A wave of nausea came, and she tried not to vomit. Her ears hummed. Her body started to feel prickly all over. She wanted to scream but nothing came. She got to her feet and began to beat her fists against the hard dirt walls. Her hands were soon bruised and bloodied, but she couldn't see them. She was in such a state of shock she didn't feel the pain. She didn't stop beating the wall until she was spent. Finally, she opened her fists and placed her hands and face against the wall. "Matt," she cried over and over. "Oh, please, God. Let me out of here. I don't want to die." She kicked the broken chair and hurt her foot. Suddenly her air felt shut off. Her legs buckled. She tried to catch herself before she fell. The minute she landed on the hard ground she began to sob. She curled into the fetal position. All she did was sob and moan.

Piper couldn't see the rat staring at her with its glassy eyes. She was moaning too loudly to hear the nervous squeaking it made. When she moved her legs again the rat flinched, and then it jumped. Piper held back a scream when she felt tiny claws dig into her flesh and begin to crawl rapidly up her torn pantyhose, onto her skirt, and then onto her chest. She covered her throat with her hands and closed her eyes tight. She could feel the rat's claws on her hands now, and then it started sniffing around her chin. Clinging to consciousness, she tried to visualize

313

Matt. Her lips began to tickle. She opened her eyes and looked down her nose to try and see. She could tell that the rodent had reached her mouth. His damp feeling tail brushed her cheek when it turned around and climbed onto her chest, stopped for a minute, jumped to the ground, and scurried off.

Piper inhaled deeply to calm herself and only took more smoke into her lungs. She became aware that the room was filling with it. She heard a crackling noise and looked overhead. Sparks, looking like a squadron of fireflies, were falling through the cracks now, and Piper knew that she was going to suffocate. She quickly inched her way across the floor on her bottom until she bumped into a wall. Her eyes stung and watered. Her throat felt dry. Smoke rises, she remembered, and quickly stretched out on the hard floor, keeping her face down, praying the rat was gone. That's when she felt a rush of cold air hit her in the face. She followed the draft with her hands until she felt the outline of a door. And then her fingers touched a thick metal ring. Forgetting her injuries, she quickly got onto her feet and using both hands yanked on the ring with all her might.

Old hinges screamed when the door opened, and cold air rushed past Piper, providing more of a draft to fan the flames above. She went through the narrow opening and quickly shut the door behind her in hopes of escaping the fire. It was so dark where she was that she couldn't see a thing. She inhaled to clear her lungs and with both arms outstretched she touched solid walls on both sides. Feeling the surface, she could tell that it was probably made out of bricks. And then she knew that she must be in an underground passageway, used for runaway slaves and long since forgotten. Hope returned. "I'm going to get out!" she cried. And then Mona came to mind. Death still stalked her. Still, she had to take a chance.

Moving slowly, Piper went forward into the darkness, now putting both sore hands in front of her. She walked on, praying she would see a light at the end of the tunnel, like in the movies she'd seen. Thinking about Matt helped her keep her sanity. "I have to get out," she said over and over. After what seemed an endless tunnel, she walked into a wall and bumped her forehead. Frenzied, she began to feel about, searching for an escape. Her spirits soared as her fingers touched what felt like hinges. Freedom ruled her thoughts as she traced the outline of a wooden door, but she couldn't find a knob. Defeat pounced on her. "I can't open the goddamned door," she screamed and beat her fists against the hard wood. She considered turning back and knew if she did she would surely burn. There was no way out; her fate was sealed. She sat down on the hard ground and leaned her back against the useless door. Her death was immiment. "Oh, God," she prayed. "Please make it fast. Please. I love you, Matt," she cried and suddenly felt faint. She closed her eyes and saw her parents and Kelly. "Hi, Piper," Kelly said and smiled warmly. "I've missed you so much." Piper sighed and then everything went black.

Outside, the firemen had hoses aimed on the blazing barn. Every so often, one soaked the shed and the house, just in case the wind shifted and the fire spread. Experience had taught them that they would be there until early morning. Their faces were sooty; their feet were freezing having been soaked by the water, and they craved a cup of coffee.

Meanwhile, Matt arrived at the Maine General Hospital. As soon as he parked his car, he shut the engine off, turned and faced Crutches, who was curled into a ball on the back seat. "I hate to leave you," he said. "But I have to tell John and Nellie what's happened." Crutches stared at him and whimpered. Matt climbed out of the car and walked towards the hospital. He had no idea how he was going to break the news to the Stolls. Just before he went through the door, he spied a black hearse come around the corner, and then he recognized the driver. He couldn't bear

315

to look and ran inside.

Once Matt reached Nellie's floor, he stopped at the desk and told the head nurse that he had to tell the Stolls that their barn had burned and that a friend had died in the fire. The nurse immediately phoned Nellie's doctor to get permission for Matt to tell the Stolls and to find out what she should do in case Nellie needed medical attention. When she hung up she told Matt that the doctor said that it was okay to inform them about the tragedy and that the doctor had ordered a sedative for Nellie in case she needed one. "I have to come with you," she told Matt.

The nurse was the first to enter Nellie's room. Matt could hear laughter coming from a television set hung high on the wall. The minute he stepped inside he saw John sitting on a hard chair beside Nellie's bed. They were holding hands.

"Well look who's here," John said to Nellie. "Nice of you to drop by."

Matt didn't say anything. Both Nellie and John could tell by the way he and the nurse acted that something was dreadfully wrong.

"Come in, Matthew," Nellie said. The nurse took her place on the opposite side of the bed from John.

"What's the matter, young fella?" John asked and became aware that he felt a thud in his stomach.

"I'm afraid I have some bad news," Matt said and got right to the point. "Mona Hadley murdered Pi-Piper. She set your barn on fire. It's burned to the ground."

Nellie gasped and grabbed her chest. The nurse was ready. She felt for her pulse. Nellie shooed her away. "I'm okay, I'm okay," she said. "Dear, God, no! I can't believe it."

John sat there in a stupor. Matt noticed that the old man's hands had started to tremble. He wasn't certain, but it looked like his bottom lip was quivering. John kept clearing his throat. He wanted to talk but no words came out of his mouth.

Tears started down Nellie's wrinkled cheeks. "Piper,"

she cried. "That poor dear child. Oh, God! Where is Crutches?"

"He's fine," Matt reassured her. "I have him in my car. I'll take him home with me tonight."

John nodded and then he found his voice. "Are the other animals . . . ?" His voice cracked.

"The livestock escaped before the fire, but I don't know how. One of your neighbors put them in the shed for the night."

John nodded. "Piper," he said softly. "I can't believe it." He hung his head so nobody could see him crying. His voice cracked again when he said, "I hope she didn't suffer." He was sorry he said that. He really couldn't bear to know the answer.

But Matt didn't say a word. He was too upset to continue and left the room without saying goodbye. He didn't bother taking the elevator. Instead, he found the stairs and quickly made his way to the lobby and outside to his car. Crutches saw him approach. The minute Matt opened the car door and sat behind the wheel he felt a rough tongue slide over his cheek. "Okay, okay, boy," Matt said. Crutches stopped. Matt wiped his face with his sleeve and said, "Nellie's feeling better. She and John send their love." He patted the dog's head. "We're going to my place now. It's not like the farm, but it will have to do." He put the key in the ignition, started the engine, and drove off. He never spoke another word to the dog all the way to his cabin. His thoughts were consumed with Piper. He hadn't experienced such black depression since his mother died. Once again he wanted his own life to end.

The minute Matt and Crutches walked into the cabin, Matt was aware of how lonely it felt without Piper there to greet him. He tried not to think about her. After a quick hot shower he made a bed for Crutches out of some old blankets. The dog stood in the middle of the floor and watched Matt with a curious expression on his face. Matt had to coax him over to the bed and to get down onto it. The dog was obviously tired because he sighed deeply and closed his eyes in seconds. Matt sat beside him and stroked his massive head until he was certain he wasn't going to wake up. When Matt was sure the dog was asleep, he quietly got to his feet, pulled the covers back, and climbed into bed, avoiding the side that Piper had slept on.

Sleep didn't come to Matt. He just couldn't get Piper out of his mind. Finally, he took the pillow that she'd used and clutched it to him. He smelled her perfume and felt a lump in his throat. Now they were making love. He was holding her in his arms and kissing her again. Grief seared his soul and kept him awake until long after midnight.

Nightmares plagued Matt. He saw Piper in a dark place, crying out for him. She was cold, smeared with blood and she cried, "Help me, Matt," over and over while Matt moaned and stirred in bed. His eyes popped open and he froze when he felt something cold and wet touch his nose. He turned his head and felt hot breath on his face and his cheek was washed. "Crutches," he said, sighing with relief. "Jesus, you scared me." The dog sat on his haunches and stared at Matt. He was panting and his tongue was hanging out. Matt turned and looked out his window and was blinded by the early morning sunshine. He closed his eyes and when he did Crutches barked at him. Matt turned his head and opened his eyes to see Crutches making ready to kiss him again. He dove under the covers, slid across the bed to the other side, and climbed out. He wasted no time getting dressed. He couldn't erase the memory of his nightmare about Piper.

Crutches limped over to him. "Hungry, old boy?" Matt asked. "Don't worry. I'll feed you just as soon as I get you home. But first, I have to call headquarters and then I want to call Nellie and John to see how they're doing." Crutches cocked his head and barked.

Matt dialed headquarters first and talked to Paul, who told him that there was no sign of Mona Hadley. He could tell that Matt was disappointed by the way he exhaled into the receiver.

"I'm going to the farm," Matt said. "I want to look

318

around in the daylight to make certain we didn't miss anything last night."

"Are you sure you want to do that alone?" Paul asked. "I'll go if you're not up to it or I'll meet you there."

"Thanks, Paul," Matt said. "I can handle it." He dreaded asking the next question but he had to find out. "Any word from the medical examiner yet?"

"Yeah, I talked to him a few minutes ago. He's behind schedule. He can't perform an autopsy on Pi—" he caught himself and paused for a second. "On Piper until later this afternoon or this evening." He knew that he must be causing Matt a lot of pain mentioning the Jordan woman's name. "I'm sorry, Matt," he apologized.

"It's okay, Paul. Facts are facts. Look, I'm going now. You can reach me on my car radio if something comes up."

"Gotcha. Hang in there, buddy." Paul hung up feeling drained.

Matt cradled the receiver and looked at Crutches. "One more call and then we'll go." The dog barked at him, went over to the door, turned, sat facing Matt, and waited. The end of his tail slapped against the floor. Matt dialed information, got the Maine General's number, dialed again and got the switchboard operator at the hospital to connect him to Nellie's room.

Nellie answered. Her voice sounded weak and depressed.

"Hi, Nellie," Matt said. "I just called to see how you're feeling this morning." He tried to sound cheerful and failed.

"Oh, Matthew. My pain is gone, but I feel just awful about Piper. How are you doing, dear?"

"I'm okay," he lied and changed the subject. "Look, I'm going out to the farm to take a look around. Is there anything you want me to get for you or do while I'm there?"

"No thanks, Matthew. John has already left for home. He's going to tend to the animals and get me some of my

319

things. How's Crutches? Was he a good boy for you?"

"Crutches is fine. He was really well-behaved. When did John leave?"

"Just before you called. He's not going to stay long because he said he wants to get back to me."

"I understand. I hope I get there in time to help him. And, if I'm going to do that I have to hang up now. Take care of yourself, Nellie. I'll stop by later to see you."

"Thanks, dear. I'll see you."

Matt hung up and looked at Crutches, who was still waiting patiently for him. "Okay, buddy. Let's go." The dog struggled to his feet. Matt opened the door and they went outside. The temperature had warmed and the sun was rapidly melting the snow and ice. Matt opened the back door of his car for Crutches, who without assistance managed to lift his body onto the seat and immediately curled into a huge black ball. Matt slammed the door, climbed behind the wheel, started the engine, and headed for the farm.

Driving along, he noticed that there wasn't a cloud in the sky. He rolled his window down and inhaled. The air felt invigorating. Then he thought about Piper again. He knew that he would have to phone her brothers as soon as a positive identification of her body was made. And then he wondered how he'd ever find the strength to get through her funeral—let alone live without her the rest of his life. Suddenly he felt a terrible heaviness in his chest and he felt like crying. "Get hold of yourself," he said out loud. "Treat her like any other victim or you won't make it." He knew he was right. He had to set his personal feelings aside, at least until after he searched the farm. Then he'd go back to headquarters and ask his commanding officer for a leave of absence until he could function normally.

As Matt drove, he remained oblivious to the rapidly passing scenery until he reached the farm. When he turned into the driveway he saw that the fire department had left. Crutches began to whine at the sight of home. John Stoll's car was in the driveway in front of the shed but he wasn't anywhere in sight.

Matt parked, shut the engine off, unbuckled, and climbed out. He opened the back door for Crutches who jumped out and hurried as fast as his lame legs would carry him over to the porch and up the recently shoveled steps. The dog was about to put the storm door handle between his teeth when John opened it. He gave Crutches a robust hug. "C'mon in here, you rascal. I have your breakfast ready." He looked up and saw Matt. "Hi, there, young fella. C'mon in. I just made some fresh coffee. You look like you could use a cup."

Matt glanced at the barn, and then he went up the porch steps and followed John and Crutches into the house. John stood at the stove pouring two mugs of steaming coffee. Crutches was wolfing down his breakfast.

"Nellie's doing fine this morning," John said. "Blood pressure is near normal. No more chest pains. I'm telling you it was indigestion that ailed her."

"I know she's feeling better," Matt told him. "I phoned her just before I left the cabin." He was glad that Nellie was on the mend and that they'd have some more time together. He recalled how he and Piper had discussed John and Nellie's relationship that first night he came to the farm. He felt sick to his stomach when he again realized that Piper was dead. Their life together was over before it even had a chance to get started.

"The animals are in the shed. They're doing fine. I already fed them. It's going to take a while to rebuild the barn. I'll have to keep them in there for the time being. Tatjana's going to be upset over everything that's happened. I thought I'd give her a call in a little bit." He tweaked his beard. "I don't know how I'm going to break the news about Piper. She was awful fond of that girl. We all were." He could tell that he was upsetting Matt. It was time to switch the subject. "I have to go out to the barn and see if anything can be salvaged. Want to come along?"

"Sure," Matt said. "I want to see if there's anything I overlooked last night."

"Speaking of that, did you know that Steven's—I mean Mona's Jaguar is in the shed?"

321

John had his back turned and was turning off the coffee pot when Matt opened the door and bolted.

"Chicken poop all over it," John sputtered. "Serves her right if you ask me. Wonder what she used for wheels to skip town? I hope Satan threw the mold away after he made her." He turned around and saw that he was alone. He shook his head and went to put on his jacket and hat and to slip his stocking feet into his boots. The minute Crutches saw what he was doing he left his food and came over to him. John patted his dog's head. "Never a dull moment," he muttered, and he and Crutches went outside after Matt.

Chapter Sixteen

In The Shadow Of Death

John found Matt coming out of the shed. "Well, young fella," he said. "What do you make of Mona's car being in there?"

"I don't know, John. How the hell did she get away?"

"Maybe she had someone pick her up," John said. "Maybe she has a lover. I wouldn't put it past her. Never did trust her as far as I could throw her." John thought he was sounding more and more like a detective.

"Yeah, that's a possibility," Matt said. "I'd better call headquarters and tell them about the car. Damn. This is going to complicate matters. She could be in Europe or South America."

"She sure could," John agreed. "When I was a little shaver it took weeks to get across the ocean. Now you can do it in the same day. Sure is fast," he said and looked puzzled. "You don't think she'd go to a foreign country, do you?"

"Yes, I do." Matt said and frowned.

"Oh, by the way, Matt," John said. "She cut the phone cords. They're all deader'n a doornail. I'm going to stop by my neighbor's on the way to the hospital and call the phone company to come and fix them. Craziest, meanest woman I ever came across. Makes my blood run cold just to think about her. Kelly and Pi . . ." John didn't finish.

He realized that there was no use carrying on and upsetting Matt. He already looked like he'd been through the wringer.

Crutches limped ahead of the two men as they made their way to what was left of the barn. The wind picked up and raced across the fields, bringing with it the scent of charred wet wood from the ruins. The unpleasant aroma drifted past John's sensitive nostrils. "Fire's out," he said. "Can smell the wet wood. Good thing. Last night that wind could've fanned the flames and maybe spread it to the shed and the house. That would've been a crying shame. Nice old place like this should never be destroyed."

Matt remained silent and scanned everything in sight. He didn't know what he expected to find, but his experience as a detective had taught him that it might be worth the effort. Crutches was now climbing over rubble where the middle of the barn floor used to be. All of a sudden he began to whine. Matt saw him start to dig frantically at something. "John, what do you suppose he's after?"

"Who knows. Maybe he smells a rat or field mouse. We have plenty. Sometimes he makes a game out of trying to catch them." John didn't think to tell Matt about the underground dugout. He was too busy searching for some of his tools. When he found his axe with the burned handle he said to Matt, "Well, I feel better now. I can get this fixed. Had it since I was sixteen. My father bought it for me so I could chop wood for winter."

Matt nodded and then he said, "It's impossible to find any clues in here." There was nothing in the shed either, except for Mona's car. "If you don't mind I think I'll search the house again before I leave. Damn. I hope Mona screwed up and left some sort of a trail. Something has to turn up."

"Do you think you'll catch her?" John asked. "She's pretty sly, you know."

"I know," Matt said. "But I'm going to find her no matter what. I don't care if it takes me the rest of my life."

"Well, I hope you do," John said. "I can't say as I'm going to sleep well at night knowing she's on the loose. What if she decides to come back?"

"Don't worry, John. She won't show up here."

"You sure?"

"Yes. She accomplished what she wanted to do."

"What was that?"

"Well, I think Mona fits the profile of a serial killer. People like her enjoy watching people die. But they don't hang around too long for fear of getting caught. They also like to keep journals about their victims and describe in detail how they killed them. Did I tell you that one of the other detectives found a journal up in her room? She wrote freely about all the people she's murdered."

"You mean Kelly, Steven and Piper?"

"Yes," Matt said. "And others. I think there's no doubt about it. Mona fits the profile."

"But why? What made her that way?"

"Who knows," Matt said. "Usually, they're white males in their early thirties. They have a mother hang-up. As for Mona—I haven't the slightest idea why she ended up so twisted. Some even take trophies from their victims."

"Like what?" John asked.

"I'd rather not say. Let's put it this way. Some take sex-related body parts."

"Lord, God, Almighty!" John said. "I hope they're aren't too many of those bastards out there."

"I'm sorry to have to tell you this—but there are more than you would think."

"Jesus," John said. "What's happening to this country of ours? Makes me want to take Nellie and leave it for parts unknown."

"That's not a bad idea," Matt told him seriously. "Sometimes I think it's only the beginning. There are more and more serial killers every year." He waited for the bitterness he felt to pass.

"Honest?"

"I'm not kidding."

"Jesus," John said and caught his breath. "Say, Matt. Do me a favor will you?"

"Shoot."

"Don't tell Nellie about what you just told me. I just don't think it would be good for her, under the circumstances. And she'd be scared to death of her shadow."

"I won't say a word, I promise."

"Thanks, Matt. I appreciate it." John stopped walking and pulled his pocket watch out of his pants and said, "It's getting late. I have to go inside and pack a suitcase for Nellie and then get back to the hospital. She'll probably have to be in there another day or two and I'll stay with her. My neighbor said he'd come by and feed the animals. He'll take Crutches, too. The kids love him and the feeling is mutual."

The two men walked towards the house. The further away from the barn they traveled, the more upset Crutches became. He lay on top of the burned rubble where the trap door used to be. At first, he whimpered softly. But when John and Matt went into the house he became louder. Before long he started to bark nonstop. Shortly after John went upstairs to pack for Nellie, Matt went out on the porch to try and get the dog to shut up. "Come here, boy," he yelled. Crutches wouldn't move. Matt tried again. "C'mon Crutches. Let's go inside." Crutches ignored him. Matt decided to go and get him. The closer he got, the more excited Crutches became. "What's the matter?" Matt asked gently and patted his head. "Get away from there. You're getting covered with soot and you've got a bunch of junk tangled in your coat. Come into the house with me before you get splinters or nails stuck in your paws." Crutches acted like he wasn't there.

Matt's temper flared and he shouted, "Damn, it, Crutches. What the hell is wrong with you?" And then he felt bad that he had gotten angry. He wondered if the dog was near the spot where Piper had died. He'd heard of dogs doing that kind of thing. He'd once read about a Collie that wouldn't move from his master's grave. "Let's go," he said more gently. "I have to search the house. In a few minutes, you're going to the neighbor's place. John told me that you love the kids there." Matt started to walk away. He'd taken no more than five or six steps when Crutches began to bark. Matt stopped, turned around, and tried to coax him over to him. Crutches wouldn't budge. He continued to bark.

Matt heard a door slam. He looked and saw that John was coming down the porch steps carrying a battered brown suitcase. Crutches was making so much noise Matt couldn't understand what John was trying to say. Finally the old man yelled, "Damn it, Crutches. Stop that racket. What in tarnation is the matter with you?"

Crutches stopped and looked up at his master's old face with the same worried expression he'd given Matt. "I'm leaving," John told Matt. "But I have to ask you another favor."

"What's that?"

"I remembered that Crutches can't go to my neighbor's. His dog is in heat. I know he'll come over and feed the other animals for me. Could you keep my dog for the night?"

"Sure. He can stay with me today and I'll take him home with me later. In fact, I'll keep him until Nellie gets out of the hospital." Matt looked at the dog. "He might mind staying with me."

"Naw. Don't worry. He'll enjoy himself. Thanks, Matt I appreciate it." John was quiet for a few seconds and then he said, "Look, Matt. I know what I'm about to ask you is going to be upsetting but there's no other way around it." Matt heard him inhale deeply and then he blurted, "When do you think Piper's funeral is going to be?"

Matt flinched. He was quiet for a second and then he said, "That all depends on her family. I'll let you know as soon as I find out."

"Nellie and I would appreciate that. And we'd both like it if you'll keep in touch."

"I will," Matt told him. "Now, I'd better search the house and then get back to headquarters and take care of some paper work."

"I'm not going to wait around for you to finish," John told him. "Nellie is going to fret if I don't get on my way pretty quick." He started toward his car, turned, and said, "Don't bother locking the door. If someone wants something bad enough they'll find a way to get in. Give us a call as soon as you know anything."

Matt nodded. He watched John climb into his car. The poor old guy seemed to have great difficulty lowering his body into the seat. Matt heard him groan as though his bones ached. He watched until the car faded from sight.

"C'mon, Crutches," Matt said. "I want to put you in my car while I search the house. That way you won't start barking and carrying on." The dog didn't move. Matt tried to coax him and failed. He grasped his collar and tugged. Crutches reluctantly followed alongside. When Matt opened the back door of his car, Crutches sat down and refused to get in the back seat. Matt tugged on his collar again. Crutches finally lifted his heavy body onto the back seat. Matt rolled down all four windows for enough air flow. The dog continued whimpering while he sat up in the seat, he never took his eyes off the barn. "Okay, Crutches," Matt said gently. "We both miss her. I don't know how we're going to learn to live without her."

Matt left the dog and went inside the house, proceeding slowly from room to room searching for something—anything that might provide a clue to Mona's next destination.

The downstairs was void of any clues. Upstairs, Matt searched Mona's bedroom thoroughly and found nothing. He went into John and Nellie's room and came out of there disappointed, too. It was time to search Piper's room. He turned the knob, opened the door, and stepped inside. The air was filled with the scent of her perfume. Matt's throat tightened and his hands shook as he walked over to her bed and sat down on the edge. His gaze went from object to object. There wasn't any sign of a struggle. He held his face in his hands, shut his eyes for a minute, and took a deep breath.

Sweet memories of Piper came now. He looked up, scanning the room again, and on top of the bureau he spied the pink blouse she'd worn that first night they'd made love. A slight smile appeared as he recalled finding her asleep on his bathroom floor. Her image seemed so real that he unconsciously reached out to touch her. He knew he had to stop.

Matt was about to get up and leave when he noticed a small pad of paper on the nightstand beside her bed. He picked it up and what he read caused him more agony. Piper had scribbled, "I love Matt Carter." He put the pad back where he found it and then he picked up her pillow and hugged it tightly. He could smell the sweet scent of her again. A deep ache filled his soul. Her image danced before his eyes. "Piper," he cried out. "Oh, Jesus, Piper." He buried his face in her pillow and waited for the feeling of deep sorrow to fade. When it finally passed he felt completely spent. It was time to go. He put the pillow back in place, got to his feet, and slipped quietly out of the room. He charged downstairs and ran outside.

The minute Matt stepped onto the porch, Crutches spied him and began to bark again. Matt decided to go back into the house to get him a treat to try and shut him up. He found a soup bone on the floor. Back outside, Matt held up the bone so the dog could see it. Crutches acted uninterested. Matt opened the back door of the car and before he had a chance to stop him, the dog jumped out and limped as fast as he could back to the barn.

Matt was losing patience. He unbuckled his belt, pulled it off, removed his holster, and placed it on the front seat. Now his belt could be used as a leash to control Crutches.

As Matt drew closer, the panting dog began to dig furiously with both front paws. "Okay, okay," Matt said. "You win. Let's see what's underneath this mess to make you so frenzied." Matt made a half-hearted attempt and failed to move the heap of charred remains that were once handhewn oak beams. Now he was covered with soot. "Ouch," he yelled and looked at the palm of his left hand. A huge splinter had been driven deep underneath the skin. "That's it," he yelled at the dog. "C'mon, we're getting out of here." Matt started to walk away.

Surprisingly, Crutches followed. He grabbed hold of Matt's pant leg and pulled. Matt went one way—the dog the other. He heard his pants tearing. He stopped abruptly and yelled, "Crutches! Damn it! Let go of me. What the hell is the matter with you?" The dog tried to drag Matt in the direction of the barn. Matt continued on his way to the car, opened the back door, and told the dog to get in. He ignored Matt's order and limped back to the barn. Matt watched. Crutches sat down in what looked to be the same spot as before and began to howl.

Matt slammed the car door and went after him. The minute he was within reach, Crutches whined and began to dig. Matt doubled his belt, dropped it over the dog's head onto his neck, and gave it a firm tug. "Come," he said. To Matt's surprise, Crutches didn't balk and limped along at his side. Just before they reached the car, Matt remembered that he didn't have any dog food at his house. "Damn," he sputtered to Crutches. "We have to go into the house and get your food."

The minute the two stepped into the kitchen, Matt let the dog go and put his belt around his neck to keep it ready when needed. Crutches ran panting to his bed and flopped. Suddenly Matt remembered that he hadn't notified headquarters about Mona's car having been found. He walked over to the wall phone, lifted the receiver to his ear, dialed, and heard nothing. He looked down and saw the problem. Then he remembered that John had told him that Mona had cut the cords. He hung the receiver back on the hook and started across the room to put his belt on the dog again so they could leave. But Crutches was already on his feet and headed in the opposite directon. He stopped in front of the cellar door and sat on his haunches. He kept scratching the door and he looked up at Matt as if to say, "Open this thing for me will you, pal."

"Jesus, Crutches. Now what? You're as undone as I am." The dog ignored him and kept right on scratching. Then to Matt's surprise, Crutches grasped the knob between his teeth and gave it a twist. When the door was opened enough he gave it a nudge with his nose until it moved completely out of his way. He looked one last time at Matt and lumbered down the dark cellar steps.

Matt turned on the light and walked down the creaking steps. Once he reached the bottom, he had to duck to keep from bumping his head on the low ceiling. The damp cellar had a granite foundation and a dirt floor. Everywhere Matt could see, there was an accumulation of household items from generations past. He passed by four chrome kitchen chairs with torn red plastic seats, an old brass floor lamp with a yellowed, ball-fringed shade, some orange crates full of rusty tools and a stack of car tires. He finally spied Crutches around the corner in an alcove. The dog was seated and staring at what appeared to be an old wooden cabinet painted dark gray. It was so large that it reached from the floor to the ceiling. As Matt approached Crutches barked.

"You're nuts, do you know that?" Matt said. "What kind of a stupid goose chase have you taken me on?" He had his belt ready and was about to put it on Crutches when he thought he heard a faint pounding noise. Crutches barked again. "Hush," Matt said sternly. The dog wouldn't stop. Matt was about to yell at him, but before he could Crutches began to scratch the cabinet door. Matt was really puzzled now. He assumed that Nellie kept a supply of dog biscuits inside. "This better be worth all this trouble," he warned the dog as he gripped the white porcelains handles and yanked both doors open.

"Crutches," Matt scolded. "There's nothing in here but a bunch of preserves." The dog looked at Matt with sad eyes. Matt softened. "I'm sorry, old fellow. I guess I'm tired—I guess you are, too. Let's get out of here now. What do you say?"

Crutches panted heavily and dropped to the ground and stretched out at Matt's feet. "What are you doing?" Matt asked exasperated. "For Christ's sake will you get up?" Crutches refused to move. Matt was about to use his belt to leash him again when he thought he heard another noise. "Jesus," he said. "I'm beginning to get spooked." And then he heard that sound again—and this time he knew where it was coming from. He stared in disbelief at the inside of the closet. All that he could see were six shelves of teal-colored preserving jars full of tomatoes, green and waxed beans, and carrots. Each bore a white label on the front identifying the contents and the date. Matt also noticed several jars of strawberry and blueberry jelly. There was absolutely nothing in sight that could possibly cause the noise he'd heard. "Damn it dog," he grumbled. "You probably heard a rat or mouse. C'mon. It's time to go." And then, just as he was about to close the closet door, Matt heard more pounding. Crutches struggled to his feet and tensed. Matt noticed that the dog's gaze was still fixed on the preserving jars.

"What the hell," Matt said, dropped his belt, and started removing jars from the cabinet. Crutches was making so much noise Matt couldn't hear anything else. When the shelves were finally empty he saw that they weren't attached with nails. One by one, he pulled the dusty boards out and threw them across the floor. When he was better than halfway finished, he saw what looked to be a metal ring on the right and two rusty hinges on the left. After the last shelf was removed he pulled the metal ring. The door was stuck. He tried again and again. Finally it swung open. "Piper!" he cried and couldn't believe his eyes.

Piper lay in a crumpled heap at his feet. Crutches licked her dirty, blood-streaked face. Matt got down on the floor and tried unsuccessfully to get the dog out of the way. He gently lifted Piper into his arms and rocked her back and forth. He kissed her cold brow. "Jesus, oh Jesus," he repeated. She didn't seem to hear him. Matt held her closer. He had no idea how long he sat there cradling her before he came to his senses. He realized that she was injured and he knew that he had to get her to the hospital right away.

He laid her carefully on the ground. She looked as though she were sleeping. Matt touched her cheek and then he kissed her lips. For an instant he thought she responded to his touch. He kissed her again. Nothing. He squeezed her cold hand. Still nothing. His fingers felt for a pulse and found a weak one. Next, he stood up; with all of his might he lifted her into his arms, and he made his way across the cellar to the stairs as Crutches followed. Matt was halfway up the steps when he almost fell backwards from the weight of Piper's body. A square-headed nail sticking out of the wall caught his shirt sleeve and raked a rusty, bloody path up his arm. He was exhausted now and it was only through sheer perseverance that he finally made it to the top.

Standing in the kitchen, he tried to position Piper's body so he could make it outside to the car without falling. That's when he heard her moan. He knew she was in pain and that he must try to be more careful how he moved her in case she had internal injuries. "Hold on, baby, hold on," he crooned, thankful to hear the sound of her voice. Slowly and steadily, he moved across the kitchen toward the door. Crutches was ahead of him now. He put the knob in his mouth, gave it a twist, and nudged the door open. "Good boy," Matt praised.

Crutches walked onto the porch and waited. Matt came out with Piper and went down the porch steps. The dog followed and stayed close to Matt's side as they made their way across the driveway. Matt was so exhausted he staggered and stumbled along the way. When he reached the car he bent over and felt for the handle with his right hand. He opened the door and laid Piper carefully down on the back seat. She moaned again and her eyes fluttered open.

Everything was blurry. She tried to speak and to lift her

left hand to rub her bruised chest and couldn't. A sharp pain tore through her head, she was freezing cold, and then she began to remember what had happened. *Mona!* she cried inside, and then she felt someone's hands on her. Her eyes flew open—expecting to see *her*. When she could focus, she couldn't believe her eyes. She said "M-Matt?" Her voice was so faint he hadn't heard her. She wondered if she was dreaming. "Matt," she managed to say a little louder.

Matt heard her and looked down at her tenderly. "Yes, baby it's me." He kissed her clammy forehead. "Hush. You're going to be okay." But Matt wasn't really sure she was going to be all right. He didn't like the pale color of her skin; how cold she felt to his touch! He knew that she was in shock. He had to get her to the hospital as quickly as possible. There was no time to wait for an ambulance.

"Don't move," he told her, but she hadn't heard a word he said because she'd passed out again. He removed his jacket and covered her chest. She remained oblivious as Crutches leaned his head inside and began to sniff her hair.

"Watch her carefully, Crutches," Matt told the dog. "I have to go to the house and get some blankets." He ran across the driveway, up the porch steps, inside, and upstairs to the closest bedroom which happened to be Nellie and John's. He yanked their bedding off the bed, dropped the light blue flannel sheets onto the floor, taking a green wool blanket and a patchwork quilt with him. He charged downstairs and out of the house.

By the time Matt reached Piper he was terribly out of breath. She was still unconscious. Crutches was right where he'd left him. "Good boy," Matt told him and wrapped Piper in the quilt and blanket. Crutches cocked his head and wagged his tail.

Piper stirred, opened her eyes, and looked at Matt and then up at the heavens. She was too weak to talk. And then she smelled charred wood and remembered the fire in the barn. She tried to ask Matt what had happened but a sharp pain tore through her head and then everything went black.

Matt closed the car door and ran around the other side to get behind the wheel. Halfway he looked down and saw that Crutches was right by his side. He ran around to the other side and the dog followed. He opened the front door and told the dog to get in. Crutches obeyed and managed to climb onto the seat the first try. Matt slammed the door. Seconds later he sped out of the driveway and headed for the expressway to Portland. He used his car phone to call the hospital and let them know that he was on the way. Then he called the dispatcher at headquarters and checked in.

As soon as Matt hit the expressway he floored the accelerator. No more than two miles down the highway he glanced in his rear view mirror and saw a state police cruiser, blue light flashing. The cruiser pulled alongside him and the trooper waved. It was Frank Nelson, who had taken Nellie and John to the hospital. Nelson pulled ahead of Matt, slipped in front of him in his lane, and led the way to the hospital, siren blaring, light flashing. Crutches rode sitting up all the way. He was so big that his head touched the roof of the car.

Upon arrival at the hospital, Matt and Frank found two nurses with a gurney and a doctor waiting in the emergency area parking lot. Matt pulled his car to a shuddering stop, threw it into park, switched the engine off, and got out. He opened the back door and stepped aside. The medical team quickly lifted Piper out and onto the gurney. She was whisked through the double doors into a curtained cubicle.

Matt stuck his head inside the car and spoke to Crutches. "I'm going to have to leave you for a while, old boy. I'd bring you with me but only seeing eye dogs can go into a hospital." Crutches barked at him just once, as if to say he understood. Matt quickly rolled down all four windows for him so he would have enough air and then he rushed into the emergency room.

After Matt gave the receptionist, who wore a name tag that said "Judi," the necessary information about Piper, he paced the floor waiting for word about her condition. He repeated a silent prayer that she would live, for he knew that she could easily slip away and die. He'd seen it happen too many times.

Fifteen minutes later Paul Reynolds come through the double doors. "Hi, Matt," he said soberly. "I got your message from the dispatcher. How is she?"

"I don't know, Paul. They're working on her now."

"Where did you find her?"

Matt told Paul the story. During the course of the conversation, Paul kept shaking his head as if he couldn't believe what he was hearing.

When Matt finished, Paul whistled. "Unbelievable. Christ. If that dog hadn't gone downstairs she never would've gotten out."

"That's right," Matt said, not wanting to dwell on that morbid thought.

"I've been thinking about getting a puppy for my kids," Paul said. "What kind of a dog was that at the farm?"

"A Newfoundland. I think they're used for rescue."

"I believe it," Paul said. "After what you just told me, I'm sold. By the way, the medical examiner called right after you did. The autopsy on that body found at the farm is scheduled for two. The only way they can identify who it is is through dental records. I sent Judd out to the Hadley house in Cape Bethany to see if he can find out who Mona's dentist was. If he finds out he's going to get her records and bring them to the medical examiner. Judd said he'd call and let us know what's happening."

Matt nodded. He was about to say something about Mona, when a doctor came through the double doors from the examination area. He walked over to Matt and Paul. Matt recalled that he was the same one that was out in the parking lot when he arrived with Piper.

"I'm Doctor Wheeler. Are you a relative of Miss Jordan's?"

"We're engaged," Matt said. "How is she?"

"Jesus, Matt!" Paul said before the doctor had a chance to talk. "I didn't know. Congratulations."

"She's going to be okay," Doctor Wheeler reassured both men. "We've taken X-rays. No broken bones. No internal injuries. Her body is terribly bruised and she has a few lacerations, but nothing serious. She's in shock, but she's going to make it. I've called in a psychiatrist. I don't think anyone can endure what she's been through and not suffer some panic disorder, but I may be wrong. I just think it's better to be safe than sorry. I'm amazed that she made it through. She's very concerned about the Hadley woman. Has she been found?"

"We don't know yet," Matt said.

Doctor Wheeler nodded. "Miss Jordan will have to spend a couple of days here so we can make certain she's okay. She's been asking for you. You can see her for a minute before she goes upstairs to her room and then you're welcome to go with her. But, remember. She's been through a terrible ordeal. Don't tire her whatever you do and don't alarm her."

"I'll wait here in case Judd shows," Paul told Matt.

Matt didn't say anything to Paul as he disappeared through the double doors with the doctor.

"She's in there," Doctor Wheeler said and pointed to the first white curtained cubicle on the left. "Remember what I said. Go easy."

Matt waved and slipped through an opening in the curtain. Piper's eyes were closed. She had been cleaned up and was wearing a light green hospital johnny and her cheeks had more color now. Matt tiptoed over to her and gently held her bandaged hand. Her skin felt much warmer to the touch. He kissed her forehead, the tip of her nose, and then her lips. When he stopped he studied her face. That's when her eyes fluttered opened. "Hi, baby," he said huskily.

When Piper could focus she blew Matt a kiss and whispered, "I love you, Matt." She tried to sit up and fell back. Her throat had never felt so dry.

"I love you, too," he said and gently lifted her into his arms. He kissed the top of her head and heard her weakly ask, "Where's Mona?"

"I think she's dead," he whispered. "The barn burned. She must've gotten trapped. We found a body but it's burned beyond recognition. We'll know in a couple of hours." He had to catch his breath. "But I think it's her so you don't have to be afraid. I'll stay with you until we are certain."

Piper didn't say anything as she cuddled closer against Matt's chest. Inside, she prayed that Mona was dead. It had to be over. Suddenly the curtain was pulled back and a male attendant slipped into the cubicle. "We're ready to take you up to your room now," he said with a pleasant smile. "You can come, too," he told Matt.

Within a couple of minutes the three were on the elevator going up. Piper rested on the gurney with her eyes shut. Matt still held her hand as he stood beside the gurney.

The elevator came to a jerky halt and then the door opened. The attendant pushed Piper into the corridor and wheeled her briskly down a wide corridor with a highly polished cream colored tiled floor. Matt kept pace at her side, holding onto her hand. She finally opened her eyes and stared at the ceiling as it rushed past.

Nellie was watching the Phil Donahue Show on Channel Six, and John was snoring in an uncomfortable-looking vinyl chair beside the bed.

Nellie's gaze left the television and rested on the empty bed beside hers. She wondered if she'd have a roommate before she went home. Suddenly two nurses came into the room and woke John up. One carried an arm full of clean white sheets and a tan blanket. The other carried the standard hospital kit—a green plastic wash basin, soap, mouth wash, paper slippers, and a johnny. "Am I getting a roommate?'' she asked the two women.

"Yes, indeed," the one carrying the sheets said.

"A woman?"

"Course, Nellie," John answered. "This hospital isn't co-ed."

"Young or old?" Nellie wanted to know.

"You'll see," said the one with the sheets who had almost finished making the bed.

"She'll see what?" John asked.

Both women ignored him and left the room.

Nellie was about to tell John that she didn't care much for guessing games when she saw his mouth fall open and then he jumped to his feet and said, "Jesus! I can't believe it!" She saw him rub his eyes.

She looked to see what had caused John such a fright. "Dear heaven! It can't be!" she gasped. "I must've died and gone to heaven!"

"Where did you find her?" John asked.

"It's a long story," Matt said. "But you can thank Crutches for my finding her." He almost left, he thought. Good God. She would've died and never been found.

"Remember the dugout you showed me, John?" Piper asked faintly.

John nodded.

"Well I hid from Mona down there. Did you know that she tried to kill me?" Her voice quivered but she didn't cry.

John nodded. "But you would've burned to death down there." He just couldn't understand how she could've survived a fire like that.

"I found a tunnel."

"You don't say. Jesus."

"What dugout? What tunnel? What are you talking about?" Nellie interrupted.

"I'll explain later, sweetie pie," John told her.

Nellie was still so stunned that she kept repeating Piper's name over and over. Tears slid down her wrinkled cheeks. "Is she hurt bad?" she asked the attendant.

"I'm okay," Piper consoled her. "Don't. It's not good

339

for you to get so upset."

"I'm fine, dear," Nellie said. "Oh, I just love happy endings."

"Me, too," John said.

The same two nurses reappeared. They grinned happily at Nellie and John. With the help of the attendant, they carefully lifted Piper onto the bed opposite Nellie. Once they had her tucked in and had taken her vital signs they made a hasty exit.

Matt stood next to the head of Piper's bed and stroked her hair. She looked up at him and smiled.

John was so excited he began to pace in front of both beds. "Well, Matt. Looks like we've got our women right where we want them."

"Where's that?" Matt asked.

"In bed," John said with a wink.

"Cut that out, John," Nellie scolded and looked at Piper with a grin.

"Okay, Nellie, okay." John said and stopped pacing and pulled on his beard and said more to himself than to anyone in the room, "Crutches is really something. Best dog I ever had. Jesus!"

"John!" Nellie said. "Stop taking the Lord's name in vain."

"I can't help it, Nellie. I just can't believe it. What a dog! And did you know that God spelled backwards is dog?"

"Really, John?" Nellie asked with awe.

John switched the subject. "Where's Mona?" he asked Matt and saw Piper flinch.

Before Matt had a chance to answer the phone rang. Nellie answered. "Yes. He's right here. Please hold on a second." She looked at Matt and said, "It's a Detective Paul Reynolds."

Matt took the phone. "What's up?" he said.

"Good news, buddy boy. I just spoke with Judd. He knew that you were interested so he called right away. He found the name of Mona Hadley's dentist and the medical examiner has already compared her records against those

340

of the body found in the barn. He says it's definitely her. Oh yeah, one more thing," Paul said and caught his breath. "The medical examiner won't be able to finish the autopsy until tomorrow, though, cause he's overloaded."

"Thanks, Paul," Matt said and inhaled deeply. After cradling the receiver he looked at Piper and said, "You don't have to worry any longer. Mona is definitely dead."

Piper sobbed uncontrollably from the rush of emotions that swooped down on her. She was free at last.

Chapter Seventeen

The Preparation Room

Charles Timothy Watts woke early in his bedroom in the living quarters located at the rear of his funeral home. The minute he stepped out of bed he felt a twinge of excitement. He'd experienced such sensations often. After each episode, something special happened. He walked quickly to his window and gave the old fashioned crocheted window pull a tug. The dark green shade rolled with a fast snap, and Watts squinted from the glare of the sun.

When he could see, he lifted the window as high as it would go and inhaled the crisp morning air to energize his soul. He noticed that all the trees were barren of leaves. Scrawny limbs waved wildly in the breeze. His glance rested on top of his garage roof. Several pigeons strutted across the black shingles, and there was hardly a spot that wasn't covered with bird droppings. Watts made a sour face and closed the window.

Wide awake now, he made his way into the bathroom to take a shower. Before he jumped into the shower stall he admired his surroundings. A faint smell of fresh paint still lingered in the air. He inhaled and was once again reminded that he had always loved the aroma of new paint. He loved the color of the walls and woodwork— salmon and peas, his favorite meal. He clapped his hands with delight, remembering how good it felt when he found out from the contractors he'd hired that there were enough peach tiles and green paint left over from the preparation room to do the bathroom, too. Never, ever had he expected to be able to save so much money. And, business had picked up considerably, what with the Stewart girl and Steven Hadley; Mona Hadley had fattened his wallet considerably when she wrote a check for Steven. "A blue lining, yet," Watts sputtered. "That bitch."

Watts shook his head and erased Mona from his brain before he got angry. Thoughts of the future came to mind. Pretty soon there would be enough money in his bank account to purchase a new white Caddie hearse he'd admired in the undertaker's catalog last month. It cost $58,000 plus tax, but it would be a refreshing change from boring black, and besides, white used to be the funeral color for the Chinese. He wondered if it still was as he stripped off his candy-striped pajamas, shivered from the chill, and walked his naked body into the shower. He must remember to call a Chinese restaurant and ask if white was still in.

After Watts showered, he dressed in his usual attire of a snow white, stiffly starched shirt, black tie, suit, socks, and shoes. He needed a shine before his ten o'clock funeral. The old man he'd fixed down in the preparation room the night before had turned out grand—on his stainless steel table that is. The makeup had taken twenty years off the guy's face. But the suit—that was all wrong. Double knit, right out of the sixties. And what a homely shade of gold. The minute the bereaved widow handed over the suit he knew that it was going to make the old man's skin look yellow, and he'd been right. Darn. And after all the time he'd spent on his makeup and hair.

The phone rang. Watts answered. It was his friend, Martin, in the morgue at the Maine General Hospital, calling to tell him that the medical examiner had a body for a Freeport funeral home but the undertaker there was sick. Martin had suggested Watts. The name on the body bag said Hadley. Not again! Watts said to himself. It's just not possible. Or is it?

Martin told him to pick up the body as soon as possible because they had a full house and needed the space. Before Watts had a chance to ask about the details, Martin hung up.

Watts looked at the clock on the nightstand next to his bed. If he left right away he'd have more than enough time to get back for his ten o'clock funeral. But before he went anywhere, he would have his breakfast. No matter what happened in his life he always made sure he ate three meals a day.

And, as usual, he strolled to the Victory Deli and Bake Shop on Congress Street to have his breakfast. He sat at his favorite table, which overlooked Monument Square, and ordered the breakfast special. For $1.99, Howard fixed him two fresh eggs—over easy—homefries, molasses oatmeal toast, and a slice of fresh orange garnish. Of course, his glass of freshly squeezed orange juice and hazelnut coffee cost extra, but he couldn't resist. Watts admired the cleanliness of the place. Sometimes he ate supper there (his mouth watered, as he thought about Ken, the baker's, chocolate truffle). And Anna, the cashier, always smiled at him. He loved such friendliness. Such a lively place, he thought. Not at all like his business. He wondered if he should've been a cook instead of an undertaker.

One hour later, Watts had his hearse loaded and was driving away from the Maine General Hospital. He hadn't been so happy in ages. He'd felt this way ever since he learned that the body was indeed another Hadley, Desdamona Hadley to be precise. Watts glanced over his shoulder and chuckled at the sight of the body bag. "Desdamona," he said. "Wow! What a classic. That would've been a great handle for Bette Davis.

"I know that you and Steven don't have any relatives, but you had lots of money. Once, when Steven and I went golfing at the club, he told me what law firm represented

344

him. I'll have to file with probate court to get paid for your funeral and that could take a while. No matter," he sighed. "It will be worth the wait. Don't you worry, Desdamona, dear. I'm going to see to it that you have all the trimmings." He was so happy that he began to sing "Amazing Grace." He always sang that one when he was really pleased. When finished, he glanced at Desdamona's body bag again and said, "Just goes to prove that you can be here one minute and gone the next. Yes, indeed. Snap, crackle, pop! You're out of here."

When Watts arrived at the funeral home, he unloaded the body bag, wheeled it into the preparation room, and placed it on top of his stainless steel table. Next, he removed his gloves and washed his hands with a special germicide soap, meanwhile glancing at his watch. Desdamona would have to wait. It was time for the ten o'clock service. Watts blew the body bag a kiss and went upstairs.

During the entire funeral service, Watts was anxious to get back to the preparation. The thought of preparing Desdamona Hadley excited him more than any other corpse that had come his way. Finally, after the interment at the cemetery, Watts and his assistants returned to the funeral home. He told everyone they could leave for the day. After they left, Watts' stomach told him that it was time to have lunch. He went into the spotless kitchen in his quarters and opened his refrigerator and selected some leftover barbecued chicken he'd cooked on his gas grill the night before. Four cold, delicious pieces later, he was ready to go downstairs to Desdemona. He got up from the table and suddenly felt so full that he had to loosen his belt two notches.

Down in the preparation room, Watts turned on the overhead lights and fans. "Bless fans," he said to the body bag and proceeded to put on his protective gear, including a white mask that covered his mouth and nose. Burned customers do have a strong odor, he said to himself and made a face as he struggled to put on his plastic gloves. When he was ready to look at what was left of Desdemona he gave the body bag zipper a quick sweeping. Sometimes such zippers snagged. This one moved easily. When it was open the smell of burned flesh was so strong it penetrated Watts' mask and made him ill. His face flushed and his eyes watered. God, he thought. What a grisly sight. What a way to go! I wouldn't wish what happened to her on my worst enemy. Then he recalled in detail the hard time she'd given him over Steven's funeral and he had second thoughts. "I guess that's what happens to some women who are witches spelled with a b," he said with a sound his mask muffled. "Darn, Desdamona, you've cremated yourself! No embalming necessary." She reminded him of the grilled chicken he'd had for lunch. All of her hair was gone. "No eyebrows—no lashes," he muttered. "No face—no fingers—or toes." Watts knew that her insides had to have been seared, too, along with her throat, lungs—everything. He shook his head, sighed heavily, zipped the bag closed, and left the room. He took the elevator to the second floor to choose just the right container for poor Desdemona.

Up in the selection room, Watts selected exactly the same casket as Steven's. His muscles strained when he tried to maneuver the casket onto the bier. When he'd finally positioned it just right, he pushed the contraption through the door, being careful not to damage his woodwork. Getting onto the elevator was another problem. It always was a tight squeeze, but he made it. He closed the elevator door and once again he hit the round button with the initials P.R. The elevator lurched and started to descend. It seemed to take forever for it to reach the bottom. To pass the time, Watts sang. "Old Mac-Donald had a farm eey-eye eey-eye O. And on this farm he had a barn, eey-eye eey-eye O." He wasn't sure if he had the lyrics right. No matter. It pleased him and it fit the occasion—considering how Desdemona Hadley had met her demise.

In the preparation room, Watts pushed the bier alongside the stainless steel table. He opened the casket with the beige velvet lining and with great difficulty lifted the body bag into it. He slammed the lid and then he wheeled Desdemona's remains to the elevator. He was exhausted. But then this part of his work was always tedious. "Upstairs, downstairs, upstairs, downstairs," he grumbled. He looked at Desdemona's casket, scowled, and said, "You were boring. I hope my next customer is more challenging to prep." The elevator came to a shuddering halt.

Watts opened the door and carefully wheeled the bier into the corridor and stopped to ponder the situation. There was no need to put her in the large room because he knew that she couldn't possibly have had many friends. Instead, he wheeled her into a tiny room just opposite his office. Once the bier was in place he backed up a few paces to take a look. He shook his head and looked frustrated. "Biers always look stark before the flowers arrive," he muttered. "No orchids for you, sweetie," he said to Desdemona. "Assorted bouquets will do. Carnations and daisies." He knew he was being mean. Desdemona loved orchids. "Oh, well, serves you right," he said. "Assorted flowers it is." And then he had an idea. "I'll be right back," he said. "Don't go anywhere." He ran out of the room.

Watts returned carrying two huge sprays of assorted flowers. One had a white ribbon with gold lettering that said "Father." He pulled the ribbon off and stuffed it in his pocket. He had intended to donate the flowers to a local hospital and to one of his favorite nursing homes that sent a lot of business his way. But not now. He placed the baskets at each end of the bier and then he admired his decorating. "That's better," he said softly. He opened the casket, looked down at the body bag, frowned, and said, "Well, Desdemona. I guess this is it." Charles Timothy Watts had a broad smile on his face when he slammed the lid shut for the last time. "Ashes to ashes," he quipped, clapped his hands, and said, "And, that's the end of loudmouth Hadley."

The phone rang. Watts quickly left the room and ran into his office and picked up the receiver. "Hello. Watts Funeral Home. May I help you?" When he finally cradled the receiver he whistled. Business was booming. He could see himself driving that white hearse sooner than expected. "Maybe I won't order a white Caddie. I might get a Mercedes. Yes, indeedy," he said happily. "Now that would be doing things up in Desdemona's style." He had a smile on his face and he did a little jig on his way downstairs to the preparation room.

Epilogue

After spending two days in the Maine General Hospital, Piper was discharged. Nellie was going home, too. John was coming to get her. "Are you coming to the farm?" she asked Piper.

"Probably," Piper said and picked up the phone to call Matt to tell him that she was being released.

"Detective Carter here," he answered.

"Hi, Detective Carter. It's me. The doctor said I can leave this morning."

"Great!" Matt said.

"Nellie has been released, too," she told him. "John is coming to get us and he's bringing me some clothes."

"Don't go with them," he said.

"Why not?"

"Because you're going home with me. I'll be there just as fast as I can." Piper didn't get a chance to say another word because Matt hung up.

After she cradled the phone Nellie asked, "What did Matthew say about our being discharged, dear?"

"He said I'm going home with him."

"I knew it!" Nellie said with confidence. "John did, too." She sighed and laid her gray head on her pillow. Oh, she thought. *If only John and I were young again we'd . . .*

It was late afternoon when Matt and Piper reached the cabin. He opened her car door for her, lifted her into his arms and carried her inside. He gently laid her down on the black leather sofa. "It's good to have you here," he said, kneeling by her side. "God. I thought I'd lost you forever." He kissed her lips.

When they parted she reached up and touched his dark hair. They kissed again.

"Marry me soon," he said huskily.

"Say when," she said.

"A week from today, right here in the cabin. John and Nellie can stand up with us."

"You've got a date," Piper said, and they kissed again. Suddenly she pulled away. "What was that noise?" Fear consumed her.

"I didn't hear anything," he said and buried his face in her hair.

"Wait! I heard it again." She held her breath.

"Oh, that," Matt said and got to his feet and opened his bedroom door.

A little black puppy with a bright red collar came bounding out and reached Piper before she had a chance to shield her face with her hands. A small pink tongue washed her face, and a stubby tail wagged happily. Matt had to come to Piper's rescue. He picked up the pup and said to Piper, "Well, what do you think?"

"I think he's adorable."

"She," he corrected.

"Where did she come from? Whose is it?"

"I bought her," Matt said proudly. The puppy squirmed so much he had to put her down. She immediately bounded back to Piper for some more loving. "And she's yours."

"Really, Matt?" Piper patted the dog's silky head.

"Really."

"She's a Newfoundland, like Crutches. Only her hips are in good shape—so far. Do you like her?"

"I love her. Where did you get her?"

"John put me in touch with Crutches' breeder. It just so happens she had one puppy left from the last litter. She was going to show this little girl here, but I talked her into

350